A GRANITE SILENCE

Also by Nina Allan

The Rift
The Race
The Harlequin
Spin
The Silver Wind
Ruby: Stories
Microcosmos: Stories
The Dollmaker
The Good Neighbours
Conquest

A GRANITE SILENCE

Nina Allan

riverrun

First published in Great Britain in 2025 by

riverrun

an imprint of

Quercus Editions Limited
Carmelite House
50 Victoria Embankment
London EC4Y 0DZ

An Hachette UK company

The authorised representative in the EEA is Hachette Ireland,
8 Castlecourt Centre, Dublin 15, D15 XTP3, Ireland (email: info@hbgi.ie)

Copyright © 2025 Nina Allan

The moral right of Nina Allan to be
identified as the author of this work has been
asserted in accordance with the Copyright,
Designs and Patents Act, 1988.

All rights reserved. No part of this publication
may be reproduced or transmitted in any form
or by any means, electronic or mechanical,
including photocopy, recording, or any
information storage and retrieval system,
without permission in writing from the publisher.

A CIP catalogue record for this book is available
from the British Library.

Hardback 978 1 52943 557 3
Ebook 978 1 52943 558 0

This book is a work of fiction. Names, characters, businesses, organizations,
places and events are either the product of the author's imagination or used fictitiously.
Any resemblance to actual persons, living or dead, events or locales is entirely coincidental.

1

Typeset by CC Book Production
Printed and bound in Great Britain by Clays Ltd, Elcograf S.p.A.

Papers used by riverrun are from well-managed forests and other responsible sources.

To the memory of Helen Wilson Robertson Priestly (1925–1934)

and Jessie Seymour Irvine (1836–1887)

and to Michaela Geal

'Listen, listen to the wind in the trees. Tell her I am dreaming of other times.'

(Susana Solovey, *The Ice Dragon*)

CONTENTS

Part 1: I Did Not Do That

A Photograph	3
A Journey	8
City in Limbo	15
Lunch Break	24
Dunnottar	32
Gone	36
The Dark Man	41
Look at the Bag	50
Someone about the Door	57
He Did Not Do That	70

Part 2: Myths and Legends

The Cream Ware Bowl	79
Inventory of Items Taken by Police Officers from the Donalds' Apartment at 61 Urquhart Road between 25th April and 9th May 1934	90

1B	92
Ambition: A Fairy Tale	116
Last Seen Wearing	131
Tommy Southern's Night Out	150

Part 3: A Crime of Almost Unspeakable Cruelty

I Want a Story with a Murderer in It	161
Avengers Assemble	166
The Stormy Petrel	174
Proof of the Sack	220
Strange Days Like These	228
She's Been Used	236
Gallowglass	243
Who the Hell is Phyllis Kingdon?	255
Guilty	260

Part 4: Jeannie in the Afterlife

The Escape Artist	274
A Model Prisoner	290
An Unnatural Reserve	299
Mrs Donald's Story	312
Coconut: A Ghost Story	315

Acknowledgements	339

Part 1

I Did Not Do That

A Photograph

YOU ARE LOOKING AT a photograph, a photograph showing the interior of a room. It is an old photograph, almost a hundred years old at the time of writing. It does not have the clear resolution and adjusted lighting you might be used to. This photograph has the quality of a historical artefact, a piece of evidence. Even before you examine it in detail, you will find yourself assuming certain things: whoever took the photograph is most likely dead now, and whatever happened here, happened a long time ago. There is a possibility that the house that contains this room is no longer standing.

Hold that thought, carry it to its logical conclusion, and you will see how this photograph, indeed any photograph, can function as a time machine. The picture not only proves that this space existed; it can carry you back there. By examining the photograph you inhabit the room and scent its aromas: dust, old newspapers, yesterday's braised beef. You hear the sounds drifting in from the hallway and from the street outside. You experience the textures of fabrics, the patina of household objects, the faded spring light.

You have stepped, however briefly, over the threshold of a different time. Your perception of the world is altered as a result.

The room you are standing in is known as the parlour. The parlour is a public reception room, a room for entertaining guests, traditionally situated at the front of the house, as is the case with this one. The room has a dingy aspect, an impression you might ascribe partly to the outdated technology that has been utilised in capturing its image, but mostly comes down to the way the room is furnished. Today, a room like this would be painted in pale, neutral colours, the floorboards stripped and varnished, a soft-minimalist aesthetic designed to take advantage of the natural light spilling in through the Georgian windows.

At the time the photograph was taken, the fashions tended towards the formal, towards sobriety. Heavy, textured wallpapers in grey or green; small spaces crammed with furniture, shelves stacked with ornaments and family keepsakes. If this room feels familiar to you at all, it is probably because it reminds you of your grandmother's house: every object dusted and neatly in place, yet the room as a whole still managing to generate an impression of endless Sunday boredom and benign neglect.

If you are old enough, you will remember boarding houses that looked like this: dilapidated seafront terraces in Brighton, Blackpool or Bridlington, intrusive landladies who unpacked your luggage without being asked. Who – you never said anything at the time, you were only a child – you suspected of poking about among your family's possessions while you were dragging your feet along the rainy promenade or taking refuge in the pier head café, tea and bread and butter and haddock and chips.

At the centre of the room stands a table, and the sturdy build of it, the dark varnish reminds you of a table in your grandmother's house, the kind that could be expanded with a pull-out panel to make room for extra guests, folded up against a wall when not in use. That table is living a new life now, as in the bedsitters and shared apartments of young working people thousands of other, similar tables have taken on new roles as writing desks and computer stations, dumping grounds for sports equipment, aquarium stands.

Sturdy, workmanlike furniture, built to last. A little dull, maybe, but there was a time when you would have been proud to own a table like this, and you can see how the table in the photograph is given pride of place. The one leg that is properly visible gleams with polish. The tabletop is protected with a velvet cloth. Velvet, with a silken fringe, typical for the period, and it is easy to imagine its colour: sage green, or autumn gold, or sable brown.

There are three chairs. One has a leather seat, held in place with brass studs, and the chair's straight arms are also leather-covered. This kind of chair is known as a carver. It would normally have been placed at the head of the table, from where the head of the household – usually a man – would have carved the meat on Sundays. In the photograph, the chair is standing against the wall between an internal door and a large wardrobe, or armoire. To the left of the armoire stands a second chair, with wooden arms and slanted, candytwist arm supports. The chair's legs are lost in the gloom and cannot be described. To the right of the table and just inside the photograph's frame you can make out a third chair, perhaps the partner of the second, although not enough of it is visible to be able to confirm this. Both the second chair and this third are upholstered with cushions in what looks like a chintz pattern. They are plump and pretty, these cushions. Like the table and the other furniture they seem well looked after.

Positioned between the first two chairs, the bulky, free-standing armoire has a central, mirrored panel, two carved side panels and a deep drawer beneath. The dark wood of the armoire, like the table leg, is polished to a high shine. The front is slightly bowed, and the top is decorated with a carved pediment. The mirror, similarly polished and free of dust, clearly reflects the table that is standing in front of it.

To the left of the table you can see what looks like a padded bench, or pew, with turned struts at the back and a pull-out bed or ottoman behind it, with a quilted cover. To the right of the ottoman is a wash stand with a plant pot in a pottery bowl. On the wall behind, two framed paintings hang from the picture rail. The paintings are of landscapes, possibly Highland landscapes, although it is impossible to say for sure.

On the back of the internal door hangs a child's dress, with what might be a fur stole, or a scarf in a lighter material wound around the hook. The dress has long sleeves and is dark in colour. In the corner of the room, between the wash stand and the door, stand two tall, white, cylindrical objects. They could be rolls of paper, or of fabric. It is difficult to discern anything further about them.

The room is crowded with things. You would probably describe it as overcrowded, a room in a house where space is at a premium. The people who live here are not well off. By today's standards, they would be described as poor. Yet the pride they take in their home is unmistakable.

This is a photograph of a crime scene, taken by one of the police officers who are in attendance. The only reason this photograph exists is because one of the people who lives here is about to be charged with murder. If this murder had not occurred, you would not be standing in this space now. The house, the room and its contents would have vanished into history, like millions of others. You would not know it existed, and neither would I.

A Journey

IN THE SUMMER AFTER the second lockdown, I travel north to spend a week in Aberdeen. It is early July. The evenings are long and white, the nights indigo and barely there, the days slipping by as they do in the north, when the weather is fine, when the light is like the light of another world. My journey is not essential, which is why I am making it. I want to travel on board a train, arrive in a place I have never visited before, check into a chain hotel and order Chinese food from a local takeaway. Explore a network of streets that are new to me. Catch unexpected glimpses of the lives of others. Is this not what writers do?

I dwell on these matters obsessively, on how absurd it is that stepping on to a train has come to seem like an act of rebellion. I have to keep reminding myself that my desire to go to places and look at things is normal, that it is this shadow-life we have slipped into that is the absurdity. This is the third summer in a row that I have travelled to the far north of Scotland for no other reason than wanting to go there. Last summer, when I had to change trains at Inverness, the concessions on the station forecourt were all closed and shuttered, and with an hour or so between trains I decided to leave the station and get a coffee. In a branch of Costa not far from the centre I had to give my name, address and mobile number before being allowed to sit down at a table by the window. It was the only indoor table, and there were no other customers.

What has disturbed me more than anything through the period of the lockdowns has been the swiftness with which accustomed behaviours, accustomed thought processes have been overwritten. I have observed a palpable eagerness among some people, to obey, to conform, to see normal individual actions, behaviours and thought processes legally circumscribed. I have found this willingness to be controlled both fascinating and terrifying.

During both these summers of the pandemic, I have been determined to travel outside my home area as soon as possible, as soon as such an activity is once again permitted. The juxtaposition of the word travel with the word permitted suggests its opposite: not just that permission to travel is required, but that to travel without permission has become the exception rather than the rule. The rapidity with which this has not only happened, but become accepted – that is what I find frightening. Not the pragmatic fact of not being allowed to do such and such a thing, but the existential fact that it is possible to have the legal right to do whatever it is rescinded at a moment's notice and with no rebuttal.

Most disturbing of all is that no one who is not a fringe theorist, a COVID-denier or a militant libertarian seems to be interested in talking about this. It is no longer socially acceptable to question the fact that the right to have a cup of tea in someone else's kitchen has been taken away. One unexpected side benefit of this situation is that there are fewer people on the trains, and because everyone is wearing masks, the threat of having to talk to anyone has been removed. My own mask is made from cotton – green, with white flowers; scant protection against the virus, but a welcome layer of social insulation between myself and other passengers. One of those reappraisals of reality that will later be described as era-defining. What will we remember of these days of burlesque in ten years' time?

Broughty Ferry, Carnoustie, Arbroath. The brackish waters of the Montrose Basin, oyster catchers and eider ducks flap and float across the gleaming mudflats like drifts of confetti. Ancient places, fishing towns. In winter these hard-nosed coastal settlements will be Baltic, glittering, knifed by east winds.

I have half an idea for a novel, something about a Russian émigré writer who comes to Aberdeen to escape the Bolsheviks. Her name is Susana and I can see her quite clearly, stepping out of a taxi outside an imposing granite villa near the university. She will find lodgings in the city, begin work as a teacher. She will live in obscurity, her work known to very few. Only after her death will her experimental saga *The Ice Dragon* be recognised as a masterpiece, comparable with Andrei Bely's novel *Petersburg* or Blok's long poem *The Twelve*. Books are wilful, fickle things, though. They change shape when you least expect them to, and almost without my realising, Susana slips from her seat and into the buffet car, drawing sentences about herself like the dense, woollen fabric of her overcoat, brought with her from Russia, where a new war is already being spoken of behind closed doors.

All the way from Glasgow I have been absorbed in an anthology of Aberdeen murders called *Blood and Granite*. The book is engrossing without being challenging, a compendium of facts that have become established over time, of details repeated so often their edges have been worn smooth, like shards of glass tumbled in the icy waters of the North Sea. There is a lulling immutability to these accounts of old crimes: this happened, that happened, the thing played out like this. The older the cases are, the more they seem like ghost stories, distant and bloodless, almost comforting, yet with that frisson of the uncanny that makes them live on.

The text is illustrated with black-and-white photographs, ordinary people immortalised through their misfortune. If the captions from the photographs were removed, it would be impossible to tell the victims from the killers, though it is not the faces that compel me so much as the crime scenes: houses, pubs, side streets, places where nothing happens until it does.

As the train pulls away from Montrose, I become captivated by a story from 1934, about an eight-year-old girl named Helen Priestly who was sent by her mother to buy bread from a local bakery and never returned. Almost at once I begin to wonder if this is the story the Russian émigré latches on to, the story that sits – like an ice dragon – at the heart of her novel.

Even before I reach the city, I can feel my sense of the narrative shifting and changing, being reshaped within the contours of this real-life crime. By the end of the day I recognise, with a feeling close to panic, that I am going to write about what happened to Helen Priestly. Even before I begin work I am wondering if the story I am about to start writing is too difficult to tell. I keep asking myself why it nags at me, why it won't stay in the past where it belongs.

I arrive in Aberdeen soon after three. The streets are quieter and emptier than I have been expecting. At first, I put this down to the continuing uncertainties of the COVID situation. But as I walk up Bridge Street and on to Union Street, I begin to get the feeling that there is more to it, not just an interruption to normality but a realignment, an inexorable slide from a previous state of existence towards something other. On Union Street a fitful wind is gusting, scattering litter across the concrete outside a pizza restaurant. Men and women sit cross-legged on the pavement, chugging Stella and Black Label cider straight from the can. They are not talking much. The sound of heavy drilling spirals upwards from the wasteland of ongoing building works that is Union Street Gardens.

The air smells dusty, warmed-over, as if recycled. The whole place seems somehow disconsolate, caught out, and I cannot get past the feeling that I have come too late. The Aberdeen I am searching for is gone, the muscular northern seaport of the years between the wars. The gloom and grit of the old city, its windows blackened by ancient dirt, its sailors packing the grimy alehouses that throng the harbourside. Before the end of paper and textiles and before the oil boom. Before the trams were set on fire and replaced by motor cars. Before the Union Square shopping mall exploded from the station forecourt and swallowed it whole.

I dump my bag on the built-in luggage stand. I feel attentive to my surroundings, energised by the sense of freedom I always find in being alone in a place where no one knows me. I take a shower, then order a meal from a takeaway close to the hotel. I cannot stop thinking about the crime scene photographs in *Blood and Granite*, in particular the one of the front room of a tenement flat at number 61 Urquhart Road, the same house where the Priestly family lived, and from where eight-year-old Helen Priestly disappeared. The dark wood furniture, the crowded accumulation of personal possessions reminds me of my grandmother's house.

The photograph of Helen Priestly's killer, taken from a news report in the *Aberdeen Press and Journal*, is spotted and blurred by time and from poor reproduction but there is an immediacy to it, still. It is hard to look away from.

I lay the book aside, put on my mask and go downstairs. Outside, the streets are empty and, except for the gusting wind, the town is quiet. I find the silence unnerving. It is as if the city is wary of self-exposure, suspicious of outward displays. A hard-bitten, battened-down outlier of a place that even now, a week after midsummer, is permanently braced for rain.

I walk slowly through the squares and wynds in the vicinity of Union Street, looking into the windows of shoe shops and betting shops, various pubs and restaurants, a dodgy-looking nightclub. The light is pastel-thin and roseate, faintly eerie. A church clock strikes nine. In the Sainsbury's Local on Bon Accord Street I pick out a packet of stilton-flavoured crisps and a bottle of pinot grigio. I stand silently with the other customers at the self-service checkouts, masks pulled up to our eyes.

You will write about her then, you have decided? says the Russian woman. She has appeared from out of nowhere, walking beside me up the steps from Flourmill Lane. This city, she says. I will never be in love with it, not ever, but that does not matter. It is the writing about it that matters. Words on the page.

City in Limbo

THE FOLLOWING MORNING, THE wind drops and the heat begins to rise. I walk out along Regent's Quay into the belt of builders' yards and storage facilities and fuel depots that have proliferated in what was once the warehouse district, the buffer zone between the docklands and the inner city. Fuel tankers and forklifts roll back and forth across concrete forecourts, warning signals flashing and beeping as they enter and exit the loading bays. From somewhere closer to the water I can hear the dull, repetitive clanging of hammer on steel. Aside from occasional guys with clipboards wearing hi-viz jackets, there are surprisingly few people about. I feel curiously at ease. I imagine applying for a job at one of the depots, a continuous stream of days spent checking shipping manifests and assigning load numbers, acquiring an intricate, esoteric knowledge of container ports and freight destinations. The prospect attracts me, as the activity of all specialist, practical workplaces attracts me, their low-key efficiency, their quiet expertise. Repetitive tasks that keep the world functioning but that are rarely understood or appreciated by those not in the trade.

I have always found reassurance in repetition, an aid to thought. Old photographs of Aberdeen docks show a diverse, rambunctious ecosystem teeming with life, a maze of lumber yards and cattle sheds, warehouses and sawmills, a complex, symbiotic machinery geared towards the transport of timber and textiles and livestock, including people. The docks are still busy. Ferries leave for Orkney and Shetland throughout the day. Container ships call at Aberdeen regularly to unload their cargoes. Service vessels bound for the rigs are still based here in the harbour. And the old names are everywhere: Hall, Hood, Duthie and Russell, the great shipbuilding dynasties of Aberdeen's past embedded in its present, in its street names and parks, carved permanently into the granite from which the town was raised.

And yet I cannot help feeling that there is less of everything now than this city is used to: less noise, less dirt, less profanity, less stink of fish and cow shit, less talk of the sea. Less sense of a place in the scheme of things. Less money.

I continue along Waterloo Quay, turning left into Church Street and then right into St Clement's Street. Directly in front of me is the church of East St Clement's, designed by John Smith, an Aberdeen architect, in 1828. The church has a tall, square clock tower surmounted with pinnacles. The churchyard, home to a number of sturdy, well established trees, is the only visible green space in a landscape of grey.

I had been hoping to see inside the church, but the door is padlocked and boarded over, sprayed with graffiti. The sight is both sad and unnerving, another reminder of the changes that have taken place here. Later, when I return home, I will stumble upon a collection of vintage maps and plans of Aberdeen that can be freely accessed through the website of the National Library of Scotland. By some strange coincidence, the cache includes a town plan printed by the Edinburgh Geographical Institute in 1934, the same year that Helen Priestly was murdered. The map was provided by the Association for the Advancement of Science to delegates at their annual conference, which that year was taking place in Aberdeen.

The map is like a window opening, as revealing as a photograph and somehow more powerful. Names are like spells, words to raise the dead, to conjure the scents and visions of a time that is gone. Labour exchange, fish market, harbour offices, Salvation Army Citadel, barracks, gasworks, police office. Newcastle and Hull steamer wharf, London steamer wharf, Leith, Orkney and Shetland steamer wharf. I imagine walking down to the quayside with my neatly packed suitcase, bound for Chatham. The dockers cursing and the stink of the fish stalls sprawling the length of Commercial Quay and all the gulls, screaming.

By the middle of the last century, Aberdeen was the largest fishing port in Scotland and, after Hull and Grimsby, the third largest in the whole of the United Kingdom. Dozens of trawlers, thousands of seamen and traders, canners and smokers all dedicating their lives and their livelihoods to the catching and selling of fish, twenty-four seven.

Beyond the London steamer wharf, the shipyards. Wood and steel, varnish and resin, paint and oil and pride and leather and canvas. Perpetual motion and vaunting ambition, a future emboldened in the present, enshrined in the past.

What happens to a thriving city when you cut its heart out? When you tell a man who has worked his whole life here, his father before him and before him his grandfather, that his calluses no longer have value, that he must *learn new skills?* When you break the hulk of a hundred years of craft into zero-hours scrap? To be without purpose is to be without worth, to be untethered and cast adrift in the vacuum of time. The Lady came and saw and conquered and then she went, carted off in the back of a Daimler, the Iron rusted to wreckage, the Lady herself now ten years dead. Yet still the nightmare lingers and the stain remains.

There are rumblings and rumours of a new aerospace industry in the north, a pioneering home-grown spaceport together with a thousand subsidiary money-pots to keep the engines turning. I imagine a woman – let's call her Lena – whose grandfather was a welder in the Aberdeen shipyards, about to begin work as an engineer at the fledgling shuttle complex. Your granddad never got over it, her mother says, the way they trashed the yards and laid off the men. Lena recalls her grandfather only dimly, a grey figure bent with age, his fleshless fingers quivering as he lighted a cigarette.

He was kind, the woman remembers, but he was sad. A living shadow. Now Lena sees him walking beside her on her way to work.

I am standing on the quayside at Footdee, pronounced Fittie and named for St Fittick, the patron saint of gardeners. The village once known as Fishtown, a couple of dozen low-slung cottages bolted together around the grids of their own backyards. A forgotten enclave, you'd be forgiven for thinking, a broken twig of the city's great tree, but you would be wrong. Footdee is ancient, Mediaeval, older than the shipyards and older than Union Street, a place with a history that stretches back centuries and still continues. Fishtown, with its hard-boiled pub and fish and chip shop, its shiny new four-star restaurant, its glass-and-concrete lighthouse that is more like a spy station, the port's roving eye, its washing lines strung from open windows, its scrubby patch of greensward is where the city begins.

I fall in love with it instantly, as I tend to do with coastal places, especially obscure ones. New Pier Road and York Street, Pilot Square and North Square, the bus stop outside M-I Swaco on Pocra Quay – I am half-afraid that if I don't take note of how I got here I might never find it again. An orange-bellied tanker on the horizon is an alien visitant, a messenger from another universe. I find myself wondering what this place will look like a century from now.

According to the Plan of the City of Aberdeen prepared for the Post Office Directory of 1879, the village of Footdee is home to an ironworks, a lifeboat house, the Sandilands Chemical Works, the Aberdeen Rope and Sail Works, and the Footdee Sawmills. Close by lies a goods yard and station, a direct connection with Aberdeen Central and busy with freight. In 1879, Urquhart Road is a simple thoroughfare linking the already populous King Street in the west with the Queen's Links, along the shoreline, and an area of open fields and woodland known as Broad Hill. King Street, where Helen Priestly will go to school in fifty years' time, is home to two hospitals: the Epidemic Hospital and the Boys' Hospital, built on the site of what will one day become the Robert Gordon University.

On an earlier plan, published by J&W Emslie in 1862, the Footdee Ironworks, the Sandilands Chemical Company and the Rope and Sail Works are all already in operation, but Urquhart Road as such does not yet exist. It is visible on the map as an unnamed pathway, running from the much less built up King Street across open fields to the Links and then on to Broad Hill. There is no Epidemic Hospital, no buildings at all this far out from the city's centre, just the powder magazine, something called the police dungyard, and the ominously named Gallows Hill.

The one constant is East St Clement's, sacred ground since the 1300s and marked on every map as far back as I can go. The church's graveyard is the final resting place of the composer and organist David Grant, who helped to compile *The Northern Psalter*, a celebrated anthology of Scottish hymn tunes published in 1872. A brass plaque set into the church wall honours him as the composer of the hymn tune 'Crimond'.

As a child, I remember being fascinated by the names of the hymn tunes we sang in school assembly: 'Monk's Gate', 'Slane', 'Repton', 'Old Hundredth'. There was something solemn and portentous about those names, the name 'Crimond' most of all, an austere and chilly resonance that seemed at odds with the stoic, consoling beauty of the words and tune. I did not realise at the time that the names, which seemed so mysterious, were often the names of places connected with the composer, in the case of 'Crimond' a village in Aberdeenshire to the north of Peterhead.

Crimond, I discover, was once the home of the tune's actual composer. Not David Grant, who wrote only the harmonies, but Jessie Seymour Irvine, daughter of the parish minister Alexander Irvine and herself a talented musician. In 2002, four etched glass panels were installed in Crimond church to commemorate Jessie Irvine as the rightful composer of the tune that bears its name. Jessie, who was born near Stonehaven, is buried in Aberdeen, in the churchyard of St Machar's Cathedral, alongside her father.

Were the Priestlys churchgoers? I have no way of knowing, though I feel certain that Helen would have sung Jessie's hymn as I myself did, if not in church then at school. Walking back through the docks and harbourside towards my hotel, I find myself humming it in time with my footsteps, that familiar and gracious three-quarter-time tread.

Yea, though I walk through death's dark vale, yet still I fear no ill.

I like chain hotels because I find them comfortable. I appreciate their cleanliness, their restful neutrality, most of all their anonymity. The certainty that no one will bother me or even particularly notice that I am there. The one thing I dislike about them is the underhum of white noise that tends to permeate their spaces, the whirring of aircon units and bathroom extractor fans, impossible to eradicate or to ignore.

Mercifully the room I am staying in is free of such torments, though my ability to sleep, unreliable at the best of times, is still compromised by the simple fact of being in an alien environment. I turn the radio down to a murmur. Someone is talking about ecological depletion, about insect die-off, and suddenly I find myself thinking of the spider that appeared in my office towards the end of January, circumnavigating the ceiling, walking a tightrope up by the picture rail above my desk. I called her Louise. A winter spider, spectral and grey, she was up there for days. I felt an affinity between us, an unspoken mutual knowledge that was somehow sustaining. I have always been interested in spiders, their actual selves and their mythical selves, Arachne, protector of weavers and spinner of snares, wilful and contrary transformer of thoughts into words.

About a week after first noticing her, I entered my office to find Louise tumbled, dead, against the skirting board, her limbs folded into her body, brittle as dried charcoal. I felt sad and for some reason guilty for not knowing her time on this planet was almost done.

I feel different from the writer I believed I was becoming. Writing now feels much closer to how it did in the beginning, when I first began dreaming up stories at the age of six. Self-defining, as if only by putting words on paper did I truly exist. I did not call myself a writer, I simply wrote.

What I feel now is the same precariousness and blind compulsion, the stubborn insistence on forging a path that might lead nowhere. Having scarcely a clue about what I am doing but having no choice.

It is four in the morning. Curled on my side on the too-firm hotel mattress, I begin naming crime novels for each letter of the alphabet: *American Tabloid*, *The Black Tower*, *Catharsis*, *Devil in a Blue Dress*. Floating uneasily in a greyish penumbra that resembles unconsciousness but lacks the restful oblivion of the genuine article, I begin to repeat letters, misplace others, forgo the order of the alphabet altogether. Perhaps this is why most people count sheep instead — it's that much less complicated. When sleep finally comes, there is an odd quality to it, an underlying scent of the uncanny, the feeling of eerie displacement that comes over you when, searching for the lavatory in a strange house, you wander into somebody's bedroom by mistake.

I am afraid that my body is undergoing a radical change. Metamorphosing into that of a winter spider, an ageless, charcoal-grey creature with hooded eyes.

I wake up still thinking about what happened in that overcrowded tenement house on Urquhart Road. I tell myself that my interest in the crime is normal, no different from my interest in the provenance of the hymn tune 'Crimond', or any other aspect of the city's history. That I should be free to explore my growing compulsion to write about the case, to have opinions about both perpetrator and victim, to theorise about alternative outcomes or explanations.

At the same time, I know there is something disingenuous about the claim, that even if everyone involved in the case is now dead, the facts of what happened are still private property, the remnants of a personal trauma that can never be assimilated or understood by an outsider.

If I intend to blunder in, to trespass and to steal, I should at least acknowledge the intrusion for what it is.

I have no right to this story, but I am going to tell it anyway. That is the kind of writer I am now. That is what writers do.

Lunch Break

THE CHILDREN COME OUT of school at twelve o'clock. The school is King Street Public School, Aberdeen, a two-storey granite edifice, built to last. Like so many Victorian municipal structures it is an elegant building, an emblem of stability and aspiration. King Street School was built in 1881, in accordance with guidelines laid down by the Public Health Act of 1872. The Act requires the provision of running water and adequate sanitary facilities to all new high-density housing and civic buildings, and its effect is revolutionary. Many of the children who first attend King Street School come from poor backgrounds. Most only have access to outside toilets and shared bathroom facilities. The Public Health Act is intended to change that, and in addition to the stipulations in respect of sanitation, school attendance itself is now compulsory. All over the country, new schools like King Street are beginning to offer the children of working-class families not only the chance of a decent education, but a raised expectation about what life in an evolving Western democracy ought to be like.

King Street School is located at 338 King Street, on the eastern side of the road, close to the junction with Urquhart Road. The building is set back from the street with the school yard, as is traditional, lying in front. The school has been designed to cater for eight hundred and forty pupils – infants, juniors, and seniors. The school will continue in its present purpose for a hundred years.

As the twentieth century turns the corner into the twenty-first, the school will find itself being repurposed, becoming the medical department of the newly inaugurated Robert Gordon University. In the November of 2001, Historic Scotland will award the building a Category C listing, reference LB48284. The protection afforded by this listing extends to the gateposts, railings and gates, which are all original. The gateposts are constructed from granite, the same as the building. The railings and gates are made of wrought iron, painted black.

At midday on Friday 20th April 1934, eight-year-old Helen Priestly passes through those school gates for the final time. The bell has just rung for the end of morning lessons, and Helen is going home for her dinner, the same as always. She leaves by the back entrance, taking the short cut down Boddie Place on to Urquhart Road. Her home, a first-floor tenement flat situated at number 61 Urquhart Road, is less than two hundred yards away.

Urquhart Road lies a mile or so north of the city centre, a long, humpbacked thoroughfare, a gentle up-and-down curve like the bent top rung of a ladder, linking King Street in the west with Links Road to the east. Links Road leads to the Esplanade, and to Aberdeen beach. In 1934, no one would question whether it is safe for Helen to be walking home alone. The street is a common space, a place for ball games and for loitering, a valuable and necessary extension of the family home. How else would a mother keep her sanity, cooped up in a tiny tenement with all the weans underfoot? On fine days she chases them out. On wet days they run out anyway, returning home hours later with sodden overcoats, their knees grazed and begrimed with street dirt, their boots and socks and pinafores streaked with mud.

This is a close-knit neighbourhood; everyone knows everyone else, at least by sight. At midday the street is busy with workers going home on their lunch break or heading back to work, delivery drivers and message handlers, women returning from visiting relatives or from the market. Urquhart Road is a long, grey corridor of four-storey tenements, a daunting expanse of granite, working families squashed together like pickled herrings in their narrow flats. It is not a slum, but it is not a prosperous area either. It is not as busy or as well provisioned as nearby King Street, but in 1934 Urquhart Road still boasts a shop on every corner. Butcher, fishmonger, greengrocer, baker, grocery and tobacconist, ironmonger and hardware store, each a hub of community gossip and local intelligence.

You can take a walk along Urquhart Road using Google Streetview. King Street, where the school is, has become the A956. Towards the eastern end of Urquhart Road, beyond the junction with Park Road, the granite tenements have been torn down, replaced by dismal-looking blocks of post-war flats. The blocks have been designed in what might loosely be described as tenement style, though in reality the flats are ugly and clumpish, more reminiscent of prison buildings or army barracks. To the west of Park Road and all the way to King Street the original architecture of Urquhart Road remains wholly intact. Few of the shops from Helen's time survive, though the shapes of windows and architraves and frontages offer a clearly readable map of where they once operated. On the corner opposite number 61, once known to Mrs Priestly and her neighbours as Webster's Corner, is a red pillar box. Webster's grocery store is gone, converted to a private dwelling, but the pillar box outside is still there and still in use.

The sky above is a searing blue, the windows of all the houses are flung open. Number 61 lies on the north side of the road, the penultimate house in a block about halfway along. In 1934, eight families live there, two on each floor. The building is divided by a communal hallway, known as the close. To the left side of the close going ground floor to third you have the Topps, the Josses, the Mitchells and the Gordons. To the right and once again in ascending order you have the Donalds, the Priestlys, the Coulls and the Hunts. A door to the rear of the lobby leads to the washroom, eight brick-built coal sheds, and a shared drying green, the same as you might expect to see at the back of any Scottish tenement, even today. Towards the rear of the lobby you will also find the lavatory, shared by the occupants of the two ground-floor flats. Opposite the lavatory is the stair alcove, with a cupboard under. The cupboard is used by Mrs Donald for storing potatoes, and is usually kept locked.

At the time the image was captured for Streetview, an estate agent's signboard in a downstairs window indicates that the ground floor flat to the right of the close – what was once the Donalds' flat – is up for sale. These original Victorian tenements have scrubbed up well. The area is popular with students and with young professionals looking for reasonably priced accommodation within reach of the city centre and the university. A listing on a popular property website shows a one-bedroom flat on Urquhart Road going for offers in excess of £57,000. The flat has new wooden flooring throughout as well as a recently fitted bathroom and kitchen. Similar properties in the area have recently sold for as much as £100,000.

On the opposite side of the road and across the intersection with Roslin Street you will see a Premier convenience store. If you navigate back down the street in the opposite direction you will notice something peculiar: the shop is no longer a Premier, but a Costcutter. The sky has turned grey, and the windows of the houses are all closed. You will understand that what you are seeing is simply a cross-hatching of an earlier image capture with a later one, and that you are probably not the first to stumble upon this anomaly. The effect is curious, all the same, as if the confluence of Roslin Street and Urquhart Road were some sort of time-slip.

We have an accurate record of most of what happened that afternoon because of the trial transcript, but let's set the formalities aside for the moment and imagine the scene as it might appear at the beginning of a new true crime drama on TV. The action opens upon Helen Priestly, a slight, mousy-haired young girl in a navy overcoat and knitted beret, running out of the school gates and making her way along the crowded pavement of an inner city thoroughfare. She is smiling cheerfully. She waves to someone she knows, makes a face at a boy on a bicycle, who loudly rings his bell as he speeds past. There are plenty of other children around, chattering and joshing, all of them on their way home for the midday meal.

The action switches to the Priestlys' kitchen, where Agnes Priestly is busy preparing lunch. There is a pot of vegetables on the stove, a beef casserole in the oven. The Priestlys are not well off, but they do not go hungry. A muffled banging sound can be heard, coming through from the lobby. There are some workmen around the back, carrying out roof repairs. The slaters do not actually arrive until around two o'clock, but the director has brought them in earlier to set the scene.

The kitchen door flies open and there is Helen. She is jabbering away, telling her mother the run of her morning, lessons and teachers and minor misdemeanours, games of tag that escalate into playground wars. Wash your hands, love, Agnes tells her, only half listening. She's concentrating on the vegetables, which are almost done. As she starts to dish up the stew her husband John arrives, washes his hands at the sink and sits down to eat. He forks meat and potatoes into his mouth while reading the paper, spread out beside him on the plain deal table. He tells Agnes that he might be late for supper. The job's taking an age, he says, and he needs to go to the shop to replenish his supplies. John Priestly is a painter and decorator, a fact we might already have picked up on from the flecks of dried emulsion on his trousers and shirt. The pub he's doing up, the Saltoun Arms, is still in business today, still good for a bar meal and a game of darts, though according to Tripadvisor the place is apt to turn a wee bit rowdy of a Friday night.

Once Helen has finished eating, Agnes asks her if she'll take this broken aluminium teapot – the lid's come loose, see? – and put it in the odds and ends box out the front of Lyon's the butcher's. Then after that would she go next door to Auntie Nannie's and see if there's any messages she wants taking. Auntie Nannie is Mrs Helen Robertson, who lives with her husband and two grown-up children at number 9 Roslin Street. The Robertsons own and run the sweetshop at number 25.

Helen runs down the stairs and out on to the street. She drops the broken teapot into the butcher's box and then dashes around the corner to the Robertsons. The Robertsons and the Priestlys are close. Mrs Robertson is Helen Priestly's godmother, and she and her daughter Ella are very attached to her. Bright as a button and cheeky as a monkey, that's wee Helen. Our Ella's that fond of her, she spoils her rotten. Always treating the lass is our Ella, just like today she's treating her to a new tam, and would you look at the pretty wee girlie in her smart blue bonnet, a real little heartbreaker and so grown up, so *ladylike*. How's about a spray of that nice French scent?

Ella Robertson, twenty-one, scatters the perfume over the collar of Helen's school dress. The scent is so powerful and so long-lasting the police pathologist will note its presence on Helen's clothing ten days later. Meanwhile, Helen is taking her leave of the Robertsons and dancing home. Agnes briefly admires her in her new blue tammy before sending her out again, asking if she'll nip to the Co-op for a loaf of bread. Just a plain half-loaf will do, she says, that's fourpence. Make sure they write it in the book and don't forget the message bag. She gives Helen a shilling then turns to make a start on the washing-up.

The Northern Co-operative Bakery is on the corner of Hunter Place, just a hundred yards away. The errand should take less than ten minutes – plenty of time for Helen to buy the bread and still be back at school in time for the bell.

Helen goes and she is happy to go. She has been to buy bread for her mother a thousand times before. And this is where the narrative thread begins to draw tighter. We follow Helen as she leaves the house, almost bumping into a neighbour on her way out – we will learn later that this is Mr Hunt from upstairs, returning to work. She skips down the road, humming to herself, part of a French nursery rhyme taught to her by Ella Robertson. There are lots of people about, and yet the way the camera zooms in on Helen's face makes us feel uneasy. A small group of men are smoking and chatting by the post box on Webster's Corner. Two women stand together, laughing, on the pavement outside the greengrocer's.

As Helen goes into the bakery, a bell rings. An older girl is at the counter, buying some yeast. Helen asks one of the serving women for a fourpenny half loaf. The woman wraps the bread in white paper. She writes down the Priestlys' Co-op number in the receipt book, then tears off the top copy and gives it to Helen. Helen puts the bread into the bag then leaves the shop, clutching the receipt in her right hand. Outside, on the pavement, she hesitates for a moment and then turns for home. We watch her until she disappears, becoming lost in the general activity of the busy street.

It is an ordinary Friday. The Priestlys are an ordinary family. The weather is chilly but dry, at least until the evening, when the sky will grow overcast and the rain will fall in torrents. It is a little after half-past one. Helen is supposed to be back at school by five to two, but she will never get there.

In less than an hour, eight-year-old Helen Priestly will be dead.

Dunnottar

THE TRAIN BRINGS ME into Stonehaven in less than half an hour. It is blisteringly hot. At the bottom of the hill, the neat little market square is swarming with visitors. The pubs and restaurants along the harbourside are loud and full.

I follow the steep path leading up from the harbour and walk the two miles along the clifftop to reach the castle. The sun-dried fields are shimmering with butterflies – meadow brown, heathland fritillary, small copper – and the pounding heat is blissful. I am swooning in the scent of dry grass, the antithesis of the windblown granite corridor of Union Street. I see other people along the way but not too many; most visitors arrive here by car, parking at the designated stopping place further along the coast then descending the final five hundred yards or so to the castle entrance.

No one is wearing masks and I am on a high.

I cannot go into the castle. The ticket kiosk is closed because of COVID and you are supposed to book in advance, via the castle website. I briefly consider trying to book a slot using my phone, but the thought of doing battle with an unfamiliar app is too exhausting. I do not need to go in, anyway. The view from where I am sitting is ridiculously fine, an idealised Highland tableau straight out of *Outlander*. I eat the two dry rolls I brought with me, wash them down with water then lie back in the grass. I listen to the laughter and conversation going on around me and at some point, the straps of my daypack twisted securely around my palms, I fall asleep.

A beetle's gold-sheened carapace, the herbal, high-summer scent of soil wrung dry, and I find myself wondering if Helen Priestly ever visited Stonehaven – on a picnic perhaps, a holiday outing with the Robertsons or with Agnes's sister. Beach towels and sandcastles, those thick leather open-toed Jesus sandals everyone used to wear for school. Ice creams and lemonade, pirate hats folded from the pages of the *Aberdeen Record*. Trailing back to the station at the end of the day, the wee ones are exhausted and beginning to grizzle. The skin of their shoulders and noses reddened and peeling, fingers and lips still sticky with the crystallised residue of salt and vinegar.

Agnes and Ella are carrying the picnic basket between them. Ella is confiding in Agnes about her new young man.

Agnes smiles and says encouraging words but she is feeling worn out. The lass knows nothing yet, Agnes is thinking. She is still a child, really.

There is tiredness around her eyes, though it has been a good day, the kind of treat you would remember for a long time afterwards, especially if you come from a background where such treats are rare.

I think about writing *a cloud blocks out the sun and I feel the chill* but I don't, because it doesn't happen. The sun blazes down, unrepentant, and the sky is hammered steel. Three small children run madly in circles, screaming with excitement as they tumble over each other, rolling in the grass.

Dunnottar Castle is seven hundred years old, and counting.

A fortress, with butterflies. Whole radiant days like these.

The Russian woman comes to sit beside me on the journey back. She is wearing a denim jacket, an old Marlboro baseball cap, and red Converse sneakers. She has a book open on her lap, the same anthology of Aberdeen true crime stories I was reading on my way up here.

It is like the world breaking open, Susana says. Murder. Like crossing the border into a different universe. You go to buy bread from a bakery and all the way there you are thinking about other things. You are thinking about the maths test you have to sit that afternoon, or what you are going to do when you get home from school, and while you are thinking about these things they are still a possibility, a set of feelings and actions and wishes that could still come to pass. What you don't realise is that the future they belong to is already over, that it was never yours.

The only way you can read about cases like this and not go crazy, she adds, is by secretly refusing to believe they ever happened.

I remember this guy, says the Russian woman, who came to a talk in the history department about artworks that were stolen by the Nazis during WW2. The speaker had written a book on the descendants of people who died in the Holocaust, who were still searching for their looted treasures and this man, after the talk was over he put up his hand and started telling the speaker he should write about his alcoholic brother, who was killed while he was in a homeless shelter. The guy was still in shock, you could tell. It was awful to see. Everyone in the room felt uncomfortable. The feelings he had were real, though, and they had changed who he was. They changed all of us too, a little. That is what murder does.

Gone

AGNES CAN HEAR HER daughter out on the landing, chatting to Mr Hunt, who's just come down the stairs with his little daughter Betty. He's on his way back to work, most like. Helen dotes on the Hunt kiddie, the two are playmates and that's wee lasses for ye, always dreaming over some new fancy, some secret game.

Agnes smiles to herself, clearing away the dinner things, and this is where I keep pressing rewind, searching for a clue she might have missed, a shadow in the hallway, something. I keep hearing Helen's laugh, the clunk of the heavy front door as she pulls it shut behind her. She'll be right, Agnes muses. She's a grand wee lass, my Helen. Her thoughts run on, untroubled. There is a crack in her world and it is growing wider, wider by the second but for another ten minutes at least she will be none the wiser.

She finishes the washing-up, folds the dishcloth neatly in two across the bar of the stove. John's back into work already and there's a mound of washing needs doing before he's home for his tea. She is listening out for Helen, who should be returning with the bread any second, she's going to be late for school if she doesn't hurry. Agnes is worried now, but only a little. She goes through to the bedroom and looks out of the window. There is no sign of Helen, just Ella Robertson coming across the road from Webster's. Agnes calls to her out of the window, have you seen our Helen? And Ella starts talking about Helen being over at theirs not ten minutes past and Agnes is saying no, I mean have you seen her since then? Has anybody seen her since then?

She barely waits for Ella's answer because she knows it already. She spies another wee girlie, another Helen even, Helen Mearns, who's in her Helen's class at school, and she's asking Helen Mearns if she'll shoot to the Co-op, see where her Helen's got to because she's late for school now. And when the Mearns girl comes lolloping back and tells Agnes what she knows in her stomach already, that her Helen's not in the Co-op and not outside on the street either, Agnes is halfway down the road by the time the words are out of her mouth, her girlie's coat over her arm to save her going back for it. She'll be late now all right. Where in heaven is the lass?

She's not in the shop, of course she's not. The woman serving behind the counter says she doesn't know Helen, not so she'd recognise her but then she asks Agnes what her number is, her Co-op number, and look, here it is, see, a plain half loaf, which is fourpence, it's here in the book.

Did she say to you where she was going? Agnes asks, hopelessly. The woman is staring back at Agnes like she's lost her mind.

I didnae ask, she says. She is already turning away to serve the next customer. Agnes leaves the shop and carries on up the street towards King Street School. It's all but two o'clock now and they're ringing the bell. Agnes spies the Donald girl, wee Jeannie her name is, the same wee Jeannie as her Helen used to play with before the falling-out with her mother on account of Agnes's falling-out with Mrs Coull. The Donald woman all high and mighty, her nose so far up in the air you'd think she was royalty. She wanted no part in the row, she'd said, which was exactly what Agnes would expect from the likes of her. And so there they both were, not speaking, though it was hardly the fault of the children. Wee Jeannie is a good girl, always polite, which is more than can be said for her mother.

She takes wee Jeannie by the elbow, hunkers down.

Did ye happen to see my Helen, Jeannie? Did she go into class?

Wee Jeannie shakes her head, then says she'll go have a look in the classroom, just to be sure. Agnes watches her fly, so lightsome she is, like fairy dust from all those after-school dance classes. The dance lessons are down to the Donald woman, another way of setting her stamp on things. Forever finicking and fussing with hair ribbons, forever making out her Jeannie's the bee's knees when everyone knows she's just a girlie like everyone else's, an ordinary Aberdeen lass who'll be doing well for herself landing a job at the shipping office or the council office or at one of the banks even, where there'll be men to be sure and decent ones, all looking for wives.

A live daughter, Agnes thinks. Each day with a living daughter is like a gorgeous holiday. If only mothers knew.

Wee Jeannie is coming back now, lips pinched in an anxious line. Her forehead softly creased, the tenderest of frowns.

Helen's not there. She shakes her head again. I have to go in now.

Agnes thanks her, touches her shoulder, sends her winging away.

She can feel the tears building, the gathering storm of them, the saltiness pressing against her eyelids and scouring the hot, constricted space at the back of her throat. She turns away from the schoolhouse, wondering which way to go. Along King Street to where the trams stop, or back through the short cut to Urquhart Road, the same way Helen would be coming if she was coming, but she is not, Agnes can feel it, and as the thin spring sunshine begins curdling into lumps of greyish cloud, she senses an emptiness growing inside her she has never known before.

She spends the next half hour fruitlessly searching, going about from one side of the street to the other, in and out of shops, asking her neighbours, the residents and visitors and tradespeople of Urquhart Road and Roslin Street and Hunter Place if they have seen her Helen, if they have seen anything, and the more time passes and the more people shake their heads, the more her daughter's absence becomes a foregone conclusion, a thing people already know about, a subject that is being discussed on every street corner.

Helen Priestly is missing, and her mother is in tears.

It is now two thirty. Agnes heads with Mrs Robertson to the Saltoun Arms. John is busy about his work, repainting the pub. Agnes's mind is blank with worry now, even though Mrs Robertson, who will remain by her side throughout the whole of the coming evening and the following day, is still doing her best to reassure her.

She'll be found soon enough, hen, you'll see.

She's still no' come back from the Co-op, Agnes tells John. Her face is pinched and pale, a snapshot of herself at fifty. John says to her she'd best go home — what would happen if Helen returns and there's no one there to see to her? The moment the women are out of sight, he puts in a call to the police office from the Saltoun bar. John is worried, but not too worried, not this soon. It could be his wife is mistaken, and his daughter will be found. With one of her wee pals, most likely, hiding out in the broom cupboard or in the washhouse or some such makeshift castle. That's the way kiddies are, he was one himself once. Dreaming of nonsense and wreaking havoc, forgetting such a slippery fish as time even existed.

He does not blame Agnes for being anxious but he could do without the trouble of it. They are behind with the job as it is, and now he'll have to leave the pub in charge of his prentice while he goes and sorts this out.

He cultivates his impatience, tending it carefully, like the single, tentative flame on a lump of damp kindling. John will entertain any theory, no matter how wild. Better to blame his wife for her nervous temperament than to flirt with the truth: that his loved one is officially missing, that little by little and person by person, his loss is becoming a matter for the whole town to know.

The Dark Man

And for a breathless couple of hours, the police believe they are on to something, and Richard Sutton's dark man is the talk of Aberdeen.

Richard Sutton is nine years old. He lives with his grandfather down the road at number 83. He is a schoolmate of Helen Priestly, has played with her in the schoolyard now and again. At around six o'clock on the Friday evening, he appears at the Priestlys' door and tells John his story.

John Priestly has only recently come in. He has spent most of the afternoon following in his wife's footsteps, from the Northern Co-operative Bakery to King Street School and then to the police station in Lodge Walk. He has spoken to friends and neighbours and tradespeople – the same friends and neighbours and tradespeople Agnes spoke to an hour or so before him. When every inquiry ends in failure he returns briefly to the Saltoun Arms to lock up for the night and then makes his way home. He knows he should have been back sooner, but he has forced himself to delay. There is a voice in his head, a voice that keeps insisting he should keep to his routine. That if he refuses to entertain the devil, the devil will grow bored with the game he has started and slink away to torment someone else.

He can taste the joy on his tongue: the kitchen door flung open, his girl sat there at the table with her tea plate in front of her. Bright with chatter and the same as always, the same as any other evening of the working week.

Instead of a daughter, two policemen. They are there to listen to his story yet again, and what a hollow little story it seems, the details of his fruitless enquiries as thin and pallid and faded as second hand clothes. He has had nothing to eat since lunchtime. He can barely think from being so famished yet at the same time, if anyone asked him, he would say he wasn't hungry.

The polis are barely out the door when the boy appears, a child he knows by sight but cannot name.

Ricky Sutton, Agnes reminds him, from down the street.

I sees her, Ricky says. There is a dancing light in his eyes, a fever John might have passed off as mischief-making but the lad is insisting he speak to them, he won't be denied.

The man had her, Ricky says. The dark man. The dark man had her by the shoulder and when the tram came up to the stop he made her get on. She looked scared, he adds, dropping his gaze to the floor as if the words hurt to speak.

Man? says John, attentive now, and his breathing is painful. What man?

Dark hair, and a bit of a beard, like. He was wearing this coat, with a rip in it. The coat was black. I never seen him before – he was a *stranger*.

The last word comes out as a whisper, like it's walking on tiptoe.

Agnes's hands are pressed to her mouth and she's beginning to cry again. With the thought of Helen in this stranger's grip John does not blame her but even so, there is something more than fear in his quickened breathing, a flash of triumph that rises like marsh gas, snuffing out his terror. So she has been seen, at least. Against the hours of stolid headshakes and dull-eyed nos, this child, this Ricky Sutton is insisting: yes!

You're sure now, that it was her? John scarcely dares to test his luck but he owes it to Agnes.

It were her, I swear it. I recognised her by the tammy.

And which tram were they getting on to, did you say?

I don't know the number. It were the one that goes down past the post office.

And you'll tell the polis the same as you've just told me?

And Richard Sutton nods his head, all the while with a look on him like he's done his good deed for the day and is rightfully proud of it.

A good boy, John supposes, a brave little fellow. There was no need for the child to come here, but come here he did.

It is the only lead the police have to go on and they swallow it whole, firing their questions at Ricky who is in so deep and so far he cannot wriggle free. Yes, the man was tall and dark and bearded, of middling age. Yes his coat was black and dirty-like, and torn in the back. And yes, the lass looked frightened, she were trying to get away.

She had the bread with her, the boy adds, excitedly. The bread she bought from the baker's. She were carrying it under her arm.

Children try ideas on for size, just to see how they fit. I am certain that Ricky can picture him clearly, his dark man, the sinister set of his shoulders, the painful pinch of his fingers as he grabs hold of Helen Priestly and pushes her ahead of him, on to the tram. I am certain the more Ricky thinks about it the more he imagines he saw her, mousy little Helen Priestly with her bread and her saxe-blue tammy and her shy dimpled smile. She's an all-right lassie is Helen but not one you'd notice particularly, not like the one in the paper who disappeared last year, the girl with the blurry outline and the silver hair. Ricky never took much notice of lasses before, but the lassie they called the ghost girl was something different. Like a thump in the heart different. And now the dark man dogs his footsteps and haunts his dreams.

Girl taken by unknown assailant, the headline said. Ricky wouldn't normally look at the papers, just the football pages, but suddenly the words 'girl taken' are all he can think about. He heard his granny and their neighbour Mrs Noone from over the close discussing the details, using words he has seen in the paper but never heard spoken, their voices lowered to whispers to try to shut him out.

Abducted, felon, fugitive, vagrant, raped.

Words dark as blackened cinders, as poisoned fruit. He knows assailant means attacker, but he is still not satisfied. There are other words he does not know – words that hide their secrets inside themselves, words that will not give up their meanings, even when you know what they sound like and how they are spelled. Ricky does not dare to think about what *raped* means. He knows his granny will not tell him that one, even if he asks.

The dark houses, the misty streets, the narrow alleyways and cobbled closes, all the places a girl might be lost in, the police are searching. They are searching for the assailant who snatched the ghost girl. Several witnesses at the tram stop had also seen the dark man.

I thought he were her da, said one. I supposed she'd run away and he were fetching her back.

A dirty-looking man, with a greasy black hat, said another. He looked strange to me.

When the policeman asked her what she meant by strange, the woman shook her head then pursed her lips and said she couldn't say.

Just that he were quiet, she admitted at last. Didn't say a word. Just took the girlie by the arm and marched her away.

Black hat and heavy coat and stubbly beard. From small details such as these, Ricky Sutton's view of the world is altered forever.

What the human race is coming to. His granny tuts and shakes her head. It disnae bear thinking about. She is kneeling on the hearthrug, rolling the newspaper with the picture of the blonde girl to light the stove.

Men like that, says Mrs Noone, there's something no' right wi' them. They'll no' find the lassie intact, I'll tell ye that for nothing.

The darkened houses and the rain-soaked streets and here comes the dark man, seeking his victims and stalking his prey, the lass with the blurry outline and the ghost-coloured hair. When Ricky happens to wake in the night he hears the sound of her breathing, the rapid, hunted sound of a girl on the run. Which is why when he overhears the news about his classmate Helen Priestly it's the dark man he thinks of, the dark man snatching away wee Helen with her bread still under her arm and that look in her eyes, the look he saw on the face of the girlie that were in all the papers.

And as soon as he speaks those thoughts aloud they burst into life. Not another one, says the first policeman, turning away from Ricky and towards his colleague. They both remember the girl from the papers who was taken the year before, but only the older man had been there when they eventually found her. Found her wandering without any clothes on, miles from her home and not a word was she ever to speak about how she had come there.

The dark man is not a phantom, he is a living monster, and now the police know who they are looking for they are quick to act. Already they are fanning out across the city. Already they are watching the tram stops and searching the depots. They are asking anyone getting off a tram if they have seen Helen Priestly – Helen Priestly in the company of the dark man with the filthy stubble who is become her assailant.

Richard Sutton has told a story that is bigger than he is. So big it has a life of its own, a dangerous, jagged reality that is overwhelming. And maybe the story itself is become the dark man, a shadow grown so huge it blocks out the sun.

And all through the wind-thrashed, rain-soaked Friday night of April 20th 1934, Richard Sutton, who is only a child but old enough already to know the truth from a fairy tale, lies sleepless in his narrow cot and decides that he will go to the detectives, he will go to them in the morning and tell them the truth. That he was passing along Urquhart Road on the way back to school and happened to hear two older boys speaking about Helen Priestly going missing. That they were revelling in the drama, as boys will do. That the details he later spoke about – the loaf of bread and the saxe-blue tammy – were details he stole from their tattling and made his own.

That he never saw Helen Priestly outside of the schoolyard, never gave her much of a thought before that day. And years later, when he has weans of his own, he will still be asking himself what it was that made him say such a thing, that he saw wee Helen in the grip of the dark man getting on to a tram.

And yet the bread is in her hands, he can still see it clearly – the bread, and the torn black overcoat, the frightened look in her eyes. He will tell himself over and over that his words made no difference. Yet the shame of his story still haunts him. The ragged shame of a lie, like a thorn in the heart.

And although in a sense Richard Sutton is right – his false testimony will not and cannot make any difference to Helen's fate – its initial impact on the investigation is substantial. Although Helen's classmates from King Street School – Helen Mearns and Ursula Charles, Ann McNab and Muriel Leslie – assure the police in separate interviews that they saw Helen Priestly coming away from the bakery and walking back along Urquhart Road in the direction of her home, it is Ricky Sutton's dramatic monologue that has most impact. By seven o'clock that evening, the phantom dark man is the person everyone is looking for. Helen's photograph is flashed up on cinema screens all over town, and a police appeal for information is put out on the radio:

POLICE MESSAGE BROADCAST VIA BBC RADIO
ABERDEEN 8 PM FRIDAY 20th APRIL 1934

Missing since 1:30 pm today, Helen Priestly, aged eight-and-a-half years, tall for her age, fair hair parted in the middle with a fringe; dressed in a blue serge frock with blue velvet collar, black shoes and stockings and light blue knitted tammy.

Living at 61 Urquhart Road, Aberdeen, and at the time mentioned was sent on an errand to a nearby shop. It is believed she boarded a tramway car in King Street travelling to the Bridge of Dee in company with a man. The girl was then carrying a loaf of bread wrapped in white paper.

The man is described as being of middle age, five feet nine inches in height, of a dirty appearance, dark complexion, in need of a shave. Dressed in black coat reaching about halfway to the ground, black trousers and cap, no collar and tie.

The news of Helen's disappearance travels out across the city in waves, a ripple effect. Bystanders and gawpers and would-be helpers begin to congregate in Urquhart Road for no other reason than to be there in the place where something terrible and out of the ordinary has happened. By the early evening there are several hundred onlookers, all hoping to be the first on the scene when the outcome of the disaster is finally revealed.

The men of Urquhart Road and King Street and Roslin Street head out in relays, combing the backyards and coal sheds and closes, poking into chicken houses and murky back alleyways, their wives and sisters and daughters rustling up batches of sandwiches, brewing endless flasks of tea. It is raining by now, a bitter wind streaking across the allotments, yet the searchers continue undaunted and grow in number. Many of those involved in the search do not know Helen personally. They are united not so much by compassion as by compulsion, energised by the sense of unease and hectic excitement that accompanies every tragedy and every accident, each twisted turn of fate.

Because it couldae been ma Gordy, ma Rosey or ma Madeleine, oh so easily. Dinnae say it, dinnae even think it. There but fo' the grace o' God go I.

A local landlord, William Duncan, owns a motor car. He has offered to drive John around the neighbourhood – they can cover more ground that way. The two keep up their efforts until after midnight, driving and stopping, stopping and driving through the chilly not-quite-darkness of a rain-soaked April night in Aberdeen. It is still painful to imagine John's exhaustion and his sense of hopelessness, the city itself made alien through his numb despair. His hands are shaking from cold and his eyes are smarting from staring at shadows. They call in again at the police station in the hope that some new lead has been discovered. They are told there is no news, that the men are still searching.

William Duncan has had enough. He insists they call a halt until it gets light.

You're all but finished, man. You're going to make yourself ill if you don't get some rest.

He drops John outside his house, saying he will return to collect him at five o'clock. He drives home through the rain-thickened greyness, the eerie no-man's-land between night and morning. The streets, the houses appear strange to him suddenly, as if they belong in a play or in a foreign country. Like someone's idea of a northern city, only they got it wrong somehow, they turned it into a place you no longer recognise.

Look at the Bag

[FROM THE *ABERDEEN PRESS AND JOURNAL*
SATURDAY 21ST APRIL 1934]

HUE AND CRY FOR MISSING ABERDEEN CHILD

Under the supervision of the police, a search was made of every cellar and stretch of ground in the Urquhart Road district, but the search there was also fruitless. The search also covered the Broad Hill, and many other open spaces.

Shortly after ten o'clock, organised searches were begun. Under the direction of the police, some 500 volunteers scoured the Beach and Links. Footdee was combed, and parties went round by Balgownie to Murcar, The police also supervised a search of Balnagask, and indeed few spots were missed by the searchers, who carried on throughout the night. Additional volunteers waited round Lodge Walk in the hope that some information would come to hand that would give them something to work on.

The scene at the Beach was an arresting one. Every car which came on to the promenade was stopped by the police. All over the links to the Bridge of Don the lights of searchers twinkled. Every type of torch was used, and a number managed to secure lanterns.

Despite the efforts of the searchers and ceaseless activities of the police, at an early hour this morning no trace of the missing girl had been found.

Information was received by the police early this morning that a down-and-out man with a girl had been seen in the Persley district.

Among the first to offer his services as a searcher was Mr P. Smith, Hutcheon Street, Aberdeen, the father of a two-year-old girl who last October was carried away and who was found the following morning lying at the edge of a quarry at Cairncry.

At three forty-five am or thereabouts, two lamplighters, employed by Aberdeen City Council, are extinguishing the streetlights along Urquhart Road and Roslin Street.

At four o'clock, a baker, Sutherland, is leaving for work.

Shift workers at the local gasworks confirm that by the time they leave home at four thirty it is already full daylight.

The scavenger, or rag-and-bone man, would normally be starting his rounds at six o'clock. As it happens, he is up an hour early that Saturday, because he has promised to awaken a neighbour who has a train to catch.

Alexander Porter, a joiner, lives with his wife at number 60 Urquhart

Road. The Porters are friends of the Priestlys. They made John some supper and sat up with him for a while after he was dropped off the night before by William Duncan. Alex has promised to help with the search again today. He gets up around half-past four, makes himself a cup of tea then leaves the house. He stops to chat with the scavenger and another man on the corner of Roslin Street before heading across to the Priestlys. Shortly before five, he sees a car being driven down the road from the direction of King Street – this is William Duncan, returning to continue the search as had been agreed. As the car comes to a standstill outside the Priestlys' building, Porter goes round to the driver's side and introduces himself to Duncan before walking around the front of the car towards number 61.

In an interview published in the *Press and Journal* on Monday April 24th, Alex Porter describes John Priestly as being 'in a state of collapse' at the end of a night of fruitless searching, adding that Agnes Priestly was in a 'terrible condition' following 'long hours of anguish and suspense' over Helen's whereabouts. Alongside the interview is a photograph of Alex Porter, a thin-lipped, underfed-looking man with deeply set dark eyes. His hair is cut short, and parted to one side. He is wearing a white shirt and dark jacket. A figure floating up from the past, a working man of the 1930s, reticent and nervous in company he is not used to. We know nothing about him, other than the poignant, now immortal details from what were likely among the most stressful and unpleasant twenty-four hours of his life.

His wife is not even named. She gave John Priestly a cup of tea and did her best to comfort him. That is all we know.

It is now five past five. Almost immediately upon entering the lobby of number 61, Alex Porter sees a bag, some sort of sack, lying half in and half out of the stair recess by the door to the lavatory. He runs back out into the street and yells to Duncan, still waiting in the car, that Helen's body is in a bag at the back of the lobby.

'I could hardly speak,' Porter says at the trial. 'My speech had left me. I gestured him into the lobby.'

And it is interesting to note how their accounts of those moments contradict one another. Porter claims he lost the power of speech; William Duncan insists that Porter came 'flying out, roaring'. When Duncan sees the sack for himself, he immediately begins to shout for help and bang on doors. There was a great commotion, he says, people shouting and yelling, crying out. 'I could not clearly recognise them at first, they were so upset,' says Mrs Robertson, who has kept vigil with Agnes Priestly throughout the night. 'Mr Duncan was bashing the wall and kicking at Mrs Donald's door.' A Mrs Morrison was screaming and crying, out in the street.

'Oh, look at the bag!' Porter is crying. Helen's feet can clearly be seen, protruding from the mouth of the sack. Mrs Topp – the Priestlys' downstairs neighbour on the opposite side – faints when she hears the screams. She is four months pregnant at the time, and so deeply distressed by what has happened that she will suffer a miscarriage. Mrs Mitchell from the third floor on the Topps' side comes out of her flat with her children and looks down over the bannister into the lobby. She hears Agnes Priestly screaming – 'Oh, my bairn!' – and then everything goes quiet.

Police Constable John Burnett Cassie, who happens to be on duty further up the street, is quickly brought to the scene by William

Duncan and Helen Robertson. He checks his watch as he enters the lobby: it is ten past five. The search for a missing child has become a murder investigation.

The milk boy, knowing nothing, calls at number 61 as usual just before six. At around six thirty, Alec Donald opens his front door to take in the milk. Seeing PC Cassie, he asks if there is any news of the missing child. When Cassie tells him that Helen's body has been found here in the lobby – that it is still lying just feet from where they are standing, in fact – Alec Donald says simply 'oh', then goes back inside his flat and closes the door.

Outside, a fine, clear morning; the puddles from the night before have more or less dried up.

Here is another photograph, a photograph taken in the lobby of number 61 Urquhart Road on the morning of Saturday 21st April 1934. The photograph was taken by Detective Constable James Cole. Cole arrived at the scene together with other officers after being summoned from the Lodge Walk police station by William Duncan upon the instruction of PC Cassie. The photo was taken from near the front of the lobby, looking towards the rear door leading to the wash house, the coal sheds and the drying green at the back of the property. The floor of the lobby looks to be made of stone, or poured concrete. We know from the trial transcript that Mrs Topp and Mrs Donald took turns in sweeping the lobby to keep it free of dust, leaves and any street dirt brought in on people's shoes.

The lobby walls are wood-panelled as far as the dado rail and papered above. The wallpaper appears typical for the period: sombre in colour, but of good quality, overlaid with a pattern of flowers and leaves.

On the right of the photograph you can see the stair recess, and the door to the lavatory, which has a brass knob. Directly opposite the lavatory is the door to the understairs cupboard used by Mrs Donald for storing potatoes, though the angle of the photograph obscures it from view. The distance between the two doors is a couple of feet at most, just enough to enable access to the toilet and to the cupboard. Lying on the floor half in and half out of the recess is a pale-coloured sack, or bag. The sack is curled slightly about itself, and appears lumpy, as if filled with potatoes, for example, as opposed to flour or meal.

You might argue that such details are mostly irrelevant, subjective, a self-indulgent distraction from the matter in hand. Who cares about the wallpaper and the fucking dado rail? I do. I care passionately. How can you imagine yourself entering that hallway if you don't see the dado rail, the varnished wood panelling that is still everywhere in tenement blocks in Scotland, a hundred years old and more, still warm to the touch and glowing with polish, still fit for purpose? The door to the wash house and the drying green is made of solid oak – witnesses say that the door was liable to creak quite loudly as it was opened.

Even as I try to restrict myself to the facts, I come to realise I will never stop being a writer compelled to imagine, and what if the spaces of my mind offer shelter to witches as well as detectives? What if the witches keep confounding the investigation with their sordid rituals, their endless harping on how things used to be back in their day, their insatiable hoarding of mementoes, their raucous laughter?

Writing is like drawing an outline or unravelling wool: the more you do it, the more there is, the further you can go, and I am the kind of writer who makes up stories from the contents of a handbag, who invents identities for a group of strangers standing in a bus queue, landing them with complicated back stories and webs of mad relatives. I fixate on small details – the colours and textures of cherished garments, the stuff in people's kitchens – because these are the details that nail reality into place.

A scrap of old newspaper, yellowed at the edges, is a piece of evidence, but it is also a door. I can never resist going through that door. Whether that is to the bad or to the good is immaterial – it is simply the case. Presented with a series of known observations, I insist there must be more to the story, more facts that have not been discovered yet, or that we're not being told. I could repeat the historical record, but what would be the point? What is the point of my telling this story anyway, unless I can help you to see or imagine something that might have been missed?

This photograph ought to appear innocuous, uninteresting even, though I cannot rid myself of the sense that even if you knew nothing about its provenance the image would still be disturbing, that it carries its own peculiar weather. Something about the way the light falls on the bag specifically, leaving you in no doubt that this bag is important in some way, that you are being encouraged to look at it more closely.

At the very least, you might ask yourself what is in it and who has dumped it there.

Each time I look at this photograph, I find myself thinking of the bag that is customarily placed over the heads of prisoners condemned to death just before they are hanged. It is impossible to look at this photograph and not feel pity. It is one of the saddest, most brutal images I have ever seen.

Someone about the Door

[FROM THE *ABERDEEN PRESS AND JOURNAL* MONDAY 23RD APRIL 1934]

POLICE COMB-OUT FOR MURDER

All day on Saturday after the finding of the body and yesterday, the Central Police Office has been the scene of ceaseless toil, with the constant coming and going of officers endeavouring to solve the mystery.

Every possible clue was thoroughly investigated, and all kinds of reports were sifted. Yesterday, from eight o'clock in the morning to a late hour, the police thoroughly searched the district, including the adjoining allotments, with their numerous huts, dog kennels, poultry runs, garages and other roughly built erections which cover the area between Urquhart Road, Seaforth Road, and the Broad Hill. The area is known in the district as the 'jungle'.

All day, huge crowds from every part of the town and the surrounding countryside gathered in Urquhart Road to watch. Every hut was entered, occupiers having been taken from many parts of the city to unlock the doors, and everything was subjected to a close inspection, and as this was completed a cross was chalked on the doors.

In the forenoon and afternoon the police concentrated on the outdoor search, but in the evening they turned their attention to the occupiers of the dwelling-houses within a certain radius of 61 Urquhart Road. Although certain information was got as a result of the carefully organised and researched investigation, which in cumulative effect may help to solve the mystery, no really vital clue was discovered which could be said to hold out hope of an immediate arrest.

Rumour, of course, was rife, and the arrival and departure of a motor car from an entrance to the 'jungle' gave rise to an arrest story, which spread like wildfire through the town and brought yet more spectators to the scene.

The report was to the effect that, not only was a man taken away in the car but that the police officers who had him in charge had also a parcel, which was said to contain some of the dead girl's clothes. Inquiry at the police office, however, brought an immediate denial that there was anything whatsoever in the report.

I scroll through the archive of the *Press and Journal*, transcribing the headlines, making notes about the other stories people were reading around the time Helen's disappearance was first reported.

There is a continuing impasse between Japan and the United States over the unchecked expansion of Japanese interests in mainland China. Manchuria has become Manchukyuo, a puppet state under Japanese control. The Japanese are opposing any kinds of loans made to China, whether for commercial or humanitarian purposes, thereby drastically reducing the influence of Western powers. The United States are so concerned about the possibility of war they have begun refurbishing outdated naval vessels that were destined for scrap.

The Japanese foreign minister's name is Hirota. He insists that Japan has no intention of breaching the Nine-Power Treaty, even though they are already so far in breach of it his statement is laughable.

General Goering, Prime Minister of Prussia and German Air Minister, gives an interview to Reuter's in Berlin. He is annoyed with British newspapers for characterising him as a 'bloodthirsty pig'. Questioned about German rearmament and possible contravention of the Versailles treaty, Goering maintains that 'the chief difficulty in disarmament appears to me to be that a power like France, armed to the teeth, should surrender nothing.'

Potato growers are furious about cheaper foreign imports being 'dumped' on the British market. In a tangentially related story, the imposition of British tariffs on Irish meat has led the Irish government to force a reduction in the number of veal calves. The offer to farmers of a ten-shilling bounty on every calf skin has resulted in a mass slaughter, with animals being killed in laybys, town squares and yards with hammers and stones.

At the Old Bailey, an eighteen-month prison sentence is handed down to Doris Burton, a thirty-one-year-old secretary from Mile End who defrauded a married couple named Barnett of £300. Burton claimed she had friendly connections with various celebrities, including Jack Buchanan and Noel Coward. A doctor called as a witness at her trial said that Burton 'absolutely lived in a world of daydreams and romance.'

Dole cuts and protectionism, shortages and surplus, customs and excise, rows over fishing rights, intimations of war and the misuse of power. Britannia, blinded by her own decreasing relevance, is sleepwalking into a crisis, and it is extraordinary to me, how little the political landscape appears to have changed.

It is the small stories that draw me in, the news equivalent of the flowery wallpaper and the polished dado rail in the lobby of that tenement house on Urquhart Road: the Doris Burton story and the opening of the Aberdeen-Kirkwall air service, the recovery by the salvage steamer *Artiglio* of £100,000 worth of gold bullion from the sunken P&O liner *Egypt*. And of course the appalling murder of Helen Priestly.

There is nothing about the famine in Ukraine the year before. This man-made disaster, barely reported at the time, has slipped from the news agenda entirely.

In terms of column inches, the story of Helen's disappearance is easily the biggest. It is illustrated with two photographs, one of Helen and another, larger photo of volunteers searching Aberdeen Links under cover of darkness. The photograph of Helen is one I have not seen before and will not find anywhere else. It is blurred and faded almost to a negative of itself, yet there is an immediacy about it, a quality of sweetness that is missing from the starkly delineated, rather static image more commonly printed.

Suddenly I feel I know her, or that I might have done. She looks like a friend of mine, a girl I was close to at primary school and then lost sight of. I last spoke to her on the bus, when we were about fifteen. We had drifted apart by then, and the knowledge of the growing gulf between us made me feel guilty and confused, filled with an aching sense of loss I did not know what to do with.

I find myself wondering what happened to her, as I often still do. I Google her name but the search proves futile, as it has done before.

The police begin their investigations by trying to work out as nearly as possible when the sack containing Helen's body was placed in the lobby. That the body was discovered so close to home is remarkable in itself. Contemporary statistics leave no doubt that most murders are committed by someone within the victim's immediate circle, and the police investigating Helen's murder would probably have focused their initial enquiries on Agnes and John Priestly.

John's innocence is plain from the start. You will remember that John returned to work at the Saltoun Arms while Helen was still over at the Robertsons and before she was reported missing. From the time he gets back to the pub until the moment Agnes and Mrs Robertson arrive with the news that Helen has disappeared, John is with his workmate, and he is continually in the company of other people from that moment on. John had no opportunity for killing his daughter, even if he wanted to. As for Agnes, her panic and distress through the afternoon and evening of April 20th, her distraught cries at the discovery in the lobby make the idea of her as a suspect more or less unthinkable.

Later, at the trial, an expert witness is called to give an account of the weather conditions in Aberdeen throughout the evening of Friday 20th April through until the early morning of Saturday 21st. That expert witness is George Auburne Clarke, an employee of the Air Ministry and the assistant in charge of the Aberdeen Observatory of the Met Office. Clarke reports that from around 6 pm on the 20th, the sky became increasingly overcast, with a blustery wind. Rain began to fall sometime between six and seven pm, leading to a continuous and steady downpour until shortly after midnight. The winds began to die away soon after three.

The rain that night is of particular importance to the police in their gathering of evidence, and largely determines the direction of the investigation. When John Priestly arrives home in William Duncan's car just after midnight, the street outside his house is still crowded with people. It is difficult to see how anyone would be able to pass along Urquhart Road without being noticed, much less sneak into the lobby of number 61 carrying a dead body.

Through the careful interviewing of dozens of other witnesses, the police conclude that the sack must have been placed in the lobby sometime between three and five o'clock on the morning of the 21st, the only time that night when the communal hallway of number 61 was more or less quiet.

We have already noted how difficult it would have been to enter the front door of the house without being seen. The only way of gaining access to the lobby through the rear of the building would have been to climb over the wall at the back and then walk across the drying green. Even without the almost certain risk of being caught, a risk exacerbated by the creaky back door, anyone attempting such a feat in the rain, and carrying a heavy sack, would find it impossible to do so without leaving some evidence of themselves.

Imagine jumping down on to saturated grass and not leaving footprints.

Aside from one small patch of moisture close to Helen's head, the sack containing her body is dry. Every witness who saw the bag confirms this. The floor of the lobby is also dry. Given the limited opportunities for entering the lobby from outside, the only reasonable explanation is that the sack was placed in the lobby by a person or persons already in the building.

After the citywide searches, the conflicting rumours, the excitement surrounding Richard Sutton's false testimony, the police quickly become convinced the evidence they are looking for is closer to hand.

The wider search is called off, and officers begin to concentrate their attention upon the tenement flats at number 61 and those of its next-door neighbour at number 59.

The initial forensic examination of the crime scene is carried out by Detective Constable James Cole. Cole is thirty-five years of age and with fifteen years of service he is an experienced officer. As well as taking the crime scene photographs, Cole examines the floor, the wainscoting and skirting boards for evidence of fingerprints or other marks left by a potential murderer. He finds none.

When Helen's body is taken out of the sack, the officers present discover that her knickers are missing. The blue knitted tammy given to her by Ella Robertson is also missing. There are pieces of cinder adhering to her hair and in her mouth. It is Detective Superintendent George Gordon who first notices blood in the area of her genitals.

Helen's body is removed to the mortuary at around seven o'clock. Because of the injuries to her private parts, the police are convinced that Helen has been attacked and killed by a man. They question every male resident of number 61, as well as those next door at number 59. By the time their shift ends on the Saturday evening, at least one senior resident from each household has been interviewed. Enquiries are still ongoing on the Sunday when a dramatic new piece of evidence is revealed, though only to the officers involved in the investigation. The post mortem carried out on Helen's body has confirmed that the injuries to her genitals could not have been caused by a penis, that they were most likely made by some sort of wooden implement, possibly a kitchen utensil.

The initial assumption, that Helen's attacker must have been male, is demonstrably false.

The police intensify their questioning, interviewing every adult resident of number 61 and number 59. They put in long hours. They become increasingly exhausted, both mentally and physically. They know that speed is an important factor in catching the killer, that the more time passes, the greater the risk of evidence becoming lost or passing unnoticed or being destroyed.

Neither does it help that public interest in the case is becoming more obsessive by the day. Crowds of onlookers continue to congregate in Urquhart Road and around the police station in Lodge Walk. The atmosphere is heightened, volatile, somewhere between rebellious and hysterical. People are hungry for a resolution, hanging on every rumour, most of which are unsubstantiated. What begins as genuine concern at Helen's disappearance and horror over her death morphs into something different and more aggressive: the desire for revenge.

By the beginning of the following week, most of the residents of the two adjoining tenement buildings will have been questioned at least twice. This is the moment when fatigue sets in: the same questions, over and over, prompting answers that by now would begin to have a rehearsed feel, the memory of the previous round of questioning rather than memories of the events themselves. For most of the residents of number 61, the circumstances surrounding the disappearance and murder of Helen Priestly remain as mysterious and inexplicable as ever. And still the police question, and wait, hoping for a slip-up, a mistake, a significant discrepancy between one set of answers and another, something that would indicate a gap between the story being told and what actually happened.

At around 11 am on the morning of Wednesday 25th April, Detective Superintendent George Gordon returns to 61 Urquhart Road to question Mr and Mrs Donald, who live in the ground floor flat to the right of the close and directly below the Priestlys. Gordon is accompanied by Detective Inspector Alexander Taylor and Detective Constable John Westland.

At the trial, the police witnesses maintain that at this stage in the investigation they had no reason to suspect the Donalds over anyone else in the house, that they were simply the next in line to be interviewed. Yet I keep coming back to something Superintendent Gordon said when questioned by the defence counsel, that he knew that 'certain enquiries' had been made about them, that their movements had been watched. 'Personally I did not give the instruction,' he adds, 'but there is no doubt that the Donalds were suggested'.

Which immediately begs the question: suggested by whom?

One of our most persistent myths about the past is that neighbours were more neighbourly then, that people looked out for one another. In the case of the residents of number 61 at least, the picture that comes across from the trial transcript is more ambiguous. It is true that the families who live in these flats are in regular contact, that they are aware of each other's movements and habits – for people living quite literally on top of one another, it would be hard not to be. But at the same time, these neighbours are not exactly what you would call close. Doors and gates and cupboards are routinely kept locked. Certain households within the block are at odds with one another over seemingly trivial matters that perhaps mask deeper resentments. In some cases, residents have not spoken to one another for several years, a situation that must have been pretty uncomfortable, given that they were living in such close proximity.

At the moment when Helen's body is discovered, there are several people who admit to coming out of their flats to see what is going on, but make no attempt to go downstairs or offer help to the Priestlys. The Donalds do not come out of their flat at all, except to collect their milk and an hour later – incredible though it might seem – to sweep the lobby.

When Mary Gordon, who lives on the top floor opposite the Hunts, mentions to Jeannie Donald sometime on the Saturday afternoon that people are saying it is 'someone about the door' who is responsible for Helen's murder, Jeannie makes no comment. She seems anxious to get away.

From everything I have read, I would describe these neighbours as watchful rather than close. It is true that the circumstances in which we find them are far from normal: by the time of the trial they have endured hours of police interrogation, weeks of speculation and rumour. Anyone called upon to give evidence in a murder trial is likely to sound if not guilty then at least on their guard. And yet their testimonies come across as incomplete somehow, and what I find to be missing from them is not raw information so much as a sense of how they truly thought and felt about one another.

What we get instead is a sense of unease, of thinly veiled hostility. Did someone in that house know more than they admitted? Is it possible that one of the neighbours said something to the police that gave them cause to keep an eye on the Donald household in particular?

Given that Superintendent Gordon freely admits that the police were keeping the Donalds under surveillance, it is the only explanation that makes sense.

Jeannie Donald is alone in the house when the police arrive. Her husband Alec is at work, at McKillip's barbershop on King Street; wee Jeannie – the same wee Jeannie we saw being questioned by Agnes Priestly in the school playground shortly after Helen went missing – is at school.

Mrs Donald receives the officers willingly, saying she wants to help with the inquiry in any way she can. Her statement, which will later be read out in court, is taken by DC Westland. When he asks her what she was doing on the afternoon Helen went missing, Jeannie tells him that she cleared away the dinner things and then went out shopping. She returned home earlier than she might have otherwise, because she needed to iron wee Jeannie's costumes for a dance rehearsal at the Beach Pavilion that same evening. When Westland asks her if she saw or spoke to anyone, she confirms she spoke to Mrs Topp from over the hallway, who happened to be in the lobby when she came in.

Jeannie is still being interviewed when wee Jeannie arrives home for her midday meal, followed not long afterwards by Alec. After he has eaten, Alec is questioned separately, in the parlour. At some point during the afternoon, Superintendent Gordon asks Jeannie's permission to search the house. Jeannie consents – what choice does she have? The search goes on for hours.

From the police evidence given at the trial, it appears that the arrest of Jeannie Donald and Alec Donald at around twelve fifteen am on the morning of Thursday 26th April hinges largely upon the discovery of what are thought to be bloodstains beneath a piece of split linoleum in the cupboard under the kitchen sink. Similar stains are found on pieces of newspaper dated 19th April – the day before Helen's disappearance – in the bottom of a wardrobe, and on another piece of linoleum in the understairs cupboard. Dr Robert Richards, the police surgeon, scrapes off some samples from the linoleum and looks at them briefly under a microscope. He concurs that the reddish substance is most likely blood, but he cannot say for certain until he is able to examine the samples again under laboratory conditions.

Superintendent Gordon makes the arrest. 'I did not do that,' Jeannie protests, on hearing the charges read to her. Large crowds are already gathering on the street outside, shouting and jeering and chasing after the car as the Donalds are led from the house and driven away. What is missing from most of the accounts is any mention of what happened to wee Jeannie at this point, and it is only after several hours of sifting through various newspaper accounts that I discover she was taken to be cared for at a local children's shelter.

It is painful to imagine how alone, confused and terrified she must have been, and I am relieved to find that by the time of the trial she has been removed from the shelter, and is living with her father's relatives, in Banff.

He Did Not Do That

[FROM THE *ABERDEEN PRESS AND JOURNAL*
FRIDAY 27TH APRIL 1934]

MAN AND WOMAN IN CRAIGINCHES

Sensation followed rapidly on sensation yesterday in connection with the murder of eight-year-old Helen Priestly.

Eleven hours after the dramatic arrest of a man and woman in the house in Urquhart Road in which the child's body was found, they were brought before Hon. Sheriff-Substitute M. M. Duncan in Aberdeen Sheriff Court on a charge of murder. The accused were:

ALEXANDER DONALD, and his wife JEANNIE EWEN, or DONALD, residing at 61 Urquhart Road, Aberdeen.

They were charged with:

On Friday or Saturday last, assaulting Helen Wilson Robertson Priestly, a girl aged eight years, residing at 61 Urquhart

Road, by seizing hold of her, compressing her throat and cutting or stabbing her in her private parts, and murdering her.

No declaration was emitted, and they were committed for further inquiry. Anticipating that the couple who had been apprehended would appear in the Police Court, a huge crowd of people gathered in Lodge Walk in the early forenoon, and when the doors of the court opened the limited space was quickly occupied, and many were turned away.

Their curiosity was not appeased, however, for the detained couple did not pass the bar at the Police Court.

Indeed, while the Police Court proceedings were still going on, Mr and Mrs Donald were quietly escorted from the police headquarters at Lodge Walk by a private passageway through the building to the Sheriff Courthouse.

A small group of law agents and press men, who were standing in the corridor of the courthouse, were the only persons to witness the arrival and departure of the accused.

The female accused, a woman of slender build walked without support but looked drawn and haggard. She was dressed in a dark blue coat with a brown fur collar and a light blue blouse and hat.

Her husband, a man of about five feet seven in height and slimly built, wore a heavy dark-blue overcoat, with a blue suit and light brown hat.

Both the accused are thirty-eight years of age.

Alexander Donald is a native of Banff, being the twin son of Mr Benjamin Donald, retired motor hirer, and Mrs Donald, 2 Low Street, Banff.

He served his apprenticeship as a hairdresser with Mr Robert Urquhart, 49 Bridge Street, Banff, about twenty years ago.

Thereafter he went to Banchory, where he obtained a situation and where, it is understood, he met his wife.

After serving in the war he came to Aberdeen, and was latterly in the employment of Mr Alexander McKillip, 228 King Street.

Mr and Mrs Donald's daughter, a girl of about ten years of age, is being cared for in the Children's Centre by the Aberdeen Association for Improving the Working Conditions of the Poor.

So what do the impatiently waiting and endlessly curious Aberdeen public know so far?

They know that an eight-year-old girl named Helen Priestly has been found 'outraged and murdered' less than a dozen yards from her own front door. They know that because the sack she was found in was dry, and the evening she was found on was extremely wet, the police suspect the killing took place either next door to or within the tenement building at 61 Urquhart Road. Crucially, and because the police have not released the details of Helen's post mortem to the public, they continue to assume from the nature of her injuries that Helen Priestly's murderer is a man. They have surely heard by now that shortly after midnight on Thursday morning, police arrested Alec and Jeannie Donald, the Priestlys' downstairs neighbours at number 61, and that later the same day the couple were jointly charged with Helen's murder.

Had I been following the Priestly case along with everyone else in 1934, I would have been convinced that Alec Donald was guilty of murder, that his wife Jeannie was guilty of perverting the course of justice, either by actively covering up for him or simply by not alerting the police to her suspicions. I would have assumed that Alec Donald raped Helen, then killed her either intentionally or accidentally to stop her from screaming.

It would hardly be the first time such a thing has happened, the usual casual and loathsome male violence, despicable and all the more sordid through its infinite repetition down the ages. I would not have been calling for Alec to be hanged, but I would have wanted him to go to prison for a long time. I would most likely have been feeling sorry for Jeannie at this point. Who knows what she was having to put up with, behind closed doors? How frightened she must have been, how vulnerable.

There isn't a woman on this planet who doesn't have at least an inkling about the nature of coercive control.

I would have been wrong though, about all of it. On Monday 11th June, six weeks after his arrest, Alec Donald is released without charge. His alibi checks out. Multiple witnesses, including his boss, are prepared to swear an oath that at the time Helen was killed, Alec was at work, cutting hair and shaving whiskers at McKillip's barbershop on King Street where he was regularly employed. Alec's release from Craiginches prison, sensational though it is, is reported in the *Press and Journal* without fanfare or further explanation.

He is a shadowy figure, Alec, defined by his absences. He is not in or about the house at the time Helen died. He is not there to look after his daughter in the immediate aftermath of the crime. He is not familiar with the jute sack Helen's body was found in. He is unable to report any unusual happenings about his house on the night of Friday 20th April or during the early hours of the following morning. He does not hear a sound, nor does he recall his wife getting out of bed, nor any other untoward movements, voices or swearing or other strange sounds. When Helen's body is discovered outside his own front door, he is not there either – he is unwilling to step into the lobby to see what the fuss is about.

According to Jeannie, he describes Agnes Priestly, crying for her child, as 'a hysteric'.

Alec Donald is not responsible, the police agree. He cannot be responsible, because he was not there. He is not called to give evidence for the prosecution because it is forbidden for a husband to testify against his wife. As soon as the trial is over, he disappears from the history books, returning only to die, offstage, in 1944.

Susana has come to stand in the street with the other onlookers, the casual gawpers, the gossip addicts, the true-crime junkies. She has no fixed opinion about the murder, she has simply come to listen to the conversations going on around her, to hear what people say. The city's polyphony is brazen, declamatory, performative. Factory music. A cheap counterfeit, the close presence of so much anger is disconcerting because it does not feel honestly earned.

On the other side of the street she sees someone she knows, a newspaperman named Vanny Redchow. The Vanny is short for Ivan, though he pronounces his name the British way, Eye-van Red-show. Susana has seen and spoken to him a couple of times in the bar of the

Douglas Hotel, close to where she works four afternoons a week in a shipping office, translating contracts and cargo ledgers from Russian into English and occasionally vice versa. The money she earns is ungenerous but adequate; the limited hours leave her time to explore the city's libraries and museums and other possibilities, a freedom that is almost as important to her as money.

As a woman with a foreign accent, her presence in places like the Douglas is less frowned-upon than it would be if she were a Scotswoman or even an Englishwoman. It is as if she is expected to behave outrageously, to make these faux pas. As if her morals, which must be questionable anyway, are given a certain latitude for slippage before being deemed irreparable.

When she asked Vanny Redchow about his name he said his granddad was Polish, that he had entered the city as a midshipman and never left.

I never knew him, Redchow added. Only my granny, and she was from Edinburgh.

The Russian woman's surname is Solovey, which means nightingale. The name is more common in Belarus and Ukraine, where her father's people came from, and where members of her extended family still live. She has thought about asking Vanny Redchow if there might be work for her at his paper, but she remains undecided. In some ways she prefers the work at the shipping office, because it allows her to remain invisible, and leaves her mind free.

For a writer, being invisible is a necessity, at least sometimes. Susana raises her hand to wave to Ivan Redchow, and then puts it down again.

And what do we know of this little ghost, this Helen Priestly? she writes later, in her notebook. We know she liked music, that her mother had recently, with the help of a small legacy, bought her daughter a piano. We know she liked pretty new clothes and fancy French scent. Those who knew her describe her as lively, happy, playful, a quiet wee girlie. Smiling quite nicely, tall for her age, and very shy.

We know she had a cheeky side, an imaginative streak that might occasionally have summoned darker visions. Ghosts and the traces of ghosts, a world of shadows, imaginary fiends and secret enemies.

Time is remorseless in its appetites, Susana writes, though she is determined that the past will not consume Helen.

Part 2
Myths and Legends

The Cream Ware Bowl

JEANNIE KNEW ABOUT CREAM ware, she'd read an article about it in an old copy of *The Lady* she'd found in a box put out for the church sale one time. Cream ware was a special kind of china that was invented in Staffordshire, the place where they made the flat-backed figurines like the tailor and the jester that stood either side of the mantelpiece at her Auntie Joan's. Auntie Joan was not really her aunt but she'd cared for Jeannie every second weekend while her mother was out. The man who really made his fortune with cream ware was Josiah Wedgwood, a potter and factory owner who was related to Darwin, the scientist who believed that humans were descended from monkeys.

Josiah Wedgwood went a little bit crazy thinking about Chinese porcelain all the time, which everyone wanted to buy but didn't know how to make. Wedgwood started doing experiments and after a lot of fuss and failure he came up with bone china, which looked and felt like porcelain but was made using a completely different method.

The new pottery had a weight to it, and the feeling of being reliable. And wasn't it strange, Jeannie thought, how there could be two different ways of making the same thing, and that it was Josiah Wedgwood who discovered how, who invented a lustrous and hard-wearing pottery that was the envy of the world but made right here in Britain.

In the end, Wedgwood's special variety of cream ware was renamed as Queen's ware, and Josiah, who going by what his uncle said was a jumped-up chimpanzee the same as the rest of us, was made a knight.

Wedgwood's cream ware became Queen's ware because of Queen Charlotte, who was married to Mad King George who in the end was so mad he didn't recognise her but you couldn't just throw him out, he was the king. Queen Charlotte had a raw deal in the matter of her husband, which made her like every other wife in that respect. Jeannie had seen Queen Charlotte's picture on a postcard once, the portrait by Allan Ramsay who was a great Scottish painter. Queen Charlotte hurried to order some of the new cream ware more or less as soon as it was invented, to show that she was British now and not German, and so admired British things.

Queen Charlotte placed the order with Wedgwood herself, which made the story into a fairy tale, or so it seemed to Jeannie. What could be more appropriate or more patriotic? A tea service in *finest bone china*, twelve teacups and their saucers, a covered sugar bowl, a basin for the tea leaves, which were called the dregs and lastly of course the tea pot, ground gold embellishment, raised flowers against a green background, bright and round and gleaming as a winter moon.

Wedgwood took charge of the production himself. How could he not, when the making of Queen Charlotte's tea service marked the high point of his life so far? Jeannie could imagine him clearly, prowling the factory, deep in conversation with the master finishers. This all happened in 1765, one hundred and fifty years ago, which was strange to think about. Hundreds of people had queued up to see it, Jeannie had read, to cast their eyes on the precious cups and saucers of the mad king's queen. A showroom had been hired especially, in Greek Street, Soho, which was not a good part of London these days, apparently, but things were different then.

Jeannie's bowl is a large, deep serving bowl. Classic cream with embossed blue flowers, the blue a most delicate shade, like an April sky, the flowers each individual in form and character, planted delicately upon the china as if scattered there by chance. The cream ware bowl is used once a year, at Christmas, when it is taken from the cabinet in the parlour and washed and dried and polished until its surface takes on the luminous sheen of mother of pearl.

There is the tiniest chip on the rim, a blemish so small you would never notice it unless you knew beforehand. Jeannie has owned the bowl since before she was married, from when she was working as a cook in Banchory at the Tornacoille Hotel. The management were selling off some china and ornaments and soft furnishings. Most of them were damaged, like the cream ware bowl, but none in such a way as mattered to how a thing was used. Jeannie had fallen for the bowl on the instant she saw it, for the lustrous shine of its glaze, for the magic that was in it, somehow, from being so rare. She would run her finger around the rim, mesmerised by the sound it made, a sweet, hollow booming, like an echo under a bridge. And she would feel for the chip, which with the years had never worsened, but rather seemed to grow a little smoother, so smooth as to suggest it had always belonged there.

Jeannie thought of the chip as a battle scar. She would even say she'd grown fond of it, that it marked the bowl as hers and hers alone.

Even in its damaged state, the cream ware bowl had cost Jeannie more than a week's wages, money she had drawn from out of her savings that might well, or so her mother suggested, have been put to better use. To buy stockings or winter woollens or a new Sunday dress.

A broken bowl, Jeannie's mother had said. Are you sure that's wise?

It is an investment, Jeannie replied. She spoke brusquely, more in defence of herself than annoyance at her mother. Who had the right to say if her purchase was wise? In the private regions of her heart she felt the cream ware bowl already as a part of herself, an avowal of the person she believed she would one day be. The bowl was both hers, and her, the first object she had ever owned that seemed to stand for something.

I'll be keeping it here, she added, queasy at the thought of what might happen if the bowl was left unguarded in her room at the hotel, the maids' quarters under the eaves where she lodged with Dutch Minne who saw to the fires and with Katy, who they all called Katydid, who was only sixteen and still learning kitchen duties. Those girls, so laughing and so thoughtless and so carefree. And here it was, finally, the reason for the spending of a fortnight's earnings, the sharp rebuttal of her mother's quietly spoken disapproval: the cream ware bowl stood as a secret, glowing reminder of the future she dreamed of, glinting behind glass and proudly on show, the spotless, gleaming centrepiece of a home of her own.

No matter that Miriam Reddy the housekeeper, the gimlet-eyed, lash-tongued creature the kitchen girls all secretly called the Wolf, had already ordered from Edinburgh a replacement, a perfect, unchipped impostor that could sit harmlessly on the sideboard without offending the guests with any rice-grain chip. The loudmouths up from England and the snake-tongued up from Edinburgh, the doctors and the business people, the clergymen of Montrose and the shipping men from Glasgow, the minor gentry and their overdressed acquaintances, those sycophants who believed that being seen in the company of a duke might bestow on them the burnishing of dukedom. What could they know of a miracle when to them this bowl or that was a matter of indifference, one insufficient enchantment among a throng of unnoticed others?

And their wives, of course, the disappointed ladies who sat with their spinster confidantes sipping sherry in the light of the fire or taking tea out on the veranda, who occasionally left behind trinkets and unconsidered trifles on the polished night stands in the upstairs bedrooms: a sweet pair of nail scissors, a cameo brooch, a primrose silk handkerchief adorned with the scarlet monogram V. S. L.

For the objects these women so carelessly abandoned, Jeannie felt a longing and an attraction too mysterious to describe, as if by cradling such gewgaws in her hands she came closer to becoming the kind of person who might own and handle such treasures as a matter of course. Jeannie was not supposed to be in the bedrooms, though she was forever sneaking off to the rooms in the back especially, where no one would think to look for her, not once the guests had set out on their daily escapades and even better if she had what the Wolf might call a pretext, like collecting the glasses and missing cutlery that somehow wound up there, or taking a sandwich to Mrs Godolphin who did the linen repairs and who never went anywhere.

Jeannie had on occasion kept hold of one of these baubles for most of a morning, and she would feel happy then, as if in possession of a beautiful secret, and in the moment of relinquishment, the timely surrender of the sewing thimble or the powder compact, the onyx fountain pen or tortoiseshell scarf ring to Miriam Reddy on the *pretext* of having found it *dropped, like, or simply laying there* on the terrace or in the tea lounge she would feel her happiness flare up more brightly, just for a second, before losing its light.

It was no doubt her seeming transparency in the matter of these trinkets – the woman is honest, she could imagine the Wolf thinking, which is a blessing you can never count on and especially not these days – that Miriam Reddy occasionally allowed Jeannie to hang on to one or other of them, items that according to Her Wolfship must no longer be needed, or that were damaged, like the cream ware bowl, in a way that to Jeannie seemed a version of nothing but to their previous, more discriminating owners could not be countenanced.

You might as well keep it, Jeannie. They won't be missing it.

The Wolf had never married. She was a lone wolf, and as Jeannie placed her neatly folded undergarments and work dresses and her best blouse, the same one she brought with her when she first came to work at the Tornacoille yet still felt an uncommon fondness for, inside the battered cardboard suitcase that would finally take her away from here and, or so it had been promised, into her new life, the home of her own she had always dreamed of, she could not help but wonder if maybe the Wolf had been the wiser all along. For all Dutch Minne and Katydid might laugh behind her back, pour secret scorn upon her for her thick ankles and tugged-back hair, her shoes so stout and so sensible you might walk in them from here to London and still not wear them out, could it not be that Miriam Reddy was queen of her own world and content to be so?

Jeannie considered the time, not a week since she'd handed in her notice, when she'd gone out to the yard with some scraps for the pig bin and come upon the Wolf, standing alone by the dustbins and smoking a cigarette. Not in a fancy holder like Elspeth McCreadie the doctor's wife, she with her French periodicals and fashionable friends, but gripped plain between her fingers as a man smokes, or a common serving girl, which or so it was rumoured was all the Wolf had been when she first began work here, though there's none of them went far back enough to know the truth of it.

The Wolf's eyes were on the hills, as if she was gazing into a past she only dimly remembered. For a moment she stayed silent, her eyes with that frosty glint in them, the look the younger girls quailed at but for Jeannie was part of the building, same as the fire that sparked off the top-floor windows with the sun's setting, the pondwater stink of the basement, the collection of Brussels tablecloths in the linen press that were washed and ironed every spring but that none of them, and that was including Mrs Godolphin, could remember being used.

So you're leaving us, Jeannie, said the Wolf, without turning her head.

Yes, Miss Reddy, Jeannie replied. My last day's Saturday, and later, after she'd finished cleaning the kitchen and gone back upstairs, upstairs to her room beneath the eaves for the fourth-to-last time, Jeannie thought back over what they'd said, the longest talk they'd ever had, and wondered if that was the last time she'd speak to the Wolf, speak to her in anything more than simple yeses and nos, that was. Just her and Miriam Reddy, conversing together.

And you're sure that marriage is what you want, Jeannie? You are almost thirty, are you not? I had rather thought, said the Wolf, leaving the sentence hanging like a hem that needed lifting, as if it were up to Jeannie to fill in the words, to finish the train of imagining the Wolf had set running.

There's still time, Jeannie said. Time for her to have a child, is what she meant, and she had felt herself blushing. Time to set a life in motion, time to be normal, time at last to find a proper resting place for the cream ware bowl.

Jeannie's fiancé was a barber, a plain man, but gainfully employed and reasonably paid. If the Wolf were to ask her if she loved him she would say simply yes. The Wolf did not ask, though. She dragged on her cigarette, exhaled.

I was engaged to a man, she said slowly. He died in the war.

I'm sorry to hear that, Miss Reddy. She was creased with embarrassment, not at the thought of the Wolf being in love so much as her sudden, inconceivable fancy to share the memory of it.

The Wolf had never been a person to her, so much as a legend.

Don't be, said Miriam Reddy. I believed at the time that my life was over, the pain was so harsh. Since then I've come to know there is only one thing that truly matters in this life, and that is freedom. Your own bed, your own money. Your own thoughts in the night, the Wolf adds, and no one laying down the law over what you're to dream of. There's still time, she said, with a thin-lipped smile. Men, she said, and then broke off. Well, she said after a moment. You're a good worker, Jeannie, you've a good head on you.

Don't lose your reason, she added. I'd always see to it there was a place for you, if you wanted to come back.

Thank you, Miss Reddy. But I'll be married soon. I'll have my own home to take care of.

Was the Wolf being spiteful or generous? Jeannie could not tell. On the day of Jeannie's wedding, a package arrived, addressed in the neatly curling handwriting of Miriam Reddy. Inside was a Wedgwood dressing table set, two round lidded pots and a heart-shaped dish. Shell-pink Jasperware, moulded decorations of cupids and flowers, delicate white encrustations like elaborately piped icing sugar. Pink Jasperware was less often seen than blue Jasperware and therefore more expensive. How the Wolf could have known of her love for Wedgwood, Jeannie had no idea. She looked for a note inside the packet and inside the trinket pots but did not find one.

The Wolf remained silent.

Silence speaks contempt, Jeannie thought, or was it consent? She thought of the Wolf as she had been at that last conversation, greying hair tugged back, cigarette in hand. Like a Wolf turned into a woman in one of the picture books she remembered from when she was a child. Jeannie would not think of reading such gruesome tales to any child of hers. She wondered indeed if any such book had actually existed. There had been no books at home, just the Bible, and Mrs Beeton, and a volume of Robert Burns that had belonged to her grandfather. She could not think where she might have read about the wolf-woman, though she was sure she had.

Woman as animal, animal-woman. She felt a needle of ice pass through her, though it was her wedding day.

There is but one thing that truly matters, and that is freedom, sayeth the Wolf.

And what of love? Jeannie murmured. She was brushing down her hair, her thickly growing, nut-brown curls, which erupted in a hotbed of frizz at the least touch of rain.

Her mother, out on the landing, was calling her name.

Love? The Wolf curls her lip. Love is what they trap you with.

Well, Jeannie says, I have to go now, whatever you say. It is too late not to.

Her face was pale as a cloud behind a sheet of Brussels lace. Jeannie Ewen was never pretty but she would do. She had a strength about her, a certain forbearance, not defiance exactly but something close to it. Anyone would know just from looking at her that she could cope in a crisis. That she was sensible with money, slow in voicing her opinions not because she was dull or stupid but because she preferred to think on matters a while before getting her fingers burned.

She liked to keep her own counsel. Like a woman, or so they will say of her, in possession of a secret and determined to keep it.

The world might come to an end, but what else was there to do but start sweeping up?

Remember what I told you, sayeth the Wolf. She threw down her cigarette on the concrete, ground it beneath the heel of her stout black work boot. Don't lose your reason.

Why would I lose my reason?

That's for me to know and you to find out.

In the days following her arrest for murder a decade later, the police compiled an inventory of items removed as evidence from Jeannie's home. The cream ware bowl was not among them. The officers searching the house probably didn't even notice it. The bowl had no bearing on the case, after all, so why would they? Who knows where it ended up after that? It could be anywhere.

Inventory of Items Taken by Police Officers from the Donalds' Apartment at 61 Urquhart Road between 25th April and 9th May 1934

A PORTION OF THE KITCHEN flooring, a piece of brown paper from the right-hand sink cupboard, a piece of table baize from the kitchen table, a cloth cover from the kitchen table, a quilt cover, a rug from the middle of the floor in the parlour, a bundle of newspapers found on the bed in the parlour, a press door from the inner lobby of the accused's house, a rubber apron taken from a nail on the inside of the same door, a handkerchief from the pocket of the overall, the screws from the hinges of the door, a brown leatherette message bag from the knob on the back of the kitchen door, two scrubbing brushes from the cupboard under the sink in the accused's kitchen, a nail brush from the sink, seven washing cloths in and around the sink, three pieces of linoleum from the inside lobby of the accused's apartment, papers taken from under the lobby linoleum, two pieces of linoleum from the cupboard in the lobby, a rug from the kitchen floor, a further rug from under the kitchen cabinet, an orange and an apple from the fruit dish in the kitchen cabinet, a joint deposit account book from the kitchen, a Co-operative Society share book, a paper bag, a woman's blue serge dress from the press in the lobby, a coal scuttle from the left-hand sink cupboard, articles of clothing from the clothes basket, the clothes basket, newspapers found in the kitchen, a loaf of bread found in a biscuit tin in a press in the kitchen, three pieces of paper found with the loaf, a biscuit tin, a zinc pail, a lady's overall from the drier suspended from the kitchen ceiling, a piece of paper from the gas fire in the parlour, four ladies' stockings from a chest of drawers in the kitchen, a games board, a piece of paper marked Findlay's Dairy, a lady's chamois leather glove, a clothes basket from the lobby cupboard, a packet of Lux from the right-hand sink cupboard in the accused's kitchen, a footstool, some substance from the sink trap in the kitchen, hair adhering to the bottom of the chair leg, an outer and inner mattress cover from the kitchen bed, some liquid from the trap in the kitchen sink, a handkerchief, a cloth bag containing two belts and nine cloths, some material from the floor of the right-hand cupboard under the kitchen sink, several bottles of scent, scent sprays, a jar, a bottle containing nail polish, an Aberdeen Savings Bank book, a purse and a five-shilling piece, a lady's flowered dress from the bottom drawer of the wardrobe, a tea cosy from the wardrobe, a piece of brown paper from under the sofa in the parlour, a piece of cardboard from the top of the wardrobe in the parlour, a sample of coal, a match cover, a pot of Panzone, a leather brush case, a hair-dressing comb and a hairbrush, a comb, a set of pyjamas, newspapers, a paint brush, a paper bag, a string of beads and a latch key from under the bed in the kitchen.

1B

Rose arrives in the city in what feels like midwinter. As she steps from the taxi cab on to the pavement the snow is falling, and in front of the house the street stands empty in either direction. There is no one here to meet her, though the woman from the rental agency had assured her there would be someone to show her the apartment and sign over the key.

'Where are you wanting your trunk?' the driver asks, and Rose instructs him to carry it into the hallway. The man shoulders his way through the storm doors, sets her box on the tiles. Rose scrabbles in her purse for coins. She is panicking about what she will do if she is unable to gain access to the apartment, though she cannot expect the cabbie to be responsible for that. She wonders if she might ask him to take her to the rental agency, but he is already gone.

Then the door to 1A creaks open and a voice calls her name.

'Miss Blair?'

Rose turns around smartly, her heart thumping. The hallway lies more or less in darkness, the person who has called out to her illuminated only by the weak electric light shining through the fanlight of their own entranceway.

'The woman from Royston's had to leave, because of the snow. She told me you would be coming. She asked me to give you the key.'

The figure standing in the doorway of 1A is male, and middle aged, his body swathed in what appears to be a dressing gown, or house coat, burgundy silk embroidered with Chinese dragons. Grey hair falls in untidy straggles about its velvet collar.

'My name is Inkpen,' says the man. 'I'm your new neighbour.'

He hands her a key, heavy and tarnished and attached with a piece of string to what looks like a parcel tag, '1B' scrawled carelessly across it in smudged black ink. Close to, Inkpen looks older than Rose had initially imagined him to be, sixty perhaps, with dark bags under his eyes and a puckered line of scar tissue high on one cheek. His eyes are deeply set, intelligent, though the Chinese dressing gown hints at something decadent and possibly unsavoury. He speaks with an English accent.

'Might I offer you some tea? A sandwich?'

'I shouldn't,' Rose replies, though even as she rejects him she is regretting it, annoyed that her desire to be alone should once again triumph over more practical considerations. She has eaten nothing since Glasgow. There will be no food in 1B. The thought of having to venture out into the snowy darkness is somehow appalling.

'Well, later then,' Inkpen is saying. 'Once you've settled in.' He smiles cheerfully, raising an eyebrow, as if he can see through her buttoned-up greatcoat and into her turmoil. Still, he is right to smile – the situation is not without its humorous aspect. Rose mutters her thanks and takes the key. She fumbles it into the lock of 1B, praying it won't jam. The feeling of being under scrutiny is close to unbearable. The key turns with a dull thud but the door sticks in its frame. Rose slams her hip against the lower panel – the bruise will be visible on her skin the following morning – and finds herself stumbling, almost falling into the space beyond as it gives way. She disappears inside the flat, pushing the door closed behind her without looking round.

Someone has lit the stove. Rose finds out later that this was Mrs Scudamore, the woman from Royston's, but at the moment of feeling its warmth it seems like a miracle: a fire, drawn curtains, a kettle on the hotplate, the rudiments of life. Rose waits until she feels sure that Inkpen has retreated into his own apartment then opens the door to the hallway and pulls in her trunk.

Outside in the darkness, the great houses with their granite facades stand disconsolate, the streets with their sleet-slicked cobblestones, the tobacconist's on the corner, its door sign turned to Closed.

'I'm here to write about the murder,' she confesses to Inkpen, later.

'You've come all this way for that? Don't you have enough murders in London?'

Inkpen has changed into loose cord trousers and a velvet smoking jacket. His hair, brushed back from his forehead, falls smoothly to his shoulders.

'I can't stop thinking about her,' Rose says. 'The little girl.'

'I'm not much of a one for children. Would you like a glass of port? I have cold cuts, left over from supper, if you are hungry.'

'If you are sure it's no trouble.' Her stomach growls. 'You're very kind.'

'I'm not kind at all,' says Inkpen. 'I have a penchant for interesting company.'

His sitting room is the mirror image of the one in 1B. The furnishings speak of long habitation and an appreciation of comfort: twin leather sofas and an ottoman upholstered in velvet and strewn with periodicals; silver coffee pot, Turkish carpet, fire roaring in the grate. Rose feasts on oatcakes piled with cream cheese, pickled beetroot and honey-glazed ham, a slice of game pie. She tries to conceal how famished she is, and fails utterly. Inkpen peels and nonchalantly consumes a single hardboiled egg, casting the fragments of shell into the fire.

'What makes you think I might be interesting company?' Rose asks. The food has revived her spirits considerably. Now, finally, she is curious about Inkpen, whose generous hospitality seems at odds with his sardonic smile. They have a rapport. In spite of the distance she was anxious to establish at their first meeting, Rose realises she likes him.

'You arrive in a taxi like a White Russian fleeing the Bolsheviks, for one thing. Now you announce you're here to investigate a murder.'

'You didn't know that when we met, though. And I'm not here to investigate. I'm a journalist, not a policeman.'

'A writer. I didn't realise they travelled this far north.'

'Do you know who lived in 1B before me?' Rose asks, once they have finished sparring.

'A Magnus McGraw. Some sort of businessman, I believe. He's living abroad now, South Africa. There's a rumour he killed his wife, but I don't believe a word of it. Just because a person is no longer around doesn't mean they've been murdered. Or perhaps you think differently?'

'That depends. What was her name?'

'Violet, I think.' Inkpen chuckles. 'Are you sure you're not a policeman? I only met her the once, last summer. She seemed rather shy. Nervous, even. Like a little ghost.' He laughs again. 'To tell you the truth, I felt sorry for her. McGraw's a philistine – typical businessman. I couldn't imagine a woman like that being happy with someone like him. But then you never know what goes on in a marriage, do you?'

'I am not married,' Rose says, 'so I would know even less.'

'Me neither.' He raises his glass. 'Here's to the sordid conclave of the cantankerous!'

She clinks her glass against his. She finds she is laughing, that she cannot help it. *My neighbour across the hall is rather strange*, she writes to her father later that evening, *but we get on unexpectedly well together. I cannot believe I have been in this city less than eight hours.*

When Rose told Maurice Leadbeter she wanted to write a feature on the Priestly case, he refused to commission her. He said it would be a waste of his money and her time. 'No one wants to read about a crime in Scotland,' he added. 'The public prefer their murders closer to home.'

They both understood the subtext. Rose was overstepping her brief, which was to concentrate her attention on the domestic sphere. What Maurice called women's issues. Crime was for the boys, Leadbeter's lads, the murder gang. If Freeman or Harcourt had asked to cover the story they'd be on the train already, though the chances of rooting the Beter Boys out of El Vino's were, broadly speaking, nil.

Maurice Leadbeter knew that, too.

'This is a woman's issue,' Rose protested. 'It's a woman who's been accused. She is facing the death penalty.'

'One less harridan in the world, then, winners all round,' Maurice quipped, which was when Rose lost her temper, called him bigoted and small-minded, blinded by his own prejudices.

'Not now, Rosie. I haven't got time.' Maurice sighed. He covered his eyes with his hand, as if warding off a migraine. 'You're stretching my patience to the limit here.'

Rose could feel her impatience bubbling up, the desire to laugh in his face that was really rage. Once when he was drunk, Maurice had let it slip that he admired her work, that he considered her a more interesting and original writer than half the men on his staff, only he couldn't risk giving her the stories she wanted to cover because it was liable to promote unrest.

'Promote unrest?' Rose had repeated. She had felt like laughing then, too, cackling like the fish wife he took her for then kicking him in the balls. How's that for unrest?

He told her not to get hysterical, to brighten herself up a bit. Rose had visited the newspaper's archive, read through the articles Maurice wrote when he was still on the crime beat. They were pin-sharp, perspicacious, even, on occasion, beautifully phrased. She admired Maurice – his work ethic, his professionalism, even his ruthlessness. What she could not abide was his moral cowardice, his unwillingness to rock the boat. The profession was hostile to women, so Maurice Leadbeter was hostile to women. 'What is it you want?' he had asked her once, shortly after refusing yet again to let her cover an ongoing murder trial.

'I want to write,' Rose said. 'I want to write about the things I believe are important, about what's happening now.'

'There's a dog show happening now,' Maurice had retorted. 'All kinds of things are happening now. How can you know which of them are important if you don't look into them?'

Rose accused him of being flippant, of belittling her, though she knew Maurice was right in a way, even if he didn't realise it. There was a current of seismic activity in every encounter, in every hackneyed street scene, an underhum of energy that might spill over into something darker at any moment. Rose covered the dog show, just to spite him. She wrote a humorous article comparing over-protective dog owners with stage mothers. Maurice liked what she had done. Not that he said as much to her face, but she could tell he was pleased.

As well as the piece she dashed off for Maurice, Rose spent most of the rest of the weekend composing a longer article about a woman she happened to notice while at the dog show, walking a borzoi around the arena and smiling like a film star. Something about her had seemed familiar and as she gazed at the woman's silver hair, the same colour as the borzoi's, the person standing next to her in the crowd nudged her elbow and whispered that the woman was Pauline von Blick, the opera singer they said was Hindenburg's mistress.

Rose remembered something she had read a few months previously, about von Blick being at the centre of one of the most costly divorce cases in Europe. She realised the story she wanted was right there, parading itself in front of her in a fox fur coat.

There is no such thing as dull, only a dull way of looking at things. The news is everywhere, and everything is news.

*

The furniture in 1B is hideous – dour and blockish and heavily varnished, leftovers from before the war. The flat though is larger than Rose expected, one room opening out of another like the mysterious, hidden spaces inside a labyrinth. She keeps discovering odd, left-behind items – an ostrich-feather fan, a set of Russian tea glasses in silver holders, a chimpanzee marionette – hidden at the back of the wardrobe or on the top shelves of cupboards.

Objects that can only have belonged to Violet McGraw. They hint at another life, a life Rose cannot fathom. If this Magnus McGraw really had murdered his wife, why would he have left her personal possessions scattered around the apartment? Almost as if he wanted to leave a record of his guilt, a memento of a passion that had failed.

Aileen McConnell, who comes in to clean for Marion Kennet up in 2A, has been following the Priestly case assiduously in the *Daily Record*.

'Eight years old, the lass,' she keeps repeating. 'What is it that drives people?'

When Rose asks if she will leave the morning paper, when she has finished with it, Mrs McConnell looks faintly aggrieved. She says she is in the habit of using it for lighting the fire in Mrs Kennet's sitting room.

'Marion will have her own paper,' Rose says. 'She has it delivered.'

'As you will,' says Mrs McConnell, who knows this already. She has been cleaning for Marion Kennet for most of ten years. She knows perfectly well which papers Marion takes, as well as the precise contents of her weekly grocery order from McIlvaney's, including the cakes that come in a covered basket every Friday when Marion's daughter visits, the daughter who according to Aileen is not really her daughter but an orphan child Mrs Kennet adopted at the age of two.

'Never blessed with weans of her own, which accounts for a lot. As for the husband, far be it for me to say but there were something no' right about him.'

Marion Kennet is a widow. The walls of 2A are crowded with valuable-looking oil paintings, as well as a mirror that supposedly once belonged to Queen Victoria. Marion reminds Rose of Miss Villiers, who lived down the road from them in Lambeth, and whose cousin, as she never tired of reminding people, was a Member of Parliament.

Mrs Kennet pretends a lack of interest in the Priestly murder. Like everything found in the street she considers it grubby, both in and of itself and as a matter for discussion, though Rose cannot help noticing that she has stayed abreast of developments, that if anything she is better informed about the ins and outs of the case than Aileen McConnell. Their first meeting takes place in the hallway, two days after Rose's arrival. From the rapidity of Marion's passage down the stairs, Rose thinks it likely that the older woman has been lying in wait for her.

'And you work for a newspaper, I've heard?' Marion says to her, a nugget she can only have gleaned from Aileen McConnell.

'In London I do,' Rose replies, 'but I'm here in Aberdeen as a freelance. I'm following a story.' When she mentions the Priestly case, Marion sniffs loudly as if she has been presented with something deemed foul, and is determined to test its foulness for herself. Then she asks Rose if she would care to take tea with her, in her apartment, that afternoon.

'Have you heard the latest?' Marion says, when she comes to the door. Her hallway is dimly lit, and smells faintly of aniseed. 'They're saying the husband had nothing to do with it, that she acted alone.'

She ushers Rose inside. 'It's not a good road, Urquhart Road,' she adds. 'All those children crowded together like puppies in those tiny rooms. It's hardly surprising that these things happen, with people like that.'

She moves stiffly about, arranging the tea things. Whether her awkwardness is down to infirmity or age is unclear, though there is a rigour about her also, a determination not to be outmanoeuvred by her misfortune. She runs water into the kettle, places iced biscuits on a decorated plate then covers them with a napkin. The kitchen range is a handsome green, the covers polished by Aileen McConnell to a blinding shine. A freshly laundered dishcloth hangs from the rail. Like everything in Marion's flat, the cloth is both itself and more than itself, a symbol of correctness and propriety. Of moderation, though whether chosen or forced upon her, Marion would never tell.

'You know they're saying the Donald woman caused the child's injuries herself? That poor girl.'

The kettle, on the stove top, begins to whistle, its shrill reverberations like a human scream. They drink their tea seated either side of the fire in Mrs Kennet's sitting room. The room, which would once have served as the formal reception room for the entire house, is enormous, twice the size of the sitting room in 1B. It must be marvellous in summer, Rose imagines, in the hazy, opalescent light of an August evening, though for most of the year it would seem cold, even when the fire is lit, as now. A strange, barren ghost of a place, of a time long past.

Rose finds herself wishing they had stayed in the kitchen. Marion Kennet is stirring sugar into her tea.

'What do you think of her?' Rose says. 'This Mrs Donald?'

She has seen the woman's photograph in the *Press and Journal*: an ordinary face, the face of a woman you might glimpse beside you at the butcher's counter or in the post office. Dark wavy hair and firm mouth, deeply set eyes. In her buttoned-up coat and felt hat you wouldn't look at her twice. If someone told you she was a murderer you would probably laugh and then ask them in some confusion if they were joking. Rose finds it interesting that the paper carries no photograph of the husband, that it is the woman, Jeannie Donald, people want to look at.

'She used to work as a cook,' Mrs Kennet is saying. 'A big hotel over at Banchory.' She is staring into her teacup, stirring, stirring. 'You cannot credit these people,' she says. 'I would not know what to think of her. I don't reckon I could ever come to an understanding of someone like that.' She rests her teaspoon in her saucer with an audible clink. Rose finds herself wondering if Mrs Donald will be offered tea at the police station. At the prison, she reminds herself. The latest photograph in the *Press and Journal* shows the back of a police van. The caption insists that both the Donalds are inside.

'It's not a good road, Urquhart Road,' Mrs Kennet repeats. 'The police are down there every other night, breaking up fights and suchlike. That's what I've heard, anyway. The kind of life she would have been in for, I reckon the Priestly girl is best off out of it. A child of her own by the time she's sixteen, a useless lump of a husband expecting her to wait on him hand and foot while he's spraying his scent all round the neighbourhood like a mangy tomcat? That's no life at all.'

'Not to have a chance, though? That's a tragedy, surely?'

'You're young,' Marion says, as if this closes the argument. Rose sips her tea, holding the cup between her hands in a manner Mrs Kennet will no doubt find uncouth, but she feels in need of its comfort, of the sense of warmth and sustenance between her outspread palms. She is unsettled by Marion's tone, by her class snobbery, by her insistence that Helen Priestly's death is a misfortune that was bound to happen. The tea is delicate in flavour and has a subtle aroma, unlike the tea Rose buys from the Co-op, black and coarse, quickly becoming bitter if you steep it too long.

Marion removes the napkin from the plate of biscuits. 'You must help me eat these,' she says. She pushes the plate towards her. 'They'll go stale otherwise.'

Outside, the rain is still falling, rattling against the windows as if demanding entry. The rain fell in torrents throughout the night of Helen Priestly's murder. And yet the sack the child's body was found in was completely dry. In one of the more scurrilous of the local papers, it had been reported that the child's feet could be seen, poking out from the mouth of the sack they found her in, that she had been murdered less than a minute from her own front door.

In London it is spring. The daffodils will be finished already. The white light of the north can be enthralling, but on a rainy day like this there is something bleak about it. Bleak and blank-eyed.

There is a clock by her bed, a brass travelling clock in a leather case she discovered shoved to the back of one of the shelves in 1B's enormous, multi-drawered linen press, elegant in design and beautifully made. It is Violet's, Rose feels certain. When Rose wakes in the night, the clock's soft, even ticking seems to offer her solace, the steady reassurance that she is not alone.

Rose has been making an inventory of Violet's possessions. The chimpanzee puppet and the tea glasses, the ostrich-feather fan, the brass travelling clock, a Murano glass pen set, a pair of grey silk slippers, a beaded purse, an exquisite filigree brooch in the form of a dragonfly. This last she finds, inexplicably, in the kitchen dresser, along with a set of scrimshaw napkin rings. In the back of the cavernous linen press she discovers a cake of lavender soap, a Paisley shawl and a yellow silk handkerchief embroidered with the monogram V. S. L.

The 'V' must be for Violet, the 'L' seeming to imply that the handkerchief was in her possession prior to her marriage.

Fugitive things, elusive things. Treasures hidden, yet easily discoverable, a smattering of clues. So different from Magnus McGraw's old furniture, which speaks of permanence in a way that has proved disingenuous, an elaborate veneer. The gigantic sideboard that dominates the sitting room, vast enough to climb inside. The scrolled and gilded mirrors, their pitted, luminescent surfaces swarming with the dusty light of a previous century. Obdurate, invincible, flotsam from the before-times.

When she next takes tea with Marion Kennet, Rose asks her if she had been on speaking terms with Violet McGraw.

'Why are you asking me about Violet?' Marion looks at her sharply, then glances away.

'Some of her things are still in the flat. At least I think they must be hers. I'm curious about what she was like.'

'She was young,' Marion says. 'She came from a good family. Her father died in the war, which probably explains how his daughter ended up married to a man who was twice her age. She told me she was leaving him, you know, that husband of hers, the reprobate.'

'You mean Magnus McGraw?'

Marion nods. 'Though I wouldn't be surprised if McGraw turned out not to be his name, if he had six names, come to think of it, if he was living here under an alias. He was one of those men, McGraw, the kind that lies without scruple. You could see it in the way he looked at you. As if he was trying to sum you up, trying to work out if you might be a problem to him further down the road.'

'Down the road?'

'Wherever and whenever it happened to be that his doings caught up with him, that his real nature came to light. Because it always does in the end, with men like that. They arrived here in midwinter. Their things were delivered first – all that brown furniture. Then a week later there they were and you know how it is with some people, there's something you don't take to and that's how it was for me with Magnus McGraw. Those eyes of his. Light blue, they were, like ice, not a colour you normally see in eyes and I remember thinking he's blown in on the weather, that man. Frosty, although he was polite enough, all very proper, but that sort always is. To begin with, anyway. Violet was done up in furs. She looked pale as death.'

'How long were they here? In 1B, I mean.'

'About five years. McGraw was often away on business trips, which is how I came to know Violet. They didn't seem to see many people socially, even when he was at home, and I think she was lonely. She got into the habit of nipping up here of an afternoon. She'd sit where you're sitting now and chatter on about friends of hers from South Africa, or else she'd be showing me a dress her husband had sent, from abroad, from one of his business trips. She had some beautiful clothes, Violet. They must have cost a fortune. She seemed bright enough in herself, but I couldn't help wondering if there was something behind it, something she wasn't saying. The last time I spoke to her she was completely different. A hardness to her. I asked her had something happened and that was when she told me she was leaving him.'

'Did she give a reason?'

'Just that things couldn't go on the way they were. I wished afterwards that I'd got her to tell me what exactly she meant by that, but I've never been one for putting my nose into other people's business and I wasn't about to start.'

'So what happened?'

Mrs Kennet shakes her head. 'I never saw her again. A fortnight or so later I happened to run into him in the hallway — McGraw, that is — and when I mentioned I'd not seen his wife recently he stared at me bold as you like, said she'd left for South Africa the week before and that he would be following at the end of the month. I've never forgotten the way he looked at me — like he'd put one over on me and there wasn't a thing I could do about it and both of us knew as much.'

'Do you think he was telling the truth? About her going to South Africa?'

'I try not to think anything. What good would it do?'

The trial date has been set for July 16th.

Rose has received two telegrams from Maurice Leadbeter,

demanding her return to London at the earliest opportunity. She is surprised by his persistence. She had been expecting Maurice to use her unsanctioned absence as grounds for dismissal, a prospect she had viewed with equanimity if not indifference. She cannot now imagine returning to work on the paper, or at least not without a substantial alteration of terms.

'I need more freedom,' she says to Maurice when finally he calls, the harsh whirr of the telephone bell echoing from within the depths of 2A, followed by Aileen McConnell's smart rap on her door, the interrogative tilt of her head as she informs Rose that 'a gentleman' is asking to speak to her.

'He's calling from London,' Aileen adds, accusingly, and Rose hurries upstairs. Her first thought is that it must be her father, though it turns out to be Maurice. How he has discovered her whereabouts, much less Marion's number, is one of Maurice's mysteries and not worth troubling over.

'You're wasting your time up there. I'll put you on Features and that's my final offer. You know I rate your stuff, Rosie, but you won't make me beg.'

'I'll give it some thought,' Rose says. She is thinking that Maurice is making a fair fist of begging already. 'I won't be coming back immediately, though. I need more time.'

'How much time?'

'Until after the trial at least. I'm writing something,' she adds. 'I think there might be a book in it.'

'A book?' Maurice sounds incredulous, as if the word is new to him. Rose is tempted to make adverse comment to this effect but manages to restrain herself. It would be unfair to suggest that Maurice is not well-read, and his intellect is as sharp as any she has encountered. It is his willingness to compromise it that Rose finds insufferable.

'It's my life, Maurice,' she says instead, and the bluntness of her statement seems to stun both of them.

'You'll let me know, then,' says Maurice finally, 'when you're coming back, I mean?'

'If I'm coming back, yes. Look after yourself, Maurice.' She wonders if this is the last time the two of them will speak, but once again dismisses the thought as not worth dwelling on. She replaces the receiver, says good evening to Mrs McConnell and goes back downstairs. Marion Kennet is away. She and her daughter Frances are spending a month in Italy. 'Before the tourists descend in force,' Marion said, when she announced their departure. The house feels curiously empty with just Rose and Inkpen. The attic flat, Inkpen has told her, is let to a shipping merchant none of them has ever seen.

'The Flying Dutchman,' Inkpen says. 'The ghost of the high seas.' They are in Inkpen's living room, drinking whisky. The deepening friendship between them is of a kind she remembers from her schooldays, that sense of complicity, of laughing at the world from behind closed doors.

In an unguarded moment, Inkpen tells Rose he had expected to remain without female company for the rest of his life.

'Women can't stand me, not now,' he says. 'They think I'm uncouth.'

'You are uncouth,' Rose says. She is surprised and a little unnerved by how much she has come to depend on him, not least as a sounding board for her thoughts about the Priestly case. She has been spending time on Urquhart Road and Roslin Street and King Street, talking to shopkeepers and tradespeople and others who live in the neighbourhood. The atmosphere is tense. There is a party line on the murder, which is that Jeannie Donald is guilty and deserves to hang. Even those who never knew Helen, who had never heard of Mrs Donald before the news of her arrest, are vociferous in denouncing her.

There is something terrible in the air, a feigned sense of outrage that threatens to overwhelm the facts of the crime itself. And yet Rose enjoys speaking with them, the shop workers and the schoolteachers, the street cleaners and the porters and the maids of all work. She likes hearing their stories. The tenements of Urquhart Road are overcrowded and the sanitary provisions outmoded and yet she finds she cannot agree with Marion Kennet about the character of the place: Urquhart Road is not a bad road, it is a busy road, loud with the onrush of life. Most of what she learns has little to do with the murder, yet the details seem relevant, nonetheless, what Maurice Leadbeter in his more expansive moments would call sense of place.

And in one instance at least she has struck lucky. She has managed to make contact with one of the slaters who was working next door to the Priestly house when Helen went missing. The man is named George Munro. At first he seems nervous, embarrassed, but when Rose asks him to tell her about his work his diffidence evaporates. He seems brighter and more energised, in charge of himself, particularly when he is telling her about the disasters he has witnessed, the chimney fires, the lightning strikes, the catastrophic falls from lethal heights. The job he had been called to on the afternoon of the 20th foreboded none of these things. Some minor water damage to one of the flats. A couple of loose slates that needed replacing, as well as some of the flashing that had come away.

'Nothing worth talking about,' says Munro. 'Couple o' hours' work at most.'

'And did you see anything while you were working? Anything unusual?'

'No but,' and with these words he is nervous again, examining the backs of his hands like a couple of broken tiles he has been tasked with repairing. 'I did hear something. I heard a scream. I thought it mightae been a child shouting out, falling into water. I's heard the sound before.'

'A child falling into water?' Rose feels stunned by what she is hearing, the casual intrusion of such a detail into the commonplace.

'That gasping sound,' says Munro, 'as like the kiddie were snatching for air before it went under. I goes to look in the washroom, in case it was trapped. I lifted the lid of the boiler but it was empty.'

'And did you know already that Helen Priestly was missing?'

'I found out just after we arrived. There were a woman greeting outside o' the butcher's and I heard somebody saying that's the mother.'

'And you say you've heard the sound before. When was that?'

Munro goes quiet, and Rose is afraid he will not answer, but then something shifts in him and he tells her he once saw two children drown in Rubislaw quarry.

'They were nine year old,' he says. 'Twin brothers. One jumped in to save the other and they both went under.' Munro rubs at his eyes. His fingernails are bitten down to the quick. 'Ye cannae forget a sound like that,' he says. 'That's why I goes to look in the washroom.'

'How old were you when that happened?'

'Ten or eleven. My ma wouldae thrashed me if she'd known I were up there so I never said nothing.'

'I'm sorry,' Rose says. She has forgotten, for a moment, that she is supposed to be interviewing him. She is simply there, listening.

'It were thirty year ago now,' Munro says. He folds his arms across his chest and looks away. Rose knows there are things, pieces of history, she can never hope to fathom.

'Thank you for talking to me,' she says.

'They're saying she drowned the bairn in the kitchen sink,' the slater adds. 'How can that be right?'

Rose discovers from county records that Violet's mother Iris was born in Cornwall. Violet's father, Andreas Leitner, was originally from Danzig. His whole family became naturalised British when he was eighteen. Violet meets Magnus McGraw at a party in London, at the house of a family friend. Magnus is from Aberdeenshire, the son of a factory foreman, though he seems to have been at pains to conceal his origins. The two are married at Banchory, and spend their wedding night at the Tornacoille Hotel before taking the overnight train to Southampton. From there they travel on board the steamship *Dunnottar Castle* to Magnus McGraw's estate in Cape Town, South Africa.

The Tornacoille, where Jeannie Donald was employed as a cook before she was married. Which means she was probably working there on the night the McGraws were staying. In the first week of June, Rose books herself a two-night stay at the hotel, a luxury she can ill afford but cannot resist.

Banchory is in full bloom. The hotel sits in its own grounds, surrounded by overflowing banks of pink rhododendrons. The hotel's guests are a mix of well-dressed middle-aged couples and groups of younger men who are here for the shooting and fishing. A few have wives in attendance, most do not. The hotel, all dark wood panelling and pre-war furnishings, is stylish in a way that speaks of money but eschews fashion, the natural habitat of men like McGraw, though Rose can only imagine that Violet would have been bored here, that any doubts she already had about her marriage would have been confirmed.

The evening meal is traditional, hearty, the kind of cooking she imagines Jeannie Donald probably excelled at. Rose sits up late in the hotel bar, writing up her notes. In her plain shift dress she feels both invisible and glaringly conspicuous. After breakfast the following morning she parks herself in the guest lounge to go through the newspapers. She orders coffee from one of the restaurant staff and when the woman returns with her tray Rose asks her if she remembers Jeannie Donald, or Jeannie Ewen, as she would have been then.

The woman's expression changes from one of bored neutrality to something more guarded. She is in her late twenties, Rose estimates, but it is not beyond the bounds of possibility that the two had once worked together. The woman looks about herself as if to check who might be listening, but aside from herself and Rose the guest lounge is empty.

'You're talking about the woman who's been done for murder? For killing that wee girlie over in Aberdeen?'

Rose nods. She is expecting more questions, demands to know who she is and why she wants to know, but the waitress merely glances over her shoulder one more time before launching into her story. She is clearly anxious to have the thing out before they are disturbed, as if she has been waiting all this time to tell someone, waiting ever since Jeannie's arrest, which probably she has.

'I was never here when she was. I only started here three year ago. I was on bedrooms at first, only Miss Reddy says I've done that well I can go in the restaurant, if I wanted, which is better pay so why wouldn't I? Anyway, Miss Reddy's assistant Katy McCleary's been here ten year or thereabouts and she was telling me and Mhairi Docherty about when Jeannie Ewen got into a row with Roddy Lawlor who used to see to the chickens and how when he went out to see to the birds the morning after they'd all been killed. Lying lifeless there in the coop with all their necks broken. No one could ever prove anything and Katy says Miss Reddy always had a preference for Jeannie Ewen, she were a good worker, she said, so nothing was done. Everyone knew it was Jeannie who killed those chickens, though. She was always flying off into rages on account of nothing. Like the devil were in her, Katy said, and she weren't a bit surprised when she heard about the murder. She'll have lost her temper again, she said. Jeannie Ewen was a good worker all right but she had a tongue you could light a fire with in a force nine gale.'

The waitress stops speaking suddenly. 'Would you like anything else, Miss?' she says. The neutral tone is back, though the colour is high in her cheeks and she looks faintly flustered. 'I could fix you up a sandwich if you're feeling hungry.'

'No, thank you,' Rose says. She feels reluctant to let the woman leave, and as she turns to go back to the kitchen Rose finds herself asking if she has ever come into contact with Violet McGraw. The effect is instantaneous, and remarkable. The blush in her cheeks deepens to a fierce red.

'Mr McGraw often stays here on business,' she stammers. 'But I've only seen Mrs McGraw the once.'

'It's all right,' Rose says. She can feel the woman's anxiety, the hot pulse of her shame. 'I don't know them.' She hesitates, trying to think of a reason she might give for having mentioned the couple. The truth is too bizarre.

'My neighbour was friendly with them,' she says, finally. 'Before they went back to South Africa. She told me they had been guests here, that's all.'

The waitress nods and hurries away. After lunch, Rose walks the two miles into Banchory. She buys a postcard from one of the gift shops, a watercolour image of the Tornacoille with an old-fashioned horse and carriage waiting in the drive. *This place wouldn't suit you,* she writes on the back. *Too much fresh air.* She addresses the card to 1A and drops it into a post box. It occurs to her that she has never seen Inkpen outside his apartment.

They have talked about the Donald case, for hours. Inkpen believes Jeannie is guilty, that her outburst of violence is an expression of dissatisfaction with her impoverished circumstances.

'Murder as an act of protest. You might even call it a work of art. A disruption of the status quo, like with the Dadaists.'

Rose thinks his theory is obscene and she has told him so. Yet she keeps coming back to it, tormenting herself with the question of what it might mean for the world if Inkpen is right. Even if Jeannie acted on the spur of the moment, the stresses that plagued her everyday life are bound to have exerted an influence, even if subconsciously.

And at least Inkpen is capable of applying logic in his search for answers. The mood of the townspeople has grown increasingly ugly. Impatient with the slow wheels of justice, they seek only revenge. There are many who would happily see a return to public executions. The word the papers use to describe Mrs Donald, again and again, is evil.

'There is no such thing as evil,' Inkpen insists. 'Only evil deeds.'

One of the drawers in the big linen closet is crammed with documents. Most of them are articles torn from magazines, pieces on shipping and international trade. As Rose goes through them she notices that the names of certain people and businesses keep recurring, though she cannot find any mention of the name McGraw.

Of the other documents, some are bank statements, years out of date. Buried beneath a stack of old news bulletins from something called the *Arctic Shipping Consortium*, Rose discovers a passport in the name of Violet Sara Leitner McGraw. The passport is still current, due to expire in the February of 1938. Folded inside the passport is a single piece of notepaper. There is no date, no return address – Rose conjectures these might have been on the envelope, which is not present.

Tell him tonight, or I'll tell him myself. It is dangerous to keep delaying. He may do something rash.

The note is unsigned, though the handwriting looks familiar. It is not until some days later, when she happens to spot a small pile of unstamped letters waiting on the hall table in Inkpen's apartment, that Rose understands where from.

Ambition: A Fairy Tale

Skinny malinky Vanstone
Five feet tall
Flirting with the captain
At the Christmas ball
When the captain coddled her
She laughed out loud
Kissed him on the lips
Before a cheering crowd

Skinny malinky Vanstone
Name in lights
Danced the tarantella
In her spangled tights
When the doorman grabbed at her
She screamed blue murder
Later in the court room
They claimed no one heard her

> Skinny malinky Vanstone
> Sentenced to hang
> Walking to the gallows
> When the telephone rang
> Crowds are in an uproar
> As the king grants pardon
> Now she's dancing with her captain
> In the palace garden
> (Music hall song, 1930, Anonymous.)

For a couple of weeks she was notorious. Then she disappeared into another life.

Skinny malinky Vanstone they called her at school, her breastbone sharp as a chicken's, and that skulky knock-kneed slouch, stick-arms folded across her flat chest to keep off the chill. Grey sack dress with oversized pockets and Peter Pan collar. Cracked patent leather shoes that used to be her mother's, then her sister Carol's, then eventually hers. To think that once they were shiny and new, dancehall shoes. Now they get her laughed at.

Hair the colour of mud and ink-smudge eyebrows, the first time she made up a dance she was copying a toad, a fat, lumbering toad from round the back of the coal store. Golden-eyed and stubby-toed, the careful way toads move, with an elastic-limbed, purposeful grace few people notice. And Irma is filled with it, tanked up with the greenish, pea-soupy light of the toad's secret kingdom. A king in the coat of a toad – King Toad. Irma stretches her arms and squats. Feet planted, legs apart. Swivels her head and stares, imagining gold. The gold of her bottomless eyes and the gold she is guarding – because guarding gold is what toads should do in life as well as in fairy tales.

The rush of becoming something else is like a magical potion. And suddenly Irma feels lighter because she knows the way out. Out of the schoolyard's raucous banter and the cracked leather shoes. The way a fledgling in the nest might sense the power of flight before they try their wings.

And in her later years she looks back at her time in the spotlight as a kind of fairy tale: the child of the chimney corner transformed to a goddess by her gift for movement then cast down through her own ambition once more into the dust. They were strange years. Good years, she is bound to admit, though always with a shade of falsehood about them, as if she knew in her heart even then that the fates would turn on her, as they are always bound to turn, sooner or later, on anyone they feel has risen beyond their station.

Was she ever free? Was she ever lovely? The music was lovely, and her movements, yet beneath the makeup and the shawl of feathers she was merely herself: skinny Irma with the dirt-coloured hair, and a habit of slipping back inside her childhood, with all its demons, the moment the curtain had fallen and the lights were dimmed.

Who is Irma Vanstone? the papers demanded. She with no thought in her head other than to defend herself, to escape the monster, and in this the fates had believed her, or given her the benefit of the doubt at least, for here she was, wasn't she? Free to go, as the judge had said. Free not to finish her life at the end of a rope.

Her misfortune had become the subject of a music hall ditty. Lily Morris herself had taken it out for a spin at the Hackney Empire. They were dancing in the aisles, her sister told her. Like what we'd been through as a family was some sort of joke.

As a family, Irma smiled to herself, grimly. She could see no point in reminding Carol that she'd not heard a single word from her while she was in prison.

And had he ever truly loved her, the military man? For a little while maybe, between the champagne hours of midnight and 2 am. But between those who called him a cad and those who called him a fool, Irma cannot find any satisfaction in condemning him. They had nothing in common, she and the captain, just those fleeting, dream-soaked moments, not enough to build a life on. He set himself free – so what? He did them both a favour.

She comes to Aberdeen because it is far away. So far from London it is another world, another country at least, a colder northern one. The wind along the seafront is brutal, even in September. Still, no one knows her name here, which is all that counts. And that curious, energised feeling of being a novice, filled once again with the rapture and terror of being on stage.

She is twenty-eight by then, but still looks younger. The perks of being scraggy as a house mouse, and strangely nondescript, until she starts to dance. It is easy for her to lie about her age. A charity woman who came to visit her while she was in prison has given her a contact. The vaudeville, she calls it, at the Beach Pavilion. The dancers are always leaving to get married, she says. So they're constantly looking for new girls. It's a hard life, she adds. Harder than they bargained for, most of them.

The contact's name is Madame Crossac, though Irma suspects the woman is French as jellied eels. Hair dyed black as boot polish, mouth a scarlet slit.

You're old, she says. You sure you're up to it?

Twenty-four, Irma says. I've got experience.

I bloody bet you have, says Madame Crossac – her first name is Vivienne. She strikes up the piano, a monstrous, iron-framed instrument, twin candelabras jutting upwards like bull horns, tipped with silver. The woman can play though, like a banshee on heat, and some years down the road Irma learns that French or Blackwater estuary Madame Crossac was once a repetiteuse at the Paris Opera.

She plays 'The Maiden's Prayer', that dusty teatime favourite. And it is good to dance, to stretch her limbs, to perform once again before a living person instead of prancing about in front of the mirror. After the 'Prayer', Crossac plays Ravel's 'Habanera' and Irma comes fully alive. She forgets the harsh lighting, the clammy chill of the rehearsal room, the slightly tacky surface of the linoleum floor. Irma likes to imagine the habanera as a seduction – not of a man, but of music itself, a controlled explosion. Her limbs are heavy with longing, with unsheathed desire. And no one will get to see her now, just bus drivers and their whey-faced wives, she thinks. Pastrycooks and plasterers, louche newspapermen on their evenings off, the callow sons of padres in search of risk.

And why not? Irma thinks. Why not them as much as anyone? The music does not care, and does not alter.

As Irma comes back to earth, Madame Crossac stares at her hard and crosses her arms. There is steel in her eyes, and a wealth of knowledge, but no trace of pity. The job's yours, if you want it – five bob a week. She adds that there is extra to be earned if Irma is willing to offer tuition to local schoolgirls in the afternoons.

The vaudeville girls are mostly too young to keep discipline, she explains. But I am assuming that won't be a problem for someone your age.

Many of the girls she dances with are not yet eighteen. They bicker and squabble amongst themselves, like grubby white mice. Romantic entanglements and money troubles, minor debaucheries and major feuds, the talent inherent in every rainbow for becoming a storm. And all as if time were no object, a pretty bauble, theirs to play with. Irma wonders occasionally if Crossac is right, if she is too old and too sensible now to be seen as anything but an interloper. She is at best tolerated.

There is a man, at least, sort of. Ivan Redchow, a junior reporter on the *Press and Journal*. Irma suspects he is younger than she is, though he likes to pretend otherwise, a skinny malinky himself, fingers bruised yellow and purple from the twin intoxicants of nicotine and ink.

Soon as I get my break, he's forever telling her, we can be away to London.

Burning the midnight oil, setting down his stories. Vanny wants to be a member of the murder gang. Don't they all?

In the main, she finds the schoolgirls easier to manage. Their breathless excitements and petty jealousies remind her of the faraway fairytale world of her own schooldays, though fairytales, she reminds herself, can be dangerous places. Irma should know, she was in one herself. She was almost hanged there.

Stage mothers are a fact of life, or of this life anyway, but the cold-faced woman in the flowerpot hat and the blue coat is unnerving in a way not easily explained.

Mrs Donald is poor, you can tell from the coat, the hat, the rubbed-out dignified bleakness of everything she owns. But poverty is hardly a scarce commodity, especially here. The woman should be unmemorable, the kind of person you might speak to for half an hour and then find yourself wondering what she looked like, what she said.

Mrs Donald reminds Irma of her own mother, most like – the same ugly cauldron of a hat, the same barely suppressed frustration with the sourness of her life. Her daughter Jeannie is another mouse – a measly yellow one. A hectic, quivering creature with no colour in her cheeks and a square forehead. A pretty dancer right enough but there is something missing, a want of resilience, a sense that she is not so much demanding to be seen as straining to please.

The demand to be seen is in the mother. That and the resilience, a fortitude like iron.

Mrs Donald has asked Irma several times now, how she should see about getting her Jeannie an audition for a proper dance school.

Jeannie's a mite young yet, Irma havers. Better to wait a year or even two.

She knows what the dance schools are like: harsh places, cruel places, a playground for monsters. Wee Jeannie won't survive more than a term in such an establishment, not because she lacks for talent but because she doesn't want to dance. Not for anything past a pastime and that's not enough.

The thought of trying to explain this to Mrs Donald makes Irma feel tongue-tied. She finds herself thinking about the woman even on her days off, wondering what it is that drives her, what makes her tick.

There's something not right about her, she says to Vanny.

What do you mean, not right? Vanny says. It is unusual for Irma to bring her work home with her. Mostly she likes to sew, to take a turn along the esplanade, to sit an hour or two with him and the lads from the paper in the The Old Believer. She drinks whisky and ginger wine, or a half of stout. She doesn't say much, but she likes to hear them talk. She finds their excited voices and circular arguments strangely soothing. She smiles a half smile, nips at her drink, feels the tension ebbing away from her exhausted limbs. Irma doesn't do politics. She doesn't gossip about the girls in her troupe or her pupils either. So Vanny will know enough to listen when she breaks this rule.

She acts polite but she's not, Irma says. She makes out she's grateful for the classes and for me paying attention to Jeannie but underneath she's angry. Like she's waiting for me to make a mistake, so she can go off on one. She scares me, Irma says, and she does not tell Vanny the worst of it, how she's always looking for bruises on wee Jeannie's back and shoulders, for a sign that her misgivings about the Donald woman are founded in something real. But the girl's sallow skin is unblemished, her scrawny body fresh with the smell of soap. Her hair is neatly combed, her clothing well worn but looked-after, with any small tears or pulls neatly repaired. Wee Jeannie invariably comes to rehearsal with some sort of refreshment, a sandwich or a cheese patty, carefully wrapped in greaseproof paper.

And those costumes of hers, for the galas – all sewn by hand, the colours and fabrics and trim so carefully chosen. Whatever is wrong with the Donald woman, there's nothing you could hold her to account for in the care of her daughter.

Of the children Irma has in her charge, wee Jeannie Donald is far from the handsomest but she is the most hardworking. There is a doggedness about her efforts that makes her almost noble.

Perseverance, she says suddenly to Vanny, that's the word. She strains to find something of herself in poor wee Jeannie – in their scrawny angularity they look somewhat alike. Yet if the two of them are both aliens, they're from different planets.

Irma was always on fire – with rude awakenings, with inborn talent, with the lust for escape.

Wee Jeannie is like a rock plant, holding fast to the ground she has conquered, clinging on.

The Beach Pavilion is sited at the south end of the Esplanade, across the road from the windswept seafront, within sight of the lighthouse and the lookout point at Footdee and the hosts of trawlers and steamers and cargo ships sailing in an endless relay in and out of the docks.

The pavilion first came into being in 1882, an octagonal wooden structure used mainly for small-scale entertainments and summer galas. There's a postcard from 1907, showing the interior of the Beach Pavilion in this first incarnation. The lighting is strung between the roof supports, as in a circus tent. The stage is raised behind a plywood arch, the audience sitting attentively on rows of wooden chairs.

This flimsy gazebo was replaced in 1928 with a more permanent building, a venue for tea dances and musical theatre and variety shows of the kind that had become increasingly popular through the years between the wars, an entertainment for all the family, a respectable and natural successor to the Victorian music hall. This is the Beach Pavilion as Mrs Donald and her daughter Jeannie would have known it, described on the Theatres Trust website as 'a single-storey sprawl of brick and stone clad in buff faience, in the nondescript style of municipal swimming baths and healthcare facilities.'

It was cheap to build, in other words, thrown up to capitalise on popular demand for beachside entertainment but with no particular thought for what it looked like. We might well assume that the place was ugly, and it most likely was, objectively, yet to dismiss it with such an insufficient insult would be to miss something, would be a failure of imagination that omits as much as it includes.

The summers on the Links, the clandestine meetings and sorrowful partings, the drunken birthday celebrations that spiralled out of hand. The chatter and laughter of after-show revellers, spilling out into the bleach-blonde sunshine of an endless July evening. The honk of a horn in the summer night, a shopgirl wiping her eyes as she tries to hide her pain. The ache of abandonment, the sunset of passion, the brash laughter of revenge.

The creak of dusty boards in the curtained wings, the hunched backs of stacked chairs, the piles of torn costumes and faded stage setting. A cracked teacup with a lipsticked rim. The high shrieks of the vaudeville girls, tossing an admirer's bouquet back and forth between them over the wooden partitions in the ladies' toilets.

A sparkling cardboard crown. The hiss of yellow gaslight, piercing fog. The sheeting rain that night in April, when the life of one child was forfeit, and the life of another, her erstwhile playmate, was altered forever.

And every building tells a story, even this single-storey sprawl of brick and stone. Still adhering to the wall of a bus shelter further down the Esplanade, a poster advertising a summer special three years before. The Ace of All Concert Parties, Harry Gordon's Entertainers, John Lovering, Norah Lamb, Jack Holden, Gladys Courtland, Al Stephenson, Claude Worth, the Four Pavilion Girls. Twice nightly six forty and eight forty-five, Saturday matinee at three. Prices as usual, commencing Monday 29th of June 1931.

The singer, comedian and popular entertainer Harry Gordon was famous throughout Scotland but most especially in his hometown of Aberdeen. Gordon attended King Street School, the same as Helen Priestly and wee Jeannie Donald. His company of entertainers first came together in the Deeside town of Banchory, where Jeannie Ewen once worked as a cook at the Tornacoille Hotel.

Harry Gordon died of influenza in Glasgow, in 1957. He is the subject of the 1980s stage play *Cold Today*, written by the noted Aberdeen playwright Charles Barron, to mark the centenary of Gordon's birth in 1883.

The Beach Pavilion remained in use for more than a century. The building was demolished following a fire in 2014.

*

The main item on the programme is *Scheherazade*. Millicent Raeburn is cast as the storyteller. Millie is short and slow-moving but there is a dreaminess about her that perfectly suits the part. The more difficult role of the princess goes to Jenny Orpen; the prince goes to Annabel Wright, with her strong, athletic body and pageboy hair.

Wee Jeannie is Scheherazade's cup bearer. The part is small but demanding and it is perfect for Jeannie, one of the few who can handle the complicated step sequence without getting muddled. Wee Jeannie will also take the role of ship's lookout in the storm at sea segment. Jeannie's costumes are so well finished they could pass for shop-bought.

Say what you like about Mrs Donald, she is an excellent seamstress. She has frequently proved herself useful making adjustments to the other girls' costumes, though Irma wishes she wouldn't insist on being there at every rehearsal, hovering about at the back of the hall like a disgruntled ghost.

I'm sure she does it deliberately, Irma grumbled once to Crossac. She's trying to find fault with me or something.

She doesn't care about you, Crossac said. She's a strange bird, that's for sure, but she doesn't mean any harm. Could be she wanted to go on the stage herself once, who knows? Either that or she's here to get some time out from her old man.

The final dress rehearsal is on Friday 20th. It is raining so hard that some of the ensemble dancers haven't bothered turning up. Irma scurries around in the wings, trying to sop up the water from the roof leaks before someone goes flying. Wee Jeannie has a rip the size of Aberdeenshire in one of her knee-highs. Her calf looks black with blood, but when Irma looks closer she can see it's just the way the sock has plastered itself like an ink stain around the curve of her leg.

The girl seems close to tears, which is unlike her.

You'll be all right, Irma says. Take off those socks and I'll put them on the boiler with the others. Then they'll be warm and dry for when you go home. She pats the child on the head. Her hair is soaking. She wonders briefly where her hat is and then the thought flits away. The girl's teeth are chattering. This bloody city, Irma thinks, too bloody windy, too bloody cold, too bloody wet. Not like London, where the smog might kill you, that's true, but at least you can stay out nights and not freeze to a block.

Are you sure you're all right, love? The girl nods her head, though the gesture seems more like a reflex than an honest answer. The child is nervous as are they all but there's no time to spend reassuring her because here comes trouble in the shape of the Geller girls, the bloody ship's mice. The mice are popular with the audience but Irma has asked herself more than once if adding this extra dose of chaos is worth the aggro.

Wee Jeannie's cup-bearer costume is pink and silver, a tunic dress and tights.

She seems different, Irma thinks, older somehow. Vivienne Crossac at the piano is on excellent form, and Irma hopes she will bring the same commitment to the performance proper. The ensemble pieces – the storm and the dance of the handmaidens – are more or less in sync in spite of the absences, and Millie Raeburn is a picture in her turban and gown. The rain is thundering on the roof like tin tacks but no one's thinking about the foul weather, not now. Some of the mothers have stayed behind to watch, those who can't face heading out into the wet again and Mrs Donald of course, who would have stayed behind anyway. She is sitting slightly apart from the others, her large hands clasped determinedly around the bag she brings Jeannie's costumes in. There is a sullen cast to her face, more so even than usual. Irma finds her presence oppressive as she always does.

Near the end of the storm section, Jeannie stumbles, flinging out an arm to steady herself. As soon as she is off the stage she seems all in. She folds her arms across her chest, hugging herself. Her eyelids are drooping. The child is ill, Irma thinks, caught a chill most likely. She should be at home.

Jeannie, Irma calls to her softly. The girl is weeping, the tears flowing down her cheeks in a steady stream. Jeannie makes no attempt to wipe them away and Irma realises the girl doesn't even know she's crying. She dabs at Jeannie's face with a handkerchief.

What is it, love? You did really well.

They can't find Nelly, Jeannie says. Her breath hitches in her chest. I wanted to go and help look for her but I'm not allowed. I'm not allowed because it's raining and Ma says it's dangerous.

Irma doesn't have a clue what wee Jeannie is talking about. She hasn't heard the radio broadcasts – she's been too busy here, at the pavilion, preparing for the rehearsal. She wonders vaguely if this Nelly might be a lost cat, or maybe a doll. But there are only moments to go before the final scene opens and there's no time to ask.

I'm sure Nelly will be fine, love, she says. She strokes the girl's cheek. Time to get changed. Jeannie has less than three minutes to get back into her cup-bearer costume, and her face still has that peaky, pinched look, marked by tears. Irma wonders if she should pull her out of the performance, wrap her in a blanket beside the radiator with a cup of sweet tea, but Jeannie somehow gets her act together and if anything she's better in the finale than she was at the start.

Could be the kid has what it takes, after all. Irma stops worrying about her at that point – there's too much else going on, and it's only later as they're locking up that she overhears a couple of the mothers whispering about the child reported missing from Urquhart Road.

A week or two after the trial, Irma finally tells Vivienne Crossac the facts of her own case.

I had no intention of killing him, I just wanted to get him off me, she says. The scissors were lying there on the dressing table – they were what came to hand, that's all. The whole thing was a blur.

Do you still think about it? Crossac asks. She is smoking a cigarette. The August evening is fine and bright. The scent of caramelised sugar from the doughnut stand drifts sweetly in the warm air.

Not really, Irma says. Not often. She is looking out to sea. There are ships on the horizon, heading into port. He was a nasty piece of work in any case. He used to blackmail the girls any chance he got. Some of the actors, too. Not that they said so in court. But then there's lots of stuff that doesn't get said in court, like how you did the world a favour, especially his wife.

I do think about her, though, Irma adds, that Mrs Donald. The way she'd look at you sometimes, as if she hated the sight of you.

Like the world owed her a living, Crossac says, I remember. I don't suppose we'll ever know the whole truth about what happened. That's just how life is.

Last Seen Wearing

THE GIRL'S SHOCKING DISAPPEARANCE in broad daylight, that's what gets to her, and so close to home. As if a hand had reached out of the sky and gathered her up, plucked her off the street like a dropped handkerchief, or a doll cast aside on the pavement by a disgruntled child.

Pearl reads and rereads the online articles looking for clues, an unregarded sentence with more meaning behind it than the writer intended. It is the description of Helen's clothing in particular that she finds heartbreaking: *a blue serge dress with a blue velvet collar, black shoes and stockings, a light blue knitted tammy*. The report is so stark, so precise it is almost unbearable. This child was clearly well cared for, regarded. A photograph shows her with short, side-parted hair and a lopsided smile. A child who suddenly stopped being a child, with thoughts and friends and worries, and became a part of the past. A set of movements and facial features and articles of clothing, a tragedy people would read about in their morning paper.

The newspapers at the time said the child's mother, Agnes Priestly, was 'prostrate with grief', that she had 'required medical attention'; the neat, journalistic phrases recasting personal catastrophe in the language of advertisements. Grief and rage and heartache, caught and stunned and repackaged as front-page headlines.

The weather continues to be wet. When for a ten-minute interval the sun appears, the pavements take on a silvered, mirror-like sheen. The light of spring is different, though; even when filtered through rainfall, it will not be denied.

Last seen wearing: black shoes and stockings and a blue knitted tammy. Dense and springy three-ply wool, a blue that catches the eye like a discarded chocolate wrapper, snatched by the wind and bowling ahead of you forever down the rain-slicked street. From the sixteenth century there were bonnet-makers' guilds in all five of Scotland's great cities: Glasgow, Edinburgh, Perth, Stirling and Aberdeen. The most famous of the bonnet towns though was Stewarton, in the county of Ayrshire. The bonnets made there were worn first by farmers, then by working people of all trades, the felted yarn and drooping sides designed to repel the worst of Scotland's weather. The making of bonnets was carried out in the off-season, known as winter work, with a good cash crop at the end of it, if you were skilled enough, and many labourers and diggers and planters were good with their hands. You could knit a bonnet in the round, on three needles, the same as you'd use to turn a heel when fashioning a sock. The wool was then moistened and felted and brushed to a soft, thick pile. The matted texture of this material rendered the completed bonnet close to watertight.

The yarn would be died with woad, the oldest of the blue dyes and the most home-grown. You'll remember the blue-painted faces of William Wallace and his band of Bravehearts? That's woad, the colour of the Saltire, the shade of rebellion. A blue bonnet is a Scotch bonnet, is a mark of pride. The Covenanters wore blue bonnets, they were even killed for them. The Jacobites wore blue bonnets, they were killed for them, too.

The blue bonnet became known as a tam, or tammy owing to its mention by Robert Burns in his poem or should I say ghost story *Tam O'Shanter*. This most famous of Burns's narrative poems tells the story of a feckless drunkard who gets chased by a horde of witches through the pouring rain. The verses' punchy, staccato rhythm mimics the hoof-beats of a galloping horse.

If you go on to Google maps you can follow the route Tam takes upon his windswept flight, the road from Ayr to Alloway that is now the B7024. The new church is on your left, the roofless ruin of Old Alloway Kirk is there on your right. The churchyard is shaded with trees, a green idyll, and if you go there in real life you'll find Rabbie's parents, lying together in a shared grave beneath a single stone. Fly on past the churches, on, on past the fine stone houses of Alloway and you'll see the swan's neck curve in the road before the Brig o' Doon.

When the Google car last captured its image, the river Doon ran smooth as melted chocolate beneath sunny skies. The distance between bridge and church seems laughably small in the age of the motor car, though on foot or on the back of a horse it would seem challenging enough and with a witch in pursuit on a stormy night it might well have seemed endless.

Onwards and outwards into open country and there's nothing for miles.

I don't really believe in character, said the well known writer, I believe in moments of truth, and Pearl, listening to the podcast, thought that even though what she'd said was austere, it was a perfect summary of what the writer had set out to achieve in her recent trilogy, the three novels referenced endlessly by critics and worried over by readers, searching for points of correspondence with the writer's own life.

There are many such points of contact, but they do not matter. What matters is the text as a record of incident, a forensic report designed to defy the idea of story, even as a story, however grudgingly, begins to unfold. The point is not the story as construct, but the individual qualities of the words themselves.

As a child, Pearl loved to build complicated structures out of Lego bricks: houses, pavilions, spaceships. She still remembers how it feels to handle pieces of Lego, to run her fingers along their straight edges, their moulded smoothness, the round protuberances that allowed her to slot one brick on top of another and begin to build something. The potential in a pile of individual Lego bricks is much more interesting, she thinks now, than the incompetent attempts at creation that mostly result from it, just as words in their unattached state – words divested of their corporate identity, words as works of art – contain a world of latent possibilities still untapped.

Lobby

Shadow

Sack

Sock

How can stories still hold meaning when the world is gripped by forces that warp the currency of everyday exchange? When Pearl first started writing, the power of story seemed infinite. The disease and the war and the warming seem to have made a nonsense of such complacency. There are moments of palpable evil, Pearl writes, the sense of living in a time when speaking has become so difficult that silence feels easier.

Or if not silence, the more tangible weight and volume of specific words, dropped singly into the silence like stones into water.

Rain

Leaf

Owl

Bowl

Glove

Loaf

Brooch

Pearl imagines a brooch pinned to Jeannie Donald's coat collar, an oval moss agate, set in silver. The brooch was left to her by an aunt who died when Jeannie was twelve. The brooch is not strictly real but Jeannie Donald existed, she had a life. For a brief period – ten years – Jeannie and Pearl existed within the same time frame. They had no knowledge of one another, and yet in those moments of their coexistence a mutual connection was being forged, threads twisting back from the past and into the future to be caught in the now.

The child looks up from her exercise book, surprised. She sees the rope of time unspooling towards her through the blue.

*

Pearl messages her friend Billy.

I know this sounds like it's coming out of nowhere but I'm about to start writing a novel about a historical case. A murder that happened in Aberdeen in the 1930s.

Sounds fantastic. Go for it.

Because this is how they are, she and Billy, they affirm each other's choices, no matter what. They enjoy many of the same things: true crime and curry and folk festivals and fake American diners. Hunting for antique postcards in junk shops in Blackpool and Morecambe.

Billy writes about the future: bone-lean, cutting edge satires on the rise of alt-right politics and the surveillance state. His most recent novel has just been optioned for TV. He likes to get up late and work late, the opposite of Pearl. She imagines him in his kitchen, brewing weapons-grade coffee and eating sardines on toast. His boyfriend Corrin, a paralegal, will have left for work hours ago.

Telling Billy things makes them seem possible. During one of their innumerable lockdown Zoom calls Pearl had spoken to him about how difficult she found it to write in the first person.

Because it's too revealing, you mean?

Because I am afraid that no one is really interested in what I think or feel. The third person you can hide inside. It's like body armour.

How are you doing? Billy messages, in the present. *Really, I mean.*

Fine, Pearl replies. *It's been good to get away*, and even as I write this I am still trying to decide what Billy is alluding to, what reason Pearl might have for wanting to get out of the city for a couple of days. The most obvious would be a break up, but that seems too predictable, and I'm not interested in her droning on about some guy. Could it be that someone close to Pearl has died – her brother, for instance? This would make more sense within the context of the story, and the more I think about this brother the more he comes into focus: a year older than Pearl, a business graduate, and he's gone missing somewhere. His name is Stewart, and he has gone missing in the rainforest, in Malaysia, during a hike. There's been no word of him for almost six months, and the friends who were on the trip with him don't have any answers. Pearl's mother – Mavis – is entirely wrapped up in the online campaign she has launched to look for him. Pearl is worried that Mavis is becoming isolated. The only friendships she cares about now are those she's made through the campaign message board.

The three of them worked as a family before Stew disappeared. Because Pearl and Stew were so close, the fact that Mavis loved Stew more never really bothered her. Now the relationship between Pearl and her mother is revealed as a vacuum. They will both have their own view on why this has happened, but at least here on the page I can mostly ignore Mavis, who is selfish and unreasonable and intellectually stymied by internalised misogyny.

I'm fine, Pearl replies. *It's been good to get away. The thing is*, she adds, *I know Stew would be really into me writing a book like this. He loved unsolved mysteries.*

Loves, she types, correcting herself. It is becoming harder to think of her brother in the present tense. In some ways, the fact that he went missing abroad has helped to keep him alive, the waiting simply an extension of the original, expected waiting from when he went away. Pearl is glad not to be in contact with the friends he was with, the ones who returned from the forest without him, who raised the alarm. They are all back working in their jobs now. One of them, Ben Macy – Pearl knows this through the message board – has just become a father. She wonders if they have become closer, the three of them, or whether the effect of Stew's disappearance has been the opposite, a corrosive anxiety that will drive them apart, or set them one against the other, telling tales.

That would depend, Pearl supposes, on what really happened. So far at least, none of them has gone against their original story. That Stew diverted from the main trail to take some photographs and never came back. They searched the whole area, for hours, yelling his name and setting off their phone alarms, but there was no sign of him.

It was like he'd never been there, said Daniel Okumbe, the only one of the three who had contacted Pearl afterwards to say how sorry he was, how he still felt haunted by Stew's disappearance and always would. He asked if she wanted to meet and Pearl had said yes. Daniel flew up from London. He claimed he had a business appointment, that he would have been making the trip anyway. They spent an hour sitting opposite one another in a Vietnamese restaurant off Byres Road, where Pearl could not rid herself of the feeling that he was holding something back.

When she asked him what they'd been talking about before Stew stepped off the path, Daniel shrugged, a gesture that to Pearl seemed too deliberate, affected nonchalance.

I can't remember, Daniel said. Just stuff, really. We were chatting about all sorts of things. You know what it's like.

He showed her the photos he had taken the evening before, the four of them goofing about on the hotel terrace. In one of them, Stew was staring off to one side, clutching a beer bottle and not looking at the camera. It looked like they'd had an argument, Pearl said to Billy, afterwards. I should have asked Daniel what it was about, what had been said, but I knew he wouldn't tell me. He would have pretended it was nothing, that it didn't happen.

What if it was nothing? Billy says. *What if things happened exactly as those guys said they did?*

Coming from anyone else, the question would have been infuriating, but because it's Billy it actually calms her, opens up the possibility that she's wrong about this, that there is no truth to discover but the one she has been told: prosaic and confusing and inconclusive. That the only reason she is trying to cast doubt on it is because she wants them to be lying, those friends of Stew's. If they're lying that means they know something, which means Stew might still be alive.

The official search for Stew ended five months ago. Mavis is raising money through the message board to mount a new one.

That's good though, isn't it? Billy is typing. *That Stewart would be into it. This Aberdeen story of yours, I mean. It's a way of keeping him involved in what you're doing.*

Pearl has been thinking the same thing, only she has not said so, not in those words, not even to Billy. The word story can mean many things — a newspaper report, a falsehood, a fairy tale — and she hates the idea of false comfort, of magical thinking. Billy met Stewart only the once, the Christmas before the pandemic, and so the Stewart he knows is mostly Stewart as filtered through Pearl; her words, her memories.

Billy never had time to become a part of their world, to become enmeshed in the version of reality they made together. Pearl has not said as much to Billy, but she is glad. It means her friendship with Billy still feels whole, untouched by tragedy.

I am not sure yet what has happened to Stewart. The police explanation is the logical one: that after becoming separated from his friends, Stewart wandered deeper and deeper into the forest until he met with an accident, or simply died from starvation and exposure. That through a mixture of bad luck and inadequate planning, Pearl's brother is dead. It is painful to imagine him wandering in circles, calling out at first then pounding on in silence, his panic giving way to numbness and then finally to an exhausted, almost peaceful sense of resignation, a hyper-awareness of his surroundings that is like a drug trip. Bitten by insects and scratched by thorns, he begins to hallucinate. His last thoughts are of Pearl, who somehow seems to be with him, even though there is still a part of him that knows that is impossible.

Remember that Christmas when we gave away the turkey? Pearl says, and Stewart dies, laughing.

How long might he have lasted, alone in the forest? Pearl does not like to think about this question and neither do I. It seems so senseless for a life to end this way, so avoidable, so stupid, one of those things that comes down to the equally pointless agony of if onlys.

But there is another possibility – that Stew simply absconded from his life, that he either planned to disappear, or took advantage of his misadventure to cut ties with everything. To stumble, uncomprehendingly at first but with an increasingly intoxicating sense of release, out of the jungle and into the freedom of a different future. His initial requirements would be the most basic: water and food and overnight shelter, the comfort of strangers who are able to tell him where he is. His phone is dead by now, obviously. When, exactly, does it occur to him that he means to keep it that way?

You will argue that Stew would never do this, that if he and Pearl are as close as I say they are, he would never subject her to that kind of mental torture. Is he in trouble with the law, then? I can hear you asking. Does he have a terrible secret no one knows about? You are looking for qualification, for a motive that would make his behaviour seem reasonable. I don't think there is one, though. I don't see Stew in trouble with the police, or up to his eyes in credit card debt, though one of his friends is – Marcus, who still feels guilty about Stew's disappearance because of the row they had the evening before it happened. Marcus ended by telling Stewart he could piss off, he could piss right off. The words keep replaying inside his head, pretty much on repeat.

Be careful what you wish for, Marcus is thinking as he turns his car into the parking lot of the cheap motel where he is about to meet the person who will change his life. Be fucking careful. But anyway, that's a whole other story. There is simply this wish in him – in Stewart, I mean – a desire so inflamed it is like an obstruction, the need to be free. Free of connection or commitment or the opinions of others. To book into a hotel under a different name, the pristine, knife-edged sheets a metaphor for the newly minted, box-fresh life he is about to embark on.

To begin again, from a position of knowledge. Well, maybe now he can.

*

I know I'm probably only fixating on the Donald story because I can't seem to write about Stewart, Pearl says to Billy in person, once she's back in Glasgow. I do understand that.

In the beginning, when Stewart first vanished, Billy asked Pearl if she meant to write about him and Pearl had said no. Stewart then was still so present. The idea of putting him on the page – a third-person construct – seemed wrong to her, a tacit admission that her brother was not coming back.

In the months since, the real Stew has gradually receded, cloaking himself in his own story, a distant figure on a lonely road, moving gradually out of earshot, out of sight. His story has become the property of others, the subject of intrigue and speculation whose relationship to her brother is only tangential.

If anyone is the main character in that story, it is Mavis.

I don't think it matters, Billy says. There's more than one reason for choosing a story. I think mostly it comes down to instinct – what we feel drawn to. We don't get to choose these things. Not freely anyway, not the way we think.

There was a book event Pearl went to, in which the author giving the talk maintained that most writers spend their entire lives circling the same story. Pearl has always been obsessed with stories of loss and its antithesis, memory, with the moments and details that confer identity or even reality: the opening chords of a pop song, the texture of a particular fabric, the dusty aroma of cobwebs and old newspapers. She remembers a video Stew posted on Facebook during his first year at Edinburgh of a Burns Night party piece that doubled as a drinking game. The film shows Stew reciting the Burns poem, *Tam O'Shanter*, the whole thing from memory. Each time he makes a mistake he has to down another dram. He is wearing a kilt, or someone's checked skirt, his then-girlfriend Angie's, probably.

He looks so alive, so free. Away from her, outside of her, surrounded by people Pearl does not know, and laughing in a way he never laughed at home, or only rarely, and perhaps that is the point.

He is wearing a ridiculous hat, a bright blue Tam O'Shanter with a massive pom-pom.

Indigo, from the Latin indicum, the elusive, magical colour between blue and violet.

We don't get to choose, Billy had said. Not the way we think.

Chapman
    carlin
    houlet
    crummock
    cantraip
    meikle
    usquebae
    breeks
    rigwoodie

cutty sark, which, Pearl discovers, is an outrageously short petticoat, or camisole, an expression that can be equally applied to the woman wearing the garment and with a similar suggestion of being disreputable, slovenly, or promiscuous, served with a generous pinch of nerve and a wide streak of glamour. Which tells us something about why the prosperous nineteenth-century London shipbuilder Jock Willis chose to name his sleek three-masted clipper after the lascivious Nannie in Burns's poem.

Tam O'Shanter is full of references to fabric and clothing, the cutty sark and the guid blue bonnet for starters but also breeks, plush, garters, duddies, linen, Paisley harn. Pearl has developed a fierce admiration for the Scots language: its musicality, its clashing cadences, words headstrong and thorny as thistles, as the landscape they sprout from. The poem's content is salacious, so filthy with double meanings it's like a shabby overcoat – the torn black overcoat of Richard Sutton's dark man, for instance, and it occurs to her that the story of *Tam O'Shanter* is actually a version of the story she is trying to write: Helen Priestly was on her way home after buying some bread – she was coming from market, like Tam. Only a witch chased after her and caught her before she could get there.

There were people in Aberdeen at the time who really did believe Jeannie Donald was a witch. They wanted her to hang.

Whenever Pearl is asked why she writes about murder she says she is drawn to crime stories because of what they tell us about society. Ever since watching Mike Newell's film about Ruth Ellis, *Dance with a Stranger* when she was in her teens, Pearl has believed in the value of crime fiction narratives in highlighting dividedness and inequality. As a writer though, she finds these stories compelling because of their quality of alienation, their solitary mindset. She is not interested in the violence itself – she finds violence repellent – but she is obsessed with what comes afterwards: the search for clues, the investigation of motive, the importance of detail.

Small things, like the colour of shirt buttons, the composition of fabric, the type and make of footwear revealed in the forensic examination of a careless footprint. A ticket stub dropped into the waste bin of a city laundrette. *A blue serge dress with a velvet collar, black shoes and stockings, a light blue knitted tammy.* Points of fact that would normally pass unnoticed that suddenly become a matter of life and death.

And language, of course. Did the witness say laundrette, or laundromat? Did they offer their testimony fluently, or in a stunted monotone? A certain choice of words can tell you so much – not only about where something happens and who is describing it but the attitudes of police and public to both killer and victim. Language is the key to everything, or at least it can be, the lyrics of a song playing everywhere the day it all went down.

In the case of Helen Priestly, Pearl cannot rid herself of the compulsion to keep rerunning the scenario, to keep rechecking the factual route map in the hope that the next cycle will play out differently. It is the same, of course, with Stewart. If only Helen had gone straight upstairs; if only Stewart had stuck with the group, or never gone on the trip in the first place.

According to the multiverse theory, the time-stream is infinite; there are no bad choices, only different ones. But what use are such platitudes to Agnes Priestly, or to Mavis? When Pearl calls her mother that evening, Mavis sounds down, uncharacteristically deflated. When Pearl asks her what is wrong, Mavis tells her that the DNA tests on an item of clothing found not far from where Stewart disappeared have proved inconclusive.

So we're back where we started, Mavis says. She sighs. The T-shirt, discovered hidden in undergrowth by one of the new search team, has been the first tangible gain in many weeks. Mavis is not normally in the habit of asking Pearl's opinion, but there is something in her voice, a note of appeal, that makes Pearl feel for the first time in a long time they are on the same side.

Not necessarily, she says. The DNA not being Stew's is only one part of the picture, surely? That T-shirt belonged to someone. And if they've ruled out Ben and Marcus and Daniel and no one else has come forward who knows what that might mean?

That's what Enzo says. Enzo is the head of the new search operation, an Italian photojournalist with a mass of local contacts and used to dealing with the Malaysian police.

Well, then.

I know you're right. But I really thought this might be a breakthrough. I still think it's his, you know, the T-shirt. I can't help it.

Pearl knows she should encourage her mother to give up on any idea of the T-shirt as a link to Stew, some sort of final message. And yet she cannot shake the feeling that the garment is one she remembers, that she has seen Stew wearing it. She has not said so to Mavis – that would only make matters worse – but it preys on her mind, nonetheless. The fear that she has missed something, that she is being offered information she has failed to process.

The T-shirt is a men's size medium, khaki-coloured, with a CND symbol made up of hundreds of tiny black fly graphics. Some of the flies have broken free of the logo and are buzzing about on their own like a scattering of dust motes. The design is clever and faintly disturbing, one you would remember and want for yourself, possibly, if you were into gothic.

There is no manufacturer's label, just a fringe of grey threads in the collar seam where one should have been. Enzo has posted images of the T-shirt every day since it was found, appealing for information about where it might have come from. Several people have responded, tweeting photos of themselves wearing identical garments. One, an art student named Zahir, claims he bought his off a stall on Lewisham market. The other two are both based in South Korea, but when asked where the T-shirts were purchased, both name different outlets, neither of which seems to have contact details. Enzo is following up, but even if he manages to find out where the T-shirts originally came from, what will that prove?

You could go to the outlet, Pearl supposes, show a photo of Stewart and ask if anyone remembers selling a T-shirt to this man. The likelihood of anyone recalling a random customer from more than six months ago is remote, and that's assuming any of the original staff are still there to be spoken to.

Even if they are, and they remember, where would that leave you? At some point during the three-day layover in Seoul, Stew happened to buy a T-shirt from a trendy clothing store. So what?

In the trial transcript of the Priestly case, Pearl reads that when Helen's body was found, she was still wearing the blue serge dress and the black shoes and stockings. The police agree that the shoes were clean and dry. Helen's knickers, and the blue knitted tammy given to her by Ella Robertson were missing, and never found.

One of the most significant aspects of murder, or of any serious crime is how completely it shatters the illusion of normality. On the surface, people's lives have an appearance of sameness, of routine. The reality beneath is more complex. Patterns of secrecy and jealousy, patterns of violence. When the surface of life becomes disrupted, these patterns begin to emerge. The patterns of resentment within Helen's tenement block for instance, where half the neighbours are on friendly terms and the other half aren't speaking to one another. The most concrete piece of evidence – the scream heard by the roofer, George Munro – is not even reported to the police until the Monday morning.

The scream cannot be corroborated, and must be treated as hearsay. Later, at the trial, the judge asks Munro if he did in fact hear a scream at all. Pearl supposes this would be impossible to prove now, either way, though Munro's testimony is an extraordinary thing in itself, words spoken from a world where the sudden and violent death of children is not uncommon.

I'm still not sure if I can pull this off, Pearl says to Billy. If I can do right by Helen.

You'll get people talking about her, Billy says. People who've never heard of her before, who never even knew her name. That has to be something.

I suppose so, Pearl agrees. I hope you're right. I miss Stew, she adds. I can never say that to Mum, because she'd only start telling me how she misses him more.

I wish I'd known him better, Billy says.

I've decided I want to write about him. I'm going to go out there. To Kuala Lumpur. Next year. I haven't told Mavis.

Are you going to?

No. Not yet, anyway. I want to do something for Stew that she can't. I know that sounds awful but it's how I feel.

It doesn't sound awful, Billy says, it sounds like something you needed to say, and I can see them clearly, sitting side by side at the bar with their glasses in front of them, tired now but still talking, because there's always one more thing to say, one more question to ask. Corrin has called it a night already. He's due in court at eleven and still has work to do.

By the time Pearl makes her journey to Kuala Lumpur, there will have been several new leads in Stewart's case, one of them to do with a photograph someone took at Singapore airport and sent anonymously to Enzo; the other will be connected with the khaki T-shirt. I have not decided yet where all this is going, but I can already see the hotel room Pearl will check into on her arrival: clean but basic, with a cold-water shower and a portable electric fan. A lacquered tray with a tired-looking electric kettle and two cups and saucers in blue-and-white porcelain. Spode, and quite valuable, though no one in the story has any idea of this, much less how they came to be where they are now, in a bedroom in a budget hotel on the other side of the world from where they were made.

Pearl dumps her luggage on the tubular stand and lies down on the bed. She is desperate for a shower but too tired to get undressed. She is asleep before she realises. Later, she will open a Word file and begin to write. She will make an inventory of everything in the room. Because it seems like the best place to start, and because it is details like these that compel her, things that seem ordinary, trivial, mundane, which are anything but.

Tommy Southern's Night Out
(Tam O'Shanter by Robert Burns,
Freely Rendered in a London Idiom)

YOU KNOW HOW IT is at clocking off time, when the barrow boys are calling it a day and the market traders are packing up their stalls, when it's starting to get dark and you're thinking to yourself you'll just pop across to the boozer for a quick one, see who's around, have a bit of a natter, and before you know it you're comfy by the fire, your mates are all gassing and God love you but you don't give a toss about how it's going to be later on, all those miles before you're home and the devilish weather to boot, the pissing rain and the roads like mud-chutes, not to mention the roasting you're going to get from your old lady, who'll have been brewing up her own storm to unleash on you the very second you step through that door. Dog tired you'll be and half cut, her with a face like thunder and you know she's just loving it, that she's been sitting there the whole time grinding her teeth and more or less praying you'll be late, just so she can have a go at you, because that's what turns her on.

*

You know the score. And that's the exact situation my old mate Tommy Southern found himself in one night on his way back from Ayr. Now there's a town that knows how to enjoy itself, if you get my meaning.

Tom's no fool – at least not when he's sober – but bloody hell, and I know how we like to moan on about her indoors but going by what happened I'm thinking Tommy would have done well to listen to his missus, at least on this occasion, because you can't say she didn't warn him. You're a useless bag of blubber, Tom Southern, she'd say to him, a blithering idiot, a career drunkard. You and your no-good mates, can't keep the lid on it for more than five minutes. One year's end to the next and every bleeding market day you're off down the town spending our cash like it was water and don't get me started on that Jean Kirkton you've been seen hanging around with, you think I don't know about her then you'd be wrong. You're going to end up so deep in shit one of these days, drowned in the river most likely, or else – well, you know what they say about Alloway church, how the witches lie in wait there for men like you, stumbling about in the dark with no wife to guide them.

Which was laying it on a bit thick if you ask me, all those names she called him, but there's no avoiding the facts in this case and though I'd be the last to point the finger normally, the number of lads I've seen wind up serving the devil, one way or another, you can't help thinking their wives might have a point.

*

Anyway, it was right after clocking off, like I said. There's old Tom, toasty by the fire with a damned fine pint in front of him and sat by his side who else but Johnny the Cob, Tom's *boon companion* if ever there was one. Tom loves Johnny like his own brother and you know what it's like when those two get together – week-long benders and all that and you don't need me to tell you those don't always end well. The vibe's hotting up, the beer's going down a treat, Tom's getting nice and friendly with the landlady and Johnny's off on one of his ridiculous anecdotes, landlord's laughing like an effing drain, the fool he is. It's pissing down outside by now but Tom's half drowned in booze, happy as a lord and quite honestly he don't give a monkey's. Time's flipping by like greased lightning and Tom's so royally soused he's king of the world.

But time, as wise men warn, will have its way. The poppy's red hot kiss, the rainbow's sultry curve, sweet as a queen's tit, the snow the falling snow and Lord help us, even the Aurora frigging Borealis – here today and gone next minute is what the poets say and there ain't no man on this Earth has ever discovered the secret of stopping the clock. What's coming to you is coming, rain or shine. It's almost closing time by now and Tom, like it or no, he's out in the cold. And it's dark as a miner's arse out there, the kind of night no one in their right mind would be riding out in but Tom's got no choice, not unless he feels like spending the next eight hours as a vagabond drunk in a ditch that is. The wind's screaming like it's the dawn of the zombie apocalypse, the rain's coming down like chains, thunder and lightning slicing and dicing across the heavens, loud and bright enough to scare even a grown man witless. Night like that's the devil's business. Even the littlest kid would feel it in their bones.

But if old Tom's got one ally in all of this it's his horse, that grey mare Meg. Talk about a trusty steed, I'd bet on Maggie any time, and sure enough, soon as Tom's on board she's going like the clappers. It's black as pitch out there and mud up to your knees, the storm's a right bastard but Tommy barely gives a nod to the thunder-and-lightning polka clashing all around him, he's too busy trying to keep his hat from blowing off – you know, that natty blue one, the one he sleeps in, practically – and you'll never guess what, he's actually singing to himself, some godawful din, some bit of rap he's picked up down the market and all the time he's looking over his shoulder, just checking where he's at because you know what they say about that particular neck of the woods – that it's haunted as fuck. Hideously creepy anyway, and to make matters worse he's still got to ride past Alloway Kirk, which is a shitting ghost-fest even when it's not pissing down like buggery and shrieking with owls. But he's going great guns is our Tommy, ghosts or no ghosts. Cross the ford where that door-to-door sales rep fella froze to death in a snowdrift that time, then on past the massive boulder where Carlo the drunkard came a cropper – snapped his neck as I remember it – then there's that cairn where the bikers found that kiddie that was killed and then he's on to the finish line, the blackthorn tree by the well where Mungo's old witch of a mother finally saw sense and hanged herself. Tom's almost at the river now. The Doon's thundering like Niagara Falls from all the runoff, and you'd think with the storm raging and the lightning flashing that would be plenty to be going along with, only he's forgotten about the church, hasn't he, old Alloway, which is glowing through the trees ahead of him, so bright you'd think the place was on fire, only it's not, and there's a din coming from the churchyard like it's New Year's flipping Eve.

Well of course, Tommy's so tanked up he barely notices. You know what it's like – two pints down and you rule the world, couple of whisky chasers and you'll take all comers, including the devil and whichever of his demon cohorts think they're hard enough. The laddie's not for turning, only old Maggie – and don't you go thinking I don't see the irony here – old Maggie is spooked as a fish. *Frit*, you could say. She knows when something's off, and for all Tom's kicking and whipping she's scarcely budging an inch. It's that light that did for her, I reckon, that damned unholy light that's streaming through the trees, and as they come in sight of the churchyard, well, that's when the shit really starts hitting the fan because the place is full of them, warlocks and witches, having a right knees-up and none of your ooh la la French malarkey either it's the real McCoy we're talking here, stuff to please the home crowd, a vicious jig, a devil's reel, the gay frigging Gordons. They're at it like knives, the lot of them, and you're not going to believe this, but the MC, it's only Satan himself, Old Nick large as life and twice as ugly sitting in one of them window alcoves like a beast just crawled out of the forest and – I kid you not – giving the pipes full welly like he means to keep everyone dancing till the crack of doom. The roof and rafters are splitting from the din – bet he's popular with the neighbours – and get this, you know all that shit in the Bible about the dead shall come forth, well he's only gone and done it, the devil I mean. There are coffins – you can smell the stink of them – lying open like wardrobes, and you're damned right my teeth are chattering, yours would have been, too. The corpses are falling over themselves, all dolled up in their Sunday best or whatever it was they were buried in – fucking fetid. And as for old Tommy, it's almost as if they're taking the piss, these dead guys, having him for a laugh, because they're lighting his way somehow, holding up candles or bloody marshfire lanterns, inviting him to sit down with them, share a bite to eat, only it's not food they're offering, is it, it's the bones of a serial killer, still hanging from the gibbet, a couple of dead babies – the Lord alone knows what kind of state they were in – a thief, freshly hanged, his gob frozen open at the last gasp. And then there was all this other stuff, the *murderabilia*, you might call it – five tomahawks still streaming with the claret, couple of blades recently returned from doing Satan's dirty work, piece of garter elastic looked like it might have been responsible for one of them dead babies, and just to top it off, there's a knife some ruffian used to do in his own father. What do you mean, how do I know? His greasy grey hairs are still stuck to the handle, that's how. There was a ton more of this godawful shite but I'll not say another word or they'll be carting me away.

Tommy's eyes are popping out of his head – he can't believe what's in front of him – and the whole thing's kicking off generally. The pipes are getting louder and louder, the dancers are pounding the ground like they're at a barn dance from hell, which is pretty much where they are, in fact. The queen bitch is going at it so hard you can all but taste the reek of the sweat pouring off of her, and strike me blind if she's not ripping off her togs and prancing about in her scanties! Not a sight you'd want to see, believe me. And Tom's thinking trust my luck to get a witch like that, when they could have been buxom young beauties, you know, like in *Vampirella*, all white linen and big bosoms. Give me a pretty little piece like that and she'd be worth losing my trousers over, ghost or no ghost, and never mind that I've only one decent pair in the world now, my navy moleskins, and even they've seen better days. But these old fannies, flinging themselves about like they was Hot Gossip or something? It's enough to make you lose your lunch. But like I say, that's my luck all over, isn't it? Poor old Tommy Southern, always drawing the short straw.

But yo-ho-ho, it's like the devil heard his griping, because Tom's luck is in! There's one of them at least's worth a second look, right little vamp she is. Bit of a local legend from the sound of it, sinking boats and raising havoc the length of the Carrick shoreline, dab hand with a pistol too, the number of cattle she's offed and just for hell of it, zombie Bonnie to Tommy's clueless Clyde. She's got this Paisley slip on – more like a handkerchief from what I've heard – same as she used to wear of a Saturday night when she was still among the living and her sainted gran, who I'm told was a God-fearing woman, she'd spend the last couple of quid in her pocket to treat her precious Nannie and I thank the Lord she never saw this coming, her sweet little gift-wrapped petticoat ending up as the main attraction at a witches' Sabbath.

And this is where I have to leave things to your imagination, people, because the way that girl went at it, leaping and carousing like a flipping pole vaulter, like an Olympic sex athlete, there are no words, and Tom, needless to say, is sitting there dumbstruck, bewitched, like the whole unholy spectacle is put on just for him. Even the devil's got a hard-on – you can see from the way he's sucking those pipes, in such of a lather you can just tell there's something else he'd rather be sucking on. They're all howling and clapping for more and Tom, well he must have lost it altogether because the next moment he's standing up in the stirrups and bawling out 'Come on, you strumpet!' like he's at a frigging Spurs match. Everything goes dark then, black as an ox's arsehole, and Tom's barely got a-hold of the reins again when they all come pouring out the churchyard – devil, demons, witches, the whole bloody lot of them, like when some unlucky fuck of a farmhand puts his shovel through a beehive and all the hordes of Satan's drones come barrelling forth. Like a hare running for fear of its life in front of the pack, or when someone down the market yells 'Stop, thief!' and every Tom, Dick and Harry within earshot is storming down the road like a flock of lemmings whether there was in fact a thief on the loose or not. You get my drift. Poor Maggie's doing her best Red Rum impersonation and the witches are pouring after her in a shrieking cloud.

And oh, Tommy-boy, you're in for it now. You know that scene in *Don Giovanni*, when the devil comes to drag the old reprobate down to the hot place? That's you, that is – roasted like a herring for sure, your Katie keeping the home fires burning, the poor woman with no idea of her upcoming widow's status unless Maggie can do her stuff and get you both to the bridge before you're toast. Because that's the thing with witches – they can't cross running water, everyone knows that, and once you're over the hump you can turn around in the saddle and flip 'em the vees and there's not a damn thing they can do about it. But we're not out of the woods yet – Tom's not quite at the bridge and Nannie's coming up hard, miles out in front of the rest she is and man, that girl is not one to give up on her quarry without a fight. Maggie's tail's streaming out behind her and fuck me if the witch hasn't grabbed it. She's reckoned without that horse's courage though, because Meg's leaping for the bridge and Tom – Tom's safe, by the Lord Harry, and all the witch has got for her trouble is Meg's grey tail! She's stumpy at the rear, the poor mare. Still, not a bad outcome, given the circs.

And you don't need me to teach you the moral of the story, boys, now do you? Stay away from the boozer and keep your hands off the ladies. Nine times out of ten they aren't worth the running. Poor Maggie'll tell you that for nothing and she should know.

Part 3

A Crime of Almost Unspeakable Cruelty

I Want a Story with a Murderer in It

*W*ITH THE ARREST OF THE DONALDS, writes the eminent advocate John G. Wilson in his 1953 introduction to the transcript of the trial, *sympathy with the bereaved family turned into a bitter animus against those accused of the crime, of which the howls in the street which greeted the arrest were but a symptom.*

Jeannie Donald's defence counsel are convinced that the public mood, inflamed and abetted by the constant rumour-mongering of the tabloid press, has made it impossible for their client to receive a fair hearing in Aberdeen. They apply to the Crown Office to have the trial moved to Edinburgh, where though the crime has been widely reported those called to serve on the jury will not have first-hand knowledge of the persons involved. There are one hundred and sixty-four witnesses in total. They will have to be ferried to the High Court in groups on the days they are required.

Most of those who hope to gain admission to the High Court are doomed to disappointment, Susana reads in the *Press and Journal, for the court room is not much larger than the Sheriff Court room at Aberdeen.*

The case preoccupies her more and more, not the murder itself, which is hard to think about, but the way it has roused people. Strange stories swirl in its wake – the dark man with the dirty beard, the piece of gossip about Mrs Donald, or Ewen as she was at the time, wringing the necks of a dozen chickens because of a row she had with a kitchen porter. People gather together in crowds for no reason. Rumours rise on the wind like foul smells and then die down again. The city of Aberdeen, a stern and stolid place with little patience for fantasy, has become charged with an atmosphere of danger, the kind of tension that sullies the air before a fight breaks out.

Susana first took refuge in this city because she thought she would feel more at home here than she would in London. The silver light of the north, the stink of fish and the language of sailors, which she has known all her life – these things are as familiar to her as the whipping of the wind along the esplanade, the sullen cadences of church bells, the endless, hallowed evenings of June and July. What has taken her by surprise is the town's small-mindedness, its distrust of anything that cannot immediately be seen and touched and dismissed as a waste of time or money. The brutal humour of the men, the sneering cynicism of the women give to the city the feel of a garrison town, especially in winter, a meeting place for soldiers and alcohol, that fatal recipe.

A grey people, grey as the blocks of granite the city is built from. Susana has begun to feel that greyness creeping in to possess her: ink-grey, storm-grey, mist-grey, the grey of the backs of wolves as they course through the snow. She has been working on a piece called *The Stormy Petrel*, a narrative poem inspired by the folk tales and ghost stories that were told at summer festivals in the north of Russia when she was a girl. The work is also a response to the writer Maxim Gorky, whose poem of the same name praises the revolution that so far at least has led only to bloodshed and famine.

In Susana's poem, the title figure is a rogue cavalryman, a deserter from the Red Army who has gathered around him a company of misfits and vagrants, poets and magicians – men and women of the north, determined to free their country of tyrants, whether White or Red. She has been having trouble with the poem, mainly because she feels so distant from the events it describes. Exile is like that, one of the clerks at the shipping office has warned her. It robs you of everything: first your country, then your language and finally your thoughts.

The Donald case has sparked her with a new enthusiasm, the sense of a story unfolding around her in the present tense. The city feels different with the story inside it, a gaunt grey giant that had seemed dead but was only resting. Resting and waiting to be woken from its winter stupor.

The giant's name is Aberdeen. She imagines its granite forearms, the angry glimmer of mica in its colourless eyes, and wonders if this is the story she has been waiting for all along. *They called him the stormy petrel*, she writes, *because he blew in on an ill wind, and the wind was murder.* The Russian word for stormy petrel is buryevestnik, which means bringer of storms. Scholars who have studied the epic poems and folk tales of northern Russia claim that even the most fantastical have a basis in fact, in historical conflicts and journeys of exploration and in real people. Is this what Susana is trying to do with the Donald case, to transform a pitiful local crime into a legend?

She already has her murdered princess, her enraged villagers, her witch. Who then is her magician, her bringer of storms?

She has the feeling that she has not yet met him, that if she means to find her magician she must go to his castle. Susana has time off owing to her at the shipping office, and when the date of the trial is announced, she finds herself asking her boss, Mr Bright, if he could recommend to her a reasonably priced guesthouse in Edinburgh where she might stay for a week, without attracting unwanted attention to herself.

What she means is: where would she be safe from the eyes and hands of importunate men. Susana has never been inside a court room before. She tries to imagine what it might be like – the hard wooden seats, the burnished panelling, the susurrus of voices, murmuring, like an incoming tide.

The judge is coming, the judge is coming, the judge is here.

You'll be wanting to see the sights, then, says Mr Bright. Susana nods and agrees. As a reason for her journey, wanting to see the sights is believable and sound.

I have not been to Edinburgh before, she says. I would like to visit the castle, and the university. A friend of my father was at the university, she adds, which at least is true. She writes to the guest house Bright has recommended, reserving six nights' accommodation with breakfast and evening meal to be included. She uses the shipping office's headed notepaper, hoping this will stop people asking her questions about why she is there. I am travelling for work, she will say, which she is, only not for the shipping office.

The cost of the trip will be substantial, but she has managed to save a little, if only because she has all but relinquished the possibility of ever going home. Since the death of her father, the gates of her own city have been closed to her. Her brothers write from time to time, when they remember, though she understands that leaving as she did she has become unreal to them. For news, she has come to depend on her cousin Marina, who understands her decision to emigrate, though she disapproves of it.

Marina is a newspaper journalist, like Vanny Redchow. The last time Susana heard from her she was travelling to Kyiv, to report on the food shortages there, though she has not had a letter from Marina in almost a year. There has been some reporting of the grain shortages in the British press but not much, not as much as you might hope, and the series of articles that do appear are later dismissed as fakes, or lies.

Russians hungry but not starving, runs the headline of consensus.

There are rumours that a maverick journalist from Wales who did report on the famine has been kidnapped and murdered, though it seems that no one here is interested, either way. Susana wonders if Ivan Redchow, perhaps, would be interested. She has not had sight of him since she spotted him in the street outside the police station, though she supposes he will be travelling to Edinburgh to attend the Donald trial, the same as she is.

Avengers Assemble

THE COBBLED STREET OUTSIDE the court house is awash with reporters: murder gang stalwarts in tweed jackets and loafers, ties loosened and all of them smoking, smoking, deep in conversation yet watchful, waiting, alert for the moment when the doors are opened and they surge inside. Crowds of onlookers, mothers, fathers; gawpers seeking to make themselves exceptional simply by being there. The morning is bright and crystal clear, the light softer and less prurient than the salty northern glare of the place they are from. The wafting aromas of frying bacon and fresh morning rolls, the ebb and clamour of voices, the splash of sunlight, yellow as paint, across the court's stern facade.

Somewhere inside the building there is a woman, waiting. To be on trial for your life is to be stripped of your soul, of any small power you had to make your fate your own. You remember the games you played as a schoolgirl, cop and robber, killer and gaoler, roles you once made sport of before trailing home for dinner in the grey evening light. Potatoes fried in their skins for extra nourishment, crisped fat, bacon rind, your mother yelling stop now with your blethering, sit yersel' down.

To rest in the hand of your Lord, and as flies to wanton boys are we to the gods. One God, or many gods, or no god at all, the internal disorder, the stomach's cramping is insurmountable. How did it ever come to this? How does it ever?

The judge presiding is Craigie M. Aitchison. The counsel for the prosecution is Wilfrid Guild Normand, the counsel for the defence is Daniel Patterson Blades. The waiting woman does not know these men, and they are all men. I can find no record of how the jury was split in terms of men to women, but let us not forget that no woman ever sat on a Scottish jury until 1921. Scotland's first woman advocate, Margaret Kidd, was not called to the Faculty of Advocates until 1923, where for the following quarter-century she sat alone. And get this: no female Professor of Law in a British University until 1970, no female judge at the Old Bailey until 1972. First female judge in Scotland? 1992.

Read it and weep, ladies, read it and weep, and be sure that to enter a court room in 1934 is to enter upon the threshold of the dominant masculine. The first to address the bench is Mr Blades, the future Solicitor General for the whole of Scotland. He confirms that Mrs Donald is sticking to her plea of Not Guilty, and in this moment, before the trial is properly underway, Jeannie's defence team have made their biggest mistake. Unbeknownst to the public gallery – to Vanny Redchow and the rest of the murder gang, to the families and witnesses, to Susana Solovey and the two hundred or so public spectators who travelled down that morning from Aberdeen hoping to get into the court room and being, for the most part, disappointed – the chief forensic witness, Professor Sidney Smith, has already reached out to the defence team, inviting their client to change her plea from Not Guilty to Culpable Homicide; in other words, Manslaughter.

Smith's offer is significant – it means he knows something about the prosecuting evidence that the defence are not aware of – but Mrs Donald's team have rejected his suggestion out of hand.

Jeannie does not enter her plea herself. She does not speak at all. The words she offers in her own defence, when we get to hear them, will be spoken by a man.

The first person to appear on the witness stand is a sixty-six-year-old architect named John Ross McMillan. McMillan has been commissioned to draw up plans detailing the rear elevation of numbers 59 and 61 Urquhart Road, the ground floor layout of number 61 and its position with regard to other streets and businesses in the neighbourhood. A reproduction of this street plan is included with the trial transcript, a neatly-folded pull-out section that clearly shows the location of the Northern Co-operative Bakery as well as the Robertsons' confectionery shop and Webster's grocery store.

Maps, street plans, architectural drawings – as evidence, there is something incontrovertible about them, an authenticity that is difficult to challenge. In their intricacy, their exactitude, their helpful references to scale and compass bearing, their listing of symbols and annotations they are beautiful things, tactile things, the way they fold into themselves, compressing a large amount of information into a small paper rectangle that fits easily into a backpack or even a pocket.

Daniel Blades questions John McMillan at length about the plans he has created, and in the careful back-and-forth of cross-examination the internal and external spaces of 61 Urquhart Road are revealed to us in detail. We learn that the rear of the house, bounded by stone walls, would have been difficult to access from any of the neighbouring properties. We learn that the Northern Co-operative, which comprises a butcher and grocery store as well as the bakery, lies precisely two hundred and eighteen feet from Helen's front door. Going further, Blades asks McMillan to confirm the height of the wash rooms and coal stores behind the house as well as the height of the fence around the drying green, the width of the rear door, even the distance between the rear door and the door of the lavatory.

The proliferation of such minutiae would have been tiring for a jury, especially when, as Blades well knows, the majority of the detail is irrelevant. We might argue that he is playing for time, blinding them with science, though in fact he is trying to fill their minds with alternative scenarios. An unknown assailant, climbing over the wall, or scrambling across the roof of the neighbouring wash house. A back door left ajar, a window jemmied open – the more possibilities the jury can imagine, the more they are likely to remain undecided about what really happened.

In his defence of Jeannie Donald, Blades's most effective weapon will be the stubborn stain of doubt.

Lost in the barrage of facts are two pertinent details. Firstly, the glass in the upper right-hand panel of the rear door has been broken at some point and replaced with plywood, meaning that the ground floor lobby is darker than it would have been otherwise. Secondly, the measurements of the cupboard under the sink in the Donalds' kitchen. *The cupboard is one foot six inches from front to back*, McMillan confirms, *four feet five inches from east to west and two feet eight inches in height. The sink impinges on that height to the extent of about eight inches, whilst the sink trap impinges still further.*

A cramped, awkward space, not dissimilar from the cupboard under the sink in any modern kitchen and containing the same variety of assorted detritus: wash cloths, scrubbing brushes, cleaning materials. This cupboard was also said to have contained a wooden box, used for storing cinders – Jeannie used cinders for doing the laundry, an old fashioned, time-consuming process that was soon to die out through the introduction of modern detergents. The cinder box, the witness insists, had since gone missing.

This cupboard will crop up again later, so keep it in mind.

But first, the prosecution must establish what happened from the time Helen is reported missing until the moment her body is discovered in the downstairs lobby. And though it is the men, as we have seen, who control these proceedings it is the women of the house who have most to tell us, because they, unlike their husbands, were on the spot throughout. Washing and cleaning, shopping and sweeping, clearing the dishes, preparing meals, their testimonies overlap and coalesce, a Greek chorus of memories and impressions, each bolstering the other, the small differences between them of lesser account than the fact that in their essence they all concur.

Mary Topp and Jane Joss especially are central to our understanding of that nightmarish fifteen hours, and it is surely no coincidence that

Mrs Joss lives opposite Mrs Priestly on the first floor, and Mrs Topp lives opposite Mrs Donald across the ground floor lobby.

The two are very different women. Mary Topp is twenty-eight, expecting her first child. She has lived at number 61 for just two years. She is in and out of her flat a lot that afternoon – cleaning her windows, instructing the slaters, popping down the road to visit her mother. When Mr Blades asks her about the creaky back door, Mary confirms that you could hear the sound it made even when you were inside your own apartment. Most crucially, Mary Topp is the one person who saw and spoke to Jeannie Donald in the earlier part of the afternoon, when news of Helen's disappearance was just beginning to circulate.

She describes how, coming in through the rear door, she saw Jeannie standing in the lobby outside her flat. Whether she was entering or leaving Mary could not be sure, though she is almost certain that Jeannie had her coat on.

Jeannie tells Mary that she is 'back early', though where she has returned from, she does not make clear. 'We did not speak many minutes,' Mary says. She does not tell Jeannie about Helen Priestly going missing. She is anxious to get to her mother's house and has no desire to be delayed in further conversation. It is only later, when she returns from her mother's some time after five, that she speaks to Jeannie on the subject of the missing child. 'Mrs Donald said that Mrs Gordon had told her,' Mary explains. 'She said she nearly collapsed.'

Jane Joss is sixty-two. She lives with her two sons and one daughter-in-law, all of them together in the same small apartment where she has been head of the household for twenty years. Jane is nobody's fool. When questioned about Richard Sutton she says yes, she saw him come to the house in the early evening to speak to the detectives, and no, she didn't believe a word of what he said. She refers to Ricky's dark phantom as 'a man that goes singing about the street,' as if for her the dark man was no abductor, just a local oddball with no connection to the crime or to anything else.

She makes clear that Mrs Donald and Mrs Priestly were not on good terms. Jane herself has not spoken to Jeannie in three years.

As the afternoon wears into evening, the neighbours are drawn increasingly into the whirlwind of activity and speculation around the missing child. The men leave the house to join in with the search; the women huddle in conclave around Agnes Priestly, avid for news.

Only the Donalds are not to be seen. Alec is still at the barbershop. Jeannie has taken her daughter to her dance rehearsal at the Beach Pavilion. The whole family arrive home at around eleven, and go straight to bed. Later, Jane Joss tells of the moment the following morning when Helen's body is found. Mrs Priestly is struggling and screaming in the arms of Alex Porter, desperate to reach her child. Mrs Joss comes to help Mr Porter take her back inside. 'I helped Mrs Priestly upstairs,' she says, 'I never was out of her house until the detectives came.'

Her recall is intense and detailed. She responds to questioning in a confident and forthright manner and there is no doubt in our minds that she knows what's what. She seems particularly incensed by a suggestion made by Jeannie Donald in her statement, that at the instant of the body's discovery, Jane is heard to cry out the words 'she's been used, she's been used'.

The defence counsel seem obsessed with this detail, though every time it is brought up again, Mrs Joss is adamant she said no such thing, that the words were never spoken, in fact, by anyone.

'But is it not the case,' insists Mr Blades, 'that after the little girl was found that morning, that that was the opinion you all had?'

'It was the opinion that the whole of Aberdeen had until it was found out properly,' retorts Mrs Joss. 'That is not to say I said it. Don't put words in my mouth.'

This strangely heightened space of hours in which so much is seen and observed, so little known. But what we all must know by now is that someone is lying.

The Stormy Petrel

HE BLEW IN ON an ill wind, and that wind was murder. His hair, prematurely grey, had helped to cement the nickname, though mostly, John believed, it was the aura he carried, the sense that bad news followed him, or that he followed it. The newspaper coverage of the Ruxton case had made him instantly recognisable – the silver hair, worn long, the wire-rimmed spectacles – and people would approach him in the street, asking him to sign the book he had written about the forensic investigation. Those who had not purchased the book, or did not have it with them would offer for his signature a photograph clipped from a magazine, a copy of a local paper that had covered one of his cases, anything that came to hand.

For a certain section of the public – those raised on Sherlock Holmes stories and bloodthirsty tales of Jack the Ripper – Professor John Glaister, or Dr John, as the papers dubbed him, was a source of fascination and regard. For others, John suspected he stood more in the model of Victor Frankenstein, conjuring something from nothing, raising the spectres of dead men who would best stay buried. In either case, he was noticed, applauded, confronted, and in spite of his insistence that he himself was of little account, that the advancement of science was a matter of teamwork and the sharing of knowledge, there was little John could do to banish the public portrait of himself as a medical mastermind.

His wife Isobel, who everyone called Muff, said he should not let his minor celebrity become a source of concern.

'You are a scientist, Johnny,' she said. 'Most scientists remain invisible, but you are seen. If being seen helps people understand the value of science in their own lives, then that is a good thing.'

John knew Muff's arguments were sensible, compelling even, though he remained uneasy. Whatever his work was about, it was not about him. A long time ago, when he was still a student, John had made a bargain with himself, that the business of his life, the study and practice of pathology, should occupy within him a separate space. A sacred space, he thought privately, into which the desires and human weaknesses of his personal life should not intrude. The autograph hunters, the public lectures and radio interviews felt like an intrusion, a dangerous mixing of the public and private he had not been prepared for.

'Don't knock it,' his lab assistant Andrews laughed off his concerns when he tried to explain. 'You're an asset to the department, or haven't you heard? You know what that means.'

And yes, John did know. Being an asset drew outside investment, money from on high that many of the university's cash-strapped departments might literally have killed for. What they did in medical jurisprudence was seen as *relevant*, directly translatable to the business of ordinary life. Hence the state-of-the-art pathology lab inaugurated last year, the tranche of lucrative international studentships, not to mention the string of high-profile conferences that he and various of his colleagues were regularly invited to attend.

If you can't beat them, join them – that was what Muff said, but even as others drank and partied, determined to enjoy the red-carpet treatment while it lasted, John felt determined at the very least to keep his youthful ideals in view when he stood on the stage. The audiences who flocked to hear him speak were eager to hear about the Ruxton case in all its unsavoury detail, and while he would not deny them what they had come for, John also did his best to convey something of the background drudgery, the painstaking disentangling of evidence from inference that was the backbone, the bread and butter of decent forensic work.

An autopsy is a search for truth, he liked to remind them. A truth that benefits the living and the dead alike. Cutting up bodies is a serious business, and the dead do tell tales. It is simply a matter of learning their language, and taking care to listen.

'How does it feel,' a reporter once asked him, 'knowing you have the power to send a prisoner to the gallows?'

John had thought only a short time about his answer before replying that he had a job to do, and that job concerned the analysis of certain facts. Whether those facts determined guilt or innocence was up to the jury, and how a jury's verdict was translated into sentencing was a matter for the law.

'It is the judge who decides, not the pathologist,' John said. 'More than that, it is the criminal themselves.'

On whether he personally approved of the death penalty, he would not be drawn. His father had advised him at the outset that whatever his personal feeling it was unwise to let himself become involved in politics. Whichever side of the debate he came down on, it would inevitably lead to assumptions about his practice. John could see the sense in his father's reasoning, though in truth the death penalty appalled him, not only as a man but also as a doctor.

To be a doctor was to understand the multitude of irreparable disasters that could befall the human body. Whether through disease, mishap or accident of birth, death could arrive in a thousand guises and was ultimately unstoppable. To order the deliberate destruction of a human animal seemed to John a form of sacrilege, like taking a beautiful watch and purposely grinding it to pieces beneath your heel.

John did not believe in God, or at least his faith was a pallid thing, so insubstantial and unreliable as to be irrelevant. He heard the voice of the numinous as a background echo, the ghost of school assemblies and harvest festivals, the glimmer of frost upon the frozen lawns of Carronhill on Christmas morning. A feeling, more than a fact, and yet it seemed to him that human beings were too fallible, too limited and too credulous to be charged with making any final decision in the matter of life and death.

It seemed to him that their very hunger for putting an end to one another was in itself a disqualification from this kind of authority. But who was he to say? John did not, as a rule, lose sleep over the matter. He understood that his personal feelings would have no bearing on the outcome of a trial, either way, so there was no point dwelling on them, though that was easier in some cases than in others. Buck Ruxton, for example, had been a lost creature, a murderer with so much blood on his conscience that death at the hands of the state had seemed a kind of mercy, as much for society at large as for the man himself.

Other cases had proved more troubling, both at the time of his being called to give evidence and for a long while afterwards. Poverty, greed, fear, the sweet stench of opium or the foul breath of alcohol – the reasons for murder were often as pathetic as they were despicable. Should a man face death for an error of judgement, or for losing his temper? If anything, John found such questions more difficult to answer as his career progressed.

This Donald woman, for instance. Her guilt was not in question, but why had she acted in the way she had, what had possessed her? Guilt, as John was coming to learn, was but one aspect of a case, a garish banner that advertised one thing whilst obscuring others.

John's job was such that he often had no idea of the background or circumstances of a case until he was standing up in court beside the other witnesses. He did not mind this – in fact he preferred it, had spoken in many interviews of how ignorance in such matters is often the best preserver of objectivity. All this was true, and yet, when she turned, when she looked up to where he stood in the witness box John felt a chill fall upon him, and then a flush of heat, as if a great bird had flown over, casting its grievous shadow before speeding away.

Those eyes, that hair. More than that, the way she stood, so straight and so tall, though she was not tall, or not particularly, she was of medium height. The firm set of her mouth.

I did it. So what?

John could have sworn for a moment that it was she, Edna McCrae, though of course that was impossible. He had not seen Edna McCrae for twenty years, not since the war, not since Egypt. He did not know if she was still living even. The time he had spent in her company was time he was pleased to be done with, that he would not wish back. Had he spoken to Muff about Edna? He did not think so, though his memories of those months were unreliable on account of his illness. The fever had swept him up like a gigantic hand, dangled him momentarily over the abyss before setting him down, depleted but alive, in quite another country and a different time.

He found that the war was over and he weighed five stone less. He was married – he remembered that all right – and the monastery in the desert, that desecrated paradise, was so far away in his past it felt like a dream.

The woman in the dock, Jeannie Donald, was thirty-eight years old. Five foot six or thereabouts, high cheekbones and dark hair. Decent-looking, normal, yet she had almost certainly murdered the child of one of her neighbours, a little girl whose ordinary school uniform and bloodied undergarments now formed part of police evidence. The child had been raped and then asphyxiated, though the autopsy revealed that the assault on the child had most likely been carried out with a kitchen utensil, or other wooden implement. There was no semen present, and the division between vagina and anus had been all but obliterated.

John's mentor, Professor Smith, who had performed the post mortem, was of the opinion that whoever had perpetrated the attack had done so with the specific intention of averting suspicion from themselves.

'If the motive for the attack on the girl was found to be rape, then it stands to reason that the attacker must be male,' he said. 'If the attacker happened to be female, then simulating a rape might be her best way of putting herself in the clear.'

John listened to the evidence, the parade of next-door neighbours and shop girls and factory workers who had seen or spoken either to Jeannie Donald or the girl's family on the day in question. Their recall was partial, suspect, as it was bound to be. Like every other witness statement he had ever heard, theirs were strewn with absences, details they had either forgotten or were never in a position to know. And yet in spite of the messiness of it all, a picture had begun to emerge, as it always did. The picture was not a proof of what had transpired, though it gave a fair impression of how events had progressed. This happened, that happened, so-and-so did the other, as in a scene from some dreadful play by Marlowe or Webster.

Jeannie Donald's expression remained impassive throughout. *So what?* her eyes seemed to say. *Yes, and?*

As if she was having a joke at their expense. As if the murder was nothing more than a piece of pantomime.

John was still in medical school when the war came. He wanted to join up immediately – like most young men his age who have never actually experienced armed combat, he saw the conflict as an opportunity to prove himself. His father though was adamant that he continue his studies, and so for the early part of the war John's time was divided between the military hospital at the Hyde Park Locomotive Works and the dissecting rooms of Glasgow University.

The emergency hospital was soon overwhelmed. Each night the trains would pull in, loaded down with wounded men and their unfathomable suffering. Even for the doctors in charge, men hardened by years of experience, this deluge of hopeless cases was difficult to stomach. For John, though he could not know it, the months at Hyde Park were simply a foretaste of what was to come. He continued to work his shifts for as long as possible, resigning his position just three months before his finals. He was exhausted, both physically and mentally. He promised himself that when he returned to practical doctoring after his exams he would do better. In the meantime, he proposed to Muff. To his joy and satisfaction he was accepted.

Three days after being notified that he was licensed to practice, John received his call-up papers. He was being posted to Gaza, to assist in the treatment and repatriation of soldiers fighting the armed insurgency in the east, as well as any prisoners that were taken. He was glad at least that the waiting was over, to have a verified mission. Glad also that he was not being sent to the western front, where two of his closest comrades had already died. Stewart and Rab, both fellow medics, had been like brothers to him. When he thought of the senselessness of their sacrifice, the store of talent and humour and compassion now lost to the world, John found his anger to be almost greater than his personal grief.

He discussed his feelings with no one, and for the whole of his journey east – the commandeered steamship, the shambolic caravan of decrepit motor vehicles and ancient donkey carts – he hardly dared to think about what might await him. What awaited him, in fact, was nothing – a hospital that was not a hospital at all, but an abandoned monastery, surrounded by desiccated thornbrush and hilly scrubland. A joke of a posting, the monastery's gaunt, crenellated walls reminding him of nothing so much as the haunted castle at the centre of the novel by Bram Stoker that Muff had found so thrilling but John had merely frowned at.

'What is the point?' he had asked her. 'How can those bloodsuckers be frightening when they don't exist?'

He remembered his words, here in his room, as far from the centre of war as his grandfather's elegant drawing room, lighted with candles and fragrant with roses, as the dew-jewelled, beech-fringed lawns of Carronhill, and was forced to admit that in spite of his own blunt assertions to the contrary there was something uncanny about the place, a quality of déjà vu that was deeply unsettling.

As if he had been here always, awaiting an influx of dying warriors who never came.

As with most aspects of the war, the eventual reality was both more terrible and more ridiculous than anticipated. The dying warriors, when they finally arrived, were all Turkish prisoners, soldiers so badly wounded in the fighting they could do nothing but lie sweating and shivering in their unguarded dugouts until the shooting subsided enough to bring them to safety. The extended interval without food, without sanitation and without even the most basic medical care meant that most of the men were already past the point of no return.

They were brought in on camel-back, some two hundred of them, slung two to a beast in makeshift canvas hammocks. Within twenty-four hours of their arrival, John informed the CMO that he suspected many of the men were infected with typhus. Every precaution was duly taken, but the basic conditions of the monastery together with the disastrous medical condition of the men made it more or less inevitable that the disease would spread. It ripped through the camp in a matter of days, with little the young medics could do but tend to their patients the best they could and separate the dying from the already dead as efficiently as possible.

By the time the outbreak had run its course, just eleven of the original two hundred prisoners remained alive. Several of the doctoring staff had also perished. As with the deaths of Stewart and Rabbie, John found his emotions crippled by the pointlessness of it all. So many men dead, some of whom would have gone on to make fine doctors. Their deaths, sordid and agonising, had served no one.

He felt weak with longing for home, for the comforts of clean hot water and familiar food. He had several weeks' leave owing, but his release order had gone astray and as the camp readied itself for the next onslaught of wounded he found himself once again in limbo, waiting and thinking and frustrated by his own powerlessness.

It was during this tense, depressing interval that Edna McCrae arrived among them. Her presence in the camp was unwelcome; an irritant at best, at worst a source of divisiveness that threatened to spill over into open hostility. Nor did it help matters that they had little else to think about at the time. One of the men, a junior medical officer named McNab who had only narrowly escaped death during the typhus epidemic, took an instant dislike to Edna McCrae, a hatred so pathological it at first amused and then later unsettled the rest of them.

'The woman is evil,' McNab insisted, more than once.

'Leave over man, you're still delirious,' said Sharpin after one of McNab's more colourful outbursts. Sharpin was an old soldier, a RAMC man for more than twenty years. He had seen a great deal, most of it unpleasant, and John had learned much from him. He also found his company congenial. Sharpin took most things in his stride, but even he found McCrae disconcerting, John could tell.

'The camp's no place for a woman,' he said, a common enough sentiment among the serving soldiery but there was more to it than that. Edna McCrae was watchful and intelligent and she held strong opinions. She did not agree with the war and found no hesitation in saying so. Sharpin had no time for McNab and his panic-mongering but even so, he did not like Edna McCrae because she did not know her place as a woman should.

John was called to the Donald case some three months after the arrest. He had no knowledge of the prisoner at the time. He did not approve of tabloid sensationalism, though the Donald business had been so widely reported it was difficult to avoid entirely. He knew the child's body had been found in a sack, that it was on account of this sack, or rather its residual contents that his expertise in forensics was being called upon. The sack itself was something of a mystery. A canvas flour bag printed with the brand name 'BOSS', the sack had originally been supplied by the Luken's Milling Co, Atchison, Kansas. Since the imposition of tariffs this firm had been sending its flour to Britain through their Canadian mills. The bag was unusual, not commonly sold in Aberdeen. This should have made it easy to track down, though in practice it proved the opposite.

John had met with Professor Smith at the university forensic laboratory in Edinburgh. Here he was given a number of samples of hair and fluff recovered from the inside of the sack, together with similar samples of fluff collected from inside the Donalds' flat and another, larger sample of hairs taken from a hairbrush that had been handed to Jeannie Donald in her prison cell.

The fluff inside the sack, the same fibrous, greyish waste matter you would find at any place of human habitation, was actually made up of some two hundred separately identifiable fibres, hairs and skin particles, of which twenty-five were identical with parts of the sample taken from the Donalds' home. A good percentage, John thought, remarkable even, and one that went some way to proving that the sack the child's body was found in was likely to have belonged to Jeannie Donald.

The hair from Jeannie Donald's hairbrush proved more conclusive still. Not only did it share the same mid-brown pigmentation as the hair recovered from the sack, but when he examined it under the microscope, John found that both samples of hair showed an unusual and irregular bulging of the cortex.

The hair samples were so similar as to be identical; the hairs from inside the sack could only be Donald's. The discovery sent a wave of shock through him, as such discoveries still did, a tremor of recognition that was equal parts vindication and déjà vu. There had been many such moments during his time working on the Ruxton business, and this one, now, came as a reminder that the Donald case, like most murder investigations, was a game of two halves.

Professor Smith and Professor Shennan and Dr Richards had

travelled a good way down the road to discovering how the child had died, just as the officers involved in searching the lobbies, kitchens and parlour rooms of number 61 Urquhart Road had arrested Jeannie Donald as the person most likely to have brought that death about. Now they were looking to him, John Glaister, to provide the proof that linked the person that had been arrested to the crime that had occurred. Not through gossip or hearsay or from movements partially glimpsed through a downstairs window but through material evidence.

He had proved that the hairs from inside the sack were the same as the hairs on Jeannie Donald's head, just as Smith had observed that the small hole in the corner of the 'BOSS' sack was identical with the holes in other sacks found hanging from a nail in the understairs cupboard used by Jeannie Donald for storing potatoes.

When taken together with the other, more circumstantial evidence, Jeannie Donald's guilt seemed all but certain.

Edna McCrae came to Enab as the sun was going down, walking slowly towards the guard post at the entrance to the camp ground. She wore desert khaki: a dusty flying suit, buttoned cape and a wide-brimmed hat. A strange get-up, made stranger by the Gladstone bag she carried. It was difficult to understand how she had arrived there, so many miles from anywhere that might reasonably be called a settlement and with no supply transport due for at least five days.

Going by recent experience, it would be longer.

The woman claimed she had journeyed north from Riyadh, first by camel train, then with an army convoy en route to Damascus, then by camel train again.

'I was told I could arrange transport to Cairo from here,' she said. 'I have friends awaiting me in the capital.'

'They'll be awaiting you some time yet, then,' said Major Waterhouse, who had been called to the guard post. 'What was your business in Riyadh?'

'I am an archaeologist,' said the woman, 'travelling with a party sponsored by the University of Oxford. We have been making a study of prehistoric settlements to the south of Riyadh.'

'There is nothing south of Riyadh,' Waterhouse said. He glanced briefly over her shoulder, as if he expected to see others – men, vehicles, hostile marauders – come teeming out of the scrubland in her wake. He looked thoroughly displeased. Edna McCrae was not on the schedule, and from his body language it was clear he did not believe her story. John could not see that her story mattered, either way. They could hardly turn her away, and what threat could she pose in any case, a lone woman? Even if she was a spy, there was nothing at the camp for her to spy on. Even if there were, she had no means to communicate her discoveries to the outside world.

They were stuck with her. John realised he was glad, or at least not unhappy. He was sick of the hospital, heartsore and careworn in the wake of his illness, tired out by the endless jabbering in Turkish of the recuperating prisoners, the spats and petty rivalries among his colleagues. All of this was inevitable and could not be helped. Edna McCrae, whoever she was and wherever she came from, would at least be something different, someone new to talk to. He told Waterhouse he would show her to the bunk room, a small, high-ceilinged chamber that was out of the way of the Turkish soldiers and reasonably clean. There was a camp bed in there, most recently slept in by a man named Farquhar who had been invalided out not long before John's arrival. The official diagnosis was heat exhaustion, though according to Sharpin the man had wandered away from the camp and almost died of exposure in the cold desert night.

'He lost it,' Sharpin said. 'Some people do.'

John told none of this to Edna McCrae. There was a fine dust over everything, the pervasive sense of emptiness and ruination that clung to the building like a miasma, that surged back in to fill its spaces the moment they were vacated. 'It's all a bit basic, I'm afraid,' he said. He had become used to the place, he realised, for good or for ill. He could not imagine how it must look to Edna McCrae.

She laughed. 'I've known far worse, believe me. There's no need to stand on ceremony with me, Captain . . .?'

'Glaister. My name is John Glaister.' It struck him how rarely he had found himself in the company of a woman who was not related to him somehow, either in the strictest sense of being family – sisters, mother, grandmother, aunt – or in ways that were almost as rigidly defined. Through being his patients, for example, the poor women of the tenement slums he had attended in their wretched confinements through his years at medical school. Then there were the mothers and sisters of friends, the wives of hospital benefactors and visiting lecturers. Even Muff, whom he had known since his schooldays, after a brief and thrilling interlude of chaotic suspense was now as closely defined by him as he was by her.

There were female medical students, a few, anyway, but in John's particular year group there had been none.

Edna McCrae stood before him merely as herself, a woman he had met for the first time less than an hour ago and of whom he knew nothing at all except what she had told them: that she was an archaeologist, and on her way to Cairo. Both seemed not so much unlikely as fantastic. To be carrying on such a life during wartime, in the midst of such hostile territory, alone.

John struggled to understand how he should relate to her. Stumbling beneath the weight of his own embarrassment and lack of experience, he grasped at the only solution that seemed available to him: he addressed her as if she were a man.

'Canteen's at six thirty,' he said. 'We all eat together here. There are some Turkish fellows – prisoners of war – but you won't mind them.'

'I'll be happy to meet them,' said Edna McCrae. 'We had a Turkish man in our outfit. He was a doctoral student before the war, a most brilliant young man. Now he is on the run from the military police.'

John stood silent, unsure of what he might add. He would not have said that McCrae was attractive, though he would not have said she was unattractive, either. The dark brown hair, pulled back from her face, looked as if it might not have been washed in several days but then, he reflected sombrely, neither had his. The desert, the endless waiting – the place could put the devil in you, if you weren't on the lookout for him. McCrae was smiling slightly, as if she had guessed his thoughts exactly.

'Forgive me,' she said. 'I am sure we have all had enough of politics, for the time being at least. Is there somewhere I might wash before dinner?'

'We have a cold-water shower. The men have a rota for washing, morning and evening. The facilities will be free now. I will see to it that you are not disturbed.'

He escorted her to where he and the other officers had their water closet, the stony chamber known as the sluice room where their engineer had rigged up a hosepipe and connected it to a water drum. The water pressure was non-existent but the set-up worked.

As John stood guard at the entrance to the passage, he found himself trying to imagine what McCrae's body was like beneath her outlandish clothes, the long legs and strong forearms with their large, almost mannish hands, the surprisingly narrow waist and curvaceous hips. He had not seen a woman naked since Blackpool, the night before he departed on active service. The whole business had been a mix-up. John had gone to Egypt in place of his brother Joe, who shared the same initials. Joe was in London, about to complete his doctorate – it was inconceivable that he should throw over his studies, and John had agreed to take up the commission in his stead. It was only by luck that Muff had even been there – a hastily arranged weekend party, with no idea what was to befall them at the end of it.

When considered in hindsight, their decision to sleep together, taken on the instant and in such emotional circumstances, was probably a mistake. John, nervous about his own performance, still felt he had not taken care of her properly, had not asked himself sufficiently if this was what she really wanted.

Their coupling had been brief, and if not disappointing exactly then certainly confusing. He sensed that both of them felt more at ease once they had put on their clothes again. He had replayed the scenes in his mind a thousand times, imagining how different things might have been had they been on their honeymoon, rather than wedged into a narrow bed in a cheap seafront hotel, the noises from the kitchen and the public bar rising in a continuous clamour from the floor below.

The feeling came to him from nowhere, that Edna McCrae would have relished the unexpectedness of it all, that she would have revelled in the very tawdriness of their surroundings. He listened to the stop-start-honk of the makeshift shower, thinking that he barely knew her, that the woman was so unlike Muff she barely counted as a woman at all.

She emerged from the sluice room dressed in a traditional ankle-length garment known as a thawb, the khaki flying suit she had been wearing hanging in damp folds over her arm. Her hair trailed wetly down her back in unruly tendrils. The next time he saw her, in the canteen, it had been gathered into a bun at the nape of her neck.

Waterhouse seemed resigned to her being there, determined, as was Waterhouse's way, to make the best of things. No doubt he felt concerned that if anything untoward were to arise from the situation, the blame would be laid at his door. But in spite of his superior rank and long experience, Waterhouse was as bored and rattled as the rest of them. He was happy to be distracted, if only for a while.

McCrae herself seemed completely relaxed. Seated between Waterhouse and Sharpin, she talked animatedly about her journey to the hospital, riding on camelback in the company of nomads through the hills of Judea. The Turkish prisoners, seated at their own table, watched her with interest, but either she did not notice or did not care. The men were quieter than usual in any case, on their best behaviour. Only McNab seemed downcast, shrunken within himself. John put it down to the lack of news from home: another day past and no letter, no word from his fiancée, Mabel, of whom he had talked incessantly when they first arrived there.

The war was hard on a man, for all sorts of reasons, and John felt sorry for him. He wondered if he should speak to Waterhouse about McNab, suggest a period of leave, though he knew in advance what Waterhouse would say: if everyone in need of leave took leave, there would be no one left on duty to sign them out.

In the days that followed, John would wish many times that he had trusted in his instincts and said something. Of all the stories he recounted to Muff when the war was over, what happened to Leonard McNab was the one he left out.

The newspapers made much of the defendant's silence, suggesting that her refusal to speak in her own defence was an admission of guilt. A callous silence, some called it, a haughty silence, claimed others. John knew it was more likely that Jeannie Donald had been advised by her counsel to let them speak for her, and with good reason. Even when they were innocent, the defendant was rarely the most convincing speaker on their own behalf. They were often nervous, inarticulate, easily confused. Worse, they could turn aggressive, aggrieved, determined to batter the jury into submission. In a case like this one, the situation was further complicated by the accused person's refusal to accept or to intuit the danger they were in. John suspected that Jeannie Donald would still be protesting her innocence, even as the noose was tightening around her neck.

For Donald's plea to be carried, the jury must be made to believe that Donald could not have murdered the child because Donald was not in the house when the child died. She believed, as did her counsel, that if she could put together a strong enough story about where she had in fact spent the relevant part of the afternoon in question there would be insufficient evidence to convict her. Public knowledge of what could be proved by forensic science was still – like the science itself – in its early infancy. From the testimony that he had heard – from the witnesses and from the police, from the statement that had been read out on Donald's behalf – John felt bound to admit that she had made a good fist of it. The evidence in the kitchen, on the face of it, was minimal, and the case for the prosecution had not been helped by the police rushing to conclusions about what had initially looked like bloodstains under the sink.

Donald had made a good job of cleaning up after herself, added to which there was no one – no neighbour, no passer-by – who saw her confront the child, or shake the child, or speak to the child even, at least not that day. No one saw Jeannie Donald at all from the time her daughter left the house at one until Mary Topp spoke to her in the lobby at half-past two.

I'm back early, Donald had said. *I have all wee Jeannie's dresses to iron for the Pavilion tonight.*

In her statement to the police, Jeannie Donald claimed she had left the house at ten past one to go out shopping, arriving home again sometime between a quarter and half past two. After speaking to Mary Topp she went into her apartment, where she immediately made a start on ironing her daughter's costumes for the dance rehearsal that evening. Her husband Alec came in for his tea at around four o'clock. She and wee Jeannie set out for the Pavilion at twenty past five.

A good story, enriched with details that sounded authentic because most of them were. A prosaic account of mundane actions, made hideous and strange only when you stopped to consider the possibility that the body of the murdered child had been lying concealed in the apartment for the whole duration.

While Donald was ironing her daughter's dresses, the body was there.

While her husband was eating his tea at the kitchen table, the body was there.

When Donald and her daughter left the house to go to the Pavilion, the body was there, just yards from where neighbours and friends and family were desperately searching.

Jeannie Donald would have known this. Her hands would still have carried the invisible traces of what she had done. How could it be possible that she continued to cook and clean and sew as if this monstrous derangement of normality had never occurred?

The more the truth was revealed, the more the woman's stolid silence began to grate on him. John saw her silence as a disguise, a means of preventing access to her soul. She looked so very much like Edna it was uncanny, and yet in the essence of her person she was disturbingly other. When Edna McCrae fell into silence, John had always felt that she was doubly present, intensely alive, a whole world unto herself.

Jeannie Donald's silence seemed to him a dead thing, blank and chill as a bricked-up window, as a slab of granite.

John could only imagine that most women would be horribly bored at the camp; quite apart from the heat and the sandflies and the primitive bathroom facilities, there was nothing to do but play cards and drink the pallid, fermented barley water that passed for beer.

Edna McCrae did not seem bored. When she was not in the bunk room she could be found walking in the area of walled scrubland that had once been the monastery garden, making intricate line drawings of the plants that grew there, pencil studies of the very insects that drove the rest of them crazy. When it became too hot to walk outside, McCrae retreated to the decaying back rooms of the monastery, which still contained prayer books and heaps of old Bibles, strange little pieces of statuary representing the saints, the things that were left behind when the monks, sensing the end of their time in the wilderness, had upped and left the monastery and returned to Damascus.

The artefacts were broken, worthless, the disused rooms with their piles of junk claustrophobic and airless. When John asked McCrae what she hoped to find there, she laughed.

'The same as you when you examine a sick person, I would imagine. Clues to what went wrong.'

'The whole enterprise was misguided from the start, surely? Who could survive in such a place? Who would want to try?' In the days since she arrived, John had noticed a change in Edna McCrae, not a mellowing so much as a settling. Though with her curious dress sense and disregard for propriety she was as careless of convention as before, she seemed more welcoming of conversation, a fact John found himself taking advantage of increasingly often. In the way she seemed to enjoy sparring with him, she even reminded John of Rabbie, the fierce debates they'd had over whether it was possible to be a scientist and still believe in God.

'This land was once fertile, you know, and a sacred place for Christians, the place where the Ark came to rest after the Flood. The monks would have considered themselves privileged to be here. Desertification drove them out, and that is man's doing, not God's.'

'You are a believer, then?'

'I believe in science and the pursuit of knowledge, the same as you do, Doctor. There are those who would argue – even scientists – that the existence of God is a necessary fiction, a bulwark against the void. I find the void itself to be interesting enough for one lifetime. I keep my nose out of God's business, so long as he keeps his out of mine.'

'God helps those who help themselves, in other words,' John countered. 'That's what my father says.' He could not remember ever having spoken this way with Muff. They had known one another so long he took her like-mindedness, her sympathy towards his worldview for granted. Muff went to church, she sat in the family pew every Sunday, though John had always assumed that this was a ritual she kept for the sake of appearances. Muff's father was the Town Clerk, for whom faith was a matter of tradition as much as belief.

He felt ashamed, suddenly, for not ever having asked her what she believed. That he did not know for sure seemed a gross omission. He had said nothing of Muff to McCrae and that too shamed him, though equally he knew nothing of her own personal attachments, or lack of them. Their relationship existed entirely in the present tense, and that was where it must stay, he reminded himself. He was not attracted to McCrae in the way a man normally finds himself attracted to a woman, but he was forced to admit, all the same, that since she had come among them she had seldom been far from his thoughts.

Because she is not of this place, he reassured himself. Because she reminds me there is a world beyond, that the war cannot go on forever, that there are other ways of thinking.

McCrae walked and talked and spoke like a man, in that there was no apparent division between what she said and what she believed it was fitting to say, although when he asked her about her time in Riyadh, the expedition she had been with, she became evasive. She told him she had been part of a team attempting to excavate the Roman ruins of old Jerash, in Jordan.

'It is an incredible place,' she said. 'The modern settlement is not much. But the old city was once a significant Roman stronghold, a vast and wealthy outpost of Western civilisation. There is evidence that much of the original architecture survives. I more or less sold my soul to get a place on the dig, but some of the people in charge made matters impossible. The atmosphere became soured and in the end I decided to leave. A small group of us collected supplies and headed south, to Riyadh. Have you heard of the Empty Quarter?'

John admitted that he had not.

'On the face of it, it's a kind of hell. Nothing but sand, heat, desert for hundreds of miles. There are legends though, of another city, a lost city. The man who funded the expedition was convinced we would find it. A place where no human being has set foot for hundreds of years.'

'Did you uncover anything?'

'He was not a well man,' she said, not answering. She was cupping a flower in her hand, a specimen of the dirty yellow weed they called desert buttercup, the spiky leaves tickling her fingers, like the bent legs of spiders. Her eyes were downcast, gazing at the plant as if it was something rare and precious and infinitely longed-for. 'We ran out of water.' She sighed. 'I shouldn't still be here, really. I need to get home.'

'Home?'

'To London, I suppose. I was born in Ayr but my parents moved south when I was a baby. They settled in Banbury.' She smiled. 'Banbury. Can you imagine? It's hard to remember what it feels like, to walk those streets, to hear the church bells, to feed the ducks on the duckpond. When I think of Banbury I think of those old black-and-white etchings you find in books, illustrations of days gone by. I sometimes find it hard to believe it still exists.'

'My grandfather owned a house near Thornhill, in Dumfriesshire,' John said. 'A stone house with rambling gardens and many rooms. We used to spend summers there, as a family, and the Christmas holidays. My father often had to stay behind in the city if there was an important trial underway but my mother was always there to take charge. My brothers and sisters and I used to run wild for weeks at a time, the six of us, building hideouts in the woods behind the house, playing at hunters and spies and Christopher Columbus, games with complicated storylines and endless lists of rules only we children understood. I remember at Christmas especially, the excitement of going down to Carronhill. My father was not an extravagant man, as a rule, but at Christmas it was as if he became a child himself again. He seemed determined that we should enjoy ourselves, that we should lay down memories to help sustain us through whatever the future held in store. He would begin his preparations months in advance, ordering marzipan and chocolate from Lübeck, in Germany, sugarwork baskets and crystallised fruits from Fortnum & Mason. Then this mountain of provisions had to be transported down to the country, a journey that was often difficult in winter, with the railways beset by ice storms and the road from the station to Carronhill close to impassable.

'I remember the aroma of burning logs and the scent of paraffin, the tattie scones and fried bacon and mushrooms we were served at the kitchen table when we finally arrived. The bedroom beneath the eaves I always shared with my brother Joe, its polished, uneven floorboards and snarl of black beams. And then the frost, the following morning, the tracery of crystals that secretly covered the windows during the night. I don't know why I am telling you this,' John said. 'Maybe because I can imagine there are moments like this for you, in your memories of Banbury. And because the war has taken so much from us – from all of us, without a by-your-leave or an excuse me or a simple sorry. We are all in no-man's-land, I think,' he added. 'This sounds unpatriotic, I know, but I have seen too many men in pain to go on believing that love of country is anything more than a shameful swindle. If this shocks you, Miss McCrae, then I apologise.'

The truth was that he was shocked at himself, at the guileless outpouring of images and memories, of thoughts he scarcely knew he had, let alone dwelled on. His father had served in the Boer War and his brother Joe was in the medical corps, the same as him. John knew them as he knew his own skin, and yet he had rarely if ever spoken to them of the mixture of guilt and anger he felt at the needless, sordid waste of so much human life. Of human life and dreams, for would not the Turkish prisoners who had died on his watch each have secreted within themselves their own unspoken, beloved version of Carronhill, a time and place that was sacred and inviolable, a portion of their soul?

Would not the Germans, come to that? There was a fellow John had briefly spoken to at medical school, a student doctor on an exchange programme from Heidelberg. He had on walking shoes, John remembered, and carried a guide to the city's churches. He wondered where that man was now, what hell he might be enduring, or escaping.

'I would be shocked if you did not feel that way,' McCrae said quietly. 'The war is madness. An infection, like typhus. Until the rest of the world can see that, we are lost.' She touched his arm, very briefly, then took a step back. For a moment it seemed as if she might say something more, and though his own lips felt frozen shut, John yearned to know what it might be. His heart raced, as if he had taken something, some false antidote. Edna McCrae murmured some words he did not quite hear, then turned and walked away.

'I've seen you talking to her,' said McNab. 'You should be careful.'

The man was unshaven, and his fatigues were spotted with grease, or motor oil. Rangy and silent and increasingly sly, McNab now had an aspect of the feral dog about him, forever hanging about the place on the lookout for titbits of gossip, for scraps of ill will. He was bad for morale, unsettling because he was unsettled, though what might be done to ease the tension remained unclear. Once again, John found himself wishing that McNab could be sent home on leave, or to another encampment. Anywhere but here.

'I'm not sure what you mean,' he said. He kept his tone even, relaxed. McNab's aggression was liable to surface on the slightest pretext.

'We know nothing about her, do we? Or where she came from.

What if she's a spy? I think she probably is a spy, don't you? A woman like that.'

'Like what?' John said, in spite of himself. The man was infuriating.

McNab smiled his twisted smile. 'There's nothing for you there, Johnno. You can always tell with these New Women. There's a smell comes off them – like rotten fish. The whole camp stinks of her.'

'That will do, Sergeant.' John hated to pull rank. He believed strongly that the success or failure of a set-up like this one, hundreds of miles from any authority and thereby any help, depended as much on trust between the men as on protocol, if not more so. The sense that McNab was slipping away from him – from them – was more than palpable, it was pervasive, a kind of slow decay. John thought of sending McNab to clean the latrines in the Turkish barracks, but the thought of resorting to such antiquated notions of discipline made him feel weary and incompetent, impatient with himself. He asked McNab to make an inventory of supplies instead, a job that actually needed doing, and that McNab, who had a head for figures, might even enjoy.

He hoped it would suffice, at least until the next consignment of patients arrived, at which point Edna McCrae would leave the monastery with the departing convoy. Waterhouse had said as much. John could not suppress a pang of regret at the thought of her going, even as he felt relief.

Throughout that evening and the following day, Leonard McNab appeared subdued but stable. When he failed to appear in the canteen for the evening meal, Waterhouse sent one of the Turks to go in search of him. Within a short space of time it was established that McNab was nowhere in the camp.

The light was going, the sky the mangled purplish blue of a deepening bruise, the shade that presaged its rapid progression to total darkness. If they were going to find McNab they must do so quickly or wait until morning.

'What do you reckon, Glaister?' said Waterhouse, and it struck John that though they would routinely confer on every matter from the allocation of rations to the trustworthiness of the latest war rumour, Waterhouse had never asked for his advice outright, nor had he seemed so disconcerted, not even in the midst of the typhus outbreak, when men were dying hourly and his own health hung in rags through lack of sleep.

There was no accounting for it.

'I'll take the Turks,' he said. 'Comb the periphery. If McNab has decided to go AWOL, he won't have got far. There's nowhere for him to go,' John added, though both of them knew that did not exempt a man from getting into trouble, especially out here, especially at night.

John organised the Turkish soldiers with lanterns and they began making a general search of the uneven, brush-covered land that lay behind the monastery, working their way out into the scrubland in expanding circles. He could hear the distant shouts of Waterhouse and Sharpin, walking the stony track that wound its way from the guard post out into the desert, calling McNab by name at measured intervals, and it seemed to him that McNab was less a name now than a sound, spiky and brutish and devoid of meaning. Though he scolded himself inwardly for falling prey to such melodrama, he had a bad feeling. Pushing forward into the dusk, he kept expecting to stumble across the sergeant's bloodied remains, the unlucky victim of a knife attack by one of the vagrants that came by regularly, begging for food. Or worse still, felled by his own weapon.

He told himself he had not realised things had reached such a pass, though he suspected he had known, and still done nothing, and the idea that he was responsible for whatever fate had befallen McNab became a torment. His thoughts spun inside his head, unleashing a tide of distress and self-doubt he had not experienced before. What kind of doctor was he, if he could not recognise the depth of suffering closest to hand?

What brought him back to himself was McCrae, or rather her voice, not just the edge of panic he detected in it but the unexpectedness of her outburst, borne to them where they were searching through the humid evening air.

'Here! Over here!'

John had given no thought to Edna McCrae since McNab had gone missing. That she had joined them in their search was a matter of surprise, given the animosity McNab had expressed towards her, a malice he made no attempt to conceal, even from her.

But then, as John reflected later, so many things about that night were unexpected. He started back towards the camp, his lantern swinging in front of him in a dizzying arc. As he reached the guard post McCrae came running to meet him. Her hair had come undone, and John felt the urge to restrain her, to catch her in his arms. He remembered her talk of the ruins of Jerash and it came to him that the woman before him embodied the spirit of that ancient outpost, her body and thoughts as one, and seething with life.

'He's in the supply stores.' McCrae sounded breathless. 'He's unconscious. I can't seem to rouse him.'

John followed her back to the stores, a stone outbuilding where they kept the less valuable and less easily damaged supplies: canvas groundsheets and tarpaulins, stretcher poles and camp beds, empty oil drums. McNab lay collapsed in the narrow alcove behind a stack of wooden crates.

'Hold the lantern,' he said to McCrae, addressing her brusquely as he might a driver or an orderly. She seemed not to notice, and as he bent to examine McNab their shoulders briefly touched. McNab was not deeply unconscious, though in every sense that mattered he was dead to the world. He seemed to breathe in fits and starts. Now and then a low moan puttered out through his lips, which were bluish and flecked with saliva. When John placed his hands on his torso he could feel the man trembling.

'He's taken something – or else he's been poisoned.' He felt horrified, more so even than when he had first detected the symptoms of typhus in the Turkish casualties. Given the conditions they were forced to endure, an outbreak of contagion had been inevitable. But whatever was wrong with McNab, there seemed no sense to it. 'Let's get him inside,' he added. Two of the Turks had appeared with a stretcher, so quickly they might have been conjured out of the air. They laid McNab in a side room, what had once been a wash house. John thanked and dismissed the Turkish soldiers, asking them to fetch Waterhouse, who was there within minutes.

'Has he been shot?' Waterhouse asked. From the look of the man – his face drained of blood, his low, cathartic mumbling, John could easily understand how Waterhouse had reached such a conclusion. He shook his head.

'No discernible injuries,' he said. 'But look at this.' He pointed to what his initial examination had revealed: a pinkish, raised welt on McNab's right side, the comma-shaped mark at its centre an angry red.

'Rattlesnake?' asked Waterhouse.

'Could be. But a snake bite would normally leave two puncture wounds, not one. I think this is a spider bite.' As so often, John felt grateful to his father, who from the beginning of his studies had encouraged his nascent interest in toxicology. 'Latrodectus renivulvatus – that's the North African variety of what is commonly known as the black widow spider. The venom acts on the nerve endings – that's why he's cramping. Look.' John pointed to McNab's hands, which had gone into spasm, clenching into fists as if McNab were preparing to defend himself against an invisible enemy. 'This will get worse before it gets better,' he said. 'All we can do is keep him comfortable while he rides it out.'

'And will he – ride it out?'

'He's young,' John said. 'He can survive this. We'll have to wait and see. Keep him hydrated while the poison works its way out of his system. I'll sit with him.' He felt he owed it to McNab, that what he saw as his earlier negligence made him responsible. There was no logical basis for the feeling – McNab had gone out to the stores for some reason and come into contact with a venomous spider. It could have happened to anyone. Had he warned the men about black widow spiders? John could not consciously remember doing so, but they were part of camp lore, everyone knew about them, even if few of the men had ever seen one. The spiders were shy creatures, hiding in out-of-the-way corners and undisturbed crevices.

Short of accompanying Leonard McNab everywhere he went, there was nothing John could have done to prevent such an accident. Nothing anyone could have done. Yet the feeling of guilt persisted. The thought flitted across his mind that it had been Edna, and Edna alone, who had known where to find him. Edna who made drawings of the creatures, both benign and hostile, that inhabited the overgrown vegetable garden, the stone outbuildings and supply stores. Edna who knew the common and Latin name of every one.

Black widow, John murmured absently. But then the thought was gone.

'How is he?'

John started violently out of his doze as if he had been struck.

'You,' he said dazedly. He stared up at Edna McCrae, who was holding a mug of tea, offering it to him as if he was the reason she had come here, after all, not to check on McNab but to check on him.

He took the cup from her hands. The tea was strong and sweet and not too hot and he gulped at it eagerly.

'He seems a little easier,' he said. 'But I'm worried we've not seen the worst yet. I wish I knew more of his medical history. If there is any kind of physiological weakness there, this toxin will exploit it.'

'What kind of weakness?'

'Heart condition, gastric condition. Anything, really.'

'The son of our translator was bitten by a spider,' McCrae said. 'When we were in Riyadh. He was five years old. He died, and his father turned his back on the expedition. I think that's when things began to go wrong for us. We were all downcast.'

'Children are more vulnerable. Their strength can fail quickly.'

'It was as if he was on fire. His whole body wound up with tension, like a piece of jammed machinery.'

'That's what it does to you.' He wished she had not told him about the child. The angel of death, he thought. The black widow. He brushed the thought away. 'There is no need for you to be here,' he said. He glanced at his watch. 'You should take your rest.'

'And if I want to be here?' she said, and only then did John become aware of how quiet it was in the wash house, the night thick as a blanket around them, just the shallow, uneven breathing of Leonard McNab, not sleeping so much as simmering, to intrude on the silence.

'You can stay, of course,' he said. 'I would be glad of the company.' He remembered one of the innumerable, sordid nights during the typhus outbreak, when after watching three men die one after the other he had snatched ten minutes outside the tent, meaning to find some food for himself and instead stared up at the moon, the pale silver disc of her, so like a queen, he had thought, so sunk in majesty she is outside our sphere, beyond our ken, and though the words inside his head seemed close to nonsense they had comforted him nonetheless, granted him some sort of promise that this time would pass. That it would pass, and waking from sleep would mean a new day, free from the stench of faeces and the fear of contagion.

'If this man dies, it will be my fault.' He had promised himself he would not say so, that to express a sentiment he knew to be false would be self-indulgent. And yet the urge to confess his fear was overwhelming, and who better for him to confess to than Edna McCrae, a woman he barely knew and who, once this chapter of his life was over, he would never see again.

He expected her to deny him his guilt, to insist that what had happened to Leonard McNab was an accident and everyone knew it. Instead, she inclined her head in the direction of the man on the camp bed and merely nodded.

'There are moments in life when talk of guilt is beside the point,' she said. 'We see things happen, and fail to prevent them. That is all. I can tell you what happened in Riyadh, if you would like to hear it,' she added. 'Then you can judge for yourself if I am to blame.'

'I am no judge of anyone,' John said. 'I have seen enough of the law to understand its limitations. I would like to hear your story though, if you would like to tell it. He needs water, but I can't make him take any,' he added. He laid his palm against the forehead of the man on the camp bed, who shifted away from him, then groaned.

'Let me try,' said Edna McCrae. She took a handkerchief from her pocket, soaked the corner in the jug of lukewarm water John had placed on the rickety trestle beside the bed and then squeezed the sodden material over McNab's parched lips. His tongue darted out to catch the drops; whether in reflex or conscious need seemed not to matter. He had taken the water, that was all. McCrae wet the handkerchief again and repeated the process.

'We had so little water in the end it was all we could think about,' she said. 'There's a madness that takes over, a kind of dream state. I kept thinking about that story in the Bible, the one where Moses takes his staff and beats on a rock and brings forth water. I lay in my tent through those endless nights, more and more convinced that there must really be a way of getting water from stone and driving myself mad wondering how I might discover the secret. There was one of our party, an American, who kept seeing visions of fountains, far off in the desert. In the end he wandered away – we couldn't stop him. He'll be bones now. And do you know the strangest thing? When I first came here and saw that room with all the Bibles in it, the first thing I did was look up that story. It's in the Book of Numbers. *There came the children of Israel, even the whole congregation, into the desert of Zin in the first month, and the people abode in Kadesh. And Miriam died there, and was buried there.*'

McCrae quoted the verses from memory, her eyes half closed, as if the words were imprinted on her eyelids and she was reading them back. '*And why have ye made us to come out of Egypt unto this evil place? It is no place of seed or of figs or of vines or of pomegranates, nor is there any water to drink.*'

'You have an excellent memory,' John said. 'I was never very attentive during Bible classes.'

'I have always despised the Church. Organised religion is a system of power, nothing more. But even as a child I loved the Bible. Not for being the word of God but for its stories. There are no stories more marvellous, or more terrible. The spite God shows to Moses, and to Aaron, men who have followed him faithfully. And then that line about Miriam, dying out there in the desert, so far from home. The words are so simple and yet so pitiless. I cannot forget them.'

'What happened to your party?' John said.

'After Mehmet died – the boy I told you about – there was a lot of disagreement among us about what we should do. Some said we should remain behind in Riyadh, postpone the expedition until we could hire a new translator and take on extra supplies. Others argued that unless we kept to our schedule we would run out of money anyway, that the whole reason for our being there would be undermined. I was one of the ones who wanted to go on. I had become obsessed with finding the lost city. And with the desert too. I was in love with it, I think. Insane with desire.'

'So the party split in two?'

McCrae nodded. 'There were eight of us who went on, five who stayed behind. I don't know what happened to them – only that when the camel drovers brought us back to Riyadh they were nowhere to be found. Only three of us survived. Arturo is still in the hospital in Riyadh – he was too weak to travel. Miriam said she would stay with him while he recovered. She implored me to leave, to get back to London. She said it was important, and I chose to believe her.'

'Miriam?'

'Quite a coincidence.' McCrae laughed, a harsh, dry sound. 'Miriam is a scholar of Islamic and early Judean art. She has a passion for learning languages. I was in love with her, too.' She reached beneath her chair to where, John now saw, she had stowed her Gladstone bag, the same one she had been carrying when she first arrived. She lifted it onto her lap and undid the clasp. 'On the third day out from Riyadh, we found this. Well, it was Derwent who found it, the American. Everything was all right then. We still had plenty of water and our hopes were high. Derwent stumbled over what he thought was a piece of rock, buried just beneath the surface of the sand.'

She opened the bag and took out something wrapped in what

looked like a pillow slip, stained yellow along the edge from lack of washing. 'This is why Miriam insisted I should leave, so that what we found would reach the university, no matter what. It has to be one of us, she said, and you're the stronger one. What she meant was that of the two of us, I was the more likely to make it back alive. I told her I wasn't leaving without her and she said I had to, that it was vital we passed on our discovery. In the end I agreed. But the real reason I left was because I could not bear the thought of dying in that alien place.'

McCrae unwrapped the bundle, spreading the fabric flat across her lap. At its centre lay something bright, a cylindrical object roughly the size of a pocket flashlight. It looked to be made of silver or some other light-coloured metal. As he leaned in to inspect it more closely, John saw that the object was covered all over with a pattern of engraving, a close-knit tangle of lines and curves, as if its surface had been carved with the intricate, finely wrought map of an impossible labyrinth.

The object was compelling, even as its purpose was obscure.

'Touch it if you like,' McCrae said. 'It's very cold.'

Even as he was thinking that he would not, that he had no desire to, the object was in his hand, and he understood. The thing was cold as ice. The pads of his fingers prickled with a sensation that was not quite pain, not quite discomfort even, but that was curious nonetheless, and so unexpected that his first instinct was to shy away, to put the object down, no matter how attractive, and it was only then that he realised something else, that the object was weightless. Not weightless in the sense that it was without substance – like paper say, or straw. The cylinder impressed its presence upon him as a bar of gold might, or a piece of lead piping, and yet his hand, the chill aside, felt not the slightest effect, was not pulled downwards with the force of gravity as it normally would be, did not transmit the heft to his shoulder and thence to his brain.

It was as if the object he held was an idea, and not the real thing. As if he was attempting to carry a portion of empty air where its substance might be.

Surprised, he let go of it, and though he half expected the thing to float upwards, it fell back into McCrae's lap with a soft thunk, as if it truly was made of metal, after all.

'It must be hollow,' John gasped. He noted with displeasure that his voice was unsteady. 'A canister of some kind.'

'I don't think so. Listen.' McCrae picked up a pencil that was lying on the trestle and tapped it smartly against the object's side. Instead of the ringing sound John would have expected had the object been hollow, there was a dull knocking. 'Derwent had a theory, that it had fallen from space.'

'Was that before he started seeing mirages, or after?'

'After, I suppose. But his ideas were strange from the outset. He believed the place we were looking for was the last outpost of a vanished civilisation, that the city's ruins – should we ever find them – would provide evidence that Earth had been visited by beings from another world. It was Derwent who found us our translator. He had been in Riyadh before, trying to buy his way on to another expedition. We were unfair to him, I think.'

'Unfair how?'

'We none of us took him seriously. We thought of him as an amateur, a rich man's son with money to spend and no sense of how to spend it. You know how it is, within a close community. Small differences become exaggerated, a source of conflict. It is easy for a person to become isolated, a focus for hostility.'

'With ideas like his, I am hardly surprised.'

'All the same, we should have been more compassionate. Derwent was unwell, that was obvious. But we were all unwell by then. When he wandered off into the desert – I do not want to say this, but I think one or two of us might even have been relieved, not to have to listen to his ravings any more. The things he said, out there in the night, so far from everything we knew. He frightened us, more than a little. After he disappeared, Arturo found the object, wrapped in his groundsheet. We all thought he had taken it with him. I almost wish he had.'

'Arturo is the one who is still in Riyadh?'

She nodded. 'He is a quiet, sane man, a native of Rome. He has been writing about old Jerash for years, about its place in Roman history as he and other scholars believe it to have been. It was always Arturo's dream to see the ruins before he died. I think his mind will recover, once his body is rested. If he gets better, he will go back, I feel sure of it.'

She rewrapped the silver cylinder in its fabric covering and replaced it in her bag. John felt relieved, glad, in fact, to pretend he had never seen it. His younger sisters especially had always enjoyed the stories of H. G. Wells and Jules Verne, tales of creatures from other planets and journeys into space. John himself preferred his adventures closer to home. He did not, on the whole, see the point of fantasy. Why look to the stars when there were nearer wonders, still to be explored?

As for the silver cylinder, he had no doubt that science would explain its provenance, if the object could be brought to an institution with the means to deal with it. He was of a mind to use what influence he had to arrange safe passage for Edna McCrae and her troublesome cargo, and if some of his motivation lay in ensuring that the woman left the hospital at the earliest opportunity, then what of that? Her presence in the camp had already been more trouble than it was worth.

She should leave before things get worse, John thought, and he was wondering how he should best convey his thoughts to Edna McCrae when Leonard McNab began to shake and moan, his body hitching together beneath the thin blanket as if galvanised.

'He's having a fit,' John said, 'a grand mal.'

McNab came suddenly to consciousness, or seemed to, sitting upright in the bed with his right arm raised. His eyes were wide and staring and as John moved swiftly to quiet him he pointed straight at McCrae.

'You,' he said. 'You killed him, you. You murderer.'

His voice was harsh and barking, almost mechanical. Sweat gleamed on his brow as he thrust himself backwards against the pillow. 'She's the worst kind of thing,' he added. 'Can't you see it, Glaister?' and thinking about those moments so many years later, here in the High Court of Justiciary in Edinburgh where he stood in attendance at the trial of Jeannie Donald it seemed to John still that it had been McNab's use of his name that had been most frightening and most extraordinary. What stronger evidence was there that McNab, in spite of his delirium, knew where he was and who he was speaking to, that he remained, despite the gravity of his condition, not only aware of his surroundings but determined to warn his comrade of imminent danger?

John remembered the way McNab had looked at Edna McCrae, as if she were the devil and his soul was in jeopardy, and it came to him that he had seen the same look more recently, in the eyes of the dead child's father as he gave his evidence.

I had one child, the child Helen Priestly who is now dead. She was a healthy child, well grown for her age. I never had any trouble with her health. My child had never given any trouble by going away from home. When she played she played in the neighbourhood of my house.

'Steady, man, steady,' John said to McNab. He pushed gently at his shoulder, tried to make him lie down again. 'Don't excite yourself,' he said. 'You need to rest. I will stay with you.'

Even as he spoke, McNab's eyes seemed to empty, rolling upwards in their sockets like the picture cards in one of the slot machines in a seafront arcade. His shoulders sagged, then slumped. 'I think he's had a heart attack,' John yelled. He thumped the man in the ribs, then turned him on his side and began compressing his chest.

'There's no point,' McCrae said quietly. 'He's gone.'

When John looked up at her, he saw that she was crying.

'He must have had a weak heart,' John said to Waterhouse, afterwards. 'Myocarditis. Exacerbated by the spider venom.'

'Could anything have been done differently? If you had known about his condition beforehand, I mean.'

'Not really. Certainly not out here. Would you like me to write to his people?'

'I'll do it,' said Waterhouse. He was the senior officer, and John felt grateful to him for shouldering the burden, relieved that the news of McNab's death would not come from him, that his involvement in the case would remain mostly off the record. They buried McNab in the scrubland behind the monastery, marking the spot with a wooden cross. A week or so later, someone – John had the feeling it was one of the Turkish soldiers – decorated the grave with a statuette of Saint Luke, reading from his gospel, one of the relics left behind by the departing monks.

Edna McCrae was no longer with them. The day after McNab's funeral, an army vehicle bumped its way along the dirt road to the guard post. The truck was scratched and dented to a degree that was abnormal even for the time and place but like so many vehicles of its kind it was somehow still functioning. It had reached a steady state, John supposed, where to keep going was somehow less of an effort than breaking down.

At the wheel was an Egyptian woman, dressed in khakis and a straw boater. She introduced herself as Miriam Salah.

'I am from the archaeology department of the University of Alexandria,' she said. Her English was peerless, perfect, with just a touch of an American accent. 'I understand a colleague of mine has been staying with you. I am here to offer her transport back to London.'

McCrae was outside, making more of her drawings in the scrub, when the truck arrived. As she came around the side of the building and caught sight of it a change came over her, an expression of such lightness and candour she seemed almost a different person. Waterhouse asked Miriam Salah if she would stop and share a meal with them. She was a handsome woman, John could not help noticing, with an imperious expression and shining blue-black hair. But both she and Edna McCrae seemed determined on leaving immediately and that was what happened.

McCrae went as she arrived, dressed in her peculiar army surplus and carrying her Gladstone bag. The truck jounced into life and drove away. Once the vehicle was out of earshot, it was difficult to believe it had ever been there.

Two days later another convoy arrived, a mixture of Turks and Arab men, all prisoners of war. John's leave was officially cancelled. He ought to have minded, but war was war and he did not complain. There was a part of him that felt relieved. His duty, once again, became all consuming. There was no time to think about anything else, least of all Leonard McNab or Edna McCrae.

John remained at the camp in the desert until 1918, when he was invalided out. He had suffered a prolonged bout of amoebic dysentery, and had lost so much weight that Muff, who was there to meet him at Glasgow Central, failed to recognise him. By March of the following year he had recovered enough to set himself up as a general practitioner, working out of the apartment he and Muff had taken the lease on, in North Kelvinside.

He was a young doctor and a new husband. The war was finally over and the world had moved on. John rarely thought about his time at the monastery. He was shaken by how the Donald trial brought it all back to him. It was not simply that Jeannie Donald looked like Edna McCrae; it was the atmosphere she carried, that same sense of self-containment and defiance that nothing could penetrate. Donald was not relaxed, exactly, though she did seem confident, smiling at odd moments, exchanging words with her defence counsel and even the police as if she was there in the dock by invitation, rather than standing trial for her life.

It was only when she caught sight of her own daughter in the witness box that the mask seemed to slip. Wee Jeannie Donald, with her neatly brushed fair hair, was an appealing witness. More than that, she was a reminder of the other child, her playmate and exact contemporary, who was no longer there. The questions put to wee Jeannie by the prosecuting counsel were mostly about bread: what kind of bread did they normally have at home, what kind of bread had the Donalds eaten with their supper that April afternoon? Wee Jeannie replied to every question carefully and politely. She had no idea what her answers meant, but the court knew, and so did Jeannie Donald: they had eaten the loaf that Helen bought, bread of a different type and cost from their usual purchase.

Jeannie Donald's face turned pale and she began to weep. Not just at the sight of her daughter, John suspected, but at the manner in which her innocence had been subverted. She hid her face between her hands, and John knew there would be more shocks in store from the silent witnesses that had been summoned to speak against her.

The hairs from Jeannie's brush and the hairs in the sack.

The traces of blood and intestinal bacteria on the cleaning cloths that had been taken from the cupboard beneath Jeannie's sink.

The sheet of newspaper from the day before the murder, and the blood upon that.

Mute objects that told their own story, that were undeniable.

It was not John's task to sit in judgement – that was for the law – but as he watched Jeannie Donald's agonised face it was Leonard McNab he thought of, his anguished cry.

You. You murderer.

What had McNab seen in the face of Edna McCrae? What had he known? John had no trust in the ineffable, then or now. He had always preferred science, which was the guard rail on which his life ran. But still, McNab had intuited something, just as John had felt the weightless pressure of the silver cylinder, had sensed its uncanny chill in the tips of his fingers. If John's vocation had taught him anything, it was that not seeing a thing with the naked eye did not necessarily mean it was not there.

Could McCrae have hated McNab enough to do him harm? There was no logic to it. She had known the man as little as Jeannie Donald had known little Helen Priestly.

Time will tell us the truth of that mystery; time, and science. But John Glaister's part in the drama is played, and he has a train to catch.

Proof of the Sack

PROFESSOR SYDNEY SMITH WAS born the son of a road builder in Otago, New Zealand in 1883, and began his scientific training by working as an apprentice to the local pharmacist. Smith learned well and studied hard, eventually winning a scholarship to read medicine at the University of Edinburgh. He qualified as a doctor in 1912, soon afterwards taking up a position as assistant to Sir Harvey Littlejohn in the Department of Forensic Medicine. Just a year later, his keen observational skills and growing expertise in forensic techniques helped to solve the mystery surrounding the murder of two young brothers.

In 1917, Smith became head of medical jurisprudence at the Egyptian Ministry of Justice in Cairo, where in 1924 his particular interest in ballistics, together with a new technique he devised for the side-by-side comparison of microscopic slides, helped to apprehend and convict the gang responsible for the assassination of Lee Stack, Commander-in-Chief of the Egyptian army.

Smith returned to Britain in 1928, where he was appointed chair of forensic medicine at his alma mater. Almost immediately he became involved in investigating a series of high profile murder cases, several times clashing with the famous pathologist Sir Bernard Spilsbury, whose considerable reputation was at its peak.

Spilsbury, who came from a more privileged background, was as single-minded in his pursuit of knowledge as Smith, but his more flamboyant and increasingly dogmatic personal style was very different. Spilsbury clearly enjoyed his celebrity status, and did nothing to discourage the image of himself as a man of genius. Smith, although he too had garnered public attention since his success in the Stack affair, was more of a pragmatist.

He was appointed to the Donald case by the Procurator Fiscal five days after Jeannie and Alec were arrested. Though the public did not know it, the case was in danger of going under. Certain key suspects – most notably Alec Donald – had been dismissed from the investigation more or less immediately, and even the question of Jeannie's guilt was far from decided. The supposed bloodstains under the sink turned out not to be bloodstains after all, and it was only later, as police began to investigate the finer details of her statement, that they discovered Jeannie had lied about her activities on the afternoon of April 20th.

She told the police she had gone to the market straight after dinner. But the prices she quoted for the items she purchased – eggs, oranges – were only accurate when compared with the week before. More damningly, the haberdashers she claimed to have visited in order to price up dress material for Jeannie's dance costumes happened to be closed that Friday.

Still, telling a lie is not the same as committing a murder. If the police were to prove Jeannie's guilt, they needed something more tangible, and as it happens, the most significant aspect of the Donald case is that it was one of the first in history to be proved by the new and evolving techniques of forensic science.

When Theodore Shennan and Robert Richards carried out their original post mortem on Helen Priestly, they found bruises around her throat, and traces of vomit in her windpipe and airways. From this they were able to deduce that she had died by asphyxia. With her stomach still full of the mostly undigested remains of the beef and mashed potatoes she had eaten for lunch, the two doctors were able to go further, concluding that Helen's death had occurred less than an hour after she was last seen coming down Urquhart Road on her way back from the bakery.

Professor Smith was aware of the rumour, now generally circulating, that the Donalds and the Priestlys did not get on, and it was from this non-medical piece of information that he was able to extrapolate the events that led to Helen's death.

His own post mortem on Helen's body had already confirmed what Drs Shennan and Richards had previously observed: Helen Priestly had an enlarged thymus gland. The thymus gland, situated between the neck and the upper thorax, is the part of the lymphatic system responsible for the development of T-cells. As we learned during the pandemic, T-cells are vital to the human immune system, and the thymus gland is at its largest and most active in children and young adolescents.

An especially enlarged thymus, however, was thought at one time to be indicative of a condition known as Status Lymphaticus, widely held as the cause of sudden unexplained death in children and infants, including cot death. Even in the 1930s, this science was controversial.

There were doctors and other specialists who disputed the existence of such a thing as Status Lymphaticus, and by the early 1950s the theory had been dismissed by the medical establishment as grievously flawed.

At the time of Helen's murder though, it was still commonly believed. As one of these so-called 'thymic' children, Helen Priestly would have been considered vulnerable to intensified stress or a sudden shock. Professor Smith knew that Helen did not like Mrs Donald, and found himself wondering what might have happened if after buying her bread at the Co-op she had come home and encountered Jeannie in the hallway of her building.

It was easy to imagine an altercation between the two of them. Perhaps Helen had called Jeannie a name, or made a rude gesture. Short-tempered Jeannie might then have struck the girl, or even grabbed hold of her. What if Helen had passed out from the shock? Jeannie Donald, who would not have known that Helen was susceptible to fainting, might easily have mistaken the child's unexpected loss of consciousness for death.

Might Jeannie's subsequent assault on Helen have been committed out of the fear that she could be charged with murder? The simulated rape seemed actively designed to throw suspicion away from her and towards a man. Any man would do, but especially a disreputable one, like the destitute beggar she described in her statement. Or Richard Sutton's dark man.

But Helen Priestly was not dead – not at this stage. Jeannie's vicious and painful attack with a wooden spoke would most likely have revived her. Smith imagined her crying out, being sick from the shock. If Jeannie had then panicked, placed her hands around Helen's throat to stop her screaming – that would account for the vomit blocking her windpipe and the bruises on her neck.

Smith knew he was making a leap, but in cases where the facts are obscured such risks, when reasonably calculated, often pay off. He realised he would have to produce evidence to support his theory, to prove a concrete physical link between murderer and victim. It was in the pursuit of such evidence that he came to focus on the jute sack that Helen's body had been found in, the old flour bag with the word BOSS printed on it in large red capitals.

Drs Shennan and Richards had previously noted that the sack being dry suggested that Helen's killer was already in the building at the time of the murder. There were cinders in the sack, fragments of which were caught in Helen's mouth and hair, but in spite of anecdotal evidence that Jeannie Donald was the only resident of number 61 who still used cinders as part of her laundry routine, Smith concluded that the debris could have come from any of the households within the building.

He turned instead to the other residual contents of the sack, the small quantity of hairs, miscellaneous fibres and household fluff taken and held as evidence by investigating officers. Smith knew that if he could match these fibres conclusively with similar material collected from the Donald residence, it would be a significant step towards proving what he needed to prove: that Helen Priestly had died inside the Donalds' apartment.

Unlike the egotistical Spilsbury, Smith believed that the key to successful forensic investigation lay in teamwork, and when the Donald case called for expert knowledge in a specific area, Smith's first thought was to call on the services of a fellow professional.

The person he called on was Professor John Glaister, chair of medical jurisprudence at Glasgow University.

I seek out John Glaister's memoir *Final Diagnosis*, because I am hoping it might include a personal account of his involvement in the Donald case. In this I am disappointed. John does not even mention Jeannie. After telling us about his return from Egypt in 1931 – did I mention that John took over the post in Cairo when Sydney Smith left in 1928? – he fasts forward to the Ruxton murders of 1935, the case that made him famous, at least for a while, and that continued to attract the greatest number of questions from an admiring public.

In the course of my search for information about John's involvement in the Donald case I stumble across an extraordinary clip of film from the National Library of Scotland. It is May 25th 1918, and here is John Glaister with his new bride, Isobel Rachel Lindsay, on their wedding day. John is in uniform, Isobel is wearing an ankle-length wedding gown and veil. Arm in arm and smiling, they exit Glasgow Cathedral beneath the crossed swords of a regimental guard of honour. They are followed by Isobel's three excited-looking bridesmaids and an assortment of wedding guests, all dressed to the nines. I cannot help noticing that several of these people are carrying umbrellas. We are in Glasgow, after all.

There they are. I feel sidestepped by truth, ambushed by it, close to tears.

Every true account – essays and journalism, media reportage, film footage, even personal letters – is in some sense fiction, the partial version of reality that is inevitably the product of the subjective mind. Every fiction is in some sense true, because it has actually taken place inside the head of its creator. Richard Sutton's dark man did not force Helen Priestly on board a tram because there was no dark man, and so neither, in a sense, was there a tram. But if Ricky's mind is real then the dark man is, too. Within the invented space of this narrative, the dark man has as much reality as Jeannie Donald's parlour.

For those who insist on knowing which parts of *The Stormy Petrel* are 'true', here are the facts.

John Glaister did serve as a medical officer in the RAMC from the time of his graduation in 1916 until the end of the war. He was posted to Enab, in the foothills of the Judean mountains, where he worked in the treatment and rehabilitation of injured service personnel at a field hospital set up in an abandoned monastery. In his memoir, John describes the monastery as 'austere, solidly built . . . a massive, castellated building set among the rocky hills sparsely covered with dense green scrub.'

The arrival of two hundred badly wounded Turkish prisoners, slung in hammocks from the backs of camels, absolutely happened. The officers John worked with really were named Waterhouse and Sharpin, though Leonard McNab, like Edna McCrae, is my own invention.

The excavation of the Roman city of Jerash was begun in 1925. The Rub' al Khali, or Empty Quarter, is long supposed to be the site of the lost city of Iram, as mentioned in the Qur'an, though as far as we know, no alien artefacts have so far been discovered there.

When John's leave eventually came through, he dashed back to Glasgow to marry Isobel – known to all as Muff – though he had to return to Gaza, and the monastery, not long afterwards. There he contracted amoebic dysentery and, though he is too reticent to say so outright, very nearly died. The moment when Muff fails to recognise him on the platform at Glasgow Central station is taken, once again, from his own recollections.

The forensic details pertaining to Jeannie's case are taken from John's witness testimony at the trial. For the purposes of dramatic effect I have taken the liberty of shifting the Ruxton murders back in time, though given the wealth of other troubles I have invented for John, this minor sleight of hand does not seem important.

Strange Days Like These

A YEAR LATER, I HEAD north again. My partner Chris is travelling with me. It is the beginning of September, the week King Charles III ascended the throne, and I have booked a room for us at the hotel where Jeannie worked as a cook before she was married. The Tornacoille is just outside Banchory, a prosperous and attractive spa town at the heart of Royal Deeside. I still have the notebook I brought with me on my first journey, a brown A5 exercise book with a cover design of pheasants and a tatty strip of elastic to keep it closed. The notebook has been in my bag so long it is scuffed and dog-eared, abandoned plot lines interspersed with the names of hotels, the dates of exhibitions and the postcodes of restaurants.

My Russian lady could come to live on the same street as the murder, I wrote on the 28th August 2021. *The cold, the isolation, the background of mountains.*

The way I work is haphazard, instinctive, a slow accretion of thoughts and images and finally ideas. A book's gestation is random, less chronology than collision, something close to chance. It is only now, some fourteen months after I first began to think about this one, that I am coming to an understanding of what it is about.

Banchory lies decorous, steeped in the honeyed sunshine of late summer. The slopes of the hills are purpled with heather, the river's banks rustling with pine trees and mountain ash. The Tornacoille turns out to be a comfortable country hotel, more upmarket than we are used to but the atmosphere is pleasantly informal and the food is excellent. The grand old building, tastefully refurbished, gives little away. The structure aside, there is barely anything left now from Jeannie's time. I ought to feel disappointed, but I find it is enough simply to be here. The guest information folder in our room informs me that the Tornacoille was built in 1873 as a private house for an Aberdeen brewer named Thompson. It became a hotel in the early 1900s, after Thompson went bust. 'An inspection form from 1938 records the Tornacoille as having thirty bedrooms, of which just three had private bathing facilities,' reads the information sheet. 'Other guests had the use of a bathroom at the end of the corridor.'

There is no mention of Jeannie Ewen, or Donald. I have not come across any mention of Jeannie's employment here outside of the trial transcript. I doubt the hotel's present owners know anything about her, though it seems that the Wolf, the formidable housekeeper from my story 'The Cream Ware Bowl' did actually exist, a version of her anyway. According to the information sheet, the Tornacoille's general manager in the 1930s was a Miss Musgrave, who used to carve the roast in the main dining room every Sunday, dressed in a long black skirt. She had steel bars put on all the windows in the servants' quarters to stop any potential 'gentlemen friends' from calling after dark.

I am delighted by this discovery, though not surprised. I have experienced so many similar coincidences in my life as a writer, so many moments of synchronicity that the Wolf's intrusion into reality is almost expected.

When you think about a place enough, it comes alive for you.

I lie on my back on the hotel lawn, releasing the tension of the long drive, relishing the warmth of the sun and gazing up at the windows beneath the eaves, the attic rooms that were once occupied by servants and officers' batmen. I wonder if any of those rooms was ever Jeannie's. I wonder what hopes she had for her life when she first arrived here, not long after the war.

What made her agree to marry Alec Donald – sense, or sensibility?

The road that skirts the grounds murmurs ceaselessly with traffic, with the restless, constant motion of those passing through. An eagle coasts on thermals down the valley, floating high above the elegant chimneys of the buildings beneath. In winter this is a harsh place, a town cloaked in the colours of fire and seared by frost, a place that still bears the scars – hundreds of trees, scattered like matchsticks, torn out by the roots – of last winter's storms. A land of ice and granite and impassable roads. Of frozen mornings in late November, of maids lighting fires, cricked backs and broken fingernails, a lifetime of graft.

The following morning we drive east, into the city. The weather has turned, and although it is not raining, or not yet, the streets are blanketed in mist, a town of ghosts. The ships in the harbour loom enormously, their orange outlines like vast inflatables, pockmarked with rust. The traffic is denser than when I was here last, the pedestrians more numerous and more directed. Yet still the place seems suffused with the nagging unease I detected previously, a sense of desolation that seems deeper and more permanent than the scars left by COVID. The city is sullen and irritated, sick of the present. We drive east along Union Street — erroneously, it transpires; we'll be fined for it later — and then turn left, and as we begin the series of slow loops that will bring us into Urquhart Road I catch sight of the Saltoun Arms, the pub John Priestly was working at on the afternoon of his daughter's disappearance.

I had not realised we would pass that way, and the shock of recognition is bracing, almost electric. A run-down city pub, its exterior scarified with graffiti and out-of-date flyers. Glimpsed, then vanished, a phantom jigsaw piece, nondescript as a section of sky but equally vital. It is a part of the picture. Without that piece of sky the jigsaw is missing something and so is the story.

We arrive at Urquhart Road, parking east of the Roslin Street intersection on the south side of the street. I get out of the car and cross to the north side, walking west. The mist is thicker now, darkening everything. I start keeping a mental inventory of the passers-by: a couple of workmen in overalls, a young Asian man in a grey hoodie, a woman pushing a pushchair and a woman walking a dog, and as they sail towards me out of the murk it feels as if we have gone back in time — me, they, all of us, a random bunch of strangers thrown back to the 1930s, to the soot smuts and the smoggy air and the reek of rubbish.

The reek of rubbish is real: large dumpsters, placed at ten-yard intervals along the street overflow with uncollected refuse, the aftermath, the collateral damage of the recent Scottish bin strike.

Here is Roslin Street. Webster's grocery store is now a Premier Express. Lyons, the butcher's shop on the corner opposite, is now a nothing, an empty-eyed investment opportunity, its chocolate-brown paintwork chipped and dirty, its windows shielded by blinds. Two steps north and here is the low, shoebox-shaped building that was once the Robertsons' confectionery store, its window glass daubed with pink graffiti, the u-shaped scoop of its battered guttering blocked with grass. Sprouting seed heads droop and sway in their makeshift basket above the pavement below.

Roslin Street seems quieter and better kept than Urquhart Road, its houses set back from the street behind neat front gardens and low stone walls. There are trees, flowerbeds, a privet hedge or two. There is noticeably less rubbish. I walk further up the street, trying to find a place from where I can spy into the back yards and drying greens of Urquhart Road, but the containing walls make it impossible – the police were right. On the backs of the houses satellite dishes sprout like mushrooms, like bracket fungus. I find it painfully easy to imagine Helen, miraculously transported from then to now, rushing in from the garden to watch children's TV.

I return to the intersection and continue along Urquhart Road. Number 61 is closed-looking, grim. I pause outside Jeannie's sitting room, hoping to sneak a look inside, but the window is opaque, a closed book, inscrutable behind dust-choked nets. The dismal weather makes the whole house seem uncared-for, abandoned, and if it was an Airbnb before COVID I cannot imagine anyone paying much to stay here now.

The veil between my time and Jeannie's feels perilously thin. Urquhart Road then was a bad road, a place of poverty and struggle and tittle-tattle and barely scraping by. Now it is a place of transience, of hand-to-mouth existence, zero hours and pay as you go. Can a street be haunted by hardship, by loss? The sense of deprivation is so pervasive I am prepared to believe it.

Most of the small businesses on Urquhart Road have disappeared, the shop fronts altered to residential use, a row of numbered buzzers beneath each entryphone. A scattering of independent traders remain, and at the intersection with Hunter Place I discover that the Northern Co-operative Bakery is now A&P McKay, Hotel and Bar Suppliers. On to King Street, and the traffic is faster. There are more people and more small shops, poky and grubby-looking, the same as you find in any city, once you step outside of the souped-up central shopping district.

King Street Stitch Tailoring, Londis, Podiatry Studio, Wine, Whisky, Port, Mayree's Styling, Afro-Caribbean Specialist. Behind a barred-off shop window an ancient sign for DAS Hoover that might well date from Jeannie's time, though there is little else that does; at this end of King Street, almost all of the original tenements have been torn down.

Only the school remains, the King Street Public School that is now a part of the Robert Gordon University. The building is pristine, stern-faced and grey, larger than I expected and more imposing. I stand in what used to be the schoolyard, listening for the cries of children and hearing nothing but traffic. Around the back of the building, the wrought-iron gates at the Boddie Place entrance are chained shut and it is clear they have not been in use for years. There are cars in the car park, though not many, and there is nobody about.

If any of the children from Helen's class are still alive, they will be in their late eighties or early nineties. It is at least possible that wee Jeannie is out there somewhere, a great-grandmother, the same age as the queen now no longer among us.

I feel heavy with knowledge. As if I know these streets better than I do. As if I am returning to my own district.

Helen Priestly lies at rest in Allenvale Cemetery, to the west of the city centre, across the road from Duthie Park. It is only when I arrive there that I realise how huge it is, that there are thousands of grave markers. I walk down one avenue of gravestones after another, trying to be methodical, my search becoming increasingly haphazard as time presses on. I realise that unless I remain here for the rest of the day I am never going to find what I am looking for.

The names fly past, many of them familiar to me from the trial transcript: Wilson, Bain, Mathieson, Robertson, Munro, and it is as if the occupants of the cemetery are standing in judgement still, a conference of the dead, locked in a cycle of accusation and denial that can never be broken.

And yet it is a peaceful place, the headstones kept neat and tidy, the boundaries and borders of the graveyard planted with trees. Great lowering specimens, their leaves damp with rain, watching over the dead as they have done through centuries past and will continue to do.

I reluctantly give up the search. As I turn to leave the cemetery, I feel a pull towards a certain set of headstones, the sense that I am being recalled. I pass quickly along the row, glancing at each stone and dismissing it: not Helen, not Helen, not Helen. Then suddenly I come to a standstill. Here is another name I recognise, and why not? I have written it many times, communing with its owner nightly as we sit up late, talking.

Not Priestly, but McCrae. Because of course it is.

I stand still for a moment, then pass back through the gates to the world beyond. I know Helen is resting here somewhere, because I feel her presence. She has a whole city of guardians, looking out for her. She does not need me.

She's Been Used

YOU WALK TO THE Green by Urquhart Road, King Street, Queen Street, Broad Street to Union Street, Market Street, through the new market, down by the fish place and from there to the Green. You are carrying your brown rexine message bag. If you were to follow the same route now you would find it transformed. The market's gone, for a start. The building was demolished in 1971, its elegant Doric columns replaced with a cumbersome concrete edifice that together with the new British Home Stores building became one of those anti-landmarks, those importunate post-war follies that define a city's skyline through their sacred monsterhood.

Both are no more: closed for COVID during the first lockdown, placed in administration later that summer then bulldozed to the ground the following spring. It took ten weeks to demolish the market. There is a plan to replace and improve, a snazzy new shopping plaza with a mix of independent businesses, trendy boutiques and pop-up food outlets, though as yet the site is vacant, nothing but rubble.

The original Simpson's Market Hall opened in 1842. The roof

was constructed from open timberwork, the interior lit by gas, which when combined with the wood, straw, fabric, oil, hemp and other combustible materials on sale explains why the building went up like a powder keg forty years later.

The market you walk through was known as the new market. Erected after the fire on the original site, it had a wrought-iron roof support and as its centrepiece a fountain, made from red Peterhead granite. It appears in old photographs as a traditional pannier market, the kind where you could buy pretty much anything: buttons and tape measures, baskets, scrubbing brushes, Staffordshire figurines and Caithness paperweights, home-baked cakes, fabrics and haberdashery, hats, coats and walking boots. And fish, of course: finnan haddie and Arbroath smokies, prawns and crab and langoustines, kippers and cod. If you were new to the city and unsure of your way, the stink of fish from the market would surely guide you.

The smaller market across the way is called the Green. You purchase a dozen eggs and six oranges. You are able to tell the policeman exactly what you paid, though you are less precise about who served you and who you spoke to. From the Green you head up through Correction Wynd, coming out on to St Nicholas Lane where you call in at Raggy Morrison's, the haberdasher's. St Nicholas Lane today is a narrow, cobbled alleyway that runs behind the Royal Bank of Scotland. It is home to the Prince of Wales pub, established 1850, the Selera Malaysia Bistro, a Tui travel agents and a branch of Timpson's. I wonder if the Timpson's was once Raggy Morrison's, though from the way you describe 'crossing over' to Morrison's, there seems a good chance that the shop was not on St Nicholas Lane itself but somewhere close by.

At Morrison's you price up some tarlatan for wee Jeannie's dance costumes. Tarlatan is a cotton fabric, heavily starched to give it extra body. You are wanting to buy orange, green, red and white tarlatan, and Morrison's has all the colours except white for sevenpence a yard. You tell the shopkeeper you'll think about it, and then go out through the side door. From Netherkirkgate, just moments from where I will be staying at the Marriott almost ninety years later, you head back along Broad Street and into Queen Street, up King Street and home.

As you arrive back at the house, you see Mrs Hunt and Maggie from Webster's and Agnes Priestly, standing together talking at Webster's Corner. Mrs Priestly is wiping her eyes. You've heard her mother has been ill and so you're thinking that must be it, her mother has died. You enter the lobby of number 61 and you are just unlocking the door when Mrs Topp comes through from the yard with her basin and steps.

I'm back early, you say. I have all Jeannie's dresses to iron before five o'clock.

You go inside your house and shut the door. You do not see anything unusual about your house. You put the iron on the stove and when the metal glows red you begin to iron Jeannie's frocks, It is 2:15 or thereabouts, you remember thinking that you would be finished with the ironing by four o'clock. Wee Jeannie will be home for her tea then and there is so much to do. Your statement to DC Westland is a never-ending catalogue of shopping, cooking, cleaning, ironing, sewing and mending, washing the dishes, sweeping the lobby. You do not mention a single thing you do only for yourself. No interests outside the home, no friends that are not friends of the family, no time when you are not taking care of other people or attending to housework.

There is one other thing you do mention, and that is Richard Sutton's dark man. A beggar came by, you say, while wee Jeannie was at the table, having her tea. Dirty-looking, in need of a shave, an old man. He asked for something that you did not catch, and you remember your daughter asking you who he was. Coat open at the front and hands in his pockets, dark hair and dark clothing and, you think, a cap.

At half-past five you leave the house to take wee Jeannie to her rehearsal at the Pavilion. It is a filthy night, the rain like a lash, but you have Jeannie's costumes safe and dry in a suitcase and carry-bag. You grab your daughter's hand as you are crossing the road.

Wee Jeannie is taking part in five separate dance-numbers: the Highland dancing and the toe dancing, the star ballet and 'Dancing Night' and 'Sleepy Town'. Wee Jeannie has a talent for being on stage and so you cannot let her miss this rehearsal, not for the world and certainly not on account of Agnes Priestly. Agnes Priestly's not one to cross, her with her gossipy tongue on her, her row with Mrs Coull and now with young Mrs Joss, there's none of them good enough for Agnes Priestly and she lets them all know it. Whatever's happened with her girlie the lass herself will be to blame. Lost her money most like – that's what Alec says – lost her money and feart to come home. Then went and got herself missing on her own accord. Fell into mischief, no better than she should be. When a child is spoiled as she is there will always be trouble. Forever ringing your doorbell and making faces. Forever calling you every uncouth name under the sun.

Helen Priestly, driving you wild with her spying and calling. Yet when it comes down to it the girl weighs nothing. Limp and absent as a bird a cat's got, scant as a bundle of feathers and as easy to crush. A girl and then a nothing, folded inside a tattie sack like a bundle of cloth. You think of hell and you see the devil with his devil's grin but when you come right down to it hell is just silence. Silence and the fact of something you can never undo.

The hours when no one knows are the last hours, and they are all but done. You grip Jeannie's hand all the harder as you're crossing the Links Road, as if you're fearing the wind will take her and dash her to pieces. Your mouth is dry all through the rehearsal. The lass is gone now, you are trying to tell yourself, so whatever it was you did to her no longer matters. Once a body is dead you just have to deal with it. If you can hold your nerve until the morning you will know what to do.

Strange days like these, like a sojourn in hell, and nothing is real. The feeling of floating in midair made more persistent and disturbing through the sleeplessness that chases you like a coven o' witches through the hours of Friday night. The street outside is overflowing with searchers and with dog-handlers, policemen and gossips and the blackly curious, those drawn blindly to others' misfortune, pulled along like iron filings in its magnetic wake. The rain still hammering down and yet the crowds do not disperse until long after midnight. Long after midnight and nothing yet found, least of all the dark man, the phantom beggar. And still you lie sleepless, eyes cracked against the gaslight, against the ceaseless thumping and banging and going upstairs. Agnes Priestly holding court in her numb little parlour room, her narrow judgemental eyes now reddened from tears.

And you're wanting to say to all of them: old news. Old news, with no new ending, no happy release. Go home, you want to say to them, leave me some rest. And here is the darkened alcove with its pitiful cargo. And here is the weight in your arms laid down in the hall. These are secrets held only by walls, yet still there are those who question the notion that houses are haunted.

You lie back unsleeping, the only sound within the lightening chamber the ticking of the clock – tick-tock, tick-tock – upon the parlour mantelshelf. When the lobby explodes in shouting and screaming it is almost a relief. People will come on the instant and bear her away. And you say to your Alec oh surely the kiddie's been got and Alec says in an angry undertone what's the use in going out among hystericals like that?

At seven o'clock you do go out, to sweep the lobby. The policeman says to leave it, and you go back inside. You make breakfast for Alec and Jeannie, then a little later you open the window to speak with Mary Mearns.

Dancing and meeting, meeting and dancing. A weekend of laughing and nonsense, like voices in a nightmare. Mrs Muir and May Muir and Jean James and Charlie. The Beach Pavilion and then the Tivoli. Walking down to the Castlegate then back up the road and down again. So much up the road and down again. Chatting lightly as a goat springs, as a message boy whistles. Talking of nothing but the weather and then the dancing, those new plaid blankets they have at Metcalfe's, those pretty tablecloths. Mrs Muir asking about the wee girlie – she's heard there's been *a development* – and Alec bless him saying we're not to speak of that, the kiddie that's died you know that's our Jeannie's wee pal.

And on Castlegate Jimmy Hay's restaurant, the Athenaeum reading room, built by Simpson's same as the market with its fine arched windows. The windows glittering with wealth and with sweetmeats, wee Jeannie always liking to look in the windows to see what she can see. The lustre draws her as a magpie to treasure, as a bee to honey.

Oh mother, she says so properly, oh mam won't you look. It's like something out of a storybook like the colours inside a kaleidoscope like in a dream.

And when you come to stand by her side you see there's a dragon behind the glass, a fiery beastie all made from spun sugar and with a dusting of ice.

Ice in jagged crystals, glistening like diamonds. Like the frost on schoolhouse windows in the winter night.

A beastie winged and crowned and fanged and transparent as glass.

What a thing, don't you think? clamours wee Jeannie. Your precious girl your little dancer, you and she with less than a week now in each other's company.

Aye well, I remember a time when I was a boy, says Alec, but no one is listening.

He's a fine one, right enough, you say to your daughter. It's a wonder the many miracles to which a human hand can turn.

You touch her hair, for the faintest of seconds, and then you're glancing towards the building across the street: the Sheriff Court, grey and cold as a knife and sheer as a cliff.

Gallowglass

WHAT DOES THIS WORD mean, Susana asked him, gallowglass?

It's an old word. Irish, I think. It means a mercenary soldier. One known for being fearless on the battlefield, the kind who would rather die than be taken prisoner.

Gamblers, then, she said. Men who play cards. Not chess players. She tasted her drink. Bourbon, she had asked for, at least partly because she liked the word, and she was inclined to make choices based on words she enjoyed the sound of. As if by studying the sounds of words she would become more fluent in using them.

This had proved to be true, at least for her, though she had never mentioned it to anyone. The bourbon had the sheen of amber and burned her throat. Like drinking fire. Her fingertips tingled, like wing tips. She felt warmed right through.

Vanny Redchow had ordered the bourbon without asking questions. The two of them were seated in the smoky saloon bar of the Gallowglass, an alehouse and pie shop on a narrow side street close to the Grassmarket.

Gallow, and then glass, images that collided to make a new one, her gallowglass lean and slightly stooped, like Ivan Redchow, who was younger than her, five years younger at least, Susana thought, though it was hard to tell for sure. She felt glad to be away from the Royal Mile, where the crowds were abrasive and incautious and the bars were caves of man-made noise. The men of the press, the men of the law, the men of the office and of the shipyard and of the factory floor, all with their loud opinions and their loud insistence on being first come, first served.

The Gallowglass reminded her of the seamen's mission canteen bars preferred by her father, the aroma of gravy, the soupy yellow light, the reek of beer and onions and frying meat. A short walk from the Gallowglass, the place of execution, the square where criminals of earlier centuries were brought to be hanged. As they made their way to the alehouse, Susana had asked Ivan Redchow what he knew about the history of the Grassmarket and he told her it was famous, that tourists still came to drink at the Last Drop, the public house that stood next to the site of the public gallows, though the city's last public execution, he added, had taken place elsewhere, at the meeting point of the High Street and the George IV Bridge.

Seventy years ago, almost exactly, he said. The 21st June 1864. The man's name was George Bryce. He was convicted of murdering a nursery maid, Jeanie Seton.

Jeannie? said Susana. The coincidence seemed strange to her, a ripple of darkness, like an owl's cry.

Jeanie or Jeannie or Jennie is a common name in Scotland, Vanny insisted. She was baptised Jane in any case, Jeanie was just her nickname.

Did he kill her for love, then, this Bryce man?

He hated her. She called him a drunk and a liar in front of his girlfriend and being a drunk and a liar he could hold a grudge. Slashed her throat with a razor, in front of several witnesses. There's no doubt that he was guilty. Twenty thousand people came to his hanging – men, women, children, whole families including servants and grandparents and babes in arms. From what they wrote in the papers it was like a street party, Vanny said, or a war. The hangman's name was Askern – Askern of York. He cried after, cried from the shame of it. His profession, I mean. Being turned into a circus. That was the end of public hangings in this town.

You know a lot of history, Susana said.

It's my business to know. I want to write so people will remember.

He spoke the words simply, yet with intensity, as if these were words he whispered at night, from deep inside. The kind of words you come to know a person by, she thought, and then she asked him if he had always known he wanted to be a writer.

My father runs a hardware shop. I was supposed to take over the business. My sister Elly is in line for that now, which is lucky for my father because Elly could run an empire. I had no idea what I wanted until I was doing it. The Armstrong case was the first – he was a doctor who poisoned his wife and almost got away with it. The trial was in 1922 and I was sixteen. I used to go into the laundrette and the public bar of the Douglas, all sorts of places, collecting up the newspapers people had left behind. I couldn't afford to buy them myself, and I was desperate to read about the case, I couldn't get enough of it. Not the murders but the mystery behind them. I wanted to know what really happened. The story burned a hole in my brain. I knew then what I wanted to do and my father supported me. He even helped me get a job on the *Evening Telegraph*. I was only the post boy at first but I was keen, you see, and that matters. What about you? he said. Do you spy for the Russians?

Susana laughed and shook her head. She liked the way he asked his questions, so directly, as if he hoped to surprise or shock her into answering. I work in a shipping office, she said. I make translations of cargo manifests. And in the evenings I write.

What do you write?

Poems, she said. Stories. My cousin Marina writes for a newspaper, as you do. She does not see the point of made-up stories. She says the only stories that matter these days are the ones that are true. I once said to her that sometimes it is difficult to tell the difference. That made her angry, she said I was twisting words, playing with words deliberately to suit my purposes. But this murder is also a story, is it not?

A true one, though, said Redchow. People want to hear about it because it really happened. Like your cousin said.

Not everything you hear in the court room can be relied upon. That is what interests me most of all — the places where the story gets away from us, where it becomes something else. She was thinking about the words of the schoolboy, Richard Sutton, and of the words of the accused woman herself, the statement that had been read out in the courtroom by the policeman who had taken it from her, all those words that seemed so ordinary, so plain. Blunt words, like uncut gemstones, like the words of the scavengers and shopkeepers and slaters who had spoken before her, and yet the words spoken by Jeannie Donald described an afternoon and evening and night that had never happened.

There was a woman I used to know in Arkhangelsk, she said to

Vanny Redchow, a piano teacher who lived close to where my family lived, on the Street of Princes. When you spoke to her she sounded ordinary too, a dull little mouse of a person whose daily activities, in their minute details, seemed to take up more space inside her mind than they rightly should have done. Only when you shouldered the weight of your boredom and actually listened you would see she was crazy. That most of what came out of her mouth was a fantastic lie. Places in the town that did not exist. People who had died before the war. She spoke and spoke and spoke. And she played – she played the piano like an angel, this woman, like she was living her real life somewhere else, and sometimes she would appear on the street in front of you and tell you what it was like. You would have to really hate a child, I think, Susana added. To injure her in that way. Even her dead body.

There was trouble between them, though, wasn't there? Vanny said. Between the two families. You remember what the father said, about Mrs Donald watching his daughter as she went up the stairs.

Like an evil queen in a fairy tale, Susana thought. Like the big bad wolf.

Helen had a name for her, did she not? she said. She used to call her Coconut. I wonder what she meant.

Some childish nickname, I suppose, Vanny said, you know what kids are like. But who would murder a child because of a nickname?

We are never going to know, said Susana, and it seemed to her that this was the worst of it, that the truth of what had happened could never be known. The small moments of insult and personal injury that had grown into something unbearable, like a pile of trash that was waiting to be set alight.

Under the law, such secrets are meaningless. What has weight is a person's actions, and the order they come in. But if the secrets provoke the actions, surely they must count? She had tried to explain this to Marina, more than once. Marina had said she could return to her secrets and family photographs when the war was over.

People are dying, Marina had said, as if this was an argument that ended all others, which maybe it was, but Marina was furious with her in any case, for deciding to leave Russia. A writer in exile is voiceless, she said, a charlatan. Little by little, you will become nothing.

There was a pain inside her chest, so brittle and yet so fierce, like blackthorn twigs, like the diamond hardness of frost flowers, and as they sat there together, the two of them, the sounds of the alehouse going on around them, Susana began to think how strange it was to be here with Vanny Redchow, with this man who seemed as unmoved by her, Susana, as by a piece of old furniture, the table in front of her for example, scorched by cigarette burns and sticky with beer, stained by decades of blood and saliva and even tears.

The girl serving pies at the neighbouring table would be more of a temptation, her rust-red hair and transparent lashes, a smile he could dream about in secret and never have to reckon with. And she asked herself if this was what she had come for, after all, these moments alone with a person she barely knew. Did he attract her? Was she lonely? Charlatan, she could hear Marina saying, and she wished her cousin did not have to be so angry always, though her anger was one of the things Susana loved about her.

I should be going, said Vanny Redchow. She noted the guardedness in his eyes, the deliberate distancing. I'll walk back with you to your hotel if you like, and although she felt certain he was only being polite, Susana said yes. The streets had emptied out. The evening light was pale, the sky almost colourless, with the transparent, topaz sheen of a bolt of satin. There's something no one mentioned, Vanny was saying. If she hid the body under the sink, the way they're saying she did, how could she have carried it into the lobby without waking her husband? The three of them slept side by side, in the same bed. I would say it's impossible.

He was animated again, alight with the story, and when they arrived outside Susana's hotel he said he would come in for a drink, if she felt like it, if they served good whisky.

They serve good whisky, she said. They serve all kinds.

Your hair is so pale, he said, once they were in her room. Almost white. He cupped his hand around the back of her head, stroking with his thumb. The sensation was pleasurable, yet she felt impatient with him, knowing that he did not feel much either way about the colour of her hair, that it was all preamble.

It is normal where I come from. We are either very fair or very dark. My older brother is dark. He has a woman's eyelashes. She laughed, then kissed him on the mouth, which tasted of whisky and of the cigarette he had been smoking as they walked down the road. What is it you want with me? she said. I am old. Much older than you. What are you here for?

You're not old, he said. He drew back from her slightly, as if he was already regretting his impulse to come here, to be with her, wondering if she would be worth the trouble and thinking probably not. You know what this is, he said.

You mean do I understand that I have no claim on you? That once we leave here I will not interfere or cause a problem or search you out? That I am not crazy, like most women, she thought but did not say. The idea was too commonplace, so much a man's idea that she felt wearied simply by thinking it, yet she was relieved nonetheless, that he had brought them to this point so soon, that there would be no misunderstanding and no blame.

I feel the same way, she said, so we are agreed. She unzipped her dress. It was warm in the room. She had forgotten to open the window when she left that morning. The colourless light through the gap in the curtains made her skin look whiter than it was, carved from the shadowed hollows in this cheap little rented space beneath the eaves.

It was me all the time, she thought, the ice dragon. She sat down on the edge of the bed and drew him to her, the weight of him pressing her backwards on the scratchy blanket.

You are different, too, she said. You really do want to know things.

He did not answer, they were beyond the point of speaking, and as he pushed himself inside her she groaned, feeling lightness overtake her, a sense of relief that was only chemicals, she knew, but if they were chemicals her body needed then that was good, too. She raised her knees, drawing him deeper, and thought how good it felt, not to be caught up in thoughts of Danilo and the summer they'd spent in Karelia before the war.

Danilo, who was all set to join the Red Army. Susana had called him a fool and they had parted soon afterwards. She had thought she could never forget him, but really it was her idea of him she loved, her idea of that summer, which was gone now, finally, and some years later she would tell the critic and biographer Dorothy Bowes that her story 'The Catfish' had been inspired by someone else, a man she had seen on the road, briefly, and liked the look of.

She would meet Dorothy through her neighbour in Rubislaw, the historian and poet Erasmus Inkpen. Susana suspected that Inkpen had been sleeping with Dorothy, though she never knew for sure. She had few close friends in the city, people she could speak to honestly and deeply about her writing, and though there was something about Inkpen she did not care for, a coldness around his heart, she valued his friendship as she valued Dorothy's, and did not inquire.

'The Catfish' is about a woman who lives in a wooden hut, close to the mudflats of a tidal estuary. She falls in love with an enormous catfish, who she believes to be a prince. The woman has been disgraced, which is why she has come to live in the swamplands on the border with Finland. The story appeared in 1930 as part of an anthology of stories and memoir by Russian émigrés. It is Susana's most successful story, the only work of hers to be published in a mainstream edition. Her work did not sell well during her lifetime, and Susana was grateful to Dorothy, who first encouraged her to submit one of her stories to the short-lived but prestigious *Port Erroll Review*, who put her in touch with the independent publisher who supported her work through the years of World War 2.

Dorothy would compile Susana's bibliography as part of her doctoral thesis, and after Susana's death, she would arrange for her papers to be donated to the British Library. The files would include a number of unpublished stories, one longer prose work as well as letters from her cousin, the Soviet journalist and dissident Marina Belenko.

According to the library catalogue, the papers' current whereabouts are unknown.

Are you going to write about this? Vanny said. The trial, I mean. Do you think you'll get a story out of it?

I already am writing about it. Only not like you think. Not like in the newspapers. I want to write something that will describe how it feels, to think about a story so much it becomes part of your own. It is like searching through old photographs, she said. Sometimes one of them will speak to you, even though you did not know the person. I want you to know, she added, how much I have enjoyed your company this evening.

Same here, he said, and as he pulled on his clothes Susana thought how beautiful he was, not because he was desirable, to her or to anyone, but simply as himself: no longer quite young, in need of more money than he had in his pocket, thoughtful and intelligent and curious. Fascinated by a story for its own sake, for the mystery at the heart of it, just as she was.

For the scratch of pen on paper, which would go on, no matter what, and would always unite them. It is enough, she thought, and wished it could be so always, to know she would not see this man again and still not mind. To be able to think of someone living in the world, and writing. Without the pain and greed of what was called love but was really a kind of fear.

Good luck with your story, she said, and with everything.

You too, he said. He did not kiss her again and she was glad. After he had gone, Susana felt calmer, less vulnerable to ridicule. She tuned the radiogram to Radio Luxembourg, which was playing a programme of dance numbers. She found she was still thinking about what Vanny had said, about the cramped sleeping arrangements inside the Donalds' apartment.

Had they known about the murder, her husband and child? She knew she should rest, put the night in place as a barrier against this strange day, but sleep was slow in coming, and she found herself caught in the twisted pathways of the story she wanted to tell. The story of a dragon, as in the old legends, a dragon whose daughter has been captured and killed by human hunters. Tormented by grief, the dragon steals away one of the children of a local family. The child is never seen again, and the dragon is blamed. The people of the city, who are normally accepting of dragons, raise an army to drive her from her cave in the mountains and destroy her.

In some chapters, the dragon would be a fire-breathing beast with scales and wings; in other parts of the book, she would be a woman accused of murder who takes refuge in the mountains that surround the city. The chapters in which the dragon was a woman would be more like newspaper articles, a true account of the case that would not be so very different from Ivan Redchow's. Mrs Donald had been traduced in her home city, transformed from a flesh-and-blood woman to a creature from mythology – the beast, the fiend, the witch, the monster and of course the dragon. This process of mystification was as interesting and as frightening as the crime itself.

She folds away her newspapers and her grey-covered notebook, stifles a yawn. She is tired now, and though her mind still flocks with ideas, she is ready for sleep. She brushes her hair, walks barefoot along the corridor to use the bathroom. The sky, through the gap in the curtains, is a pearlescent grey, the closest it will come to darkness at this time of the year and as always for Susana a reminder of home.

And this is where I will leave her, where my road diverges from hers and she must go on alone. I did not come to know her as well as I wanted to, but the time we have spent together will always be precious. We think alike in many ways. I am going to miss her.

She is sleeping now, the light from the window striping her eyelids with its chalky bars. I did not say goodbye, I realise suddenly, but I do not want to wake her. I close the door softly behind me as I leave the room.

Who the Hell is Phyllis Kingdon?

THROUGH FIVE DAYS OF proceedings and dozens of witness testimonies, no one has been called to speak in the defence of Jeannie Donald. Then finally, on the morning of Saturday July 21st, a new witness appears. Her name is Phyllis Kingdon and she is nineteen years old. She is a stranger to the proceedings and to all the discussions about them. She is a stranger both to the Priestlys and to the Donalds. She is a stranger to Urquhart Road. No one in the public gallery has ever heard of her.

Phyllis claims that on the afternoon of Friday 20th April, she left her home and went to board a tram at Queen's Cross Circle. While she was waiting for the tram to arrive, she noticed a little girl in the company of a much older man. The man was in dark-like clothes, awful ragged, she said, and badly in need of a shave. He had a long coat on, open in front, and was carrying a bundle. The child was dressed in a blue frock, a tammy and black stockings. She seemed awful scared, said Phyllis. That's how come I noticed her – because she looked scared.

When the Lord Justice Clerk asks her what time all this happened,

Phyllis says she happened to hear a clock strike, and when she looked up at the clock on the corner of Queen's Road she saw it was half-past three. She would not have given much of a thought to any of this, had she not heard the broadcast description of Helen Priestly that same evening, at the Capital Picture House. She telephoned to the police the following morning, and gave her statement.

Phyllis Kingdon expresses surprise that she was not called as a witness. She relates how, at the encouragement of her mother, she presented herself at office of a solicitor this very Friday, offering her evidence.

And what was it that brought your attention back to the little girl you say you saw at Queen's Cross Circle? asks the Lord Justice Clerk.

By reading in the paper Mrs Donald's statement about the beggar — it coincided with the same beggar as I saw, at Queen's Cross.

There's that beggar again, the dark man who will not be banished, no matter that he is a fantasy, no matter how fake he is. The policeman who took Phyllis Kingdon's statement has only a vague memory of speaking to her. They were exceptionally busy that day, he recalls. Every murder investigation brings with it a heap, a veritable *farrago* of false leads, mistaken sightings, spurious information of all kinds. The false reports received in the course of the Priestly investigation numbered more than two hundred.

Every report is investigated, the policeman insists. Even if most of them turn out to be dead ends.

Phyllis Kingdon is the ultimate red herring. Did she really see a dark man? I somehow doubt it. And yet something makes her persist with this cheap bit of fiction. Is she looking for excitement, a chance to get in on the case that is the talk of the town? Still, I cannot help feeling sorry for her, at least a little. It cannot have been a pleasant experience, being subjected to such detailed questioning when everyone in the court room – everyone who mattered, anyway – would already have known that her account was at best a fantasy, at worst a deliberate lie.

I don't believe that Phyllis lied. I think that like Ricky Sutton she landed herself with a story she couldn't get out of. I am sure a part of her really believed that she did see the beggar. Phyllis wanted to be important, and for a moment she was. I am only sorry, Phyllis, that I can't paint a fuller picture of you here. There are no photographs for me to look at, no descriptions in the newspapers, nothing. I must imagine you for myself, then: slightly ungainly and rather tall, dark-haired, with a tendency to clasp and unclasp your hands. I see you wearing a hat – a blue pudding-basin hat, trimmed with a velvet ribbon. A hat not unlike Mrs Donald's, in fact.

You are overcome by the solemnity of the occasion. You had not expected to come face to-face with Mrs Donald, for one thing, and it shocks you a little, how ordinary she is, the kind of woman you might find yourself standing behind in the cinema queue or at the green-grocer's. You wonder briefly what it must be like, to have everything about yourself laid out for everyone to see, put on display like so many unwanted items of clothing at a bring-and-buy sale. The idea makes you uncomfortable, and there's a part of you that regrets your part in the proceedings. Luckily for you, you'll be on the train home in a couple of hours, and with a tale to tell.

I wonder what will become of you, once your moment on this lighted stage is over and played. Your story is complete nonsense, of course. If you had been following the trial in more detail, you would know that Helen Priestly was dead before you even left your house to go into town.

One detail that will never leave me: the Priestlys' Co-op number – 21657 – imprinted in blue ink on Helen's right palm. The Lord Advocate, in his summing up, describes how Helen would have been given the torn-off carbon copy of the receipt when she bought the fourpenny half loaf, that she would have been clutching it in her hand as she hurried home.

Normand makes a powerful case. He stresses the importance of the material evidence that links Helen Priestly to Jeannie Donald: the fibres in the sack, the hair from the hairbrush, the traces of blood and intestinal bacteria on Helen's underwear that are identical with traces found on washcloths in the Donalds' kitchen. The circumstantial evidence – Jeannie's bogus trip to the market, the non-existent beggar, the Donalds' lack of participation in the search for Helen – these things, he admits, are of limited evidential value in themselves, but when considered alongside the physical evidence, the certainty of Jeannie's guilt becomes overwhelming.

Daniel Blades, summing up for the defence, is left with little to say. No normal woman, he insists, would be able to commit such a heinous act, and then continue about her usual business as if nothing had happened. When he remarks on the margin of doubt left by Professors Glaister and Smith in their analysis of the material evidence, the strain inflicted upon his argument is almost tangible.

Lord Aitchison is having none of it. He insists that the jury should not dwell on the horror of the act, which he describes as 'a crime of almost unspeakable cruelty and wickedness, committed upon a young and innocent child who had done no harm to anyone in the world'. It is not their job to ascribe a motive to the defendant; they must simply decide whether they believe the woman in the dock is the murderer of Helen Priestly.

'We cannot see into the mind of another,' he adds. 'The springs of action are hidden. All we can do is judge by what men and women do.'

The jury retire to consider their verdict at 18:01. They return to the court room less than twenty minutes later, at 18:18.

Guilty

[From the *Dundee Evening Telegraph*,
Tuesday 24th July 1934]

No one who was present in the High Court of Justiciary, Edinburgh, last night will ever forget the tense scene when Mrs Donald was sentenced to death for the murder of Helen Priestly at Aberdeen on Friday April 20th.

Mrs Donald, whose wonderful self-control had been the salient feature of the six-days trial, broke down completely the moment she heard the foreman of the jury utter the word 'Guilty'.

She crumpled up as if all the strength had gone from her body. Two or three low moans – little more than vocal sighs – were heard, and she slumped heavily to her right against the shoulder of the stalwart policeman beside her in the dock.

She buried her face in his sleeve, and from that moment onwards seemed quite insensible of what was happening in court.

Her young woman attendant, who had been warned earlier in the proceedings to take a seat immediately behind the accused, rose and leaned over the rear of the dock, seeking to administer comfort to Mrs Donald.

Her words and ministrations had no effect on the prisoner, who seemed to be in a stupor. The attendant motioned for a glass of water, and one of the court officers hastened over with the carafe that is placed beside the witness box.

Between them, they forced the glass to Mrs Donald's lips, but it was impossible to say whether or not she actually had a sip of the water.

Meanwhile the clerk of the court was recording the verdict, and when he had finished he read it over to the jury.

Mr A. G. Erskine Hill, Advocate Depute, immediately moved for sentence.

Mrs Donald was still huddled up in the dock, and when the policemen were about to raise her to her feet for her sentence the clerk of the court vigorously signalled to them to allow her to remain seated.

There was a painful silence as the Lord Justice Clerk, Lord Aitchison, reached for the black cap, which was concealed below or behind him.

Bringing the awesome, three-cornered object into view, his Lordship held it just resting upon his wig with his left hand, and, leaning forward, uttered the following words in a low voice which betrayed his emotion:

'In respect of the verdict just given, I, Lord Justice Clerk, decern and adjudge you, Jeannie Ewen or Donald, to be carried from the Bar to the Prison of Edinburgh, thence to be forthwith transmitted to the Prison of Aberdeen; therein to be detained till the thirteenth day of August next, and upon that day, between the hours of eight and ten o'clock forenoon, within the walls of the said Prison of Aberdeen, by the hand of the Common Executioner, to be hanged by the neck by a gibbet until you be dead; and your body thereafter to be buried within the walls of the said Prison of Aberdeen; and I ordain your whole moveable goods and gear to be inbrought and escheat to his Majesty's use, which is pronounced for Doom.'

It is highly probable that Mrs Donald never heard a word the Lord Justice Clerk uttered She seemed quite insensible.

To most people in court, in fact, the sentence was inaudible, especially the latter half of it, as Lord Aitchison's voice dropped lower and lower until he was speaking scarcely above a whisper.

As soon as sentence was pronounced Mrs Donald was assisted to her feet by the policeman, the trap was lifted and, half leaning on them, half carried, she was borne from the dock to the cells below.

The Lord Justice Clerk, addressing the members of the jury, remarked that that closed their duty and his in that most painful case. It only remained for him to thank them for the undivided attention they had given to the case from the start.

In discharging the jurors, his Lordship said that in respect that the trial had lasted for a week and had necessarily imposed upon them a very heavy strain he would give a direction that they be exempt from jury service during the next five years.

It had been expected that the jury's absence would be a long one, and their return in 17 ½ minutes took most people by surprise.

There was a rush into court when the bell sounded, and people snatching a hasty cup of tea in the buffet in the basement scurried upstairs, some of them without paying their bills – for the waitresses had left everything and run upstairs too.

Outside in the High Street, whither news of the verdict and sentence had travelled like wildfire, a large gathering of women, with a sprinkling of men, gathered outside Parliament House.

More than half an hour elapsed however, without sign of the condemned woman appearing, and the crowd began to filter away.

Shortly before seven o'clock, a cream-coloured police van swung into the square, and the crowd streamed across the street in its wake. They jockeyed for position of vantage to see Mrs Donald leave the building.

Minutes fled past. The crowd swelled, but there was no sign of Mrs Donald. A policeman turned the corner from the police office about 50 yards away and gave a signal.

Another policeman appeared from the entrance to the High Court. The crowd realised that they had been duped. Mrs Donald had been removed from the building by another exit.

[From the *Aberdeen Press and Journal*,
Monday 6th August 1934]

DEATH SENTENCE COMMUTED
Mrs Donald faces life imprisonment
Lord Provost takes news to cell

The announcement of the reprieve of Mrs Donald, who was found guilty of the murder of Helen Priestly at 61 Urquhart Road on Friday April 20th and condemned to death at the High Court of Justiciary on July 23rd caused general surprise in Aberdeen and throughout the north of Scotland on Saturday, coming, as it did, a few hours after the news had been published that the machinery had been set in motion for an appeal against the conviction.

During the week-end it was the chief topic of conversation among all classes of the community. The question that was most in the public mind was whether or not the appeal would be proceeded with in view of the change in the situation caused by the reprieve and the commutation of the sentence into penal servitude for life.

Last night the Edinburgh agents declined to make any statement whether the appeal on behalf of Mrs Donald would go on. It is expected that an announcement will be made today.

Undoubtedly the situation is without precedent in the history of the criminal law of Scotland, as it was only in 1926 that the Criminal Appeal Act was passed. Never before has there been a case in which the official communication announcing a respite of the execution of the capital sentence and a letter intimating appeal, or a notice of intention to appeal against the conviction of the person reprieved been delivered by the same post, for it was stated by Mrs Donald's Edinburgh agents on Friday night that the appeal notice had just been posted to the Justiciary office in Edinburgh.

The official letter announcing to the Lord Provost of Aberdeen that Mrs Donald had been reprieved was sent from the Scottish Office, Whitehall, London, and reached the Town House, Aberdeen by the first postal delivery on Saturday.

When the Lord Provost arrived at the Town House shortly before noon and found the letter awaiting him, he at once made arrangements, in accordance with his official duty as Chief Magistrate of the city, to communicate its terms to the condemned woman in Aberdeen Prison.

Accompanied by the Town Clerk and a Town Sergeant, the Lord Provost went by motor car to Craiginches, where he was received by the governor of the prison, Mr W. A. Chisholm, and conducted to Mrs Donald's cell.

The Lord Provost read the letter from the Secretary of State, and that done immediately returned to the Town House.

The letter was in the following terms:

With reference to the case of Mrs Jeannie Ewen or Donald, now lying under sentence of death at His Majesty's Prison, Aberdeen, I have to inform you that under full consideration I have felt justified in advising His Majesty to respite the execution of the capital sentence with a view to the commutation to penal servitude for life.

Mr A. Donald, the prisoner's husband, was informed of the reprieve at the earliest possible moment. He and his little girl, Jeannie, have been staying with his father at Banff.

Mr Edward R. Yule, Mrs Donald's Aberdeen agent, communicated the news by telephone to Mr Donald's sister, who is employed in a shop there. Miss Donald immediately went home, and gave her brother and her father the tidings that Mrs Donald had been reprieved.

A *Press and Journal* representative called at the home of Mrs Ewen, the mother of Mrs Donald, at Glassel. He was met at the door of the house by Mrs Donald's youngest sister, and the smile on her face suggested that the news of the reprieve had reached her. She told him that they had already been informed that their sister had been reprieved.

He was unable to see Mrs Ewen, who since the arrest of her daughter has been in ill health and was in bed on Saturday, but he was told that she was overjoyed at the news that her daughter was not to die.

Another sister, Mrs Mackie, resides at Marchnear, Glassel. Mrs Mackie had not been previously told of the reprieve, and when the *Press and Journal* representative informed her she seemed stunned for a moment, and it was some time before the full import dawned on her. She made no comment, except to say that 'so far, the news was very good'.

[From the *Aberdeen Press and Journal*
Thursday 16th August 1934]

WHY WAS REPRIEVE GRANTED?
Mystifying aspects of the Donald case

We continue to receive many letters relating to the Donald case and the events subsequent to the conviction. The majority of them are inquiring why Mrs Donald was reprieved. That is a matter known only to the Secretary for Scotland and his advisers. No official reason has been given or is likely to be given.

One statement has been made to the effect that the public sentiment is set against the hanging of a woman in any conceivable circumstances. That certainly is not the case. It would be a deplorable thing if public sentiment ever reached such a point – so long, that is, as capital punishment remains a lawful sentence. Such a rigid sex discrimination would be a dangerous doctrine.

Other inquirers are puzzled to understand why the reprieve was announced before the appeal was heard. Notice of intention to appeal, it will be recalled, was posted the night before the announcement of the reprieve. Then a short time later came the announcement that the appeal had been withdrawn.

An appeal in a murder case is not lodged against the sentence. There is only one sentence which the court has to impose on conviction – death. Commutation of the sentence rests with the Royal prerogative alone.

An appeal is launched against the conviction, either on some such ground as that the weight of evidence was against the jury's finding, or that there was misdirection by the judge to the jury, or some vital point omitted by the judge which should have been brought to the attention of the jury, or on some purely legal flaw.

In short, an appeal is lodged in the hope of getting the conviction quashed, the convicted person maintaining that the jury's verdict was wrong and unjust.

The granting of a reprieve does not in any way remove the grounds of the appeal that the conviction itself should be quashed. The convict's contention, conveyed by the lodging of an appeal, that there has been a miscarriage of justice cannot be lessened by the mere amelioration of the punishment.

The trial of Mrs Donald created in the mind of many people the conclusion that while the jury justly came to the conclusion that she was guilty of the murder of Helen Priestly, she had not committed what has come to be known as murder in the first degree. In other words, she may have had no intention to kill, the actual killing being committed when she thought the child was already dead.

Strangely enough, no such defence was put forward by Mrs Donald at the trial. It was the Crown prosecution itself which brought to light the possibility of such a defence.

In all these mystifying circumstances, therefore, it is not surprising that there have been persistent rumours that while still under sentence of death, Mrs Donald confessed herself guilty of the child's death.

Inquiries have been made by the *Press and Journal* with a

view of ascertaining the truth of the report. It is impossible to get official confirmation in view of the secrecy imposed by the authorities in such circumstances.

When our London representative put the question to the Scottish Office last night, he was informed that it is a rigid rule that nothing of this nature is given out.

Thus, while the inquiry has yielded no confirmation, it is equally true that no official denial has been given.

In all the circumstances of this extraordinary case, it would clear up a conscience-troubling situation, particularly in reference to the reprieve, if, in spite of this rule, an official statement could be issued to the public.

Mrs Donald is now in Duke Street Prison, Glasgow, where she arrived yesterday to serve her sentence of penal servitude for life.

Her last half hour in Aberdeen was spent in comparative freedom as she had the privilege of a walk along about a mile of streets on the way from Craiginches prison to the Joint Station.

Although accompanied by two wardresses, she was not handcuffed, and she and her escort were in civilian dress.

This ruse to avoid public notice succeeded, for none of the many people passed on the way recognised her as the Urquhart Road murderess.

About six o'clock in the morning, the wicket in the gate of the prison at Craiginches was opened, and Mrs Donald walked out into the world again. She was dressed in the dark blue costume which she wore during her trial in the High Court.

By her side walked a wardress, and a little behind was another wardress.

A *Press and Journal* representative who was on the station platform watching the departure of the 6:45 train for Glasgow immediately recognised Mrs Donald as she passed chatting with the first wardress.

Several travellers were on the platform, while there were several porters hurrying about with luggage, but no one took any notice of the three women, indeed, there was nothing about their appearance to attract attention.

Mrs Donald's departure from Aberdeen was kept a secret even from the railway officials. There was no carriage reservation, and after one of the wardresses had been directed by a porter to the Glasgow section, the three entered a third-class compartment.

When the train left, they had the compartment to themselves. Mrs Donald was seated between the wardresses facing the engine.

Part 4
Jeannie in the Afterlife

[From the *Aberdeen Evening Express*,
Monday 24th July 1944]

MRS DONALD RELEASED

Mrs Jeannie Donald has completed her sentence for the murder on April 20th 1934 of Helen Priestly of 61 Urquhart Road, Aberdeen and has been released from prison.

After trial at the High Court of Justiciary in Edinburgh she was condemned to death on July 23rd 1934. Her execution was fixed for 14th August of that year at Aberdeen but the capital sentence was commuted to penal servitude for life while she was awaiting execution at Craiginches prison at Aberdeen.

The Escape Artist

ON THE NIGHT OF Wednesday 20th September 1896, the People's Palace theatre on Aberdeen's Bridge Street was destroyed in a terrible fire. The catastrophe began to unfold during the evening performance, when parts of the stage scenery were set alight by the gas jets that powered the stage lighting. Fire quickly spread to the curtain. Within less than an hour, the entire building was in flames.

When the audience realised what was happening, there was a mass stampede. Seven people perished while trying to escape, and several more died from their burns in the following days. Given the speed and ferocity of the blaze, most people agreed it was a miracle there were not more fatalities.

Two years later, a new theatre opened its doors on the site of the old. The Palace, which retained the original facade, cost £15,000 to build, and seated 1,800 patrons in a two-tier auditorium. Charlie Chaplin performed there, so did Harry Lauder. The young Winston Churchill – then a Liberal – addressed a political rally there. In 1911, the Palace was sold to the Rank cinema chain. Much later it became a ballroom and then a nightclub, which it still is today.

Bridge Place is just up from Aberdeen station. Aside from the dumpsters and the graffiti, the area looks more or less as it would have done in Jeannie Donald's day. The Palace Theatre is vast, its Victorian detailing still more or less intact. Like much of Aberdeen's architecture, the building is imposing without being inviting, though it is difficult not to admire its low-key elegance, its air of muted disdain for the modern world.

In 1909, the Palace played host to the legendary stage magician and escapologist Harry Houdini. Houdini had come north to pay homage to his lifelong inspiration Henry James Anderson, the stage magician popularly known as the Great Wizard of the North.

On July 1st, to celebrate his arrival in the city, Houdini performed a daring underwater escape in Aberdeen harbour. The sea on that day was so rough he was told it would be impossible to make the dive in the bay as originally planned. Not wanting to disappoint the enormous crowd that had gathered along the waterfront, the great magician insisted he would go ahead regardless, eventually entering the sea from within the harbour enclave where the conditions were marginally less treacherous.

Newspaper photographs show him heavily manacled, arms bound behind his back with a padlocked chain. Disappearing beneath the waves, Houdini resurfaced in less than a minute, handcuffs held triumphantly above his head. Wild applause broke out along the quay and continued until the tugboat, *John McConnachie*, dropped him safely ashore at Pocra jetty, Footdee, where the Handcuff King jumped into a cab and disappeared into the city.

Among the crowd on the jetty stand two young brothers. The boys are twins, thirteen years old, the sons of a motor mechanic from Banff, a handsome but chilly fishing town to the north of Aberdeen. Banff's white sands face the arctic, the granite cottages along the harbour front gaze straight out on to the icy waters of the North Sea. The boys have travelled south to the city just a handful of times, to visit relatives of their mother and once to a mackerel fair: pie stalls and roasted chestnuts, troupes of dancers and fish-headed jugglers jouncing and singing their way through the cobbled streets. A land of goods yards and department stores, of tankers vast as countries in their rain-swept berths.

Today they will see something special, or so their da says, a miracle they will remember as long as they live. Slipping and sliding on the leather upholstery, they sit in the back of one of the motor cars their father has a share in. Their mother and aunt and their cousin Caren have already left for the city on the morning train. Their Aunt Mildred is from Edinburgh. She and their mother are treating themselves to a slap-up lunch at Hay's in the Castlegate. Then they're going shopping. They are not interested in the escapologist. They believe his act is fakery, a way of extracting money from the poor and credulous.

Credulous – that was Mildred's word. Alec looked it up in the dictionary in the Banff town library. It means gullible, or stupid. But it must be Mildred who is stupid because Houdini's act is real.

Mildred's twelve-year-old daughter Caren does not look like anyone they know. She has eyes like marbles, grey-green, and will grow up to be a beauty, or so her mother says. Mildred dresses her daughter in frocks and petticoats like a spoiled princess, though Caren does not care much for fancy dresses, Caren likes playing at soldiers like anyone else. Mildred's forever on at them for getting her filthy, threatening to keep her inside, but Caren won't have it, she'll winkle her way out the window, run wild along the backs with the rest of the laddies. She's a picture is Caren.

Alec remembers standing beside his brother, craning his neck to catch first sight of the escapologist and thinking about his cousin's shining, pixie-led face reflected in the polished glass of Falconer's department store. Alec never realised what his brother felt for her until they went to inform his uncle that they were getting married, his brother new and bright in his uniform and Caren a whip-tongued lassie fresh out of school.

Mildred was horrified as they'd known she would be but what could she do, there was a war on.

Alec is no longer thirteen, he is forty-eight. He knows that he is dying, and what is it folk say about dying, about your whole life flashing before your eyes? And though Alec has never believed that, never believed in God if you come right down to it, he cannot resist the force of this slow unravelling, this careful unrolling of memories and sights and knowledge he believed was gone forever.

Vanished like his brother. Into the motor trade like their father and then overseas.

Not because of you, brother, he had said to Alec over the telephone when he broke the news. Not you and not your trouble, neither. But

I'll no' have a son of mine joined up to this new war. Alec told him he should go, and with his blessing, that he was best off out of it. He's free, Alec thought, and the gladness rose from him like a kite-tail and with the same kind of tug. The bonds that tied them were tighter than an ocean could split, and wherever went his brother, there he was also. Those who lacked twin brothers might laugh at his fancy, but what was that to him?

And so it seemed like it was meant, when he met his Jeannie, that the year of their birth was shared if not quite the month. Him waiting a decade and more after Caren and thinking never, not for a fortune would he think of another, for what would be the point? Then came this woman with the eyes of a hawk and the strength of an ox. Green eyes flecked with gold, and seeing everything. If Caren were the wind, racing along the backs, then Jeannie was the frost. The frost glittering upon all the doorsteps before a soul was awake.

You'll catch your death if you don't come in, she had said to him, when they first met. You can dry your coat on the boiler and I'll brew a pot of tea.

Why was he even there at that swanky hotel? A pal of his from the barber's, getting married. Alec walking the two-mile from Banchory station, caught in a sudden downpour that might've sunk the Ark. And he should have said no – though the offer of tea was kind, he had a toast to raise, over there across the way where the singing was coming from. But there was something in the way their eyes met, like magnets making contact and then refusing to part. Not love, he had come to believe, so much as fate. And what is fate but time seen as a line, chalked as plain as your name on the ground in front of you?

What is to be done, Alec?
What is to be done?
What is to be done.

Thirteen years old, and the boys raise stares wherever they go because of their likeness, a fact of their lives they cannot escape and do not wish to. Their twinhood is simply a part of them, like an arm or a foot. They use it sometimes to their advantage, to play tricks on their schoolmasters mostly, though as they grow older their amusement at such duplicity goes into decline.

One of the good things about being in a crowd is how quickly Alec and his brother become unremarkable. They are here to see the escapologist, like everyone else, and for once in their short young lives no one looks at them twice.

The noise of the crowd is like a bubbling cauldron, like embers waiting for a blast from the bellows to set them ablaze. There is no need for them to strain their voices, to make themselves heard. Each brother feels the other's excitement as a tension in the stomach, a flutter of breath. They are magic mad, the boys, ever since the coming of the conjuror to the Theatre Royal in Banff the year they turned ten. As the curtains opened, the magician spoke not a word, and yet the way he stood, his face made angular and threatening in the glow of the footlights, made him appear as a visitor from another world.

He picked out a girl from among the audience – yellow-haired and scrawny, Alec thought, though his uncle, sitting beside him, sat up straighter at the sight of her and the applause when she returned to her seat was like a pounding waterfall. The girl did nothing but pick out cards, which with a wave of the conjuror's wand were turned into roses. What Alec remembered was the look on her face – like she'd been given the moon, like she had been transformed as well as the flowers, and as the crowd spills, pours, froths along the jetty like a thousand-headed beast, Alec sees his cousin Caren as she might have appeared in the glow of those same footlights: a queen apparent, conjured from a garage man. A princess in disguise.

Did they tell one another I love you? The words were foreign to them as garlic butter or curried mutton, a flavour they were unused to and did not much like. Their fellow feeling was a different matter, a fact of their lives that once brought into being could never be altered.

His lass, he used to say, back before she was with child, and the words would make her eyes shine with a warmth like the glow of horse chestnuts among the autumn leaves. Treasure, if you knew where to look for it, and Alec had known. What he'd not guessed was her sorrow for the bairn she had miscarried. The child they'd had was the light of her days, but the loss of the other had opened a void that nothing could fill.

She had not told him of the loss for several days.

The babby's not coming, she had said then, at last. The Lord called him back.

The Lord, she said, as if the god she still had faith in were a well-to-do neighbour of theirs, the kind who'd call around and offer you his cast-offs like he was doing you a favour. Alec couldn't be doing with God, but his lass still let herself hope that if she said the right words and said them nicely then the Lord might give them back what he had taken away.

Her eyes were dry but the rims were reddened. Her hands clenched and unclenched, the knuckles raw from scrubbing, and as he lay dying Alec found himself remembering those words of hers, the words the policeman had written down in his crabby black hand. *We had just the one child. I never had any more.* And each time his Jeannie saw their wee one playing with another girl she would think of the lost one, their girlie's baby brother, and the world would darken around her to a foretaste of hell.

What is to be done, Alec?
What is to be done.

Long ago before the war, the Christmas of the conjuror, the brothers had imagined for themselves how they might become magicians, how their twinhood might make them their fortune, not as freaks of nature but as *illusionists*. How they might travel from town to town, taking their magic with them, earning their keep. A life of draughty theatres and freezing town halls, the wheeze of gas fires in the overpriced back bedrooms of seaside boarding houses.

Alec could well imagine the hardships, yet for a while at least he allowed himself to dream of that way of being, of something other than a life spent behind the counter of a butcher's shop, or selling sewing machines, or mending motors and hiring them out like his uncle and father. Forever in service to those with fuller purses or better fortune.

A travelling magician, with a girl who loved him. What distances might you cross, what hopes fulfil?

Were they simply not good enough, or did they not try hard enough?

The brothers' passion was real, but what was passion when put through the mangle of ordinary life? The brothers' natural dexterity, their eye for the look of a thing and the feel of a thing, their lightness of touch – the kind of talents that are hard to put a name to, until they find a new name such as barbering, or engineering, and before that the mending of rifles and the careful setting-to-rights of blown-out machines.

You always think there will be time, but there never is. The glitter of fairground lights, though, the sweet groaning of the hurdy-gurdy and the scent of fried onions. Alec gazes up at the window, waiting. There is the sound of the rain outside but there is another sound, too, from further away – the sound of circus music.

The crowd on the jetty begins to stir – a thousand-headed snake. The ancient tugboat, with its precious cargo, is drawing nearer.

Will he really do it, do you think? his brother murmurs. Alec hears his voice clearly in spite of the din. He can feel his own heart fluttering, his breath coming in gasps as they gaze out over the grey water, the lumpy great sea with its angry white crests, like foam flecked across the snarling lips of an irritable post horse.

July, and yet the water is maddened, perilous as it will be in November.

But if the ocean is determined the magician is more so. For here he is at last, bare-chested, arms chained, wind clawing at his hair. From this distance he could be anyone, yet still the crowd cheers. He drops from the side feet first, plummeting into the harbour like a granite boulder, and Alec finds he does not want to imagine it, the icy shock of the water, the drowning weight of the chains, dragging him down.

A GRANITE SILENCE

The crowd sighs with excitement, united in a terror that is not true terror but a gaudy facsimile. Everyone watching believes the magician's escape is a foregone conclusion – who would attempt such a feat, if the risk of death were real? But Alec, who has read every article about Houdini he can lay his hands on, understands that the risk is what drives him, the knowledge that each performance might be his last.

Every artist should be willing to die for his art, the magician has said, the escape artist most of all. How can we know the value of freedom unless we are prepared to give up our lives in pursuit of it?

Alec shivers. He feels the pressure of his brother's fingers, clutching his elbow. They are here together, as they are always together. There is nothing they can do but wait and see.

Houdini is gone for scarcely a minute but it seems an age. The thudding of the clock, its weights and coils, a mute moment when the world threatens to spin out of kilter and never regain its axis, or never completely.

He rises from the depths like a merman, like a sea monster, the silver chains that were used to bind him held high above his head. Bright droplets of water fountain about him as he waves, briefly framing his face in a halo of stars.

Long live the king! Long live the handcuff king!

The crowd is exuberant, vindicated. They have got what they came for and Alec, who will not live long now, still remembers the wonder of it, this resurrection from the land of Davy Jones. Like Christ, the magician had vanished from the land of his people and been born anew.

If only it had been the same with that wee girlie.

Alec had not understood all the science, all those medical words, though he had sat with the newspapers afterwards trying to make sense of it. How the child had something wrong with her that had caused her to faint. To seem dead, but not be dead. If left to herself then she would have been well again, eyes opening and letting the light in like frosted buds of spring.

Scabbed knees and sticky fingers and dirty-socked toes, same as any other child, same as their own. Up and off to the supper table, telling her tales. *The ogre-lady had it in for me, the dragon downstairs, ol' Missus Coconut.* And who would mind what she said, it were nothing but child's talk, and did no harm.

Another life, like the life of a magician, never to be his. He can still feel the ache, these ten years later, the weight in his heart that can never be shifted, the murderous downward drag of iron chains.

What is to be done, Alec?
What is to be done?
What is to be done.

Would ye look at that? says his brother. Would ye look at that.

He punches Alec on the shoulder then raises his hand. His brother is waving, waving with everyone else at the creature in the sea, the black head bobbing like a lifebuoy in between the waves as the crew of the *John McConnachie* sail to his rescue. The crowds gathered along the jetty are in glorious uproar. A ladder is lowered, and as the demigod grasps the rung the cheering intensifies.

Cold day for it, right enough, says Alec's uncle, and the two men chuckle. For them the magician's daring exploit is merely a stunt, a means of passing an hour or two, a break from routine. As Houdini scrambles to his feet on the deck of the tugboat their minds are already turning to the snug saloon bar of the Baltic Tavern: the fugged-up windows, the soft click of pool cues, the amber taste of beer.

They hurry the boys along the promenade towards the beach road, not wanting to be delayed in the general exodus, though for Alec the pace of their departure is like an act of robbery: too soon and too fast.

The feeling of living in the here and now is headier than beer, and one he will not experience again until the start of the war. Da, wait, he says sullenly, too quietly to be heard. How can he ask his father to wait if he cannot explain the reason he is supposed to be waiting? His brother's presence beside him is a steadying arm, though the two do not speak. The thought that they are the same – that their hearts are thrumming in unison – is like a call to arms. His brother knows how he is feeling, and as they enter into the Castlegate he feels his spirits lift.

The boys wait outside on the street while their father and uncle go into the restaurant to fetch the women. Alec stares absently into the lighted window of the delicatessen, his eyes ranging at random over the stacked packets of Indian tea, the jars of honey and handmade preserves, the cured meats and smoked cheeses, the chocolate gingers on their decorated platters, the exotic names and alien scents, the brightly coloured packaging.

At the centre of the window stands a work of art, a sparkling, impossible creature that at first makes no sense to him, its glittering volumes and edges only gradually resolving themselves into a shape he can comprehend.

An ice dragon, he thinks, though in fact the beast is made from spun sugar, a masterpiece that seems the more miraculous for being impermanent.

Would you eat him all up, if you could? says a voice beside him, and when he turns to look he sees it is his cousin Caren, gazing into the window in her Sunday dress. Her hair, so neatly pinned that morning, is becoming unravelled. There is a flea-shaped smear of chocolate at the corner of her mouth.

Because you could, you know, she says. The whole beastie is made from sugar, even his crown.

Crystalline skeleton, honeycomb wings. An orange-red conflagration of translucent caramel. The dragon roars as if in protest at being so sweetly diminished.

Alec shakes his head.

Naw, he says flatly. I wouldnae.

Caren laughs and ruffles his hair, her unthinking touch a gift that scorches his soul.

They'll be out in a minute, she says. Your da an' mine are going down the Baltic, so youse are coming with us to the indoor market.

I don't mind, Alec says, and all at once it is true. All at once there is nowhere else he would rather be.

The fates were not kind to him, him and his Jeannie, though he has stopped believing in fate, as he refuses any more to believe in God. You make your own fate, his da used to say, although the passage of time has taught him that the effort is futile. Misdirection, that's all it is, Alec thinks, as he waits for her. Tricking God into looking the other way.

Alec cannot understand why God keeps creeping into his thoughts like this. Only that he is dying, and a dying man's resolve is easy to shake.

She never once allowed him to visit in all these years, nor their lassie neither. Prison's no place for a child, she wrote, though she seemed glad to have the photographs: wee Jeannie on the harbourside at Banff, where she spent her summers with Mildred even after his uncle died. She's all I've got left, Mildred would say, flinging the words at Alec like she blamed him still for everything, for her Caren going overseas, and all because of a vile mistake that were never even his.

Not that he minded wee Jeannie being out of the city. The crisp salt air and the vanishing horizons, the lush high teas her auntie put on, the frocks and books and other gewgaws she would insist on buying her. Wee Jeannie had given up her dancing when her mother went away. Out of grief, Alec believed, though the lassie herself insisted that were nowt to do with it. She was through with dancing, that's all, bored and out of patience with the hours of practice. She preferred to study her lessons instead. She wanted to get a job. She wanted to travel.

Such a meek wee girlie on the face of it, and yet she had a head on her, a way of knowing her mind that came straight from her mother. Now with her posting in the WRNS she was travelling every which way: America, Denmark, Amsterdam and devil take the U-boats. Every other week she was packing her suitcase and yet still there came her letters, *darling Dad*.

She never spoke much about her mother, yet Alec knew she thought of her. He knew it from that faraway look, which had more to do with thoughts of home than with sailing away.

*

The day he heard his wife was not to hang was like a slow exhalation, the sound you might make when you're in seawater out of your depth and about to drown. When you're struggling in the depths and your heart is bursting. When suddenly the chains are off and you can breathe your fill. And as the present day draws in towards darkness it comes to him that it was his Jeannie all along who had been the escape artist. The handcuff king had played his games with death, but they were games he knew the rules of, and for a dozen years and more he had been death's master.

His Jeannie had walked through the shadow of death and then come back into the light. The black cap had been lifted, and in another hour or less he would see her once more.

The Lord is my shepherd, he thinks distractedly. The light is all but gone from the sky and he is growing tired. He thinks of his brother, who would be by his side even now were it not for the war. He could not get a passage, or Caren would not allow him to risk the U-boats and Alec tries not to mind. From his chair by the window he can see the moon rise. The same moon, he likes to remind himself, that his brother will similarly gaze on in eight hours' time. He recalls the feeling of his brother's shoulder, so close against his, as they sat open-mouthed on the plush velvet seats and watched the Christmas conjuror perform his miracles.

He had turned playing cards into roses, Alec remembers. He had taken a silver cylinder from a wooden casket, made it rise like a miniature zeppelin into the air.

Ladies and gentlemen, the riches of Araby. A priceless treasure from the tomb of the Pharaohs, this object remains a mystery to the entire Western world . . .

He turned his hands so his thumbs faced upwards, the silver cylinder hovering in front of his face. Alec strained forward in his seat, hoping and trying to see how the trick was done. There were no cords, no hidden mechanisms, or none that he could see. Alec grinned in what he realised was pure delight, he could not help himself. When he turned to look at his brother, he saw he was smiling, too.

A Model Prisoner

JEANNIE DONALD IS RELEASED from prison on 24th July 1944, almost exactly ten years to the day since being convicted. Alec Donald is terminally ill with cancer, and Jeannie is granted her freedom on grounds of compassion. Whether she is expecting to be recalled to gaol after Alec dies, we shall never know, though the public attitude towards her, so vindictive at the time of her imprisonment, seems to have become indifferent.

Headlines in the *Evening Express* on the day of Jeannie's release refer to the Soviet advance on Warsaw, Allied gains following the Normandy landings and demoralised German troops being compelled to renew their oath of allegiance to Adolf Hitler. WW2 is nearing its endgame; the country has other things on its mind. It could be there is a feeling that Jeannie Donald has served her penance. Certainly she was considered by those who knew her in prison to be a model inmate. One of the warders who had close dealings with her judged her to be 'the best they'd ever had'.

Jeannie leaves prison quietly. In the *Aberdeen Press and Journal*, the news of her release is relegated to page 4, appearing alongside stories about a teachers' pay dispute, a performance given by a close harmony singing group at the Tivoli theatre, and the marriage of a sergeant in the ATS to an RAF pilot at Ferryhill South Church.

Miss Gladys Cooper wore a gown of ivory satin cut on mediaeval lines, and carried tea roses.

After her husband dies, Jeannie moves south to Edinburgh under an assumed name, her face blending into the crowd, just one more grieving widow looking for another chance at life and a new set of memories.

Jeannie Ewen, or Donald, is gone forever.

You will have heard the myth about earthworms, that if a worm is cut in two, then each of the severed halves will become a new animal. The myth has a portion of truth in it, as so many myths do. If a worm is cut in half, so long as the division occurs behind the worm's vital organs – the orangey-brown swelling that is called the clitellum – then the head end of the worm can grow a new tail. The worm's original tail end will die, though. Without the head and without the clitellum, the tail is nothing, a stump of dead flesh. It will dry up and decompose into the soil.

I think about Jeannie waking into her new life and believing, just for an instant, that she is back in the old one. It is painful, and so easy, to dream of a world where she chooses not to get riled by Helen's teasing, where she is still in the kitchen and not in the hallway when the Priestly girl, saucy minx that she is, comes rattling along the close with her damned loaf of bread. It is not difficult to imagine how it must feel, to make a mistake there is no coming back from, that transforms the whole of your past into a kind of fiction.

When I think of Jeannie, I think of a life that was split in two by an act of violence, the old tail of itself discarded, a rotting piece of matter too repulsive to speak of. I think of the trauma Jeannie must have suffered and could never talk about. To feel your form bent out of shape to retain memories of those you loved but to have no right to them. To see the whole back half of your life, dead and decomposing like a severed tail.

Potted histories of the case online insist that Jeannie was 'abandoned by both husband and child'. We already know this isn't true, or at least not for Alec – it was because of her husband that Jeannie was released from prison in the first place. As for wee Jeannie, I haven't been able to find a single mention of what happened in her life after her mother was sent to prison.

She would have been eighteen years old when Jeannie was released. Old enough to have a life of her own, her own opinions about the future and about the past. She and her mother shared a close bond, at least before the arrest. Given the whole circumstances of Jeannie's crime, all the pieces of information that will come to light later, I cannot imagine wee Jeannie cutting off contact. Not entirely and not forever. It doesn't seem like her, somehow.

Jeannie Donald herself dies in 1976, the year of the endless summer and the plague of ladybirds, the year of 'Bohemian Rhapsody' and 'That's the Way I Like It' and 'Fox on the Run'. I am ten. My brother and I pool our pocket money so we can buy the 7" single of 'Bohemian Rhapsody'. My brother, who is eight, is obsessed with glam rockers The Sweet, and so 'Fox on the Run' is also played incessantly in our house. A summer of blue skies and dry heat. The summer I leave primary school and prepare to enter the world of streamed classes and examinations, of making friends outside my own village, of going to school on the bus instead of on foot. It seems incredible to me now, that Jeannie Donald was still in the world, that she had travelled that far into the century, into her own new future.

I am desperate to know what her life after prison was like. There is nothing on the internet, just those vaguely-worded statements about her 'disappearing from public view' after her release, and I cannot help thinking how strange it is, after all the excitement and furore over the trial, that no one seems interested in what happened next, in where Jeannie went and what she did and whether she ever expressed remorse for what she had done.

I have more or less given up hope of ever finding anything. But then I strike lucky. In a footnote to a 2018 article by an academic at Keele University, I discover that Jeannie – Jeannie as she had reinvented herself for her post-war afterlife – had given an interview to the *Sunday Mail*, the Sunday edition of the *Scottish Daily Record*. The feeling this new knowledge gives me goes beyond excitement, as if the information has been waiting there specifically for me to find. The publication date given for the article is Sunday 19th February 1955. I contact the news desk at the *Sunday Mail*, asking where I might access a copy. A day or two later I receive an email, informing me that I should be able to locate the article through the newspaper's archive, which is held at the Mitchell Library in Glasgow.

The number one single for the week of February 11th–19th 1955 was 'Mambo Italiano' by Rosemary Clooney and the Mellomen. The song is catchy and gorgeous and it begs to be danced to. I am interested to discover that it went on to accompany the opening credits to Jonathan Demme's 1988 movie *Married to the Mob*, the film Demme made immediately before his breakout blockbuster *The Silence of the Lambs*.

Other records from the same week's chart include singles by Dickie Valentine, Ruby Murray and Dean Martin. Coming in at number 10 we have Bill Haley and the Comets with 'Shake, Rattle and Roll' – the start of a musical revolution and a new world order.

In 1955, wee Jeannie is twenty-nine years old. A grown woman with a child of her own, probably. If I close my eyes I can see her dancing, her and the wee one, dancing like mad things to Bill Haley and singing along, the music turned up full blast on the kitchen radio. Is Nan there too, I wonder? Does she make them supper, the way she used to? Does she butter their bread?

Helen Priestly's gravestone, in the Allenvale cemetery, is already beginning to fall into disrepair.

The UK singles chart begins in 1952. The first official UK number one is 'Here in My Heart', by Al Martino. There's no way Jeannie wouldn't have heard that one. I find the record on Youtube and it is like catching sight of her, from a bus maybe, just for a second, or through the steamed-up window of a Glasgow greasy spoon, where I am standing at the counter, ordering a bacon sandwich and a pot of tea.

I head to Glasgow at the beginning of December. The news is full of COVID again, the new Omicron variant, and everyone is back in a state of high alert. The anxiety is as catching as the virus, but the lights of Ashton Lane, of Byres Road, the sight of people meeting and walking and shopping is an aching relief. I sit with friends around a table at Òran Mór, a wine bar I have not been into in almost two years. The outside door is left propped open for ventilation, letting in a continuous icy blast of Glasgow air.

I sit in this good place spangled with Christmas lights, sipping Laphroaig and moaning about the government. The world is the world is the world and I am glad.

I am staying at the Travelodge on Hill Street, close to the Glasgow Film Theatre and the small Italian restaurant where I normally eat dinner, a low-key, family-run place, checked tablecloths and a wooden paddle fan. I am heartbroken to discover the restaurant has closed, steel shutters pulled down permanently over darkened windows, another blameless victim of the pandemic. The feeling of regret, the underhum of restless anger is as familiar to me now as the futility of trying to explain it to anyone else.

The cinema at least is still in business, the long dark upstairs bar still serving coffee. I buy a ticket for *House of Gucci*, Ridley Scott's new movie based on the Sarah Gay Forden book about the Gucci fashion dynasty and centring upon the contracted killing of Maurizio Gucci by his wife, Patrizia.

The film is sensational in the literal sense of the word: shiny surfaces, expensive production values, evocative soundtrack. Adam Driver is unexpectedly impressive as the doomed Maurizio – intelligent, restrained, finally ruthless – but I find Jared Leto's portrayal of his cousin Paolo both loathsome and insane. I keep wondering whose decision it was to have all these Americans speaking in fake Italian accents.

I enjoy the film a great deal; at the same time, I am not surprised to learn that the Gucci family found the movie offensive, because there is something faintly repellent about the whole production. As always, I want to know more. I want to discover the personalities and predicaments at the heart of the case, to get to know their history at a level that does them justice. But there is no time for that now. It is Jeannie I have come in search of, and after a restless night's sleep I walk to the Mitchell Library in the grey and snappish cold of a Glasgow December. The newspaper archive is on the fifth floor. I fill in a permissions slip for the articles I wish to view and one of the library assistants helps me set up the reader.

The text is here with me and I am here with it. I have in front of me in microfilm a copy every edition of the *Sunday Mail* for 1955. I scroll through to February and it quickly becomes apparent that there has been a mistake: there is no *Sunday Mail* for Sunday 19th, because the 19th February was a Saturday and not a Sunday. I stare at the front page of the Sunday 20th edition and then, even though I know it is hopeless, I scroll slowly through the pages, inching my way forward so as not to miss anything, searching for Jeannie Donald in a place that she is not. After I have confirmed what I know already, I search through the remaining editions for February, as well as the issues either side for January and for March.

Finally I explain the problem to the librarian and ask if I can examine the *Daily Record*'s archive for the same time period. I have the same predetermined sense of hopelessness, but seeing as I am here I may as well check. If Jeannie is determined to hide from me then I am equally determined not to give up on the search until I have explored every avenue down to its last cul-de-sac.

The *Daily Record* is empty of Jeannie as I suspected it would be, but throughout the February and March of 1955 it is full of something else, the trial of a twenty-four-year-old freelance journalist, John William Gordon. Gordon has been charged with the murder of George Ford McNeil, a forty-eight-year-old voice actor once famous for playing the role of the businessman Mr McZephyr in the radio comedy series *The McFlannels*. The series was broadcast by the Scottish Home Service, and ran for fifteen years. McNeil's body was found stuffed inside a cupboard at his flat in Govan Cross, remaining there undiscovered until some three weeks after his death.

Gordon had fled to Spain, from where he was later extradited. There is a strange atmosphere around the trial, as if there are aspects of the case no one wants to talk about. Much is made of Gordon's troubled background – the fact that he spent periods of time in care is brought up repeatedly. Digging deeper into the case, I discover that McNeil, who is described in witness testimony as a youth worker, had been assigned some sort of guardianship role with regard to Gordon, and had offered him a place to stay on his release from Borstal.

A witness from the Iona Community, of which McNeil was also a member, speaks regretfully of the actor being involved in 'this sad business of homosexuality'.

There is so much here that is not being said. Was McNeil a latter-day Jimmy Savile? Gordon – like Jeannie – was originally given the death sentence but later reprieved. As with Jeannie, there is much hedging around the reasons for this, but reading between the lines, it seems that although Gordon was undoubtedly guilty, then so was

McNeil. Of sexual abuse? Exploitation of minors? There is a truth here that demands to be known, but for now at least I have to let it go.

One final irony: John William Gordon ends up serving his sentence in Craiginches, the prison Jeannie Donald was originally taken to following her arrest. As I scroll through the reams of tabloid headlines – the murders, the celebrity gossip, the prurient little thinkpieces on female morality – it strikes me that this blurry roll of microfilm is like a dry run for the internet. There is so little difference in what people are talking about it is like déjà vu.

An Unnatural Reserve

THE NOTABLE BRITISH TRIALS series was published by William Hodge & Co. There are eighty-four volumes in all. The first of the run, *The Trial of Madeleine Smith*, was published in 1905. The series ends in 1959 with the now infamous trial of Christopher Craig and Derek Bentley.

Each volume includes an extended introductory essay written by a leading lawyer or legal commentator, followed by the complete transcript of the trial in question. The series is well known among legal scholars, social historians, true crime enthusiasts and also writers. Even if you are not particularly interested in murder, any volume in the series will give you a unique insight into the workings of the British legal system as well as the rapidly evolving social background against which these trials took place.

The Trial of Jeannie Donald is No 79 in the series. It is a scarce book and rather expensive. Some of the volumes have been reprinted, but this is not one of them. It was published in 1953, and is introduced and edited by John Gray Wilson, a Scottish advocate who, as well as being a distinguished lawyer, was an accomplished painter and an enthusiastic participant in amateur dramatics. In 1945, he stood as the Liberal candidate for Glasgow Hillhead, the seat most famously won by Roy Jenkins for the SDP in 1982.

Wilson was born in 1915. I can imagine he remembered Jeannie's trial well, that as a gifted and dedicated law student, he took a keen interest in its vicissitudes. His introduction is written with poise, elegance and a punctilious attention to detail. People rarely talk about the poetic beauty of legal language, but I find Wilson's use of English so deft and so capable it makes my heart race.

My copy of his book is in fine condition, the red cloth boards and gilt lettering clean and intact. It is signed by the author, with a dedication 'To Miss Isabel Sinclair, Advocate, as a belated token of appreciation for her devilling, from John G. Wilson.' The dedication is dated December 1953, which makes it seem likely that the book was given to Isabel Sinclair as a Christmas present.

It feels strange, to hold it in my hands, almost like being in contact with Wilson himself.

Wilson wrote two other true crime books: *Not Proven*, an examination of what another, more famous lawyer, Sir Walter Scott reviled as 'the bastard verdict', and *The Trial of Peter Manuel*, an inquiry into the psychopathic mind and the morality of the death penalty. He also wrote a novel, *The Old Innocent*, based around the Sandyford murder of 1862, a case famous for being the first to be handled by Glasgow Police's newly formed detective division, and another trial ending in a death sentence that was later commuted to life imprisonment.

Wilson's novel is told largely in Scots, with the character of the eighty-seven-year-old narrator and probable murderer, James Fleming, inspired by that of Holy Willie from the poem by Robert Burns.

According to those who knew him, Wilson always felt a kinship with Burns, who had lived for a time in Irvine, the coastal town in Ayrshire where Wilson was born.

I am keen to get hold of *The Old Innocent* – I am interested both in Wilson and the Sandyford murder case – but I cannot find a single available copy listed online and the book, supposedly published in 2016, appears to be out of print. I email the publisher, a printing company based in Berwick-upon-Tweed, asking them if they have any idea how I might obtain one. I have no great expectation of hearing back, but as things turn out, I receive an email from their marketing manager more or less immediately.

They do not have any copies, he informs me, as the publication in question was a private commission and the book was never on sale to the public. Then he offers to put me in touch with their client directly.

This is how it happens that, seventy years after John G. Wilson wrote his account of Jeannie's trial, I find myself exchanging emails with his youngest son Mark. He describes how he rescued the typed manuscript of *The Old Innocent* from where it had languished for years in his brother's attic. Although the typescript was faded and almost illegible in places, the work seemed to be complete and after retyping it in its entirety, Mark decided it should at the very least be preserved as a properly bound document in case of future interest, whether from the family or from a prospective publisher, a task he entrusted to the printing firm in Berwick-upon-Tweed.

Mark Wilson worked for forty years in social services, while both of his brothers became teachers, each of them continuing in their own way to further John's passion for justice and public service. 'My youngest son Jonathan did take up the writing profession, and is now a successful screenwriter,' Mark adds. 'Some of my father's skill must have passed down to him.'

Jonathan Wilson, I will discover later, has worked on several high-profile TV series including BBC Scotland's gritty Glasgow-based drama *River City* and Netflix's international blockbuster *The Crown*. As I listen to a podcast in which Jonathan discusses his involvement with the series and in particular his award-winning script set against the background of Thatcher's Britain, I am in no doubt that the family passion for social justice is alive and thriving.

Mark tells me that of all the trial accounts his father published, he found the trial of Jeannie Donald to be the most fascinating. John had always concurred with those who believed Jeannie's reprieve had been granted because the authorities concluded Helen's death had been unintentional. Jeannie's actions on that fatal afternoon had not been premeditated, but were the result of an unlucky chain of events that could not have been foreseen.

Appalling as it was, her crime could not properly be described as murder, or at least not as the word was most commonly understood.

When John G. Wilson wrote *The Trial of Jeannie Donald* in 1953, there was still no public right of access to court records. The documents pertaining to Jeannie's reprieve were the property of the Scottish Office, and though even at the time there were rumours that Jeannie had made a confession to the prison chaplain, John had no means of verifying his theory. Following the Freedom of Information Act (Scotland) in 2002, Mark realised it might now be possible to discover the truth. In 2006 he and his wife Alison travelled with Jonathan to visit the National Archives of Scotland in Edinburgh. Here Mark was finally able to read the words that lay bare what happened in Jeannie's front parlour at 61 Urquhart Road.

Following her removal back to Craiginches on 24th July, Jeannie's defence team let it be known that they are intending to launch an appeal against the death sentence. There is no sympathy for Jeannie Donald in her home city; no public petition, as there had been for Edith Thompson in London in 1922, no barroom barristers protesting her innocence. Instead, there is an outraged satisfaction that the monster in their midst is about to be served her just deserts. 'If ever a woman deserved hanging, it is the woman Donald,' proclaims the *Aberdeen Bon-Accord* on August 10th.

For Jeannie herself, the time remaining to her between her sentencing and date of execution must seem absurdly, terrifyingly short. Whether it was Jeannie herself who insisted on sticking to a Not Guilty plea, or whether the course was one she was advised to follow by her defence counsel is of less importance at this stage than the fact that as a strategy it has failed.

Alone and under sentence of death, Jeannie finally comes to the conclusion that her only hope lies in revealing the very facts she has persistently denied. She asks to speak to the prison chaplain, requesting that he write down her confession for the official record.

COPY STATEMENT WRITTEN BY CHAPLAIN AT REQUEST OF CONVICT, signed by witness W. A. Chisholm, prison governor, Saturday 28th July

On Friday 20th April at 1:30 pm or thereabouts I was dressed ready to go out when the child Helen Priestley [sic] came into the lobby with a loaf in her arms. She made a face at me and my anger getting the better of me I struck her on the face and she fell and turned a purple colour. Aghast at this I made to go upstairs to tell her mother but in my fear I came back and trailed her by the arms into my house. As the child seemed to be dead I used a wooden spirtle to mutilate the private parts of the child thinking that perhaps this might lead people to think that a man had done this. Immediately after I went out and got a bag from the recess under the stair and putting the body into the bag put the bag and contents under the room bed where it remained until moved out into the lobby. The effect of all this and the sudden fear after I had taken the child in I felt everything to be 'black' and took a helping of whisky. Thinking my husband was sleeping I shut the kitchen door and put the sack in the lobby somewhere between 3 and 4 a.m. I purposely kept the secret from my husband as I did not wish him to think I had done such a thing. For 3 or 4 years Mrs Priestley [sic] had treated me shamefully by insult and gossip which must have had a very bad effect upon my temper.

Signed J. Donald

Words hidden for so long, truths buried for decades, and I cannot help thinking about all the other silos of knowledge that are still restricted, kept in basement rooms of locked-up file cabinets behind closed doors. Words walled up for no other reason than that they grant the keeper an advantage that does not belong to them. Truth is power, and knowledge is power, and the suppression of truth is a power-grab, an act of oppression.

Were Helen's parents informed of Jeannie's confession, or were they, like the rest of the country, left to draw their own conclusions about the reprieve? The effect on Agnes Priestly of not knowing what happened to her daughter would have amounted to mental torture, and I hope someone took the time to explain what had taken place.

I would like to know more about what happened to John and Agnes Priestly after the trial. Did they stay in Aberdeen, or move away? Did they stay together, or drift apart? Did they have more children? I can find no further trace of them. Just this hideously brightened window on their personal tragedy. We can only be sure that their lives afterwards were never the same, that the killing of their daughter Helen altered them forever.

For Jeannie herself, I can only imagine it must have been a relief to have spoken the truth. Two elements of her confession stand out at once: firstly, her insistence that Alec knew nothing, and secondly, the fact that Helen's body was kept hidden under the bed in the parlour – a bed that Jeannie in her trial statement describes as being used only occasionally, by visiting relatives – and not in the cupboard under the kitchen sink, an assumption that had been made, and moreover relied upon, throughout the trial.

That dram of whisky, that all-consuming feeling of black despair. The details seem so pitiful, so vivid still, and I find myself dwelling once again on the closed, secret life of that tenement house, where to fall out with your neighbours is itself a kind of prison sentence, one that would be difficult if not impossible to ever escape.

Hoping not to encounter your enemy on the stairs. Constantly suspecting that your possessions are being interfered with. Waiting silently behind your front door for a person in the apartment opposite to leave the building. A depressing, circumscribed existence, and here comes Agnes Priestly, with her piano-playing daughter and her better-off friends, her malicious gossip, her constant sniping and railing at imagined slights. Jeannie's resentment becomes embedded, like an ugly weed. The slightest provocation will be enough to make her explode.

The wooden spirtle or spurtle is a uniquely Scottish kitchen implement, used for stirring porridge. Spurtles are typically made from beech wood, says Wikipedia. The rod-like shape makes it easier to prevent your porridge from congealing and forming lumps. Spurtles come in a range of sizes. The traditional spurtle will be topped with a carved thistle. Modern spurtles are more commonly finished with a smooth taper. According to custom, porridge should be stirred in a clockwise direction and with the right hand. The World Porridge-Making Championships awards the Golden Spurtle as its main prize every year.

And I am amazed to discover that there is more. As well as Jeannie's confession, Mark Wilson was also granted access to two medical reports, one from a Glasgow psychiatrist and one from a Dr Allison, who is clearly experienced in examining medical evidence in court proceedings. These reports were obtained by Jeannie's solicitors in preparation for the appeal that was never launched. The documents are faded and in places where the photocopy is incomplete, Mark has to fill in the missing text himself, by hand. The signature of the psychiatrist is impossible to decipher, and I am only able to confirm Dr Allison's identity because the psychiatrist refers to him by name in his own report.

The psychiatrist's report is dated 28th July, and the story it tells is remarkable. The doctor first speaks with Jeannie on July 26th, just five days after the jury's verdict has been given. At this point in time, Jeannie is still protesting her innocence, insisting not only that she had nothing to do with Helen's death, but that she did not even lay eyes on the child on the day in question. The psychiatrist notes that she repeatedly questions aspects of the scientific evidence brought against her, revealing in the process that she has a better-than-average understanding of its significance.

She takes particular exception to being questioned about her mental health, stating only that she has 'already suffered so much' that the question of her sanity is immaterial.

The following morning her mood has changed. It is obvious to the psychiatrist that what he calls 'her peculiar reserve' is on the point of breaking down, and when he questions her again on the matter of her guilt she immediately clutches his hand and begins to weep. She then describes her attack on Helen as it will later appear in her confession to the chaplain, adding that she gave her 'a good slap' on the side of the head, hard enough to propel her across the lobby and against the wall.

After Helen collapses, Jeannie's one overwhelming fear is for the shame she will bring on her family if she is branded a murderess. 'She was so upset,' the psychiatrist continues, 'that I could not do more than merely listen to her statement. There is no grounds for supposing she bore the child any ill will and certainly she had at first no intention of doing more than repaying the child's grimace with an honest slap.'

He refers again to her 'unnatural reserve', adding that 'there is in her case a degree of what I can only call pig-headedness, such that once she commits herself to a position she feels constrained to adhere to it through thick and thin.'

Dr Allison's report is dated July 27th and his account of what Jeannie tells him is more or less identical with the prison chaplain's. As a doctor who has conducted 'many post mortems' on children who have died suddenly from conditions associated with the enlargement of the thymus gland, he deems it 'entirely possible' that Helen Priestly might have collapsed as the result of Jeannie slapping her. Most crucially, he believes that the purpling of the features that so terrified Jeannie might well have been brought on by Helen choking on her own vomit – vomit produced not as the result of the simulated rape, as the prosecution insisted, but at the moment of her collapse.

'The bruising on her neck is only slight,' Allison explains, 'and might reasonably have been the result not of throttling, but of the original slap.'

When Allison questions Jeannie about what happened to Helen's knickers, she claims that she burned them. The simulated rape, she insists, had not resulted in further bleeding, and so there had been no need to mop the floor with a washing cloth. The sack Helen's body was found in had been lying on the rug, and if the sack was on the rug, Allison contends, then it is reasonable to assume the hairs and household fluff so central to the prosecution's argument could have been transferred to the sack from there, rather than from Jeannie herself or from Helen's body. Such a transfer could have happened at any time.

With regard to the biological trace evidence, Allison is careful to distinguish the traces of blood on the washcloth as human albumen, not haemoglobin, and too insubstantial to be reliably attributed to any one person.

They could have come from anyone in the household, Allison maintains, and further notes that Jeannie was menstruating at the time.

In every and whichever scenario, Ella Robertson's blue knitted tammy was never found.

I have read both reports many times now, and I still find them shocking. The facts of the case remain largely unaltered: Jeannie killed Helen. Jeannie concealed Helen's mutilated body in an old flour sack then dumped the sack in the lobby under cover of darkness. Jeannie went about her normal business for four whole days afterwards, all the while denying that she had seen or heard anything out of the ordinary. This is all still true – what is more, Jeannie herself now admits it to be true. What is different comes down to emphasis and nuance, the very things that so often go missing in any controversy, not to mention the charged atmosphere that often prevails inside a courtroom.

The portrait of Jeannie presented at the trial shows a cold, calculating woman who committed a heinous crime then made desperate attempts to escape the gallows by denying all knowledge. A woman who callously ignored the tragedy on her doorstep, even while fussing over her own daughter's dance costumes and going for drinks at the Tivoli with family friends. The Jeannie Donald presented for judgement by the prosecution committed horrific injuries on Helen Priestly, then cruelly smothered her when she regained consciousness and cried out in pain.

The real woman we are able to glimpse in the doctors' reports is rather different. Anyone reading those reports today will understand that Jeannie is suffering from PTSD. Where the psychiatrist speaks of unnatural reserve, pig-headedness, a display of apathy, what we see today is shock, a devastation so numbing that it has shut down Jeannie's ability to respond. Her only concern is for her family and for her husband. She can scarcely bear to think about the child she has killed.

Helen was suffocating, there in front of her, but Jeannie did not realise. Had the child been placed in the recovery position and her airways cleared, she would most likely have recovered quite quickly, but Jeannie did not – could not – know this. She believed what she had meant as a harmless slap had somehow killed her – which in its way it had.

And what about the scream? you might be asking. The scream heard by George Munro, the slater, at around two o'clock? Surely the scream is evidence that Helen did revive after all, and that Jeannie throttled her.

But we have to remember that the scream reported by Munro was never corroborated. Not one other witness admits to having heard it, which is strange, given that Mary Topp at least was in and around the lobby for the whole of that early part of the afternoon. I am not suggesting that Munro is lying. I think it far more likely that he – like Richard Sutton, like Phyllis Kingdon – might have allowed the drama of the situation to get the better of him.

Who can say if the scream was real or, even if it was, that it came from Helen? Munro's evidence is as questionable as the evidence of the supposed bloodstains under the sink.

We have already seen how Jeannie's case is important to the history of forensics. We should not forget that it is also a lesson in how forensic evidence can be misinterpreted. Our fascination with true crime stories has led us to believe that evidence presented on the basis of science must be infallible. But the same set of clues can be used to support theories that differ radically, or even oppose one another. Forensic traces – like the traces of blood and bacteria on Jeannie's washcloth – are often minimal, leaving plenty of room for error as well as for doubt.

Personally, I find it noteworthy that neither Dr Allison nor the psychiatrist see anything unusual or particularly reprehensible in the fact that Jeannie Donald slapped Helen Priestly, slapped her pretty hard, too, by the sound of it. In 1934, the physical chastisement of children was a fact of life, and scarcely worth a mention.

It would have been interesting to see the reaction of the jury at Jeannie's trial, had they known that in future years and in the same courtroom, the slap alone could have landed the plaintiff in the dock on a charge of assault.

Mrs Donald's Story

THE DAY AFTER MY abortive December visit to the Mitchell Library, I email the academic from Keele University and ask her if she could check the date of Jeannie's interview in the *Sunday Mail*. In her reply she tells me she has retired, and that many of her papers are now in storage. She promises to come back to me after Christmas, once she has had the chance to look for the relevant article.

I find it invigorating and enlightening to talk with her. In a strange way, I feel our conversation has already brought me closer to Jeannie. Early in 2022, she visits the storage facility where her papers are and discovers what I have guessed already: the date given in the footnote to her article is out by one year.

She sends me a scan of the interview, published in the *Sunday Mail* on Sunday 19th April 1956. It is not a long piece, a thousand words at most. The byline is Liam Regan. He describes the now sixty-year-old Jeannie as 'a frail-looking, gentle old woman', a 'respectably dressed housewife' living under a different name in 'an east of Scotland town', where no one has any idea of her previous identity as a convicted murderer.

The first time I read the article, I feel disappointed. The piece seems so anodyne, almost sanitised, lacking in any real insights or revelations. I even wonder if my passionate pursuit of it has been counter-productive, robbing my story of its central mystery, the perplexing enigma of Jeannie Donald herself.

The more I study it though, the more interesting the article becomes. The whole interview seems choreographed, not by Liam Regan but by Jeannie herself. She is not playing Regan exactly, but she is keeping part of herself hidden, letting him know only what she wants him to know, and I sense again that self-reliance, what the prison psychiatrist refers to in his report as Jeannie's peculiar reserve.

In spite of everything, she has survived. Moreover, she is still herself, a woman with interests, and hobbies, and a life to live.

She has a new husband, described as a contractor, and three grandchildren, though whether these are wee Jeannie's children or children from her husband's side of the family, Jeannie does not specify. She is active in the church, and friendly with her neighbours. She seems content, and I do not mind admitting that I am glad.

The closest she comes to expressing unguarded emotion is when she talks about Alec. Though she received and wrote many letters while she was in prison, she discouraged visitors. Far from being 'abandoned' by her husband, it was she who would not allow him to come and see her.

'It was my own fault,' she says. 'I knew I couldn't face my family again and see them leaving. I would have broken down completely when we parted.'

When Alec died from cancer, she felt bereft. 'I did not know where to turn,' she said. 'We were very attached to one another.'

When she talks about her time in prison, Jeannie seems to recall those years almost with happiness, and speaks affectionately of the prison staff, with whom she still keeps in touch. 'Everyone from the Governor to the most junior wardress was very kind to me. When we meet, we talk about old times,' Jeannie explains. 'They are the only people who know my secret, and they have kept it all these years.'

A photograph of Jeannie at the time of her release shows her as well preserved, sturdy-looking, anything but frail. I find Regan's description of her as a 'little housewife' annoyingly patronising. I am more concerned with the words Jeannie herself uses when she first hears that the *Mail* is intending to publish a story re-examining the details of her trial.

'I almost collapsed,' she says, and my mind flies back to what Mary Topp said in court, about Jeannie's reaction to the news that Helen Priestly had disappeared.

Mrs Donald said that Mrs Gordon had told her. She said she nearly collapsed.

There are words and phrases peculiar to each of us that help mark out our identity, and it is these few words of Jeannie's that most convince me that the interview is real. That it presents a version of the truth that Jeannie would recognise.

I can find no record of the journalist, Liam Regan, though there is a Liam O'Regan who was the editor of a regional newspaper in County Cork. He held the post for fifty years, making him the longest-serving newspaper editor in Irish history. I suppose there is a chance he cut his journalistic teeth at the *Sunday Mail*, though I strongly doubt it. The coincidence would be too wild. I have to let this go.

O'Regan died in 2009. His daughter Nadine is an arts and music journalist living in Dublin.

Coconut: A Ghost Story

HELEN HASN'T THOUGHT OF her in a while, years in fact, but here she is again suddenly, the brute, perplexing fact of her. There's nothing definite about Mrs Donald you could put your finger on, but that had always been the trouble, especially back then. She's like a character in a dream, which is all she is now in any case, or at least that's what Helen believed until she happened to catch sight of her, sitting in the window alcove of Griffin's tea shop.

A woman in a blue hat, drinking tea and sitting alone, the living life of Mrs Donald, the living life.

Was it possible to be haunted by a memory? Of course it was. Haunting is what memories do. You could even say that memories are what ghosts actually are. But this haunting is more than a memory, it's a person. Helen knows the person can't really have been Mrs Donald, who would be old by now, if she is even alive still. And if she is alive, why would she be here in Edinburgh, staring into the ether as if she was trying to spirit herself away to somewhere else?

When she was a child, Helen used to tell herself that her dislike of

Mrs Donald was on account of her ugliness. Those hard lines around her mouth, lines that insisted she had found the root of all evil and was determined to tear it out of the soil with her own two hands.

Jeannie Donald was not really ugly, though. Put her in different clothes and she would be good looking. Statuesque, they would say in the magazines. High cheekbones and firm skin. Hair with the lustrous sheen of polished mahogany. No one ever had a penny back then, not on their street, but she looked after herself, Mrs Donald, skirts pressed and even stylish. Agate brooch pinned to her coat collar. Never a missing button or a dirty cuff.

Back from her lunch break, Helen tidies the magazines, the copies of *Vogue* and *Marie Claire* she keeps on the counter. The magazines are her own idea, a personal touch she came up with back when Muriel Aitchison was still head of Millinery and the very thought of innovation, especially from the likes of a new girl like Helen Priestly, was scarcely to be thought of.

They show the latest fashions, Mrs Aitchison, Helen had explained, her enthusiasm as carelessly indecent as if she'd left her slip showing. The ladies who shop here like to see what the ladies are wearing in Paris and London. They'll place larger orders, she remembers, hastily. They'll fall in love with the newest styles and spend more money with us.

And you would know best, I suppose? Muriel Aitchison had said. She sniffed the air as if she found the smell unpleasant, her steely eyes boring into Helen like bolts of blue light. She let the magazines stay though, the stack always dishevelled and thumbed-through come close of business, limp from all the page-flicking, the wistful smiles, the sighs of regret.

Another world, Paris. Helen has never been there, though she longs for the city of light as she has seen it reflected in a thousand heady images, in the ravishing, musky aroma of French perfume. The fountains and courtyards and cobbled streets, the glittering shop fronts and corner cafés, the marble columns and stern-faced doormen of the Place Vendôme. An antique button, lace like hoarfrost, a particular hue. Smart ladies sitting alone or conversing in pairs, skin fragrant and smooth and polished as their peerless footwear.

Even as a child, Helen noticed clothes, the way they could hide you or thrust you forward or celebrate your joy. Clothes are her passion, the passion that brought her to the capital and gave her a living. With a dram of whisky or two inside her she might even say that clothes are her vocation.

Vocation, from the Latin vocare, which means to call.

A good hat and a pair of gloves will open any door for you, she had gabbled breathlessly at her interview, cheeks aflame. Aitchison's eyes were like bayonets, lips pursed with distaste at such unmitigated zeal. Mr Birnam had liked her though, Helen could tell.

Here at Darling's we are after something different, he said, to Aitchison's visible fury. What we are looking for in our staff is a sense of style.

Oh yes, Helen breathed. I know what you mean. There is more that she could say but she bit back the words, dissuaded at last by the hardened line of Aitchison's mouth, the lips sucked up and under in a tight little wad, and it was Mrs Donald she thought of then, too, the strange woman who had lived downstairs from them through most of her childhood. Like a spider lurking in the doorway, ready to come flying forth at a moment's notice, the corners of her mouth turned permanently downwards, like Muriel Aitchison's, in displeasure at the world at large and with Helen Priestly in particular, or so it had seemed.

She had laughed too loudly, or something. Some irreparable act of insolence, some misplaced smile.

Coconut, Helen had called her, coconut, though she cannot now remember where the nickname had come from. Something about the roundness of her head, the upright stance of her, like the wooden Aunt Sally down at the beach at the summer fair. The hollow clop-clop of wood striking wood, the garish lips still grinning even as she toppled, the boys and girls shouting and cheering at her indignity.

What had it been between them, that strange enmity? Nothing but a childish fancy, though Helen still feels the shame of it, that she had taken such pains to let the woman know she was disliked. Like knocking on doors and running away, dashing through the streets and closes with the devil on your tail, Helen had called out after Jeannie Donald without knowing why.

Can I help you, sir? she says to the man who is standing at the counter. She tries to keep her expression professional, friendly but detached, anything to avoid admitting that she has been expecting him. He has been in three times this week already, Mr Albert Ferguson, with his neatly parted hair and dove-grey eyes. He first appeared at her counter a month ago. A birthday gift for his mother, he said. He asked her to choose for him. I'm hopeless with presents, he said. With anything, really.

Then you must tell me more about your mother, Helen had smiled.

How can I choose a gift for someone when I haven't the least idea of what they might like?

She cannot fathom now what came over her, to act so familiar. Something in the way he seemed to hesitate before addressing her. In the way he seemed out of place, not just in the Millinery department of Darling's department store but in the midst of life itself.

He must be forty, or thereabouts, not an old man but not young either. Too old to have been to war, unless he is a soldier by profession, which does not seem likely. Smooth, ringless hands, a gold watch, a well cut navy trenchcoat with a tartan lining. He wears spectacles, but they suit him. A doctor? A teacher? A lawyer, maybe? Not that any of this is her business, whatever he is. She shows him three pairs of gloves: one in classic black calf's leather, the same pair but in mustard, another pair in grey merino wool with pearl buttons at the wrist. These last, which have just come in, are by the designer who created the going-away gloves for the Princess Elizabeth.

Don't you think they are a little young? says Albert Ferguson. Helen nods slowly. Possibly you're right, she says, though she loves these gloves, she has shown them to him because of that, because showing him the gloves is the surest way she knows of revealing her true nature. He chooses the mustard, as she somehow knew he would. Helen boxes up the gloves and that is that.

Except it is not, because Albert Ferguson keeps returning, first to buy an umbrella, and then a scarf ring. His choices are unremarkable – quiet things, you might almost say dull things – although the items he selects are well made, expensive, the kind of choices a gentleman would make unthinkingly, without a glance at the price card. Helen suspects that Albert Ferguson is spending more money than he would normally spend, that in some strange, inadmissible way he is spending it on her.

Helen feels disquieted at the idea, almost panic-stricken. And Mrs Donald, so long absent, keeps appearing on the street in front of her as she makes her way home.

Do you like him? asks her friend Ruthie Gleckna, who works in Cosmetics. Ruthie is from Glasgow, the same age as Helen, though in terms of worldly wisdom she seems light years ahead.

Like him? Helen says. He's old.

Not that old, from what I hear.

What do you mean? Helen's cheeks are flaming like August roses.

Nothing you don't know already. I would make the most of him, if I were you, this white knight of yours. Count yourself lucky.

Ruthie Gleckna reminds Helen of Ella Robertson, that raucous, carefree laugh. Helen does not speak of Ella to anyone, not even Ruthie.

There was a girl who used to look after me when I were a bairn.

Ella Robertson could dance the Charleston and she knew about boys. She took Helen tobogganing on Broad Hill, shared the cosmetics she got cheap from a friend who worked in Binns department store. Ella Robertson laughed at everything, especially Helen's nervous, prickly mother Agnes, so anxious about her daughter's safety she'd see highway robbers around every corner from her kitchen to the Castlegate.

If I were ever to lose you, Helen, and there'd be tears in her eyes like crystals, like the drops in the chandelier behind Tikaram's bar. Like she was seeing the end of the world, or seeing a different world, one where her child walked out one evening and never came home.

And Ella would laugh her risky laugh and say not to worry, she'd be looking out for her, and there were times when Helen found herself believing that her mother had been seeing the future, after all.

Yes, you can help me, says Albert Ferguson. I was wondering if I might take you out to tea.

What for? Helen says, though she is not expecting an answer to this question and Ferguson – standing, waiting – does not give her one. It's my half-day next Thursday, she adds, scarcely knowing why, only that in some strange, pre-ordained way she feels she has to.

What about Griffin's? Say three o'clock?

All right, then. She hopes she does not sound too ungracious. Albert Ferguson can have no way of knowing that Griffin's has recently become the haunt of a ghostly Mrs Donald. She tries to focus instead on what she might wear, which is an easier subject to dwell on than why she said yes to him. Does she like Albert Ferguson? Does she mean to let him court her, if this is what he intends? And what other purpose could he have in inviting her? Men like Albert Ferguson do not lure young women into tea shops on false pretences.

Men like Albert Ferguson do not strangle you when you insist you would rather not kiss them.

Or leave your murdered body crumpled behind the waiting room at the King Street tram depot.

Helen tries to imagine Albert Ferguson's not-quite-handsome face contorted with fury and blotchy with effort, with the extraordinary physical exertion that murder demands. She is relieved to find that she cannot do it, though Ruthie has said to her often enough that any man is capable of anything, if he is angry enough. Angry enough, and scared of being laughed at for a fool, not-quite-handsome Albert Ferguson included.

She can feel her thoughts speeding away from her, spinning unstoppably, like running threads as they so often do. She is not afraid of her thoughts, she is too used to them for that, though she wonders why it is that when it comes to the subject of men it is always Ella she sees before her and never Clive.

Do you have someone? Ruthie had asked her on their second encounter. Someone you care for, I mean. A laddie? And Helen, who when asked the same question in a different tone by Muriel Aitchison had bitten her lip and shaken her head now found herself saying well, there was a boy, and when Ruthie pressed for further details told her about Clive. Clive Cameron, who'd been five years older than her, the organist of St Clement's East in Footdee. Who'd been studying Theology at the university and thinking about training for the ministry, though it was a big step to take, Clive said, what with the war on. Not the right time for making decisions that were liable to affect you the whole of your life.

Clive, who felt it was his duty to join up, even though all war is man's war, not God's, or so he'd insisted, and there's nothing to be improved by yet more killing. Ours or theirs, it's the same evil, the surest way of telling Satan he has the upper hand. And though I walk through the valley of death I shall fear no evil, for He is with me, Clive said, and did Helen not know that 'The Lord's My Shepherd' was written by a scholar who played the organ right here at St Clement's? The same as me, he added, my brother in God.

He began to play then; softly, slowly, joining one note on to another until the familiar, beloved tune shimmered and coalesced in the surrounding air. Clive had been her piano teacher, but only for a while. Listening to him play had cured her of music, had led her gently to understand that there were other things she was better at, and that was all right.

He's too old for you, Agnes said, though she had not denied Clive Cameron permission to write to Helen, and neither had her father.

A steady lad, John Priestly had judged him. Too serious for his own good if you ask me but these are serious times.

Was he killed in the war, then? Ruthie asked, her eyes wide with the drama and romance of it, and Helen was tempted simply to nod, to fall silent and lower her gaze. To let Ruthie believe that the tragedy of Clive was too red and too raw still for Helen to talk about. But even then, so early in their friendship, the thought of lying to Ruthie repulsed her more than the sorrow and shame of what had really happened.

With the end of the war came the hunger, the longing for Clive in the parts of her she barely knew yet. His letter, when it finally came, levelled her so completely that for a couple of hours at least she had tried to pretend to herself she had never received it.

Through these months of our separation it has become clear to me that it would be wrong for us to marry. To hold you to your promise, in the knowledge that I am not made for marriage, would be a sin, not on your part but on mine.

He would soon be returning to the city, he wrote, to pick up his studies.

I know you will ask if we can meet as friends. I am certain this would be a mistake, and you will not persuade me otherwise.

At the age of eighty and coming upon this letter by chance while sorting through a large accumulation of photographs and personal papers, Helen reads Clive Cameron's words for the first time in sixty years and thinks how blessed she is, to be able to encounter them again and feel nothing but the vague, almost comforting sadness that is not quite nostalgia, not quite regret but the blunt ache of time's passing, as familiar as the pain that arises in the back and calves after hours kept standing, an ordinary reminder of the need for rest.

She had loved him, for a time, but he had not loved her. She would never know the reason, not for certain, but it no longer matters. This seems to Helen like the greatest and most suitable reward for a life well lived.

He must've met someone else then. What a so-and-so, Ruthie exclaims.

I don't think so, Helen says. She sees the pity in her new friend's eyes and feels a little older. Clive would never have lied to her. That is the only thing about him she still feels sure of. Part of the reason she left Aberdeen was so she could be sure of not meeting him, of running into him accidentally, though it was unlikely. Like her and Albert Ferguson, they were from different worlds.

Edinburgh, her mother wailed, when Helen told her about the job at Darling's, her pride outstripping her sorrow, however narrowly.

The day before Helen left for the capital and her lodgings in Churn Street was the day she first glimpsed the stern and upright figure of Jeannie Donald, standing in front of the cupboard in the downstairs lobby. Helen knew she was not mistaken, even though the Donalds had moved away some time before. Before the war, even. She wonders, out of nowhere, what had become of little Jeannie, Mrs Donald's daughter. Had she gone on the stage like she said she would, or had she faded into the background like everyone else?

They had been friends once, she and wee Jeannie. They had played together in the street in front of the houses and out the back by the coal sheds, wee Jeannie a Russian princess, Helen the court illusionist and also a spy. The games children invent for one another, the secret languages. Her mother's pink quilted dressing gown, a string of plastic beads – commonplace things, trifles without value, and yet there was magic in them, or there had been. Enough to turn her into a different person. Perhaps this was the root of it after all, her love of fashion. Pretending she was somebody else. Disguising herself as someone she could never be.

I shall wear the brown dress to meet him in, Helen decides. It is plain but it fits her so perfectly, those sweet gilt buttons. When she arrives, Griffin's is crowded and noisy, most of the tables already occupied by a tour group who have been visiting the castle. Helen wonders what will happen if they are turned away, whether Albert will care enough to protest, or whether he might use it as a pretext to call off their adventure. Alone in her lodgings, she had looked at herself in the mirror and felt almost glamorous; now she is here with him outside the tea shop, she feels like what she is: a twenty-four-year-old shop girl in a cheap dress. Surely he will notice, if he has not already, the lack of anything that would make her interesting to anyone, least of all himself.

Behind the counter at Darling's, she is lifted out of reality and into a dream world. Surrounded by fine things she could never afford, the conjuror of a thousand possible futures or objects of desire, Helen can see how she might appear to Albert Ferguson as romantic, mysterious even, like one of the characters she played in her games with wee Jeannie Donald. Here on the pavement in the blank grey weather she is merely herself.

She hangs back from the shop entrance, the ornamental sign board that instructs prospective customers to wait to be seated. She half-expects Albert to be as flustered as she is – on their previous meetings he has seemed shy, uncertain of his authority – and yet she realises almost at once that she has been mistaken. His voice, when he speaks, is firm and confident, assuring the young man working front-of-house that they have a table reserved.

Ferguson, he adds, though the young man in his pinstriped blazer is already nodding, already leading them through the maze of tables to an alcove at the rear. The table looks out on to a side street, a narrow, lightless close, but it is at least quiet. The young man takes her cape, a soft-as-cashmere heather-coloured tweed, a ridiculous extravagance but it had been marked down for having a button missing and she could not resist it. The missing button was easily remedied, not with a near-match as most might have aimed for but with an ostentatious contrast, a domed brass naval button embossed with an anchor and acquired by chance, as such delectable rarities often are, from a basket of oddments outside an antique shop, all priced at a penny.

She finds herself wondering if Albert will notice the button, not merely on account of its alluring shine but in its manner of otherness, the way it marks out the garment that bears it as one that has been chosen for its beauty and quality. In how skilfully these attributes have been emphasised by the addition of an element that ought not to fit but unaccountably does.

An element chosen deliberately, by her. Helen does not think of making this choice as making art, though that is what it is. She does know it is ridiculous to hope that Albert might see these things – what man, outside a Paris atelier, notices clothes?

I like your dress, he says as they sit down, hot colour flooding his face a second later. The familiar shyness is back again, and such a contrast with the assurance and entitlement he had shown in dealing with the young man in the pinstriped blazer that it is almost as if she is seeing two different people.

The shyness is about her, Helen realises, her alone, and the knowledge reddens her own cheeks, though not as brightly as his.

Talking is easier once the tea comes. Helen learns, as she half-expected, that Albert is a junior partner in a city law firm. Not exactly what you would call a meteoric rise, he says, but I'm getting there. I like the work, which is the main thing. Mother says Pentland – he's the head of chambers – takes advantage of my good nature but as I keep having to remind her I am not my father.

Do you live with her? Your mother?

Not any more, Albert replies, and there is something in the way he says it that makes it clear the subject is difficult for him, or painful, or possibly both.

A good nature will serve you better than an ill temper, Helen says. That's what I believe, anyway. She feels astonished at herself for speaking so openly – she barely knows this man. Yet it would be pointless to deny that there is something between them.

Why am I here? she asks, finally. They have been sitting at the table for more than an hour. Why would you want to know me, to spend time with me?

When I first saw you in the shop I felt I had found something. Something I'd lost, something precious. I knew I had to speak to you, that I would be angry at myself for the rest of my life if I did not.

He is staring at his hands, the fingers tensely entwined on the white tablecloth. I'm sure you must think me mad, he adds, glancing up at her finally, his eyes clear and grey and dauntless, like a knight in a fairy tale, and she sees how vulnerable he is, how open to hurt. And he could be hurt, Helen realises, so easily.

She imagines Ruthie, her mouth wide open, laughing. Imagines how a single gust of laughter might blow him away.

All my life, she says, from when I was a little girl, I have had the strangest feeling. That I shouldn't be here, that I don't exist. I have never told anyone, not even my— There was a man, she stumbles. I don't see him any more.

You'll think me rotten for saying so, but I'm glad.

I hardly know you, Helen says.

But I think you do.

*

Albert wants to walk her back to her lodgings, but she says no, she will not hear of it, he must have other important business to attend to. In truth she is desperate to be away from him, to be breathing different air, to remember her life as it had been before Albert entered it. The rich cake and unguarded words have made her feel disorientated, as if looking in on her own life from somewhere outside.

As she comes in sight of her house, a gate opens on the street in front of her. The gate leads to a side passage that acts as a short cut between her street and the next. Lying between the two is a coarse, unkempt area of waste ground her neighbours call the park, though Helen cannot imagine anyone walking there for pleasure.

A woman steps through the gate and on to the walk. She is tall, wearing a blue coat with black shoes and stockings. Brown wavy hair spills from beneath her hat, blue and slightly squashed-looking, the same as the hat she had seen on the woman taking tea in Griffin's the week before, and as the woman turns towards her Helen sees that it is Mrs Donald – the same hard expression, the same contempt in her eyes, as if she can see into Helen's past, present and most likely her future too and find only defects and bad intentions and many a wrong turning.

Helen falls back a step. She can hear herself breathing, and she thinks how peculiar it is and how terrifying, that her ability to continue existing is so dependent on her body's willingness to keep taking in air, hundreds of thousands of breaths a day and ordinarily without notice or conscious aid.

I am seeing a ghost, she thinks, and it is awful. She is overwhelmed by the desire to run, yet at the same time she is entirely calm, her mind fully and intently attuned to what is happening. She feels the hard ground beneath her feet, smells the faint stench of drains, sees the bright red flag of a tablecloth billowing from the upstairs window of a house across the road. Its colour seems heightened, charged somehow with magic. She has never felt more aware of herself or of her surroundings, except perhaps when she was with Clive, and Helen wonders if that is what it is, to see a ghost, a kind of falling in love, not with the ghost or with death, but with its opposite: with the world, with the reality of living.

She is amazed at how ordinary the woman is, by how much ghosts are simply people, the same as herself. She stares at Jeannie, trying to take her in. The woman stares back.

I think I must have lost my way, she says. I was looking for Ewen Street.

Her voice is quiet, unthreatening. Helen realises she cannot remember what Mrs Donald sounded like, not properly, just the look in her eyes and her upright posture, the way she seemed to judge your every move. For a moment, Helen finds herself speechless. Then and with a palpable effort her own voice emerges, cracked and dry, as if the sun were blazing down and she were very thirsty.

Ewen Street is back down that way. Across the road at the bottom, first on your right. It's where I've just come from. She turns and points, noting the brooch on the woman's lapel, an oval moss agate in a silver setting. Elegant, if a little old fashioned, and powerfully familiar.

My own wee girl is at the dance school there, the woman says. She's on a scholarship. My husband says I should stay away, leave her to settle, but I miss her that much. You don't realise what they mean to you until they're gone.

I don't have children, Helen says, and all at once she is thinking of Albert, of how he'd said that finding her had been like finding something precious, something he had believed was lost forever. She glimpses a life to come, a life that can be hers if she wants it. She need only say yes.

I can't imagine not having children, the woman says. Once you have weans of your own you'll understand.

She moves stiffly to the side of the pavement and starts back down the street. Coconut, Helen whispers, the word spoken more inside her head than aloud. Cocococococonut. The woman keeps walking, makes no indication that she has heard, and the further away she gets the less Helen is certain that she is Mrs Donald, that she looks like Mrs Donald even. This woman is thinner, surely, her shoulders more relaxed inside her coat.

Helen exhales, the breath rushing from inside her chest like a gust of wind. When she breathes in again she feels more present, steadier on her feet. By the time she gets back to her lodgings, the light is leaching from the sky. The interior of her room is dust-coloured, with a faint hint of mauve. She lights the lamp. There are no outward signs of disturbance, though there is an odd atmosphere in the room, as if a stranger has been searching through her possessions while she was out.

She takes off her cape, and as she steps towards the wardrobe to put it away her shoe brushes against something soft that is lying on the floor, an item of underwear or other clothing left out by accident.

Helen stoops to pick it up. Because of the dim lighting, she does not recognise what the thing is until she is holding it in her hand: a hat, the blue knitted Tam O'Shanter that was given to her by Ella Robertson the day she died.

Helen has searched for it periodically over the years, taking her clothing out of wardrobes and sorting through drawers long after knowing that the search will be fruitless, that the tammy is gone. Are you sure you can't remember seeing it? she has asked her mother. It is pointless asking her father, who would not be able tell the blue tammy from her old bobbled grey one, but Agnes would know. Agnes had seen the hat and admired it when Ella gave it to her.

Ella was always giving Helen small keepsakes – items of clothing, pieces of jewellery, sweet treats of shortbread or jammy dodgers from Huntley & Palmers. Had Agnes felt sore at the sight of the presents – gifts that she, Helen's mother, could only rarely afford? Helen cannot believe it – her mother and Auntie Nannie were closer than sisters. But still, it is strange, that Agnes claims not to know where the hat went, that she barely even remembers what it looked like.

It was hard to speak of Ella at all, afterwards. The way she died was a source of shame as well as agony. The rage Helen feels about this silence has grown with the years. That people would rather pretend Ella had never existed than talk of what happened. And here the tammy is at last, like a coded message. Helen knows that this cannot be *the* tammy, any more than the woman in the street was Jeannie Donald. Yet still, she was, and it is. Helen does not doubt it, even for a moment. The wool is soft and beautifully pliable between her fingers, and that colour, the exalted, saturated hue of pure ultramarine.

See how it makes your eyes shine, Ella had said. You're a bonny lass, so you are. Don't let anyone tell you otherwise.

Helen strokes the hat against her cheek as if to prove to herself that it is real. Why here and why now? she asks the empty room. The sound of her voice is starkly alien, almost someone else's. As if she has been the ghost all along, and the world has moved into a future she can never be part of.

How did it go, then? Ruthie says. They are in the works canteen, both on their dinner break. Ruthie's face is flushed, her eyes full of mischief. She wants to know about Albert, about the rendezvous in the tea shop, who said what to whom.

It was nice, Helen says. In the five days since their meeting, she has not seen Albert Ferguson again, though she has received a letter from him, a note on smooth white paper in an envelope stamped with the crest of his law firm, saying how much he had enjoyed Helen's company and that he would like to take her for a drive out to Cramond the following weekend.

If the weather is fair and you are agreeable, I will collect you at two.
I don't know if it's me, all this, she says to Ruthie.

Me, my arse. Are you telling me he has a motor car?

I think it might be his mother's. I'm not sure I'll be going, though.

Why would you not? Whatever it is you've got, it's clear he wants more of it. He sounds like a decent fellow, Ruthie adds, and not at all bad looking. He even seems kind.

He is kind.

Well, then.

I'm twenty-four years old, Ruthie.

And what of it? You'll be telling me next that's young yet, and you would be right, it is young. But chances like this don't come every day, not for the likes of you and me, they don't. You'll not have to work, that's for sure. You can sit around thinking fancy thoughts to yourself all day long if you're of a mind to. Taking tea with all your posh ladies, including me.

She laughs, takes a sip from her water glass, little finger extended. I'm thinking of you, hen, she adds, her expression serious suddenly. I know enough of men to know he's a good one. You won't want to lose him.

I don't know. It feels different from what I expected, Helen says. Different from when I was with Clive. She wonders what Ruthie would say if she were to tell her about the woman in the blue hat, the red tablecloth billowing from the upstairs window, how the world had seemed lit from within. How her conversation with Albert Ferguson had been nothing like that, how what excites her most about Albert is knowing how much he is looking forward to seeing her.

But Ruthie seems to intuit this without being told.

Settle your future first, then fall in love, if you want, if you still think it's worth the trouble. I know what I'm talking about.

If you could travel anywhere in the world, where would you go? Albert asks her.

They have been walking along the shoreline at Cramond. A narrow road takes them away from the village and out towards the sea's edge, winding down between stone cottages towards the harbourfront. This is the first time Helen has seen the coast here and she is struck by the gentleness of the place, the soft greens and muddy browns and gentle ash greys, rose campion scattered like pieces of confetti amidst the marram grass. So different from the caustic, steely aroma of rain on granite, the screaming of the gulls over Aberdeen beach on a winter's morning.

The motor car, as she had guessed, belongs to his mother. Albert has the use of it every other weekend, unless Moira Ferguson needs it to get to a bridge party, a contingency that seems to arise more often than not.

Albert tells Helen about the summer excursions to Cramond that defined his boyhood, back when his father was still alive, back before the war. I liked to pretend I was running away to sea, he says, on board a pirate ship, like one of the brave young scallywags in Robert Louis Stevenson.

Albert laughs, and she realises it is the first time she has seen him do that, his head flung back, his mouth full of sky. The gesture ought to be joyful, carefree, but there is something awkward about it, disconcerting. As if he is acting out of character and not particularly enjoying the experience.

As they head back towards the village, Albert asks her his question about travel and Helen says Paris.

Paris? He looks surprised, as if it would never have occurred to him that Paris was somewhere she might long for, would ever think about even, and there is a tightness inside her chest, the sense that whatever feeling had been growing between them has been uprooted.

He does not see me, Helen thinks, and an image comes to her mind, the school photograph her mother was so proud of and that Helen had secretly hated. She was nine years old when it was taken, and no one had warned her about the flash bulb, the glaring white light that had left her unable to see for several seconds. In the photograph, she seemed less than she was, a neat little doll to be taken out and fussed over whenever the fancy arose. As if her image was more appealing than the real child.

A photograph is always the same. It can never disappoint you, or surprise you. You can fill it up with your dreams and it will never complain.

Why not show him who you truly are, then? she can hear Ruthie saying. The man is a man of brains, and he can learn.

I will always be in his debt, though, Helen thinks back at her. I will never be allowed to step outside that frame.

It's from Paris, Albert says. I wanted to say sorry.

Sorry for what?

I have the feeling I upset you the last time we met. I'm not sure how, but I know I did. Your friend in the Cosmetics department helped me choose. I couldn't very well try it myself now, could I?

He is holding a small, neat package wrapped in the gold paper stamped with roses they use by the yard downstairs in Cosmetics and Perfumery. Did Ruthie tie the ribbon for you, too? Helen laughs. She has no idea how Albert knows about her friendship with Ruthie, but the thought of them in cahoots is unexpectedly amusing.

The package contains perfume, Ma Griffe by Carvel, the delicious scent she has inhaled a thousand times from used-up test samples, eked out sparingly through the course of a year from a bottle someone left behind in the ladies powder room. Each time she smells it, Helen sees herself wafting in tailored linen through the marble-floored entrance of a Parisian department store, her dreams reflected in the mirrored counters of the perfumery aisles. It would be enough for her simply to be there, to observe the women – fashion buyers, journalists, coffee importers – now claiming the space in the world that has always been theirs.

She thinks also of Ella Robertson, robbed of her life before she could think about claiming anything, of how the scent of French perfume could still be detected on the collar of her blouse ten days after her death.

None of the policemen or doctors seemed to know which perfume it was, though the bottle would have been there on Ella's dressing table for anyone to see. Definitely not Ma Griffe, which was first released in 1946, soon after the war. The absence of this particular detail from the record still gnaws at her heart, if only because it is exactly the kind of detail that would have mattered to Ella.

I've done it again, Albert says. I've upset you.

No, Helen says. It's not your fault. It's just that the perfume reminds me of someone I knew when I was a child, a girl who was murdered. Everyone told me she'd had an accident but it wasn't true.

And she finds herself telling him everything: how Ella Robertson went out dancing one evening in April, how her body was found behind the tram depot the following morning. How no one seemed to know anything – where she was going or who she met or where they went after that. How no one was ever apprehended, and how Ella's mother Helen Robertson suffered a nervous collapse, refusing to speak to anyone for over a year.

That was never talked of, either.

How Jeannie Donald, according to Agnes, had gone round saying that Ella Robertson was fast and no better than she should be, that she'd got what she asked for.

Ella was strangled, Helen said. It rained that night. Her clothes were soaking wet. She used to let me try on her perfume. She loved nice things.

When did this happen? Albert says.

A long time ago now. Before the war. When people say before the war, it's as if they're talking about a different world, a world we can never get back. But things that happened in that world still matter.

Of course they do, says Albert. Tell me how I can help.

You listened. That helps. And thank you for the present. It's lovely.

I don't know what I want, Helen says to Ruthie Gleckna. Only – not this. I want to make something. I want to discover something. I want to go somewhere new.

He would give you children. Do you not want children?

Not yet, Helen says. Maybe not ever. How can I know?

The woman in the blue coat is walking away from her down the street. Down the street and towards the main shopping area, the tram depot and the train station, the road south, the world beyond.

Coconut, Helen calls after her. Cocococococonut. Her voice, freed from its moorings, flies out upon the evening air, bright as mercury, weightless as spider silk. Sound travels at seven hundred and sixty one miles per hour, fast enough to catch her. Fast enough to catch anyone.

But she does not turn.

Acknowledgements

The book that started me down this road was *Blood and Granite* by Norman Adams (Black & White Publishing 2003), which opened my eyes to the city's illustrious past as well as to some of the brutal and tragic crimes that have occurred there, each and every one of which deserves a book of its own. I could not have written *A Granite Silence* without immersing myself for weeks at a time in *The Trial of Jeannie Donald*, edited and introduced by John G. Wilson (William Hodge & Co 1953). Pick up any of the Great British Trials series and you will find yourself immediately captivated, drawn back in time to people and places with an immediacy that has not lessened since the case went to court. Wilson's urgent, compelling and humane overview of Jeannie's case did much to persuade me that here was a story that deserved to be better known.

Medical Detectives: the Lives and Cases of Britain's Forensic Five by Robin Odell (The History Press 2013) was vital in filling me in on the development of forensic science in Britain and in particular the achievements and (mostly) friendly rivalry of Bernard Spilsbury and

Sydney Smith. *Final Diagnosis* by Professor John Glaister (Hutchinson 1964) was invaluable in granting me an insight into the reality of working in medical jurisprudence in the early part of the twentieth century and I can only hope the good doctor would not take objection to the curious tale I have conjured from his daily reality, occasionally and rather cheekily borrowing his own words.

My background reading on the history of Aberdeen has been varied and wide. Two texts in particular were often on my desk and in my hands, namely *Scotland's North Sea Gateway: Aberdeen Harbour 1136–1986* by John R. Turner (Aberdeen University Press 1986) and *Sea State* by Tabitha Lasley (Fourth Estate 2021) both of which helped bring me closer to the city I was exploring.

I would like to offer my thanks to two people in particular, without whose openness, generosity and enthusiasm this book would most likely not exist in the form it has taken. Dr Anette Ballinger's excellent paper 'A Crime of Almost Unspeakable Cruelty and Wickedness: gender, agency and murder in Scotland – the case of Jeannie Donald' (Social and Legal Studies Vol 28/4 Sage Publications 2019) not only granted me valuable insights into the case, it also tipped me off to facts about its aftermath that were not then generally known and that shaped my narrative in ways I could never have predicted. Anette's writing on women and the justice system is of an exceptional quality and I would highly recommend her book *Dead Women Walking: Executed Women in England and Wales 1900–1955* (Routledge 2000) to anyone with an interest in this subject.

Mark Wilson, who kindly allowed me to make him and his family a part of this story, has helped bring this book to life in ways I could not have dared hope for nor adequately describe. Anette and Mark, thank you so much for your time, your trust and your bounteous goodwill. Apologies for the long wait – I hope you like what you read!

Bottomless thanks, as always, to my agent Anna Webber for her insights, advice, and thoughtful comments, and to my editor Jon Riley and the whole team at Riverrun Books for their continuing belief and support. With hugs to my mother, Monica Allan, for her own unique self and infinite love to my husband, Christopher Priest, who is everything and all.